ERIN KAYE

Second Time Around

AVON

AVON
A division of HarperCollins*Publishers*
77–85 Fulham Palace Road,
London W6 8JB

www.harpercollins.co.uk

A Paperback Original 2012
1

A catalogue record for this book is
available from the British Library

ISBN-13: 978-1-84756-202-9

Set in Sabon by Palimpsest Book Production Limited,
Falkirk, Stirlingshire

Printed and bound in Great Britain by
Clays Ltd, St Ives plc

MIX
Paper from
responsible sources

FSC www.fsc.org **FSC™ C007454**

To Janet Marie, my elder sister

Chapter 1

Jennifer walked through the door of The Lemon Tree on busy Donegall Square in Belfast city and noticed him straight away. Conversation competed with piped pop music, somewhere a phone rang, and fleet-footed staff clattered noisily up and down the open metal staircase. Yet, there he stood, behind the brightly-lit bar, dark head bent, arms folded across his chest, listening intently to a black-shirted waiter. Athletic shoulders strained against the yoke of his pink shirt and the rolled-up sleeves revealed pale-skinned forearms, thick with dark hair. His lower half, clad in jet black jeans, was slim, almost thin. And he had to be ten years younger than her. Jennifer, trailing behind her friends, and surprised by the sudden yearning he stirred in her, blushed and looked away.

A waitress wearing slim-fitting trousers showed them to their table, a wooden tray clasped against her chest like a breast-plate. Jennifer slid onto a bentwood chair and the waitress, businesslike, thrust a menu into her hand. She opened it and tried to concentrate on the words swimming before her eyes. What was she doing, eyeing up a guy so much younger than her, a man who wouldn't give her a second look? And even if he did, she'd run a mile. She'd forgotten how to flirt. And the rest of it. It had been three years since she'd been with a man.

'I know it's Friday lunchtime but I think you need a birthday cocktail!' suggested Donna, a full-figured bottle blonde.

Jennifer smiled her assent, determined both to enjoy the company of her best friend – and to give her the courtesy of her full attention. They did this – went out somewhere nice for lunch – twice a year, on each of their birthdays. And, because they lived in Ballyfergus, a town some twenty-five miles away, it felt like a very special treat.

'The food's supposed to be fantastic,' said Donna who, despite being over forty, retained an enviably youthful complexion. 'Donegal oysters are just coming back into season now September's started, aren't they?' She went on without waiting for an answer, 'I wonder if they're on the menu yet . . .'

The drinks came, they ordered food and Jennifer took a sip of the cranberry-coloured cocktail. She smiled as Donna related a funny story about one of the receptionists at the clinic where she worked who came in so hungover she threw up in a plant pot. But, in spite of her best efforts, she could not ignore the man behind the bar. She kept her eyes firmly fixed on Donna but she was aware of his every move and gesture, her attention drawn to him against her will. For the first time in her life she wished she was younger, that she could start all over again. That she could make a man like that desire her.

'Are you okay, Jennifer?' said Donna. 'You seem a little distracted.'

Jennifer's face reddened. 'Sorry.' She ducked her head of dark, straight hair and blurted out, without thinking, 'It's just that I feel old this birthday. For the first time ever.' She

2

looked around the restaurant, suddenly aware that the two of them looked out of place, dressed up in heels and smart clothes while the tables all around them were taken by younger people in casual, summery chic. Even their choice of sophisticated drinks marked them out as from a different generation. She looked down at her slim black pencil skirt, tight across the hips, and her black satin-trimmed jersey shirt, and felt foolishly, inappropriately, over-dressed.

'You're only as old as the man you feel,' said Donna suggestively and, when this elicited a feeble smile from Jennifer added, more soberly, 'Your fortieth birthday's supposed to be the depressing one, you know, not your forty-fourth. By our mid-forties we're meant to have it all sorted, aren't we?' She waved an arm in the air, the collection of bangles on her wrist rattling like chains. 'We're meant to have a family, a fabulous career, great self-image, oodles of confidence, a raging libido – oh, and a hunky man on our arm to satisfy it.' Donna chortled and paused for dramatic effect. She wasn't the female lead in the town panto every year for no reason. 'And I'd say you have it all, apart from the hunky man.'

'It's not easy meeting someone at our age.' Jennifer touched the back of her neck, momentarily shocked by the short, sharp line of hair at the nape. She was still unaccustomed to the new haircut, a sleek graduated bob that she'd only had done that morning. In a moment of madness quite unlike her she'd given the hairdresser free rein to restyle her tired, mid-length hair. It had been a good move. The style was modern and edgy, yet still long enough at the front to feel feminine. While she was pleased with it, the new hairstyle had failed to lift her mood. 'I sometimes think I never will.'

'Of course you'll meet someone,' countered Donna.

Jennifer lifted the glass, threw her head back and downed

3

the cocktail in one, wondering fleetingly if the guy at the bar had noticed her unladylike quaffing. 'Well the way things are going, it looks like I'm going to be rattling round that house on my own for the rest of my days. Matt's applied all over for commis chef jobs and, when he gets one, he says he's moving out. I don't want him to go.'

It was grossly unfair of her to expect companionship from children who were old enough to make lives of their own but she couldn't help it. Her only company for so many years, she had come to rely on them. 'I'm dreading it. It was bad enough when Lucy left for uni. And it's unlikely Matt'll get a job locally, not in this economy,' she added glumly. 'He's even applied to Dublin.'

'Well, if it cheers you any, he's not likely to get a job down there,' said Donna, 'Not with the state of the Irish economy. I hear emigration's on the up again. Apparently kids are leaving in their droves for the US.'

Jennifer looked at Donna in alarm. Far from cheering her, this news filled her with dread. What if Matt too had to emigrate to find work? To the young and dispossessed the idea of emigration was enticing, romantic even, and the well-trodden path, polished smooth by the feet of those who had gone before, was an easy one to follow.

'You know, sweetheart, he can't stay at home forever,' said Donna, a warm smile spreading across her honest, broad face. 'He has to make his own way in the world. They all do.'

Jennifer shrugged. 'I know that. And I want that for him, of course.' She paused, trying to find the words to articulate the depth of her melancholy. 'But the prospect of living completely alone for the first time in decades . . .' She shook her head.

'Lucy will still come home for the weekends, won't she?' said Donna.

'That's true,' Jennifer was forced to acknowledge. But it wasn't the same as having children living at home full time.

'And you'll still have Muffin,' said Donna cheerfully and Jennifer flashed her a grin. Donna was a glass-half-full person, the most positive, upbeat woman Jennifer had ever met. And she loved her for it. She rearranged her features into a withering look. 'He's a dog, Donna.'

'Beggars can't be choosers.'

Jennifer laughed and went on, the smile fading from her lips, 'It's made me turn a spotlight on my own life and I just think "Is this it?"'

Donna nodded gravely and said, 'Jennifer, my dear, I think we're looking at a case of ENS.'

'What?'

'Empty Nest Syndrome.'

The waitress appeared with the food and Donna ordered two glasses of white wine. Jennifer stared with no interest at the beautifully presented chicken Caesar salad she had ordered, her appetite suddenly gone.

'It makes perfect sense, when you think about it,' said Donna, who, sadly, had never been blessed with children of her own. But she was a trained psychologist and she knew what she was talking about. She picked up her knife and fork. 'Come on. Tuck in.' She popped a piece of salmon in her mouth and added, chewing, 'You're just in a bit of a rut, Jennifer. You've lost your mojo, girl, and you need to get it back. You need to get out there and meet new people.'

'You're right,' said Jennifer bravely, though beneath the table her knees would not stay still while her underarms prickled with sweat. She glanced involuntarily at the bar. The stranger was nowhere to be seen.

She thought back to the girl she had once been, a girl who'd dreamed of adventure and romance – and believed that life would deliver it. Somewhere along the way – round about the time she'd married David – she'd lost her sense of discovery.

It wasn't his fault. They'd had a baby on the way and not much money back then and dreams suddenly seemed like expensive, unattainable luxuries. David had been reliable, trustworthy, dependable – everything she thought one needed in a husband and a father. Combined with her emotional neediness and artistic temperament, it had not been a recipe for a happy marriage. Turned out what she wanted was excitement and laughter and unpredictability after all.

And now twelve years after the divorce, her life, while happy and satisfying in many ways, had become just as predictable and boring as her marriage ever was.

But if her life was a disappointment she realised, with painful clarity, she had only herself to blame. She'd been too busy ensuring that Lucy and Matt made the most of all the opportunities available to them.

Instead of swimming herself, she'd collected subs at the door on Swim Club night. Instead of going for a run on a Saturday morning, she'd stood on the sidelines in the rain watching Matt play rugby. She'd ferried them to Guides and Scouts, music, dance and art classes, panto rehearsals, hockey and football training. Not that she'd do it any differently if she had to do it over again. She'd given of her best to her family and she'd no regrets about that.

As if she could read Jennifer's thoughts, Donna leaned forward, patted her friend on the back of the hand and said, 'This is your time, Jennifer. After all the years of doing for your kids and prioritising their needs, it's time to put yourself first.'

Jennifer smiled. 'I hear what you're saying but it's a difficult idea to take on board. I don't know about you, but I feel guilty and self-indulgent pleasing myself.' She looked

6

at her hands. 'And if truth be told, when I do have time to myself, I sometimes don't know what to do with it.'

'The curse of motherhood,' said Donna wryly. 'It'll wear off eventually.'

Jennifer frowned, placed her elbow on the table and rested her chin on her hand. 'I do need to meet new people. But I don't know where to start.'

'Well I do,' said Donna decisively. 'Let's get you signed up with an online dating agency.'

'Oh, I don't think so. It, well, it seems like such an unnatural way to meet people.'

'Oh, rubbish,' said Donna. 'It's how I met Ken.'

'Oh, I'm so sorry,' said Jennifer and she put a hand over her mouth. Donna and Ken, a big, burly policeman with a heart of gold, had been together for four years. She blushed furiously and said, 'I didn't mean to . . . it's just that –'

'Oh, that's all right,' said Donna, waving away Jennifer's feeble attempt to backpedal like a bothersome bug. 'You just have to look at it a different way. It's the modern equivalent of meeting a guy in a pub. You like the look of somebody, share some information and, if you think you might get on, you arrange to meet. Simple.'

Jennifer squirmed in her seat and then a premonition came to mind – a vision of eating a lonely supper at her kitchen table, staring at the empty chairs where Lucy and Matt had sat for the last twelve years since they'd moved into the house in Oakwood Grove. No, the status quo had to change – and she mustn't be afraid of it.

And yet, she still believed in the romance of a chance encounter, the spark of chemistry when a handsome man's eyes met yours across a crowded room . . .

Something made her look up and there he was, the man in the pink shirt, only a few short strides from her. Standing in the middle of the restaurant with a tray of drinks in his hands. And he was staring at her without a flicker of a smile. No, not *at* her. He was staring *into* her eyes, his black pupils so dilated that the hazel-brown irises surrounding them were all but eclipsed. His gaze was penetrating, knowing; it touched her very soul. And she held it, startled, uncomfortable in the intensity of his gaze, but riveted nonetheless.

'Drastic times call for drastic measures,' persisted Donna, her voice breaking the spell. Jennifer, her heart pounding, broke eye contact, and the man moved away.

'The man of your dreams isn't going to land on your lap sitting at home in Ballyfergus,' lectured Donna. 'You have to go out there and get in the game. And it'll be fun. Trust me. I met some great guys,' she added, omitting to mention the many creeps she'd also encountered in her quest. 'I'll help you set up your profile.'

Jennifer, slightly breathless, struggled to regain her poise. It had been a long time since any man had looked at her that way. And none so gorgeous as him. She closed her eyes and saw him still, his clean-shaven image burned into the backs of her eyelids. His dark, softly curling locks skimming the collar of his shirt. And yet it seemed so improbable. He was so handsome. He could have any woman he wanted. Why would he want her? Perhaps she had imagined the stare. She opened her eyes. She must have. He could've been staring at someone else, or staring into thin air.

'Jennifer?' frowned Donna. 'Are you all right?'

'Yes, I'm fine. Just a little woozy. You know, after the cocktail and the wine.'

After the waitress had brought over a glass of water, Donna said with a satisfied smile, 'You won't regret this. When Matt finally walks out that door you'll be so busy having fun, you'll hardly notice him gone. Speaking of which,' she added, craning her neck to see past the diners at the next table, 'isn't that Matt over there?'

'It couldn't –' began Jennifer but she turned to look and the words died on her lips. It *was* Matt. And he was smiling and talking to the man in the pink shirt. They spoke briefly and then disappeared through a dark wood-panelled door at the back of the restaurant.

Jennifer said, as much to herself as Donna, 'What's Matt doing here?' And what business did he have with *that* man?

'Job interview?' offered Donna.

'Of course.' Jennifer pulled a face to signify irritation with her own dimwittedness as much as her surprise. Casually dressed in jeans and a hoodie, he certainly didn't look like he was about to have an interview. And he hadn't said anything to her. But why would he? He'd had lots of interviews lately and he hadn't known that she was coming here. It had been Donna's surprise. A 'happening place' she'd called it. 'Yes, he must've come for an interview,' she said, scrutinising with freshly invested interest the busy, noisy restaurant. 'And if today's anything to go by, he wouldn't be short of work. This place is heaving.'

'It always is,' said Donna authoritatively. 'It's one of the best restaurants in town. They get all their fish from Ewing's on the Shankill Road.' In response to Jennifer's blank face, she added, 'They're the finest fishmongers in the city. They supply all the Crawfords' Belfast hotels too.'

'The Crawfords?' asked Jennifer, trying not to show too much interest. Everyone but the man behind the bar was dressed entirely in black. It occurred to her that he must be the manager.

'You know,' said Donna. 'They own The Marine Hotel in Ballyfergus.'

'Oh yes,' said Jennifer, the name ringing a bell now. The

Crawfords were one of the province's most wealthy, prominent families.

'It seems they've been busy buying up restaurants too,' went on Donna. 'They took this place over a year ago and completely transformed it. It was a right dump before.'

Jennifer said casually, 'Who's that guy Matt was talking to just now?' Her eyes were drawn involuntarily to the door through which they'd disappeared.

'The one in the pink shirt? That's Ben Crawford. Heir to the Crawford empire.'

Ben. The name suited him, she decided. She liked it.

'*Ulster Tatler* voted him Northern Ireland's Most Eligible Bachelor last year,' went on Donna.

Jennifer swallowed. He really was out of her league, but still she could not help herself asking, 'And is he . . . is he nice?'

'I've never met him but I met the father, Alan, at a charity dinner once. Godawful man. Loud. Pompous. Full of himself.'

Jennifer bit her lip. Like father, like son? And he had *looked* so nice.

'Don't worry,' said Donna, placing a reassuring hand on Jennifer's. 'Apparently the son's nothing like the father. So if Matt ends up working for him, I'm sure it'll be absolutely fine.'

Chapter 2

Ben sat behind the desk in the cramped, windowless office at the back of the restaurant. He smiled at the good-looking young man sitting opposite him as he riffled through papers on the desk – and tried to put the image of the raven-haired woman out of his mind. He'd noticed her, sashaying across the floor in those black patent heels and that tight skirt, straight away. He could not believe that he'd had the audacity to stare at her like that, slap bang in the middle of a crowded restaurant. What had possessed him?

Perhaps it had something to do with making the decision about Rebecca. He'd still to act on it, of course, and he wasn't looking forward to it. He glanced anxiously at the mobile lying on the table. He'd texted her earlier to ask if she would meet him tonight for a drink. He'd tell her then.

It wasn't that he had a wandering eye. Far from it, he thought, pulling a résumé from the pile. He'd always been faithful to girlfriends and he wasn't in the habit of staring at attractive women. But this one, for some reason, had caught his eye and he couldn't stop himself. And she had stared back, making his heart race and his mouth go dry.

Pushing these thoughts to one side, he cleared his throat.

'I'm really sorry, Matt. The Head Chef, Jason McCluskey, should be here for the interview but he's been called away urgently.' His three-year-old daughter, Emily, who had a rare blood disorder, had just been rushed into hospital with an asthma attack. 'So, although this is really unusual, I'll be doing the interview today.'

'Okay.' Matt smiled for the first time. He had an open, pleasing face, the sort that inspired trust in men and admiration in women. If his cooking was as good as his looks, he'd go far.

Ben picked up a blank A4 pad and tried to concentrate on Matt. Initially impressions were not good – his hair was too long and he'd not made much of an effort in his Abercrombie hoodie and skinny jeans. Ben disliked recruiting – he felt uncomfortable with the responsibility; he did not like the fact that he held the power to determine, even to a small extent, other people's destinies. He worried that he might get it wrong. And if hiring was stressful, firing was even worse.

Only last week he'd sacked one of the waitresses, a single mum to toddler twins, for persistent, poor time-keeping. Three times she'd not turned up for work without so much as a phone call. He'd given her dozens of warnings and more chances than she deserved but in the end, for the sake of morale amongst the other staff, he'd had to let her go. And it had torn him apart. Steeling himself, he resolved to do what he always did – his best – though always mindful that he could never fill the shoes that went before him, so different in every way from his own.

Matt Irwin, he wrote across the top of the page, and settled into the brown leather swivel chair. Aiming to put the candidate at ease, he rested his right foot casually on his left knee. 'I've read your CV, Matt, so I can see you're qualified for the job. But tell me more about your practical work experience.'

'I've worked in the kitchen of The Marine Hotel in Ballyfergus since I was sixteen. It's one of the Crawford Group Hotels,' he needlessly pointed out, keen to show he'd done his homework, to impress.

'That's right.' The Marine, then rundown and in need of refurbishment, was the first hotel his father had bought thirty years ago. Now the Crawford Group had a board of directors and owned a string of top-class hotels across the province – and Alan, having done all he could feasibly do in that arena, had decided to diversify into the restaurant market. Now that The Lemon Tree was successfully established, Alan felt the time was right to establish another restaurant in the nearby thriving port of Ballyfergus. Past success, no matter how great, did not motivate Ben's father – he was incapable of resting on his laurels. He sought out new challenges – endlessly, exhaustingly. And it had only gotten worse after Ricky. 'You got a very good reference from the head chef at the Marine. Though you weren't working as a commis chef, of course.'

'That's right. I was a kitchen porter,' said Matt and added quickly, 'And there were the college placements too. At The Potted Herring. That was brilliant. They were going to give me a permanent job, you know.'

'And then they went bust,' said Ben sadly, with a shake of his head. Restaurant closures in the city had hit an all-time high the year before, and this year hadn't been much better. 'That was bad luck.'

It struck him then just how remarkable the success of The Lemon Tree was, given the depressed state of the economy. And how much of that success was down to his father's vision and business acumen. Very few other restaurateurs were in a position to expand.

'Yeah,' said Matt, 'it sucks. But I'm not the only one. No one on my course has got a proper job.' He rubbed the thighs of his jeans with the palms of his hands. 'Look, I know I don't have as much experience as you might like. As you're looking for.' He leaned forward with his large hands dangling between his spread-out legs. Ben noticed that they were shaking. 'But I'm very good. Better than good. Honest. Ask my tutors.'

Ben, doodling a series of light zig-zagged lines across the top of the page, remembered what his father said about employing staff with relevant experience. 'You don't want any greenhorns,' he'd said. 'Let them cut their teeth on someone else's time.' Ben's hand stilled and he looked at Matt. Alan Crawford would never employ this young man. And even open-minded Jason, who was all for encouraging raw talent, might have reservations. But if no one was prepared to give a lad like him a chance, how would he ever get started?

Aware that Matt had been silent for some moments and was now staring at him, Ben said, 'So tell me why I should give you the commis chef job?'

Matt took a deep breath, held it, then let it all out in an audible rush. He stared straight at Ben and said, 'Because I'm different. Because I don't just follow recipes and do things by rote. I create.' He raised his hands upwards as if tossing something into the air and his voice, quiet to start with, grew louder, the passion in it swelling like a pot coming to the boil. 'I use my imagination. I'm not afraid to experiment and try new things. And I care. Everything I do has to be perfect.'

Ben put down his pen and stared at Matt, mesmerised by the lad's self-belief.

Matt looked at the palms of his hands and a muscle in his jaw twitched. 'My hands were made to cook. This is what I was born to do. I've been fascinated by food and how to cook it ever since I was a child. Ask my Mum.' He looked directly at Ben then. 'There's nothing in the world I would rather do. And one day I'm going to have a chain of restaurants and they'll be the best in all of Ireland. My food'll be better than anything Paul Rankin or Rachel Allen or any Irish chef has ever done. You wait and see.' Then he threw himself back in the chair and blinked back tears.

Ben, slightly stunned, said nothing. He'd never before met a more self-assured nineteen-year-old nor one who seemed so certain of his path in life, his destiny. And he was filled with a rush of bitter regret. If he'd had the confidence, the passion, to fight for what he'd wanted seven years ago, he wouldn't be sitting here today at the age of twenty-eight, trapped in a job and a lifestyle he hated so much. At the time he thought he'd done the right thing, the only thing. But he'd not been true to himself. He'd sacrificed his lifetime's ambition to rescue his father, to give him a reason to go on. But with every day that passed, while Alan's dreams came to fruition, Ben's became a little more distant, a little harder to recall.

'I shouldn't have said that, should I?' said Matt abruptly and he stood up, his tall frame towering over Ben. 'Maybe I'm not the guy for this job. I'm sorry I've wasted your time.'

He turned then and started to walk to the door on the balls of his feet, hands shoved in the front pockets of his jeans.

'Wait,' shouted Ben and Matt turned round.

Ben held out his hands as if presenting this truth in them. 'I can see you're passionate and ambitious – and that's fantastic – but you have to start somewhere. You can't wade in at the age of nineteen, fresh out of college, and start running a kitchen.'

Matt nodded and said, deflated, 'I know. And that's why I'm here. I really need this job.'

Ben imagined what his father would say. But Alan wasn't here. 'I've read your references, Matt. I believe you're as good as you say you are. And there's no doubting your commitment. But there's a big difference between catering college and hacking it, day in and day out, in a commercial kitchen.'

'I know that,' said Matt.

Ben, eyeballing him, went on, 'You have to be prepared to work harder than you've ever done.'

'I am.'

'And you have to respect the hierarchy. You have to be able to take orders. If you can't do that, there's no place for you in this kitchen, in *any* commercial kitchen.'

Matt nodded and said hopefully, 'I haven't blown it then?'

Ben shook his head and decided there and then, in that moment, that he was going to take a chance on this lad no matter what his father, or Jason, might say. This project was, after all, meant to be his. 'Not as far as I'm concerned,' he smiled. 'You will have to convince Jason as well though.'

Matt's thick black eyebrows moved up a fraction in surprise. Then he grinned and punched the air and cried, 'Yes!'

'I'll put in a good word for you with him.' He'd have to do more than that – he'd have to persuade Jason to take on a boy who, on paper, was less well qualified than some other applicants. But none had impressed him like Matt. And none of the others had sparked in him the desire to help them.

Matt came over, grasped Ben's hand in both of his and shook it vigorously. 'I won't let you down, Ben. I promise.'

'Don't forget that Jason's the boss. So maybe keep your plans for a culinary take-over of Ireland to yourself for the time being, eh?'

Matt laughed. 'Okay. I understand.'

Ben got them both a coffee and said, 'Let me tell you a

16

bit more about our plans. It'll help when you meet with Jason.' They talked about the restaurant's image, the number of covers, the clientele they aimed to attract, the type and quality of food they would serve based on the province's abundant supply of high-quality produce.

'That's definitely the way to go,' offered Matt. 'Quality over price. People don't want to eat cheap rubbish any more. They want to know where the food on their plate comes from.'

Ben smiled and thought of how Matt's ethos contrasted so markedly with his father's. Alan had latched on to the 'finest local produce' mantra only because he was astute enough to realise it was what people wanted to hear – and that put bums on seats. He knew good food, but his primary interest was in the business side – menu pricing, cost control, cash flow and profit margins. But that focus, thought Ben with a grudging respect, was why he was such a good businessman.

His people skills however, while good, weren't quite as well honed. Though Ben had never spoken about it, Alan realised that he was unhappy in his job. But, unable to identify with any personality type other than his own competitive and work-obsessed one, Alan assumed Ben was bored. He thought Ben needed a new and exciting challenge and told him so. It did not occur to Alan to ask Ben what he wanted and Ben, in turn, knowing how the truth would wound his father, kept silent.

Hence the new restaurant in Ballyfergus, a start-up venture with no guarantee of success. Ben worried that he would fail, that he simply wouldn't be able to summon the necessary energy and drive to deliver what his father expected.

So, far from looking forward to it, Ben was dreading it. And not just the long hours. He'd no desire to live in a small-town rural backwater like Ballyfergus. He didn't want to leave Belfast and his flat full of books that he loved so much. Living near the university had helped him keep his dream of a teaching career alive. The only advantage he could see in moving to Ballyfergus was that it would mean getting away from Rebecca.

A short while later, as Matt and Ben strolled companionably across the pale ash floor of the restaurant towards the exit, they passed close by the dark-haired woman and her friend.

'Matt!'

Abruptly they both stopped and looked over at the table and Matt's face broke into a grin. 'What are you doing here?' he cried and, peeling away from Ben, went straight over to the table and embraced the sexy woman in black who was now standing with a white napkin dangling from her hand. How did Matt know her, he wondered. When they separated, she said, laughing, 'I could ask you the same question.'

'I came to see Ben here,' he replied, 'about a commis chef job.'

'Oh,' she said and blushed a little.

Ben came forward, not daring to look directly at the woman's face in case he betrayed his uneasiness. He could smell her sweet, citrusy perfume now and see the gentle rise and fall of her chest, and lower still, the curve of her shapely calves.

'Ben, this here's Donna.'

Ben smiled and shook her hand.

'. . . and this is my Mum.'

Mum! Startled, he looked straight at her then. This gorgeous creature was Matt's mother? It was impossible. But then he saw the likeness in the oval shape of her face; the strong jaw line; the wide, pleasing mouth. And he saw, now that he was closer, that she was a little older than he'd assumed. Her skin

18

creased at the corners of her eyes and she had deep laughter lines on both sides of her mouth when she smiled. She was no less beautiful than he'd first thought but disappointment tempered his admiration. She must've been very young when she'd had Matt. She looked directly at him, with eyes the same colour as Matt's, every pretty feature illuminated and enhanced by the warm smile her son had inherited from her. 'I'm Jennifer. Lovely to meet you, Ben.'

He managed to mumble something in reply and Jennifer said, 'Well, how did the interview go?'

'Great,' said Ben.

'I've still got to pass an interview with the Head Chef,' added Matt.

'More a formality than anything,' said Ben boldly, without taking his eyes off Jennifer, realising as he said it, that it was a lie. Yet he was desperate for some reason to impress this woman – and please her.

'Oh, that's wonderful, Matt,' she said and turned her attention to him, leaving Ben feeling as if a shadow had just passed overhead, blocking out the rays of the sun. She placed the flat of her palm on Matt's cheek momentarily, causing him to redden with embarrassment, and added, 'I'm so pleased for you. This looks like a great place to work.' She dropped her hand and scanned the restaurant. 'And Belfast isn't so far away, is it?' she said, as if trying to convince herself of something. 'You'll have to move up here, of course. Get your own place.'

'The job isn't in Belfast, Mum. It's in Ballyfergus.'

'Oh! Where?' she said, her question directed not at Matt but at Ben.

'Near the town centre,' explained Ben, hiding his anxiety behind a smile. If Jason refused to employ Matt, he'd have to tell him that he couldn't have the job. 'On the site of an old fish and chip café. Peggy's Kitchen, I think it was called.'

19

'Oh, I know exactly where you mean,' said Jennifer, her face lighting up. 'It used to be a mecca for bikers from all round East Antrim. It closed down years ago. I'd heard it'd been sold.' And turning to Matt she added, her face radiant with joy, 'Imagine getting a job in Ballyfergus! Isn't that just wonderful?'

Ben looked at Jennifer's left hand. There was no band on her ring finger, but that didn't mean anything. She certainly wouldn't look at a guy like him. She'd want someone mature, a man who was secure in himself and his place in the world, someone confident and successful.

But even though he knew he had no chance with her, he wanted to know everything about her. Matt had mentioned that he lived with his mother and his résumé listed an address in Ballyfergus. He had not been looking forward to it but, all of a sudden, Ballyfergus seemed like an attractive proposition . . .

As if he could read Ben's mind, Matt said, 'Mum has her own interior design business in Ballyfergus. Just in case you're looking for someone to design the restaurant.'

So she was both beautiful and smart. 'I'm sorry,' he said, addressing Jennifer. 'A company's already contracted to do the interior. Calico Design. We've used them before.'

She waved away his apology with a hand gesture and simply laughed. 'Good choice. Matt, stop being forward.'

'Well someone has to be,' he said good-naturedly and turned to Ben and added, 'Mum's not very good at self-promotion.' Jennifer blushed and Matt went on, 'I have to help her out now and again.'

'Oh, don't listen to him,' she said, her eyes sparkling with merriment.

Matt pulled his mobile out of his pocket and looked at the screen. 'I gotta go, everyone.' He said his goodbyes and held out his hand to Ben. 'Thanks mate.'

Then he left and Donna went to the ladies', leaving Ben and Jennifer standing alone together.

'Well, wasn't that a coincidence?' she mused. 'Us coming here for lunch at the same time Matt turns up for an interview with you.'

'Serendipity,' said Ben, unable to stop himself from staring at her. She returned his gaze without so much as a blink and they stood like that for a few frozen seconds.

A loud entrance broke the eye contact. It was Rebecca, bare legged and short skirted. Ben's heart sank. What was *she* doing here? She strode across the room, her high heels clipping loudly, her long fake-tanned legs the same colour as the varnished wood floor. She glanced from side to side, making sure everyone in the room was looking at her. And they were. Rebecca was a stunning model, signed with his mother's modelling agency, Diane Crawford Models.

Rebecca flicked her head and long hair cascaded down like a curtain of spun gold. She wore as much make-up as a geisha – and a smile like a sticky plaster.

'Ben,' cried Rebecca, throwing elongated, thin arms around his neck and, to his absolute horror, planting a kiss on his lips. He detached her arms, tentacle-like, and wiped pink, gloopy lipstick from his mouth with the back of his hand. He managed a nervous laugh and she glowered at him from under eyelashes as thick and black as spider's legs.

'Rebecca! What are you doing here?'

'Aren't you pleased to see your girlfriend?' she pouted childishly.

'Well . . . yes . . . of course,' he stumbled.

'I had a modelling job in the area – a promotional thing in Castlecourt – and was just passing,' she said airily. That explained the inappropriate make-up. She placed a proprietorial hand on his arm and lowered her voice. 'I got your text. Thought I'd pop in rather than wait till tonight.'

She flashed a fixed, professional smile at Jennifer and he said, taking her cue, 'Well, it's been very nice meeting you, Jennifer. And I hope to see you and Donna in Ballyfergus when we open.'

'You can count on it,' said Donna, who appeared from nowhere.

Rebecca hooked her arm in his and led him away to the bar. 'Who was that granny you were talking to?' she giggled, with a cool, cruel glance over her shoulder.

'Don't be so rude. And keep your voice down, for heaven's sake. She'll hear you.' He turned his back, like a shield, towards Jennifer's table, filled with an urge to protect her from Rebecca's spiteful comments.

What had he ever seen in her? Apart from a pretty face. Of course, when they'd first met six months ago – courtesy of his mother who was always trying to pair Ben off – Rebecca had been perfectly charming. Fun even. It was only fairly recently, when the chemistry between them had worn off and she began to relax around him, that her true personality had emerged.

Rebecca gave him an icy look, planted her bag on the bar and climbed onto a bar stool, her tight skirt barely covering her crotch. She looked at him calmly with almond-shaped, blue eyes. Each dark brown eyebrow was a perfect, thin arch. 'So who is she?'

'I just interviewed her son, Matt, for a chef's job,' he said, finding it difficult to make eye contact. 'She happened to be in here with her friend at the same time.' Ben glanced at the exit just in time to see Jennifer and her friend walking out.

'So she *is* old enough to be my mother,' said Rebecca. When this elicited no reaction from Ben bar a cold look, she smiled, transforming her face to photo-perfection. 'So what did you want to talk about? Oh, did you get the tickets for the *X Factor Live* show at the Odyssey?'

'I don't want to go, Rebecca. I've told you that a hundred times.'

Her face fell, like this was the first time he'd imparted the news. 'Look, this isn't the time or the place to talk,' he said, looking around self-consciously. 'I'm working.'

He should have finished with Rebecca a long time ago. Lately he'd begun to wonder if her ardour had more to do with *what* he was – a Crawford – than who he was as a person. Last week she'd given him a price list of everything she wanted, nay expected, for her birthday, a gesture so mercenary it had shocked him. And today, those cruel, unnecessary remarks about Jennifer – well, they only confirmed that he was doing the right thing.

'No you're not, you're talking to me. Anyway,' she said, casting a careless glance over her shoulder, 'they can manage without you for a few minutes, can't they? You're the boss after all. No one can tell you what to do.' And she actually snapped her fingers to attract the attention of Chris behind the bar.

Ben's face reddened with embarrassment. 'It's all right, Chris,' he said, jumping up, as the stony-faced barman approached. 'I'll get it.'

He served her drink. She made no offer of payment, not that he'd have taken it. 'I have to get back to work, Rebecca. Can you meet me later?'

'You're going to finish with me, aren't you?' she said flatly.

He ran a hand through his hair. 'Let's talk tonight, Rebecca.'

'You are, aren't you?' she said fiercely, her eyes glinting with angry tears.

'I'm sorry. I didn't want to tell you here. Like this.'

She glared at him and drummed her painted nails like weapons on the granite surface of the bar. 'Why?'

'We're just not suited, Rebecca. You're a great girl but we're not very compatible, are we?'

'Tell me about it,' she said viciously. 'You and your stupid books and old black and white movies. And wanting to sit in on a Saturday night like an old fart reading bloody poetry when everyone else is out partying. Jesus, I don't know how I put up with it.'

Ben felt his face colour. He thought she liked their nights in. Was this how she'd felt all along?

She grabbed her bag and wriggled off the stool, pulling the hem of her skirt down with her right hand. 'Well, you can go screw yourself, Ben Crawford,' she shouted, as a hushed silence descended in the room and all the diners strained to hear. 'I never want to see you again.'

Chapter 3

Lucy was the last to leave the three-storey terrace house on Wellington Park Avenue that she shared with five other second-year girls. She locked the front door and lugged the bag of dirty laundry down to the bus stop. There was a washing machine in the house but it was coin operated and she'd neither the money for that, nor to buy the washing powder. It cost nothing to do laundry at home.

She did not have to wait long for a bus into Belfast city centre. Settling into a seat by the window she jammed her knees into the back of the seat in front, nursed the bag on her lap and looked out on the overcast, calm afternoon. Already the leaves on the trees that lined the many avenues around Queen's University were starting to turn and soon the grey pavements would be littered with their crisp, bronzed beauty. The nights would start to close in, forcing her indoors to her room, making it harder to resist what she knew she must.

At the next stop a group of students, boys and girls, laden down with bags, got on the bus and she listened with lonely envy as they chatted about their plans for the weekend. The other girls in the house often invited each other home for the weekend, but Lucy was never on the receiving end of one of those invitations. And she had no desire to bring any of them home. They weren't her friends. They were house-mates, nothing more. Because try as she might she simply couldn't get on their wavelength – a mindset that seemed to revolve around dyed blonde hair and too much make-up, short-skirted fashion and boyfriends. Their conversation was so *shallow* and she didn't understand much of it anyway, peppered as it was with references to TV shows she didn't watch and music she didn't listen to. To Lucy's mind they spent far too much time partying, while she sat alone in her room most nights poring over books – not because she wanted to but because she was afraid of what might happen if she didn't.

And so Lucy was both amazed and annoyed, in equal measure, that not only had these girls managed to make it into second year, most of them had done it with better exam results than her. She attributed this to the fact that her Applied Mathematics and Physics course was more demanding, the assessment process more challenging, the examinations more rigorous – it must be so. She tried not to dwell on the fact that one girl was reading Biochemistry and another Physics – subjects that could hardly be dismissed as lacking in intellectual rigour. For the idea that these girls might be pretty, popular *and* clever was too much to bear. She would never be pretty, her singular character precluded her ever being popular and she could barely scrape a pass in exams.

Once off the bus, the strap of her heavy bag digging uncomfortably into her bony shoulder, she popped into a newsagents and, after a long deliberation, settled on a card and box of chocolates for her mother's birthday. The card, one of those jokey ones with penguins on it, wasn't exactly suitable but the selection was poor. And, at one pound sixty-nine pence, it was all she could afford. In her closed fist she clutched her last five pound note, wilted and damp from her tight, sweaty grip. Reluctantly, she handed it to the shop-owner with a weak smile. The change, when she counted it, wasn't enough to buy a sheet of wrapping paper. Outside the shop she crouched down on the pavement and stuffed the purchases into her bag with a terrible sense of guilt. Even though they didn't always see eye to eye, her mother deserved better.

She walked briskly to East Bridge Street then, her shoulders hunched against the cold, head down against the roar of the endless, screaming traffic, her shoulder-length hair, the colour of dirty straw, hanging lank round her face. She crossed her arms, feeling the wind through her thin grey jacket, and thought over the events of the past week. It wasn't that she had forgotten her mother's birthday on Wednesday, not at all. It was just that she'd forgotten to put aside some cash for a decent present – and she'd run out of money on her mobile so she couldn't even call. She was on a pay-as-you-go contract, not that her parents knew this. The phone company had cancelled her monthly contract after she'd failed to pay her bills.

She could kick herself now. She should've bought a card and present – maybe a handbag from TK Maxx – earlier in the month, before she was skint. But, to be honest, her mother's birthday was the least of her worries. She'd had to go and see the bank manager this morning, an extremely distressing experience that had her truly, deeply worried for the first time. Up until now she'd managed to keep him off her back with hints of family wealth. Her father had guaranteed her overdraft – a safety net, he'd said, for dire emergencies only.

But today, the bank manager wasn't having any of it. He'd let her have twenty pounds along with a stern warning that enough was enough. If she couldn't manage her money, then he would have to warn the guarantor, her father, that the debt could be called in. She hooked a hank of hair behind her right ear and bit the inside of her cheek. If her father started digging around in her finances, he would unearth the root cause of the debt. She could not allow that to happen.

How had she got herself into such a mess? And how was she ever going to get out of it?

On the train, two suited businessmen sat down opposite her and opened the sports pages of the *Belfast Tele*. She sniffed back the tears with determination and fingered the gold watch on her wrist, an eighteenth birthday present from her father. She could sell the watch. Better still, she could pretend she'd lost it and claim the insurance money. And then, appalled by the idea of such deception, she yanked the sleeve of her jacket over the watch and turned her back on temptation.

The train creaked into motion and rolled out of the station. She would have to seek the answer to her problem – the immediate one of money, at least – in Ballyfergus, in the form of her parents and their deep pockets. And then, she resolved firmly, though not for the first time, she would take herself in hand. She would conquer this thing. This time she meant it. She closed her eyes, inhaling slowly, allowing this resolve to fill her up. And, when she opened her eyes, she found her spirits brighter, her outlook less gloomy.

The train picked up more passengers at Yorkgate, then on to Whiteabbey, Jordanstown, Greenisland, names that, as a child, had signified the world beyond Ballyfergus. A world she had been curious, keen even, to explore until discovering that the place she loved best was her hometown.

She pulled a book on calculus out of her bag and tried

to focus. But the graphs and figures danced around the page, meaningless, incomprehensible. She put down the book and twirled a shaft of thin, brittle hair around her nail-bitten fingers and allowed herself to imagine what it would feel like to do something she actually enjoyed . . .

The train reached the garrison town of Carrickfergus, dominated by the great, grey fortress of the same name, which many considered to be the finest and best-preserved Norman fortress in Ireland. After Mum and Dad split up, Dad used to bring her and Matt here, more often than she cared to remember, as if he didn't know what else to do with them. It was marginally better than sitting around his new flat with none of her favourite things around her. It got better after Dad married Maggie and they moved into the big house. At least that felt like a home, albeit someone else's.

The train pulled into the station and one of the businessmen got off. After leaving Carrickfergus, the train hugged the coastline, the beautiful waters of Belfast Lough stretching out to the east, calm and steel-coloured on this dull day.

The rocking of the carriage had a calming effect on Lucy; the heat made her drowsy. The man across from her turned the page of his paper, the rustling sound reassuring somehow, and her mind turned to the pleasant things that awaited her at home. Her heart swelled with happiness at the thought of her brother, Matt, who would be waiting for her at the station. And her beloved dog, Muffin. She was looking forward to seeing her two little step-sisters, whom she had loved from the day they were born. Her parents too. And by Sunday night, she would be back on the train with a pocketful of cash and all would be well. For a time anyway . . .

The train rumbled along the coast through Downshire before cutting inland again through the town of Whitehead.

Then on through leafy Ballycarry station before emerging, finally, on the shores of Ballyfergus Lough.

The familiar beauty of the Lough brought a sense of peace to Lucy and she smiled at last as she caught her first glimpse of Ballyfergus in the distance. The town's origins lay in the busy ferry port, around which the town had grown and expanded. And now, with a population of over eighteen thousand, the town sprawled up the hillside, engulfing the surrounding rural townlands. A town small enough to know like the back of your hand, big enough to pass through unnoticed, and the only place where Lucy felt at home.

An hour after leaving Belfast city centre, Lucy stepped onto the platform and into a quickening westerly wind. She took a deep breath, inhaling the fresh, clean air, then hurried to the car park. She spotted her mother's red car straight away, the sound of music blasting across the tarmac even though all the windows were shut. When he saw her coming, Matt got out of the car, took her bag and threw it in the boot. Then he gave her a bear hug, nearly lifting her off her feet, and she smiled for the second time that day.

'How are you, big sis?' he said, releasing her.

'Glad to be home.'

At six foot three, Matt had, like her, inherited their father's height and slim build. He'd also inherited their mother's good looks that had so cruelly passed Lucy by – thick, dark hair, an oval-shaped face, high cheekbones, large dark brown eyes, and a smile that was impossible to resist. Lucy, with her washed-out colouring, too-skinny figure and plain face felt as though she'd been handed the leftovers. And while Matt's height was a blessing, hers was a curse. At five foot eleven, she towered over most guys, making her feel ridiculous and conspicuous. It was so unfair – why had Matt got all the trump cards?

Matt frowned. 'What are you thinking?'

'Your hair needs a cut.'

Matt pulled the cap off, ran his hands through his thatch of thick hair. He grinned, put the cap back on and said, 'I'm growing it. Lots of chefs have ponytails these days.'

Lucy gave him a sceptical look and they both got in the car. 'Would you turn that down?' she shouted above the din – of a male rapper she thought, but couldn't be sure.

'Don't you like Dizzee Rascal?'

'Not my favourite,' she grinned and rolled her eyes like she knew what she was talking about. Was Dizzee an artist? Or a band?

Matt turned down the music and Lucy breathed a sigh of relief.

She didn't care for music – of any kind. It was a language she could not understand, a code she could not crack. Background music, whether in the communal kitchen of her digs or drifting down the hall from Matt's room at home, was an unwelcome distraction, demanding her attention, interfering with her ability to think clearly. She preferred silence or the soothing sounds of the spoken word. For this reason, she listened to Radio Four – though she'd quickly learnt to turn it off when her flatmates were about.

Matt drove off, tyres screeching on the tarmac. Mum would have a fit if she saw the way he drove the Micra when she wasn't around. But Lucy would never tell, not on Matt. She stared out the window as they drove the familiar route home. Away from the town centre the streets were all but deserted, save for the odd dog walker or kids wandering home late from school. Nothing much happened in Ballyfergus and that was part of its appeal. She found the continuity of life here reassuring.

'I've got some news for you,' said Matt, interrupting her thoughts. 'I had an interview at The Lemon Tree today. I did text you.'

31

'Oh, problems with my phone,' said Lucy dismissively. 'But what about the job? Did you get it?' She clasped her hands against her chest praying that he'd been successful. Since he'd finished college three months ago he'd found only sporadic work at the local chippy. And it was getting him down. He'd started talking about leaving Ballyfergus for Dublin or London. So the prospect of a job that kept him so close to home was wonderful news.

He grinned, said nothing for what seemed like forever, and then blurted out, 'Yes!'

'Oh, Matt,' she said, her eyes filling with tears. She touched him lightly on the arm. 'That's just the best news. Now you won't have to move away from Northern Ireland.'

'I won't have to move anywhere,' he announced happily, the optimism in his voice making her blink back the tears. 'The job's in Ballyfergus.'

'Where?' she said and sent up a silent prayer of thanks. If Matt had moved away, what would she have done? He was the one person who understood her best and loved her in spite of the way she was. Mum and Dad were always trying to change her, to mould her into the popular, cool daughter they so clearly desired.

Matt told her about the interview with someone called Ben, the new restaurant opening up where Peggy's Kitchen used to be, when he hoped to start work. And Lucy listened to his animated chatter filled with joy. This was what she'd hoped for as they moved into adulthood – both of them living in, or close to, Ballyfergus.

Unlike her flatmate Fran, who came from Ballyclare, and Bernie, who hailed from Limavady, Lucy had never yearned to leave her small town roots behind. Fran and Bernie loathed the places they came from and vowed to never go back. Lucy, who listened with astonishment as they derided their hometowns, had no desire to live anywhere else.

She was not jealous of Matt. She loved him too much to envy him. But she could not help but contrast the direction his life was taking with her own. He had always known what he wanted to do while she, full of uncertainty and doubt, still had no idea.

'Mum and Donna were having lunch there,' went on Matt. 'It was a bit embarrassing. Mum went all soppy when she found out I got the job. I thought she was going to kiss me at one point but, thank God, she only patted me on the cheek.'

They both laughed heartily at this and Lucy managed to say, 'But you'd be disappointed if she did any less.'

'I guess so. Though I'm still going to move out.'

'But why?' she said surprised. 'You and Mum get on really well.' If Matt moved into a place of his own, or worse, a shared flat or house, she'd not see so much of him. 'And, it's cheaper living at home,' she argued, trying to think up reasons to deter him. 'You'll have more money to spend, and save, if you don't waste it on rent. That way you could save up a deposit on a flat of your own.'

He cocked his head to one side, considering this. 'That's true but I really need my own place. I love Mum but it can be difficult sometimes, living at home.'

'In what way?' said Lucy, astounded. She knew that it would be difficult for *her* to live at home full time. Mum was always picking on her, moaning about how she managed her money, needling her about her social life, expecting her to do things around the house she didn't ask of Matt. And though she would've died for her brother, there was no doubt in Lucy's mind that Matt was the favourite.

'Well, you know what she's like about smoking in the house,' he said, reluctantly, as if uncomfortable talking about their mother like this behind her back. 'And she's right, I guess. It's her house, after all,' he added hastily, and waited

33

for Lucy's nod of agreement before going on. 'Well, Rory had a smoke in the TV room the other night and she was none too pleased. It wasn't a big deal but it's hard living under parent's rules when you're an adult.'

'Still, I wouldn't do anything too hasty, if I was you,' she said quickly, looking out the passenger door window to hide the colour in her cheeks, brought forth by the notion of her, of all people, dishing out financial advice. If only Matt knew . . .

She yawned then, the heat of the car making her sleepy. She'd hardly slept the night before worrying about that bank manager and his threats.

'Hard week?' said Matt, leaning over to change radio channels.

'Oh, just the usual,' said Lucy nonchalantly and she thought back on the last, typical week at uni. She'd spent four of the last five nights in her pokey single room in the subdivided house. On Tuesday night she'd gone to the cinema with Amy, one of her few friends, to see a horror film.

'All that partying's catching up on you,' he said and winked conspiratorially.

Lucy forced a grin and looked out the window again. She longed to tell Matt the reality of university life – how much she hated her course; how lonely it was; how she didn't seem to fit in anywhere; how much she missed Muffin. Matt knew her better than anyone else, yet she still could not be herself entirely, even with him.

'That's the one thing I regret about not going to uni,' went on Matt, wistfully. 'The craic must be great.' He shook his head regretfully and Lucy opened her mouth to reassure him that he wasn't missing anything, but Matt, who was never down for long, brightened. 'But you know me. I'd much rather be doing something than poring over dusty books. That was never my style, was it? You were always the clever one,' he said without malice.

How could he not see the truth? She wasn't clever, not clever enough anyway. She'd failed to get the grades for vet school. And she'd never forget the look on her father's face the night she'd told him she wouldn't be following in his footsteps.

Matt's mobile, lying on his lap, flashed and he picked it up and quickly scanned the incoming text, keeping one eye on the road ahead. He chuckled.

'What is it?' said Lucy.

'It's Paul. He wants to know if I'm coming out for a pint tomorrow night.'

'Will you go then?'

'Aye, probably,' he said and she bit her lip on her disappointment. He tossed the phone on his lap and Lucy glared at it jealously. She had hoped they might spend some time together. Matt was so popular, and had a talent for making new friends. Within weeks of starting his catering course he'd been pals with everyone. And if he wasn't actually out socialising, he was never done texting and tweeting and posting things on Facebook.

'Here we are. Home, sweet home.' Matt pulled up in front of a modest detached house in a small leafy development of ten houses just off The Roddens. It had been quite a shock after the big house they'd lived in before their parents split up twelve years ago. Jennifer had tried to sell this new home in Oakwood Grove to Lucy on the basis that it was better located, but she wasn't fooled. Nothing good had come out of her parents' divorce. In fact, it had marked the start of everything going wrong for Lucy.

As soon as she opened the front door Muffin came bumbling slowly up the hall. His bony tail, the only part of him that moved with any exuberance these days, thwacked against the wall. He was a black and white collie, breathless from lack of exercise because he could not walk very far on his arthritic paws. And he was almost deaf. But his chin lifted when he realised it was his Lucy come home. He let out a little whine of delight and raised his snout in the air.

Lucy dropped to her knees, her eyes filled with tears at the sight of him, and he came over to her and sat down. He rested his head on her shoulder and let out a long contented sigh. Lucy buried her face in his coarse, dry fur, the lustrous glossiness of his youth long gone. And then he yelped and jumped back – Lucy, shuffling on the carpet, had leant her weight on his front paw.

'I'm sorry, Muffin!' she cried. She would rather hurt herself than her best friend. Like Matt, Muffin's love was unconditional. He didn't care that she was unattractive and had no friends. He simply loved her. And she him.

'Hey, what's up, old boy?' said Matt, stepping around them both. He touched the dog on the head. Muffin licked Matt's hand and sat down again.

'I accidentally knelt on his paw. Oh, look Matt. He's holding it up. Do you think it'll be all right?' She hugged the dog again and whispered, 'I'm so sorry, Muffin. It was an accident. I never meant to hurt you.' Sensing her distress the dog, still seated, licked her face and his tail swept across the carpet like a broom.

'He'll be all right in a minute,' said Matt. 'He's always hurting himself. Walking into things. Happens all the time.'

Lucy's eyes filled with tears. She struggled to her feet and Muffin ambled slowly back up the hall to the kitchen where he spent most of his time now curled up in his bed. He flopped down with a weary sigh and Lucy said, 'Oh, don't say that, Matt.'

Matt came over and patted her briefly on the shoulder. 'He's fourteen, Lucy. That's old for a collie.'

Lucy's bottom lip quivered. 'I don't want him to die, Matt.'

Matt squeezed her shoulders. 'I know. I don't either. But he's not in great shape. And you wouldn't want him to suffer, would you?'

Lucy blinked back the tears. 'No, of course not.'

'And when the time comes, we won't let him, okay?'

'Okay,' she said bravely. She remembered with sudden clarity the summer she'd got Muffin. She remembered a soft bundle of black and white fur tearing madly round the garden after the water spurting out of the sprinkler. She'd been only six then and his liveliness had astounded, almost frightened, her at times. She had loved it best when he, finally exhausted, fell asleep in her arms, his black nose like a wet pebble, his warm damp breath like a kiss on her cheek. Everything was perfect then; her parents still loved each other, and she had the best dog in the world.

After they'd had something to eat together, Matt went out. She was disappointed, but having the house all to herself was the next best thing.

Now was the perfect opportunity to raid the cupboards for food – she squirrelled two tins of tuna, a tinned steak pie and a can of corned beef in her bag, along with shampoo and soap from a supply she found under the stairs. She'd take more food on Sunday night before she left. Mum'd never notice – she stockpiled food like there was a war on. She tipped her laundry on the floor of the narrow utility room and rummaged in the under-sink cupboard for washing powder but the box, when she found it, was empty. She gave the pile of laundry a desultory kick and decided to deal with it later.

Upstairs Lucy unpacked her few belongings and put on flannel pyjamas and stood for a moment staring at her long reflection in the mirror on her bedroom wall. Pale grey eyes,

37

as dull and lifeless as a winter sky, stared back at her. Her thin, mousey hair did nothing to enhance her long face – nor disguise her sallow skin and the red-raw spots clustered like barnacles around the corners of her mouth. She turned away – no wonder people disliked her. She was grotesque. She would never have a boyfriend. She would never marry or have children. She would be alone all her life.

A little sob escaped her and Lucy straightened up and pulled herself together. Marriage and family life wasn't for everyone, she told herself sternly. She would just have to find something useful to do with her life. She had few natural talents, but an empathy with animals was one of them. How she wished that, like Matt, she'd been brave enough to follow her heart, instead of trying to please. Because a degree in Applied Mathematics and Physics, assuming she managed to graduate, was hardly going to lead her to her ideal job, was it? And yet, she could not give it up. Not now, not when the expectation of so many weighed so heavily on her shoulders – Mum, Dad, Grandad, Maggie, even Matt.

She tugged on a fleece dressing gown and slipped her feet into an old pair of slippers. Her life was a mess but tonight she would not think about it. Tonight she would try and relax. And she would not even turn on the computer because last night she'd lost seventy quid on Celebration Bingo. Her heartbeat quickened and her stomach made a little nauseous somersault at the thought. She mustn't get carried away like that again. Only she so loved the tacky, garish websites; the guaranteed million-pound jackpots; the nervous anticipation; and the adrenaline rush when she won. Oh, there was nothing like it. And she knew, she just knew, that if she could find the money to keep on playing, then one day – not tomorrow or the day after maybe, but one day soon – she would win millions and her life would be utterly trans-formed.

She took a deep breath and calmed herself. Now and again she needed to prove to herself that she was the one in control.

Downstairs, she sat on the sofa in front of the TV, ruffled the fur between Muffin's ears, and told herself it wasn't all bad. At the end of the month her allowance would arrive in her bank account, and she would be able to breathe again. Meantime, she would be strict with herself – absolutely no online gambling.

Chapter 4

Jennifer sat in the passenger seat in the car on the way home feeling decidedly downbeat. And she'd no reason to; she'd had a great day out with her best friend and Matt had a proper job at last.

'What did you think of Ben Crawford?' said Donna, suddenly. 'Wasn't he cute?'

'Was he? I hadn't noticed.'

'He was a bit young, though,' mused Donna, as if Jennifer hadn't spoken.

Jennifer blushed and stared out the window. She hadn't thought him that much younger than her. Maybe ten years. Was that too much of an age difference? But what did it matter? Nothing was going to happen between them. He wasn't the least bit interested in her and he had a beautiful girlfriend.

The car came off a roundabout and started the gentle downhill approach to Ballyfergus. In the failing light, the countryside was a patchwork of dark shades of green, interspersed with the lights of the many farmsteads that dotted the rolling hills.

And yet in spite of the calming beauty all around, her

heart was not at peace. She was troubled with recollections of the way Rebecca had kissed Ben – so boldly and right in the middle of the busy restaurant. He had looked a little embarrassed, certainly, but what man could say no to a girl like that? He couldn't wait to drag her off to the bar so they could spend time together, alone.

What was this unfamiliar emotion that troubled her so, that felt like anger but wasn't? She placed a hand on her neck, recognising it at last for jealousy. She was jealous of Rebecca. It was a ludicrous notion – that she should be jealous of a girl she didn't even know because of a man she'd only just met. But it was there nonetheless, nestled in her chest, hard and mean like a stone.

He was the first man in a long time to arouse her interest. She recalled with pleasure the way her heartbeat had quickened under his gaze. She'd thought she'd sensed some sort of primitive attraction between them, but now she wasn't so certain. Had she imagined it all? And even if there was some sort of connection between them, it clearly wasn't enough to compete with gorgeous young women half her age. And what hurt most was the knowledge that, though she was in good shape, she was past her prime. If she wanted a partner in life, it was no good looking at younger men. She had to set her sights a little lower and the age limit a little higher. And though she hated the idea of a computer dating site, perhaps Donna was right. At her age, she thought despondently, she had to be realistic.

It was almost dark by the time Donna dropped her home. She walked wearily down the side of the house and entered by the utility room, not bothering to switch on the light. She closed the door, took a step forwards in the dim light and the toe of her foot connected with something soft on the floor. She stumbled, caught her ankle on the corner of a cupboard door and almost fell.

'Ouch!' she cried out in pain, dropped her bags on the floor and grabbed on to the worksurface. Tutting crossly, she flicked on the light. A pile of laundry, Lucy's things, lay in an untidy heap on the floor and the cupboard door hung open. She could see now that she had ripped her tights and grazed her skin.

'Is that you, Mum?' called Lucy, as she came and stood in the doorway. She was wearing a pair of pyjamas and a horrible, old, grey dressing gown that used to belong to David. 'Are you all right?'

Unable to stop herself, Jennifer said irritably, 'No, I'm not. I nearly took my foot off on that door. Did you leave it open? And what's this dirty laundry doing all over the floor?'

'I couldn't find any washing powder,' said Lucy defensively. Muffin, who took an age to get anywhere these days, appeared loyally by Lucy's feet, his head cocked to one side.

Jennifer let out a loud sigh. It wasn't fair of her to take her bad temper out on Lucy. She gathered up her handbag and shopping bags. 'I'm sorry, Lucy. It's lovely to see you. Did you have a good week?'

'Yeah. Great.'

'Well, come here and let me give you a hug,' smiled Jennifer, picking her way over the laundry to Lucy. Even in three-inch heels, Jennifer was still some inches shorter than her daughter. She put her arms around her and immediately felt her stiffen. She released her and swallowed the hurt, remembering a time, once, when Lucy could not get enough of her mother's hugs. Where had that loving child gone? And what was wrong with her face? 'Those spots around your mouth look sore, pet.'

Lucy put a protective hand to her chin and turned away. Jennifer, remembering what it was like to have bad skin, felt sorry for her. Perhaps she was finding her university course hard going – stress could cause an outbreak of spots. But Lucy was no longer in her teens – she shouldn't have to live with skin like that. 'It might be acne,' she suggested, walking over to the table and setting her bags down on the worn seat of a pine chair. 'Maybe the doctor could give you something for them.'

'It's not acne.'

Jennifer kicked her shoes off, leaving them where they fell on the worn lino. 'No, you're right. It doesn't really look like acne. More like a skin infection.'

Lucy removed her hand from her face and said, angrily, 'Mum, it's not a skin infection! It's just spots. Ugly, yes. Disgusting, yes. But just spots! They'll go away soon enough.'

Jennifer took a deep breath and counted to five. 'I'm only trying to help,' she said quietly. Lucy said nothing in reply and then another thought occurred to Jennifer. 'Are you eating properly? Because sometimes when you don't eat enough fruit and –'

'Oh, for God's sake,' cried Lucy, this time raising her voice. She gripped the back of a chair with both hands until her knuckles went white. 'Don't you know when to leave it, Mum?'

Jennifer, genuinely perplexed and hurt by what she perceived as her daughter's over-reaction, said, 'Well, I'm sorry. I thought . . . never mind.' She glanced through the utility room door at the pile of laundry. 'Don't tell me the washing machine at your digs is still broken.'

'Yep.'

Lucy paid out an absolute fortune for a room you couldn't swing a cat in. 'It hasn't worked since you moved in. I feel like ringing the landlord up and giving him a piece of my mind.'

'Don't you dare,' snapped Lucy. 'I'm the one paying the rent. Do you want to make me look ridiculous?'

43

Jennifer, with no desire to see the argument escalate any further, bit her tongue. She pulled out a chair and sat down heavily. Why was Lucy still acting like a rebellious teenager? She and Lucy ought to have gotten past this stage and moved on to a more harmonious relationship, like the one she shared with Matt. 'Come and sit down,' she smiled, patting the seat of the chair beside her. 'And tell me all about your week.'

Lucy complied, folding herself into the chair with her shoulders hunched, like she wanted to disappear. She'd had an issue with her height since primary school when she'd been the tallest girl in her class. Jennifer wished she could make her believe that her height was something to be proud of. She would look so much better if she stood up straight and tall, and a cheery smile would help too – but there was no telling Lucy.

'I went out for a drink with the girls in the house a couple of times,' said Lucy, brushing crumbs off the table with the sleeve of her dressing gown. Jennifer watched them fall to the floor and decided to let the behaviour go unremarked. 'But everywhere's so expensive these days. It's nearly four quid for a glass of wine in some places. Apart from the Union,' she went on, 'but you wouldn't want to go there every night.'

Jennifer clasped her hands together and rested them on the table, trying not to look alarmed. Lucy didn't talk much about her university life, academic or social, and Jennifer sometimes wondered if she was keeping something from her. But then all students kept secrets from their parents, didn't they? She told herself not to worry so much – it was all part of growing up. But still, she couldn't help herself from commenting, 'I hope you're not drinking too much.'

'Of course not,' said Lucy evenly, 'But you can hardly go out without having a couple of glasses of wine, can you?

44

And taxis home are expensive too. You wouldn't want me to be walking home from the city centre late at night, would you?'

'Well, no. But aren't there late night buses?'

'Not always.' And for some reason Lucy blushed. Jennifer suspected she was not being entirely truthful, but, pleased to hear that Lucy had friends to go out with, she decided to let it go. 'It's great that you're going out with your friends and having a good time. That's what university's all about. So long as your studies don't suffer.'

'They don't.'

Jennifer yawned and glanced at the clock and said without moving, 'I guess I'd better go upstairs and get out of these glad rags. I'll show you what I bought tomorrow, shall I? I don't think I have the energy for it tonight.'

Lucy toyed with the frayed belt of her dressing gown. 'So, as I was saying,' she said with a note of urgency in her voice, 'things are expensive. Even food.'

'Tell me about it,' laughed Jennifer good-humouredly, and she stood up. 'Your brother just about eats me out of house and home.' She collected her bags and coat, and added, rather sadly, 'Though not for much longer.'

'So I was wondering,' said Lucy, interrupting Jennifer's thoughts, 'if I could have a hundred quid. Just to see me through till the end of the month.'

'What?' said Jennifer, doubting what she'd just heard.

'I'm a bit short, Mum. I was wondering if you could give me a hundred pounds.' She paused and looked searchingly into Jennifer's stunned face and added, 'Just this once.'

'But I don't understand,' said Jennifer, setting her bags and coat down again on the adjacent chair. 'I gave you an extra fifty only a week ago.'

'But that was for text books.'

Jennifer, confused, sat down again. 'But how can you be

short of money? Your monthly allowance is more than enough to live on. And I thought you said you would budget?' Last year, her first year at uni, she'd tapped Jennifer constantly for money. At the end of the summer they'd had a long chat about finances and Lucy had promised that she'd manage her money. And here they were, less than a fortnight into the new term, and she was asking for more. 'This can't go on, Lucy.'

Although the business was doing okay and she could meet her monthly commitments, Jennifer wasn't exactly awash with money. David paid the bulk of Lucy's living costs and education, but Jennifer contributed a hefty sum too. She rested her elbow on the table and rubbed her brow with her thumb and forefinger. 'I'm sorry, pet,' she said, feeling both guilty and resolved, 'but I don't think I can help you out. You'll have to go overdrawn for a bit and pay it back at the end of the month.'

Lucy's face reddened and she pulled the folds of the dressing gown defensively round her thin frame. 'It's only a hundred quid, Mum,' she said grumpily.

'*Only* a hundred quid!' repeated Jennifer in astonishment.

'And Dad said the overdraft was only for emergencies.'

'Do you think I'm made of money?' said Jennifer, losing it a bit. 'The car needs to be taxed and MOTed, I need to get the leak in the shower fixed and the outside of the house desperately needs painting. Not to mention replacing this kitchen.' She looked at the pale blue paint peeling off the cupboards she had painted herself when they'd moved in, the dripping tap, the cracked wall tiles and shook her head in exasperation. 'Anyway, what do you need it for?'

'I told you,' said Lucy irritably, avoiding eye contact, as she had done for most of this conversation. 'Things are expensive. Everyone at uni's in debt.'

'Well, you don't need to be. Not with the money you

have coming in. I thought you knew how to budget, Lucy. Haven't I been over it with you time and again?' Jennifer sighed heavily, got up, opened a kitchen drawer and pulled out a pen and a notebook.

'What are you doing?' said Lucy.

Jennifer sat down again and opened the notebook. 'Let's go through this one more time. It's not rocket science. I'll help you draw up a monthly budget and, if you stick to it, you'll see. It'll be so much easier to manage your money.'

Lucy put the flat of her hands on the table. 'No,' she said forcefully and then softened her tone. 'It's late, Mum. You must be tired. Let's go to bed.'

'But I can see this is troubling you,' said Jennifer with a weary smile. Perhaps Lucy was embarrassed to ask for help. 'We can have this sorted out in no time.'

Lucy's face reddened. 'No really. It's okay. I got you a present.' She got up abruptly, the legs of the chair squeaking on the lino. 'I'll go and get it,' she added and dashed out of the room.

When Lucy came back into the room a few minutes later, she sheepishly handed Jennifer a small present and a card. 'Happy Birthday, Mum. I'm sorry it's a bit late.'

'Oh, that doesn't matter one little bit, Lucy,' smiled Jennifer. 'I'm just so pleased that you remembered. Thank you.'

Lucy went and stood by the cooker, gnawing on the nail of her right thumb. Jennifer set the present on her lap – and tried not to let her disappointment show. It was sloppily wrapped in her own paper, a distinctive roll of metallic wrap with coloured butterflies on it that she kept under her bed. And it had been hastily done – perhaps just this very moment. For as she looked down at the parcel, a piece of sellotape came away and the end of the parcel popped open.

'It's not much,' said Lucy, hastily. 'Just a token really.'

47

Jennifer looked up. 'I don't expect you to buy me expensive things. What have I always told you? It's the thought that counts.'

Jennifer opened the card, an odd, humorous one that she didn't at first understand. When she got the joke, at last, she smiled and said, 'That's nice,' and set the card on the table. Then she ripped the paper off the present to reveal a small box of budget dark chocolates. The sort of thing Jennifer might put into a raffle at the senior citizens club her father attended. She set them on the table and scrunched the paper into a tight ball in her fist. 'Thank you,' she said, hoping to God that Lucy couldn't read what she was really thinking.

Lucy smiled back weakly and cleared her throat. 'I know it's not much, Mum. But as I said, I haven't got a lot of spare cash at the moment.'

'That's okay, darling. You're a student, for heaven's sake,' said Jennifer in a cheerful voice, blinking. 'The real treat for me is spending time with you. I'm looking forward to our shopping trip on Sunday.'

'I guess Matt's in the same boat,' said Lucy. 'I mean he hasn't got a lot of money either.'

'No, you're right. He hasn't,' said Jennifer, grasping at the opportunity to move the conversation on from this hurtful, thoughtless gift. It was a standing joke within the family that Jennifer hated dark chocolate with a passion. How could Lucy have forgotten?

'Matt didn't buy me anything. Not even a card,' she laughed, trying to sound light-hearted. 'He made one.' She got up and threw the ball of paper in the bin, lifted Matt's card off the top of the microwave and handed it to Lucy. It was made from a sheet of stiff white card folded in half with a funny caricature of her in black ink on the front. He'd drawn her at her office, in boots and one of the wrap

48

dresses she sometimes wore for work, surrounded by rolls of wallpaper and carpet samples. Matt was a good cartoonist. Inside it read, 'To the best Mum in the world. Love from Matt.'

'Isn't it fabulous?' said Jennifer, pressing home the fact that a gift could cost nothing – and yet mean the world to the recipient.

When Lucy had examined the card, Jennifer placed it carefully on the shelf again and said, 'Well, it's time I went to bed.'

'Mum?' said Lucy in a small voice. 'What about the hundred pounds, then?'

Jennifer's heart sank and she looked away. Didn't Lucy listen to a word she'd said? Did she have to make this any harder than it already was?

She felt the emotion well up in her chest and her throat narrowed. And her voice, when she spoke, came out hard and uncompromising and not conflicted like the way she felt inside. 'No, Lucy. I bailed you out all summer, even when you had a job at the Day Centre. You never saved a penny. I just don't understand what you do with your money. I don't think you know how to do without. When I was at –'

'Yes, yes, I know all about when you were at university,' interrupted Lucy, rage bubbling up in the face of her mother's intransigence. 'You cleaned toilets in a pub and walked there in the rain with plastic bags wrapped round your legs because you didn't have a proper coat. And your student house had no heating.'

'Well, it's true! You wouldn't put up with the deprivations I did. Your generation doesn't know how to do without.' Jennifer ran a hand down the side of her face and sighed. 'You have to learn how to budget and budgeting requires self-discipline, forward planning, and sometimes a bit of

49

discomfort and self-denial. How are you ever going to manage in a home of your own without those skills? And me giving you constant handouts isn't going to teach you them.'

Lucy scowled. 'Is that the lecture over then?'

'Oh, Lucy,' cried Jennifer in exasperation. 'I'm not trying to lecture you, I'm trying to help you.'

'If you want to help me, give me a hundred pounds.'

Jennifer looked her daughter straight in the eye, her heart pounding. 'I'm sorry, Lucy. I simply can't do that.'

'You can but you won't. There's a difference, Mum,' said Lucy coldly. 'I can't believe you're so heartless.' And then she let out a little sob and ran out of the room, leaving Jennifer feeling like the worst mother in the world.

Lucy was still in bed when Jennifer left the house the next morning for the supermarket and, when she came home, she found David sitting on the chocolate brown leather sofa in her small lounge with his long, athletic legs crossed. He wore dark blue jeans and a casual, ocean blue shirt under a tailored jacket and looked quite at home drinking a cup of coffee. She remembered that he'd come to drive Lucy over to his house for lunch with her two step-sisters – Rachel, six, and four-year-old Imogen – and Maggie, his wife of eight years.

Jennifer had been friends with Maggie for fifteen years. They'd met at an evening pottery class in the community centre, when Jennifer was trying to find an outlet for her creativity and keep her marriage together. Their friendship had blossomed through shared interests – Maggie was a talented amateur jewellery designer. Jennifer had been surprised when David and Maggie quietly started dating nearly two years after the divorce – she could not reproach her old friend on that score – but the marriage had effectively meant the end of a beautiful friendship. Jennifer wished her old friend well, but she couldn't help but be a tiny little bit envious of David. He'd gone on to start a new life and a new family and she was exactly where she'd started twelve years ago.

He set the cup on the coffee table, uncrossed his legs and said, a little embarrassed, 'I hope you don't mind me helping myself.'

'Not at all,' she said graciously, wondering how he would feel if she came into his home uninvited and made free and easy with the facilities. But she pushed this rather mean thought away. She did not want them to be enemies.

'Lucy wasn't ready when I arrived,' he explained, his pale limpid blue eyes magnified by the stylish, silver-rimmed glasses he now wore constantly. 'She said she'd slept in.'

Jennifer raised her eyes guiltily to the ceiling. She'd hardly slept herself last night, torn between the desire to give in to Lucy on the one hand, and withstand her demands on the other. But she'd woken in the morning with a new resolve.

Upstairs someone walked across the room and then the shower came on. Jennifer dropped her bag on the floor and, without bothering to take off her suede jacket, sat down on the other leather sofa.

'Matt told me all about the new job,' said David.

'It's wonderful news, isn't it?'

'I think it might be,' he said, expressing his reserved approval. David was economical with his emotions, measured, thoughtful. Qualities she had once admired and now found incredibly boring.

There was a silence as David looked around the room. She'd recently introduced a neutral colour scheme whilst retaining the costly furniture; replaced the dated curtains with plantation shutters; and hung a keenly-priced, over-sized mirror from Laura Ashley over the fireplace. Proof that you didn't have to spend a fortune to make a room

51

stylish. 'You've made some changes in here. It looks good.'

'Look, David,' she said quickly, with a glance at the ceiling, 'there's something you and I need to talk about. It concerns Lucy. She asked me for another hundred quid, last night.'

'So?' he said and gave her one of his smug, ironic half-smiles she knew so well. David was supremely self-assured, a quality that irritated her now, yet it had been one of the things that attracted her to him in the first place. Theirs had never been an equal partnership. He always knew best. And she didn't realise how much he undermined her. It was only after the divorce that she'd had the confidence to start the business.

'I didn't give it to her,' she said firmly. 'It's time she took responsibility for her own finances. She can't seem to live within her monthly allowance. Not the odd time, but consistently week after week, month after month. What did she do with all that money she earned over the summer? I never took any off her for bed and board.'

There was a considered pause before David said, slowly, 'Do you expect her to live like a nun? All students overspend.'

It was exactly what she expected him to say. Not just because he disagreed with her in principle but also, she suspected, because money wasn't an issue for him. He owned the only, very successful, vet practice in Ballyfergus. And when it came to his children, he was too indulgent.

Thankfully Muffin padded into the room just then, breaking the tension.

'Hey, boy,' said David, reaching out his hand to the collie.

The dog licked it, flopped down at his feet, silvery trails of saliva dripping onto David's scuffed desert boots. David ruffled the rangy fur between his ears. 'That's a good boy,' he said softly, reminding Jennifer how his kindness to animals

52

had won her heart. Muffin put his head on his paws and sighed contentedly. David ran his long fingers down the animal's back, gently probing.

'He's a bit thin,' he observed. 'How's his appetite?'

'Much the same as always. He doesn't want to go out much though.'

'Mmm.' He rested his hands on his thighs and, staring at the animal, nodded slowly to himself. 'Well, let me know as soon as you think he's in any discomfort.'

Jennifer swallowed the lump in her throat. 'Of course,' she said, understanding perfectly his meaning. He would be the one to put Muffin down when the time came.

'I'll make sure he doesn't know a thing.'

David looked at his watch and Jennifer, who could not let the matter of Lucy and money go unresolved said, 'She'll ask you for money, David. Promise me you won't give it to her.' And then she remembered that David never liked being told what to do.

He arranged a pained, affronted expression on his face. 'Are you telling me that I can't give my own daughter money?'

'Of course not,' said Jennifer, retracting hastily. She rubbed suddenly sweaty palms on the thighs of her blue jeans. 'All I'm asking,' she said carefully, 'is to please consider whether it's in Lucy's best interests to do so.'

He stood up, his well-built frame towering over her. Muffin never stirred. 'I think I'm capable of making that judgement call.'

Jennifer tilted her chin up and met his eye, refusing to be intimidated by his height and the size eleven feet planted firmly on her carpet. 'She's not going to learn anything about money management if we keep bailing her out every time she gets into trouble.'

He shoved his hands in the pockets of his jeans and looked down at her scathingly. 'Would you really see her short, Jennifer? Leave her without money for food and bus fares?'

'Of course I don't *want* to see that,' said Jennifer, choking up with emotion. 'But I also know that if we don't stop these handouts she's never going to learn to stand on her own two feet.'

David, who never listened to criticism of his children, said, 'Well, I for one am not going to send my daughter back to uni without a penny in her pocket. And I have to say, I'm quite astounded by your attitude, Jennifer. How can you be so mean to your own daughter?'

'I'm not being mean,' she responded robustly. 'I'm trying to be a responsible parent. And you're doing what you always do, David. Spoiling her.'

He reacted angrily. 'That is not true,' he said loudly. 'My children aren't spoiled. They appreciate the value of things, they don't take what they have for granted and they know what's right and wrong.'

Jennifer considered this, recalling Lucy's somewhat dubious moral code. Only last week she'd been undercharged in Boots but instead of pointing it out to the assistant at the time, she'd come home crowing about it. 'I'm not so sure about Lucy. And she's thoughtless. She gave me dark chocolates for my birthday.'

'Well, give them to someone else if you don't like them.'

A deathly silence followed during which they glared at each other. And then Muffin, sensing the charged, negative atmosphere in the room, hauled himself to his feet and padded towards the door. Jennifer turned to watch him go – and let out a little gasp.

Lucy stood in the doorway dressed for outside, wet hair plastering her head and a huge bag slung over her shoulder. Her eyes glinted with angry tears, as yet unshed, and the expression on her long, thin face was furious.

'Lucy, I . . . I didn't see you there,' said Jennifer feebly, desperately trying to recall exactly what, in her rage, she had said. How much had Lucy heard?

'I'm ready to go,' said Lucy coolly, ignoring Jennifer.

David gave Jennifer a sort of triumphant look, pulled his car keys out of his front pocket and said cheerfully, 'Me too, pet.'

'Do you mind if I stay the night?' said Lucy, addressing her father. 'I don't want to stay here.'

'Sure.'

So Lucy was up to her old tricks again – playing one parent off against the other, acting like a petulant teenager. Mind you, her tactics only worked because David played right into her hands.

Jennifer felt that she ought to try to resolve things between them. And so she said, damp patches of perspiration forming under her arms, 'Lucy, please. Don't be like this. I thought we could go out for something to eat tonight. And go shopping tomorrow.'

Lucy furrowed her brow and feigned confusion. 'Why would you want to go out with a, what was it, Dad? A "spoilt brat"? And I can't go shopping. I don't have any money. You know that.'

Jennifer sighed. 'I didn't say you were a spoilt brat, Lucy. I said you *acted* like one sometimes. That's not the same thing.'

Ignoring her, Lucy went on, theatrically, 'What else was it you said? That I don't know the difference between right and wrong? That I'm thoughtless?'

'Lucy, I'm sorry I said those things. I was trying to make a point to your father, that's all.' Jennifer looked to David for support but he, finding sudden fascination in a loose thread on the cuff of his shirt, blanked her.

'I heard what you were trying to do, Mum. You were

trying to stop Dad from helping me when I . . . I . . .' Her voice started to crack up and she paused momentarily, sniffed and went on, 'I don't even know where my next meal's coming from. If anyone's thoughtless, it's you.' And with that, partly covering her face with her hand, she burst into tears.

Jennifer bit her lip, her chest tight with anxiety, hard pressed to tell if Lucy's distress was entirely genuine – or partly a calculated tactic. In any event, it had the desired effect. David went over to her immediately, put his arm around her shoulder and gave her a hug.

'There, there, now. Don't cry, darling,' he cooed, talking to her like she was a toddler who'd just fallen over and scratched her knee, or some such calamity. He kissed the top of her wet head. 'Maggie's made lasagne for lunch, your favourite.'

Jennifer, watching them, was incensed. Couldn't David see that he was simply fuelling Lucy's inappropriate behaviour? And yet it broke her heart to see her only daughter standing there in tears, estranged from her. They always seemed to be clashing. Would they never be friends?

'Come on, Lucy,' said David, tightening his grip around her shoulders. 'Let's take you home.' And as they turned away, united against her, Lucy threw the briefest of glances over her shoulder. And Jennifer could almost swear her daughter smiled.

Chapter 5

Lunch service was over and Ben was just about to go home for a few hours before coming back for the evening shift when the phone in the office rang. It was Vincent Maguire, an accountant who'd worked for his father for years.

He got straight to the point. 'Ben, I've just heard that Calico Design's gone into administration.'

Ben sat down. 'When?'

'Two days ago.'

If it had been anyone but Vince on the end of the phone, Ben would've doubted his word. Ben had talked to Bronagh Kearney, the designer, only last week and everything had been rosy. 'Voluntary?'

'No. Creditors forced it. Shame really. They had a big contract for that new chain of nursing homes – McClure and Esler. When they went bust Calico were left high and dry. As soon as the creditors heard, they were onto them like a pack of wolves demanding payment. And of course, they couldn't cough up. You haven't paid any money over to them, have you?'

Ben shook his head, then remembered that Vincent could not see him. 'No, not a penny. Invoice on completion.'

'That's a relief.' Vince lowered his voice conspiratorially. 'The insolvency practitioner's a good pal of mine – we go way back – and he thinks they'll go into liquidation. If I was you I'd be looking pronto for someone else to do up that restaurant of yours.'

After he'd put the phone down, Ben sat quietly for a few minutes considering his options. It was bad news, for sure, but they'd been lucky too. At least they wouldn't lose any money. Not like Calico's creditors, poor buggers, some of whom themselves would go bust because of Calico's demise.

It did, however, leave him with the pressing problem of finding another interior designer to replace Calico at short notice. And he knew just the person: Jennifer.

He sat up straight, feet planted firmly on the ground, amazed that fate had landed this chance in his lap. Not only would he see her again, he'd get to spend time with her, get to know her. He tapped his fingers on the table, thinking how he would sell this to his father. Because he would not like Ben using someone he didn't know. Alan's intricate network of business contacts, immense and complex, like neural pathways to the brain, connected him to all corners of the province and beyond. Alan would see Jennifer as a risk. He would not like it; but on this, Ben decided, he would prevail, just as he had done with Matt and the commis chef job. Jason had been cross with him for offering the lad the job and he'd only agreed to the appointment as a personal favour for Ben.

This was the silver lining his mother, Diane, used to talk about when they were little and a toy broke or he fell over and skinned an elbow. Of course, he'd since learnt that sometimes bad things happened that were so awful, so wrong, no good could ever come of them. After Ricky, his mother didn't talk about silver linings any more.

Ben closed his eyes briefly and let out a loud sigh. He

mustn't go there, he mustn't let his thoughts dwell on Ricky, because it only led to one thing – black depression. He shook his head and picked up the big rectangular board sitting upended in the corner. Calico Design had put it together – a story board, Bronagh had called it. Swatches of fabric and wallpaper were glued haphazardly to it. Paint colour charts, the size and shape of bookmarks, fanned out like playing cards. Photographs torn from brochures and magazines were artfully displayed at angles, so completing the collage. Ben and Alan had agreed on exactly how they wanted the restaurant to look, for once working in rare harmony, and Bronagh had delivered it – in concept at least.

He set the board behind the chair once more and, one quick Google search later, Jennifer's phone number was at his fingertips.

Jennifer pulled nervously into the car park beside Peggy's Kitchen, fifteen minutes early. She parked between two cars, facing the front of the old café, and switched off the engine. She slid down in the seat, thankful for the light rain pattering softly on the windscreen, blurring her view and providing her with welcome camouflage. She'd wait a bit. Best not to look too keen – on both a business, and a personal, front.

She'd received the call from Ben a few days ago and her stomach had immediately gone into a spasm, churning like a washing machine. And even now, while she tried to talk sense to herself, she was like a love-struck teenager. Butterflies played tag in her stomach and her heart raced like a train.

'Catch yourself on, Jennifer,' she said out loud. 'Ben Crawford has a girlfriend, remember?'

Her mobile phone vibrated in her jacket pocket. She pulled the phone out and read the text message. It was from Lucy, saying that she would be getting the train home the following night. She finished with 'Luv L xo'. Was this text an olive branch? She hadn't seen or spoken to Lucy since last Friday when she'd stormed out of the house with her father – Lucy hadn't answered her calls or returned her messages. But clearly they were back on texting terms and she was coming home, which had to be a good sign.

But, in spite of this apparent truce, Jennifer was troubled by her daughter – or, more accurately, by her conflicting emotions towards her. A mother was supposed to love, wholly, fully, unconditionally. And Jennifer did love her daughter. But Lucy had a knack of arousing a whole raft of other, not so benign, emotions. Feelings Jennifer could hardly bring herself to acknowledge – irritation, intolerance, dislike, anger even. She blushed, ashamed to own them in herself. She reminded herself sternly that it was Lucy's *behaviour* that sometimes induced these sentiments – not Lucy herself. She'd been telling herself this ever since Lucy, aged seven, had a temper tantrum on Christmas morning because she didn't get a particular, expensive doll that she coveted. But Lucy was twenty now – an adult capable, in theory anyway, of marriage, motherhood, emigration, relocation, complete independence. Jennifer fretted that the behaviours she observed were, like the foundation stones of a building, an integral part of Lucy's character now.

And there was something else too – a vague uneasiness that, when it came to Lucy, everything wasn't quite as it ought to be. It was more intuition than a concrete thought, for when she tried to pin it down, it bobbed away like a Halloween apple in a barrel of water.

But she had no wish to spend another weekend locking horns with Lucy. She would put last Friday night out of her mind and try and make a fresh start. She keyed a short, warm reply to Lucy and slipped the phone back in her pocket.

Then she played with the zip on her brown leather jacket,

wondering briefly if her choice of casual chic – dark jeans, a crisp white shirt, and cowboy boots – was flattering. Then she tried to convince herself that she didn't care what Ben thought of her, except in a professional capacity.

Switching to designer mode, she flicked on the windscreen wipers and stared at the unprepossessing building opposite. It was single storey, of indeterminate age, with a steeply pitched slate roof. It might have been a workshop once. The harled, pebbly exterior was grey and streaked with water stains from a leak in the guttering and a yellow skip rested on the tarmaced forecourt. One of the front windows was boarded up and a huge, plastic-shiny sign announcing 'Peggy's Kitchen' in yellow and red hung right across the width of the shopfront. But there were plus points too – the façade was symmetrical and nicely proportioned. And the ugly glass door with metal bars on it was unusually tall and wide, and centrally positioned.

It would be relatively easy to transform the outside with a lick of paint, a tasteful sign, the right lighting, new windows and a handsome new door framed by a pair of potted trees. A sprinkling of her magic really could, like fairy dust, transform an ugly duckling into a swan. She glanced at her watch one more time and panicked. Time to go. Quickly, she flipped the visor down and looked at her reflection in the small vanity mirror. She adjusted her hair in an attempt to hide the lines round her eyes, rummaged in her bag for some gloss and touched up her lips. At last, satisfied, she collected her bag and clipboard, and got out of the car.

Ben stood at a wallpaper table in the middle of the room, wearing fashionable black-rimmed rectangular glasses. He was peering at blueprints, his palms flat on the surface of the table. When she entered he looked up and smiled broadly, revealing the little gap between his two creamy-white front teeth, a flaw that ought to have made him less attractive.

But the tiny imperfection only softened his appeal, making him more approachable, almost vulnerable. And, like Jeff Goldblum, he looked sexier with the glasses than without. Too busy staring at him, Jennifer only just remembered to return his smile. And then she looked around.

The large open space was dimly lit by two forlorn, bare light bulbs hanging from the rafters. The interior was more or less a bare shell, the walls holed and marked where fittings had been removed along with the flooring, revealing a cold concrete floor covered in carpet adhesive. In one corner lay a stack of steel appliances – sinks and metal cabinets, she thought – wrapped up in layers of clear plastic.

Ben came over and shook her hand. Then he peeled off the glasses, and rubbed the bridge of his nose where the nose pads had left small, brown indentations on his pale skin. 'Sorry about the state of the place.' In spite of the damp chill that permeated Jennifer's bones, he was casually dressed in a frayed lumberjack-style shirt over an old t-shirt, and loose-fitting jeans. It wasn't what she'd expected from the rather suave way he'd been dressed in the restaurant, but then that had been a uniform of sorts. She liked him better this way. And she liked the fact that he wasn't precious about his appearance. He sported a day's dark stubble and his hair was messed up and dusty too. 'And sorry about asking you to meet me here so late in the day. I thought it'd be best if the contractors were out of the way.'

She smiled, trying not to shiver in the cold, wishing that she'd worn a warmer coat. She followed him over to the table situated under one of the light bulbs, a temporary focal point in the room, and wrapped the edges of her jacket across her chest. 'I see they've been busy. I remember the booths and red leatherette benches that used to line the walls. Peggy's had a sort of retro fifties feel to it. Along with a smoke haze you could cut with a knife. This was in the days before the smoking ban of course.'

He rubbed his chin with his hand and smiled. 'You frequented it then?' he said, the corners of his eyes crinkled up in a smile. 'You don't look like the sort of woman to don biking leathers and smoke thirty a day.'

Laughing, she relaxed. 'I'm not. I was only in it a couple of times to pick up Matt – he had a brief fascination with bikes when he was fifteen and used to hang out here. I used to worry about him rubbing shoulders with those hard men. Luckily he discovered girls shortly after that.' She laughed and then paused, annoyed with herself for raising the subject of Matt. It would only serve to remind Ben how old she was.

She set her things on the table and said, looking skywards at the old exposed rafters and the nicotine-stained ceiling, 'I always thought the vaulted ceiling was the best thing about this place.'

'Me too. According to the architect, there used to be a second floor.'

'Interesting.' She glanced at the blueprint Ben had been studying when she came in, and said, 'Can I have a closer look?'

'Of course.'

She went and stood next to him, liking the way he was taller than her but not so tall, like David and Matt, that she felt like some sort of midget. She leaned in, their heads only a hand's width apart, aware of the heat of his body and the faint odour of a woody, masculine scent.

'These are the architect's plans,' he said and he moved his elegant hand, long-fingered like a musician's and ropey with veins, across the page. 'The main thing we're doing internally is putting in a wall between the kitchen here,' said Ben, pointing to a line on the plan, 'and the dining

63

area here. That's what the joiner's working on just now. And we're extending the kitchen into these old storerooms in the back. The toilets are in the right place – they just need to be completely refurbished of course.' The nail on his index finger was short and gently rounded, the moon a pale, pinkish-white like the inside of a shell. 'And I'm thinking of a reception desk and a small waiting area where people can have a drink and look at the menus.'

She nodded slowly, trying to take all this in, noticing that was the first time he'd used the pronoun 'I' when talking about the project. He looked at her and some uncertainty crept into his voice. 'I've something to show you. Two things actually. And I hope you don't take this the wrong way.'

'Okay,' she said cautiously, slipping both hands into the back pockets of her jeans, her fingers stiffening in the cold.

He lifted up a large rectangular board that had been lying against the legs of the table and turned it around. It was a professional mood board for a lavish interior in gold, green and deep purple. There were photographs of crystal chandeliers, close-ups of gilded chairs and silver candlesticks, distressed gilt mirrors, swatches of velvet and brocade, and expensive flocked wallpapers and deep-pile carpet. He rested the board on the table, supporting it with his left hand. 'Bronagh at Calico did this and it's pretty much spot on in terms of the brief. We wanted a luxurious, tactile design that's timeless and opulent, but warm and welcoming as well.'

Jennifer folded her arms and considered it all for some moments. 'It's going to have the wow factor, that's for sure,' she said at last.

'And this,' he said, pulling a sheet out from under the plans on the table, 'is her floor plan.' He paused to give her a few moments to look at it. 'Well,' he said, at last, pressing the knuckle of his left hand to his mouth. 'What do you think?'

She nodded. 'It really does look good. All of it.' And then, realising what his hesitation was all about, she volunteered, 'Look, I've not done this before, Ben. I mean, been called in to finish off someone else's project, but there's no sense in throwing the baby out with the bath water, is there? And let's face it, we're up against it in terms of time.'

'I'm so relieved to hear you say that,' he said, laying the board down on the table, and smiling with relief. 'I was worried you'd want to start from scratch.'

She hid her disappointment that she would not have the opportunity to come up with an original design, the most creative part of the job. But what was the point of insisting on it when Ben clearly liked the Calico design and she did too? She would enjoy the challenge of taking the basic concept through to completion on time, and, best of all, she would get to spend a little time with Ben. 'You understand that I won't be able to replicate this exactly. I may have to use different materials depending on what my suppliers have in stock and on delivery times. I might not be able to source chairs exactly the same as those, for example.' She pointed at a photograph. 'But overall, I'm confident I can deliver the high-end look you're after, on schedule and within budget.'

'I think we have a deal then,' he beamed and she smiled back, the cogs in her brain already working out whether her regular sewers and tradesmen were all available. 'I have some ideas for the exterior too,' she added and went on to outline her thoughts.

'Jennifer, that sounds fantastic,' he enthused, when she'd finished. 'What's the next stage then?'

Thinking of all that had to be done in little over two months, she said, 'Well, are you in a rush to get home?'

'No,' he said and there was a pause. The corners of his mouth turned up ever so slightly and his full lips, crimson-red against his pale skin, remained sealed. His right eyebrow, thick and black, rose just a millimetre. 'Are you?'

She blushed, embarrassed that he was flirting with her, horrified that he thought she'd been doing the same with him. 'It's just that I could do with taking some measurements of my own,' she added hastily, searching in her pockets for a tape-measure. 'In addition to the Calico plans.'

'Oh, yes, of course,' he said, a little crestfallen, and looked at the drawings on the table.

Why hadn't she given him a little encouragement instead of the cold shoulder? Foremost, because of Rebecca. But also, she was so out of practice, she'd forgotten how to respond to a bit of innocent flirtation. She got out a measuring tape and a hard-backed Moleskine notebook and looked at the row of windows facing out onto the car park. The views would never form part of this room's charm – her job was to disguise them, to draw the eye to other, more appealing, features. And, like a plain girl made beautiful with artifice, the ambience of the restaurant, vaulted ceiling excepted, would be entirely manufactured.

She lifted up the clipboard and pen and took a step forward and the notebook slid to the floor.

'Let me get it,' said Ben and he picked up the notebook and pressed it into her hand. Their fingers touched – and a bolt of electricity shot through Jennifer.

'Your hand's cold,' he said, his voice low and husky.

She trembled, opened her mouth to speak and the door suddenly burst open.

Chapter 6

When Ben saw Alan Crawford in the doorway, gilt buttons on his overcoat glinting like ceremonial medals, his heart sank. Abruptly, he let go of the notebook and took a step away from Jennifer.

Outside the rain continued to fall, harder now, framing his father with a curtain of silver grey, like the scales on the underside of the mackerel Ben and Ricky used to catch off Bangor pier. He wasn't a big man, only five eleven in his socks, yet his presence filled the room like the overpowering smell of forced spring hyacinths. And when he spoke it was as if he used up all the air, leaving none for Ben.

'Bloody awful night out there,' he boomed, running a hand over his bald head, glazed with rain. He glanced at Jennifer and flashed his showman's white denture smile, his cheeks pulled tight on either side like the string of a bow. As a boy on the family's dirt-poor hill farm near Cullybackey, he'd had only a rag and chimney soot with which to brush his teeth. This early neglect resulted in the loss of his teeth to gum disease at the age of forty-one, exactly twenty years ago. Determined his young sons wouldn't suffer the same fate, he'd stood over them with a stopwatch every night while they brushed for the requisite two minutes.

But the smile, in spite of its dazzling brilliance, did not reach Alan's grey eyes. They flicked over Jennifer like a duster, sizing her up as if she were an enemy. Ben felt his hackles rise. What the hell was he doing here? 'Well, who's this then?' he asked, striding over to Ben. The scent of the expensive aftershave he ordered specially from London wafted before him, an arresting combination of citrusy vanilla and balsamic vinegar. He came to a halt, rolled back on the heels of his handmade English leather shoes and stared pointedly at Jennifer.

Ben made the introductions. Alan, hands clasped behind his back, said with a slightly menacing air, 'Jennifer Murray Interior Design. A one-woman band, then?'

Jennifer looked uncertainly at Ben and then back to his father. Ben cringed with embarrassment. 'Not exactly. I don't have any permanent employees but I have forged very close relationships with local craftspeople who work for me on a contract basis. Curtain-makers, decorators and so on,' she said without hesitation, unnerved, but not cowed it seemed, by Alan's intimidating presence.

'And have you done a restaurant before?'

'Yes,' she said firmly, without breaking eye contact. 'Several. I can show you my portfolio.' Ben loved her self-confidence. He wished some of it would rub off on him.

Alan looked at her doubtfully. 'And you understand –' he paused and looked around, 'what we – what Ben wants? Because it is his project, after all.'

'Perfectly. And I believe I can deliver.'

'Hmm,' said Alan rudely and, shifting his gaze slowly to Ben, he effectively dismissed her. 'Let's have a look at these plans then,' he said, unbuttoning the coat to reveal a black silk shirt pulled tight across his barrel chest.

'It sounds as if you two need to talk,' said Jennifer helpfully. 'Shall I come back and take these measurements another time?'

'No,' said Ben.

'Yes,' said Alan at exactly the same time and locked eyes with his son.

Ben, startled to find boldness in his heart, repeated what he'd said. Alan's face remained immobile but his pupils contracted, betraying his anger. Softening his tone, Ben looked at Jennifer. 'Please. The sooner you get the measuring done the sooner you can get on with the job. Isn't that right?'

Jennifer smiled tightly without looking at Alan, went over to a window and noisily unfurled a retractable metal tape-measure. And to his father, Ben said quietly, 'Jennifer's doing us a favour picking up the pieces after Calico, Dad.'

He scowled grumpily. 'Well, the proof'll be in the pudding, won't it?'

The tape-measure retracted with a loud snap and both men looked over at Jennifer. Ignoring them, she took a pencil out of her mouth and scribbled furiously on the clipboard in her left hand. She was insulted and rightly so. Giving offence was one of Alan's many talents.

Ben took a deep breath and tried to make the peace. 'So, Dad, what brings you here?'

Alan rubbed his hands together, the way people do when they're itching to get started on something. 'I happened to be passing,' he said and Ben smiled at the lie. Alan had been in Portrush and Portstewart earlier that day and Ballyfergus wasn't on the way home – not unless you took the scenic Antrim coast road and more or less doubled the length of your journey time. 'I wanted to hear what you thought of the place. And see how the plans were shaping up.'

So much for Alan letting go of the reins. Without waiting

69

for an invitation he strode over to the wallpaper table and rested his knuckles on the flat surface, like a sprinter at the starting blocks. 'So,' he said, narrowing his eyes to focus more clearly – he was too proudly virile to don glasses in the presence of a stranger – 'do you agree this place is a dump?'

Ben frowned. Alan had bought the place – snapped it up, he'd said – without consulting Ben. 'It is now but it won't be by the time we're finished with it. Haven't you always said –'

Without taking his eyes off the plans, Alan cut him short mid-sentence. 'I've learned you something then.' This peculiar verb misuse, widespread across the province, marked Alan out as an uneducated man. And, whilst he knew this, and was certainly clever enough to eliminate this verbal idiosyncrasy from his speech if he chose to, he never did.

Ben, angry, folded his arms across his chest. Why was nothing ever straightforward with his father? The question had been another one of his stupid tests.

'Location,' went on Alan, raising his eyes now, and one instructive finger, 'is the most important thing, absolutely, always. Everything else can be changed. You have to look beyond the muck and filth and see what others can't.' Ben, who had heard it all before, made a swirling pattern in the dust with the toe of his old trainers. Jennifer, he noticed, glancing up, had disappeared into one of the loos.

'Tell me,' went on Alan, walking over to a window and squinting up at the sky like he was on the lookout for an aeroplane. 'What do you see when you look out this window?'

'An ugly car park?' replied Ben, stubbornly looking the other way, refusing to play the game.

Alan roared with humourless laughter. 'Depends how you look at it. That's what you see,' he said, and paused to let

Ben know he didn't think much of his vision. 'Whereas I see an asset.'

He stopped, waiting, Ben presumed, for him to offer up what that asset might be. But he said nothing.

Irritation crept into Alan's voice. 'I see convenient parking for customers. An asset that will deliver customers right to this front door of ours.'

'Right,' said Ben insolently.

Alan, who must've forgotten about Jennifer, slapped a closed fist into the palm of the other hand. 'You have to have vision, son!' he cried, his tanned face suddenly taking on a reddish hue, though it was hard to tell if he was angry or excited, both emotions producing in Alan similar physical manifestations. 'You can make a silk purse out of a sow's ear.'

Suddenly, apparently oblivious to Ben's ill temper, he chuckled heartily at his cleverness. Then he opened his arms wide and turned in a small slow circle like a contestant on *Strictly Come Dancing*, the soles of his shoes tap-tapping lightly on the floor. With his eyes closed, he might have been in a trance. 'I can see it now. Carnegie's! That's what we'll call it and it'll be the talk of the town.

'People will come from far and wide. Ballymena, Ballymoney, Whitehead and Carrickfergus,' went on Alan, reciting the local names like a prayer, the vowels hard, tight fists, so that 'Bally' became 'Balla' and 'head' came out as 'heed'. 'And from all the towns and villages up the coast as well. It'll be great, Ricky.' And he stopped spinning right in front of Ben and, smiling, opened his eyes.

Ben stared at him in horror. Every once in a while this happened. Ricky's name would slip unawares from his father's lips – the name of the child he wished was standing in front of him, not the one who was. Ben swallowed and tried to arrange some other expression on his face, something that would cloak the searing shock like a stage curtain. He pressed the palm of his right hand on his heart and felt its fierce, too-fast beat.

'What's wrong with you, boy?' said Alan crossly, the smile fading to be replaced with a frown. 'Can't you visualise it?'

'I . . . I can. But why "Carnegie's"?' said Ben, throwing the question to Alan like a bone to a dog, anything to deflect his beady-eyed scrutiny.

Alan exhaled loudly, his enthusiasm waning, it seemed, in the face of Ben's lack of it. 'Didn't you notice the old Carnegie library across the street?' he said irritably.

'Ah yes. "Let there be light",' said Ben, quoting the motto at the entrance to the first library Andrew Carnegie ever built – in his hometown of Dunfermline, Scotland, in 1883.

'Huh?' said Alan. The quote was most likely meaningless to him, yet Alan, who'd left school at fifteen, would not seek clarification. Whilst he made a big show of being true to his humble 'school of life' roots, he did not like his ignorance exposed. 'Yes, well,' he went on, 'as I was saying, it's not a library now – some sort of Arts centre or museum. Remind me on Monday to look into giving them a donation. Anyway, Carnegie's has just the right overtones for our restaurant. Classy, elegant. It has an old-school ring to it.'

Ben couldn't disagree with any of this and yet the fact that his father had proposed the name irked. 'But don't you think I should have some say in naming the restaurant? Especially if I'm supposed to be running the business.'

'You are, Ben, you are,' said Alan and he came over and placed a heavy arm across Ben's shoulders. 'Now, I know you're nervous but don't worry. I know you won't let me down,' he said, his words striking fear in Ben's heart. He removed his arm. 'Now, if you've got a better name for the restaurant, I'd like to hear it.'

Ben ventured, 'Crawfords.'

Alan's mouth puckered up like he'd just, unsuspectingly, bitten into a lemon. 'God no, not our own name. It lacks class. And you're forgetting the chain of bakery shops in East Belfast that go by the same name. Have you got any other ideas?'

Ben deliberated for a moment, then shook his head. 'Carnegie's is a good choice,' he conceded, wishing he'd thought of it.

'Good.' Satisfied, Alan darted over to the table once more and pointed at the plan. 'Now tell me about this. What's that hatched area at the front of the restaurant?'

Ben stood beside his father and saw immediately what he meant. 'That's the waiting area.'

'Waiting area?' said Alan, wrinkling up his nose the way he did when he smelled something gone off.

Jennifer slipped back into the room from the kitchen and, ignoring them both, proceeded to measure the boarded-up front window. Ben said quickly, 'Well, more of a bar area. Not that there'd be a bar as such, but a relaxing area where people could come in and order a drink while they look at the menu and wait for their table.'

Alan squinted before speaking, as if he was trying very hard to see merit where there was none. 'It'd look pretty, son. But you do know what's wrong with it, don't you?'

Ben shook his head. If he knew, would it be on the bloody plan?

'You don't have room for it in a restaurant this size. You'd lose too many covers giving up this much footage. There's room for another two tables at least here,' he said, sketching out his vision with the tip of his finger. 'And if people want a pre-dinner drink they can have it here, at their table.' He tapped the paper hard three times with the tip of his index finger as if he was giving it and not Ben a good talking to. Ben, acutely aware of Jennifer's silent presence as she went about her business, felt the colour rise to his cheeks.

His father was right of course, as he was in every damn thing. When was he going to give up this charade? Acting like he knew what he was doing when he didn't; pretending that he loved this job that he loathed.

'Now, you'll be needing somewhere to live down here,' went on Alan, who always talked as though he was ticking items off an agenda.

'Yes, I was thinking about that,' began Ben.

Alan, impatient as always, interrupted. 'Well, you don't need to. It's all taken care of. I picked up a flat last time I was down here,' he said, the way someone might comment that they'd picked up a loaf of bread on the way home. Looking very pleased with himself he added, 'You'll need to get it furnished but I'm assuming you can organise that yourself.'

When he saw the look on Ben's face he added, 'You've enough on your plate just now with splitting your time between The Lemon Tree and this place. I knew you wouldn't have time to go house-hunting. This way, it's one less thing for you to worry about.'

'You rented a flat without consulting me?' said Ben, infuriated but not taken by surprise. Was there anything his father trusted him to do?

'Of course it's not rented,' he snorted. 'Rent is a waste of money. When you're done with it, we'll lease it out. Ballyfergus has a strong rental market.'

'I'll just be off then,' said Jennifer's voice and Ben swung round to find her standing by the door with her things in her arms. 'Can I take the mood board?'

'Yeah, sure.' Ben went to get it and Jennifer said evenly, and without moving from her position at the door, 'Goodbye, Mr Crawford. It was interesting meeting you.'

'Yes, goodbye, Mrs Murray. It is missus, isn't it?'

'Actually no. It's Ms. Murray's my maiden name. I'm divorced.'

Ben, reaching down to grasp the mood board, felt his heart leap. He had to remind himself that, divorced or not, she might yet have a partner.

By contrast, Alan received this news impassively with a vacant nod, his face utterly still. When it mattered, he knew how to keep his thoughts to himself.

Jennifer walked out the door Ben held open for her, the mood board wedged under his left arm. Outside, the rain had stopped, leaving great puddles on the tarmac. Wordlessly they walked past Alan's bright red Porsche, carelessly abandoned across two parking spaces, to her car. She opened the boot and he flung the board in on top of a jumble of wallpaper books, fabric samples and a pair of muddy green wellies.

'Any chance I could get copies of those Calico plans?' she said.

'Sure. I'll send them over.'

'Oh. I haven't given you my card. You'll need the address.' She put a hand inside her jacket, pulled out a small sheaf of business cards and handed one to him.

'Thanks for coming,' he said. 'I'm sorry about my father.'

She paused for some long moments as if wrestling with something inside and then said, diplomatically, 'You don't have to apologise for your father. Ever.' Clever, because it could mean two different things, if you thought about it. Then she opened the driver's door, and regarded him thoughtfully, her eyes the colour of the chocolate velvet on the mood board. 'I'll be in touch early next week,' she said brightly. 'Have a good weekend, Ben.'

He went back inside where Alan, never one to quit until he knew he'd well and truly won, picked up the conversation where they'd left off. 'The estate agent happened to mention the flat to me when I was down looking at this place,' he explained. 'It's a high-quality new build and a good location within walking distance of here – and I got a good price. Nobody can resist a cash buyer in this climate.' He grinned, delighted with himself.

Ben folded his arms. 'It's one thing overruling me on the bar area in the restaurant. I accept that you're right about that. But the flat will be my home, not yours. I am capable of finding somewhere to live by myself.'

Alan shrugged, utterly indifferent to Ben's objections.

'Don't you see my point, Dad? I'm a grown man and you bought my home without consulting me.'

'Ach, stop moaning, Ben. I don't see what I've done wrong. I didn't buy it, the business did. And it's not your permanent home – just somewhere to kip for a year or so,' shrugged Alan. 'Anyway, I wouldn't worry about the flat if I was you, son. You're hardly going to see the inside of the place. If you're going to make a success of this restaurant, you'll be working day and night down here.' He paused, picked something off the sleeve of his jacket and fixed his eyes on Ben. 'You'll not have time for much else.'

Ben swallowed and said nothing, his heart filled with a terrible sense of foreboding. He looked around the dilapidated room and tried to dredge up some enthusiasm. But the prospect of running this place left his heart cold. He could not spend the rest of his life working for his father. But how could he tell that to him? He'd given him hope, a reason to go on, after all their hopes were lost that night.

Something bleeped in Alan's coat pocket and he pulled out his mobile. 'Ach, shite, that'll be Cassie,' he said referring to his new wife who, at forty-one, was twenty years his junior. He read the text message, and diamond cufflinks sparkled as he consulted the flashy Rolex on his wrist.

'Bloody woman doesn't give me a moment's peace.' Ben smiled and Alan said, grimly, 'Wait till you're married. You'll know all about it.'

'That's not likely to happen any day soon,' said Ben cheerfully, who'd come to see his break-up with Rebecca as a lucky escape.

'Pity,' said Alan.

Ben laughed outright at this. From what he could see, matrimonial bliss had eluded Alan. He was on to his third beautiful wife and, from where he was standing, none of his marriages had delivered up their promise of happiness.

'What're you laughing at?' growled Alan.

'Dad, come on. You're hardly one to be dishing out advice about marriage.'

Alan speared him with his gaze, his eyes like lasers. 'Maybe not. But you don't want to leave it too late. Your mother tells me that you and Rebecca have split up.'

'That's right.'

He shook his head, sadly. 'You need your head examined, Ben. You'll not find a better looking girl anywhere. And what was wrong with the one before that? Emma, wasn't it? She was a stunner too.'

Ben looked at his father in astonishment. If appearance was his criterion for a happy marriage, no wonder he'd gone so far wrong in its pursuit. 'We weren't suited, Dad.'

'Well, they both seemed like very nice girls to me,' he insisted obstinately. 'By the time I was your age, you know, I was married. And by the time I was thirty, I had a kid on the way.' At this, they both looked at the dust on the floor. The kid, safe then in his mother's womb, was Ricky. The child that had broken all their hearts.

'Steady on, Dad,' said Ben, forcing a hollow laugh. He held up the palm of his hand to his father. 'Marriage. Babies. What's brought all this on?'

Hell bent on his own agenda, it seemed Alan didn't even hear the question. 'You've got to find the girl and get married before you even think about having children. You don't want one of these high-flying career women. And don't be getting some wee girl up the spout.'

'Oh, for God's sake,' said Ben.

'No, listen, son,' said Alan, and there was no mistaking the earnestness in his voice now, as he finally honed in on the crux of the matter. 'You should be thinking about your future. Your children will be heirs to the entire Crawford fortune. And you want them to be legitimate.'

Ben took a step back, reeling from this burst of insight as if it were a physical blow or a mighty explosion in his face. It had never occurred to him until this moment that, as Alan's only surviving child, his children would be absolutely crucial to Alan's dreams. He wasn't running a business – he was building a dynasty. Without grandchildren, there *was* no future.

'What if I don't want kids?' Ben blurted out.

'Don't be stupid. When you get to a certain age, everyone wants kids,' he said in a voice that brooked no opposition. 'And everyone wants grandchildren.'

I don't, he wanted to scream. But he simply stared, struck momentarily mute by this awful understanding.

'So, this Jennifer Murray,' said Alan lightly, and he glanced slyly at Ben with those beady eyes that missed nothing. 'What made you hire her?'

'Jennifer?' said Ben stupidly. What had Jennifer got to do with a discussion about grandchildren and heirs? 'Because I think she can do a good job.' Unintentionally, his inflexion rose at the end of the sentence, making it sound more like a question than a statement.

'I see. So how did you find out about her?'

'I hired her son, Matt, first and he introduced us. When

78

I heard Calico were going under, I asked her if she was interested.'

'Sounds like you did them both a big favour, Ben,' he observed quietly, talking in the measured way he reserved for occasions when he was particularly irked by something. 'I hope I'm wrong. I hope that your motives were purely professional.'

He opened his mouth to tell his father otherwise but Alan, with words as precise as the swift, ruthless cut of a chef's knife, silenced him.

'She's a pretty woman, Ben, I'll grant you that. And I can see the attraction,' he said, as if piling Jennifer's positive attributes, like recipe ingredients, on one side of a pair of old-fashioned scales. 'But she has grown-up children, son.' He fixed Ben with a hard stare, lowered his voice. And then he tipped the scales against Jennifer, in his mind anyway, with the heavy weight of the truth.

'Her child-bearing years are over.'

Chapter 7

David drove Lucy back to Belfast on Sunday night despite her protestations that a bit of rain wouldn't hurt. It was mid-September now and the weather had taken a sudden autumnal turn. The temperature had plummeted and the rain battered the car in wind-buffeted sheets.

'So how did things go between you and your mother this weekend?' asked Dad, both hands coiled lightly around the steering wheel as if taking his driving test for the first time.

'Good,' said Lucy, thinking guiltily of the bag in the boot full of laundered clothes (a peace offering from her mother) and further supplies of canned goods. The weekend had passed off peaceably, but it had left Lucy with a sour taste in her mouth. While she had succeeded in extracting money from her father, the victory had come at a price. Things between her and Mum were quietly strained, even more so than usual. Neither had mentioned the quarrel of the previous week, but Mum didn't *need* to say a word for Lucy to know exactly what she thought. Her thin lips and toneless civility conveyed more disappointment than any words could. Once, when watching TV, she'd caught her mother staring at her so sadly, she had to get up and leave the room.

'No more arguments over money then?' said Dad, as he pulled into the outside lane, feeding the steering wheel through his hands like a rigid, circular rope. He glanced over and smiled conspiratorially. Lucy returned the complicit smile he expected, but she felt bad. She knew in her heart that winning didn't make it right. At first, she'd been filled with rage by her mother's refusal to give her more money. But later she'd thought, with grudging respect, that her mother had been right.

'No, money wasn't mentioned,' she said, hiding her shame by staring out the window at the watery view of floodlit, low-rise industrial buildings backing onto the motorway. Some were clothed in bright graffiti, the talented handiwork of kids who should've gone to art college but never got the chance.

After the fallout with Mum the week before, Dad had been like putty in her hands. Through tears, with nothing left to lose, she'd confessed how much money she needed. And to her surprise, he'd pressed a big wad of crisp twenty pound notes into her palm. He did not ask a single question, so pleased was he to gain the upper moral hand, as he saw it, on Mum. As she'd closed her fingers over the money, the feeling of relief was so intense, she'd thrown her arms around his neck and sobbed once more.

'Now you just let me know any time you're short, love,' said Dad, bringing her back to the present. 'University should be the best time of your life. I don't want you to be worrying about money. Or missing out.'

'Thanks.' Dad had always been greatly concerned that Lucy didn't 'miss out'. What he actually meant was 'I will give you whatever it takes for you to fit in.' He'd pushed her to do ballet and drama classes because that's what the other, pretty girls in her class did. As a teenager, he made sure she had the trendiest fashions and the latest gadgets

(*You want to be cool, don't you?*). He'd nagged Mum into taking her to the best hairdressers in Belfast, in the failed hope that they could do something presentable with her thin, greasy hair. And he quizzed her about her social life, wanting to know where 'all the kids hung out' and who 'her mates' were. To please him, she'd talked about the popular girls at school as if they were her friends. Sometimes she was tolerated on the fringes of this 'in crowd'; more often than not, told to get lost, or worse. It must've been clear to her father from a very early age that she was different. But, terrier-like, he persisted in his mission to transform her from ugly duckling into swan. He was a conformist.

The car accelerated away from the lights at York Street, joining the two-lane Westlink that skirted the city centre and connected eventually with the M1 on the south side of the city. 'So how's the studying going?' said Dad.

'Great,' she lied.

'You're a bright girl, Lucy,' Dad said confidently. He had never so much as brushed shoulders with self-doubt. 'If you put in the work, you'll be fine.'

Lucy gnawed the nail, already bitten down to the quick, on her right thumb. She'd lied about her first-year results. Mum and Dad were under the impression that she was on track for a two-one, maybe even a first. But the way things were going, she'd be lucky to graduate with a third, or worse. And there was always the awful possibility that she'd flunk altogether.

In choosing Applied Mathematics and Physics, she'd thought she was making a logical choice. In a world where popularity was decided on something as capricious as appearance (and a whole shed-load of other, shifting criteria, too subtle for Lucy to comprehend) maths was a solid bedrock of evolving logic and reasoning. She buried herself in numbers that appeared to deliver unequivocal answers.

But her judgement had proved flawed. Now in second year, she struggled to keep up, and the more she studied maths the more she came to realise that it didn't have all the answers. It was no less fickle than the friendship of her peers. No amount of calculus or geometry could answer the questions that preoccupied her mind, nor ease the iron grip of isolation.

Driving south, they crossed the junctions at Divis Street, where the road widened out to three lanes. Not long now. Lucy felt the muscles in her stomach tighten. Dad rested his elbow awkwardly on the narrow sill and asked, 'So, any boyfriends in the picture, Lucy?'

Lucy jolted and looked at him in astonishment. Did he know her at all? Was he blind? No man – or boy – had ever so much as looked at her. 'No.'

'Oh, come on, there must be someone,' he teased.

'Honestly Dad, there's not,' she said firmly and folded her arms across her chest.

He glanced over and said chirpily, as if her single status was something she actually had control over, 'No, you're quite right. You don't want to be tying yourself down just yet. Plenty of time for settling down later. Meanwhile just enjoy being young, free and single.' He grinned happily, content in the knowledge that Lucy was having the time of her life at uni. She couldn't bear to see the disappointment in his face if she owned up to being what she was – a social outcast, a freak.

At the Broadway roundabout they turned onto Glenmachan Street, eventually joining the Lisburn Road heading north, back towards the city centre. They were almost there. Lucy put a hand on her stomach, hard as a nut, and took a deep breath to quell the nausea.

On Eglantine Avenue she racked her brains for a way to get into the house without him coming too. Too soon, they turned into Wellington Park Avenue, lined on both sides with gardenless Victorian terraced houses. Dad pulled up outside a red-brick house with bay windows on the ground and first floor – and peeling white paint on the windowsills. Lights blazed in every window. Her heart sank – everyone must be back already.

'Here we are then.' Dad turned off the engine and took the key out of the ignition.

Lucy quickly unclipped her seat belt and cracked open the car door. 'Oh, don't bother getting out, Dad. There's no need for both of us to get wet, is there?'

He gave her an indulgent smile and, completely ignoring her, put his hand on the door handle. 'Don't be ridiculous, Lucy. Your bag weighs a tonne. I'll carry it in for you.'

He got out of the car to open the boot and Lucy had no choice but to follow him. While he'd seen the house, she'd so far managed to avoid him meeting her housemates.

When he ran up the path with the bag she grasped its handle and tried to wrench it out of his hand. 'I can take it from here, Dad,' she said firmly but he simply pushed past her with, 'Don't be silly, Lucy. Let's get out of this awful rain.'

She stumbled into the hall and watched in horror as he dumped her bag on the sticky floor – she was the only one who ever cleaned anything in the house – and headed straight for the lounge from which pounding music, and the sound of female voices, issued forth.

'No!' she cried out, desperately. 'Don't leave my bag there. It's in the way. Let's take it upstairs.'

But though he must've heard her, he paid no heed. He disappeared into the lounge. She crept to the door, moving silently like a cat, and peered into the room. Four of them were there, in the process of preparing to go out, competing sounds blaring from someone's iPod docking station and the TV. Fran was putting make-up on in front of a magnifying mirror balanced on top of the slate mantelpiece, the only original feature left in the house after its butchery of a conversion. Vicky, swaying her hips to the music, held a pair of hair straighteners in her hand. Bernie knelt in front of the coffee table, measuring Tesco Value vodka into a pint glass. A rag bag assortment of glasses, made cloudy by too many cycles in the dishwasher without dishwashing tablets, salt or rinse aid, littered the dusty coffee table, along with a carton of cranberry juice. The girls never went out without getting pole-axed first.

They all stared when Dad, looking like a lecturer in fine brown cords and an open-necked checked flannel shirt, appeared in their midst. His hands were shoved into his trouser pockets, his arms holding back the tails of the suit jacket he wore over everything.

'Hi,' he said, raising his big hand in a friendly greeting. Then, realising they could not hear him over the din, he shouted. 'I'm David. Lucy's Dad.'

Someone turned the music off and Bernie, blonde hair tied up haphazardly on top of her head like an untidy nest, got off her knees and said, all friendly like, 'Hi ya. What about ye?' No one touched the TV control so the rest of the conversation took place against the sound of *Dancing on Ice*.

'Well, well, well,' he said, surveying the state of the room – clothes strewn on the floor; an overflowing ashtray on the hearth; a tube of hair product lying on the floor, greasy contents oozing out onto the cheap laminate; the stale smell of a room never aired. The girls looked uncertainly at one another.

He looked at the bottle of cheap vodka and for one awful moment Lucy thought he was going to say something about

85

their drinking. But his face broke into a beaming smile. 'Getting ready to go out, then?'

'Yeah, that's right,' said Vicky, putting the straighteners down on a pink towel she'd draped over the arm of the burgundy sofa. Underneath was a horrible black scar where she'd already burned it. The landlord would take money out of all their deposits for that.

'Oh, that's great, Lucy,' he said, turning around and taking a step backwards to expose her to everyone's gaze. 'You've arrived just in time.'

Lucy felt her face redden as the girls exchanged puzzled glances and then all stared at her. 'Where are youse off to, then? Thompsons?' she asked, slipping into the vernacular, and dredging up the name of a nightclub she'd overheard people talk about.

There was a subdued titter of laughter. Cathy, the only natural blonde among them, looked up from her place on the sofa, where she was stretched out reading *Now* magazine. 'No one goes to Thompsons on a Sunday night,' she said evenly, her thin lips unsmiling. Lucy gripped her upper arms so hard they hurt, praying that the ordeal would soon be over.

Bernie lit a cigarette, narrowing her eyes until they were no more than slits. She inhaled then removed the cigarette from her mouth with a little popping sound. 'We're going to Kremlin.'

Pretending that this statement constituted an invitation, Lucy cleared her throat and said, 'Well, I've other plans for tonight.'

This seemed to annoy Dad for he said, sharply, 'What other plans? You didn't mention them in the car.' And he held out his arm in a sweeping gesture towards the girls, like a cinema attendant showing her to her seat. 'Sure, why don't you go out with the girls?'

What was wrong with him? Couldn't he see they hated her? Or maybe this was his awful, clumsy way of trying to force her on these unwilling airheads. He'd been doing it as long as she could remember. But she had tried to fit in, delighted that Vicky, who'd shared a maths module with her in first year, had invited her to join them – even though she got the poky room at the back of the house that never got the sun. But she'd very soon discovered, eavesdropping, that she'd only been asked because they couldn't find anyone 'sound'. After that she stopped trying to ingratiate herself with them. And in some ways it was a relief.

'I just remembered. I'm going out with Amy,' she improvised, holding up her mobile phone as evidence of some prior arrangement. Then she remembered that Amy always went to church on Sunday nights – but anything was better than staying here one minute longer. 'Look, I'd better get a move on, Dad,' she said, retreating from the room. 'She'll be wondering where I am.'

And, to her great relief, he followed her, calling out a cheery 'Goodbye' on his way. Immediately the music came back on. Lucy practically ran up the stairs, her stomach so tight it hurt, and unlocked the door to her neat and tidy room on the first floor. Dad followed her into the room and set the bag down on the floor. Lucy pulled out her mobile and, ignoring the cold water trickling down the back of her neck, pretended to read a text. 'She'll be here in a minute.'

When she'd finally got rid of him, Lucy covered her face with her hands. She'd tried so hard but she couldn't do it any more. She hated everything about her life here in Belfast, in this house. There was only one thing that made it in any way tolerable. Quickly, she got her laptop out, went over to the small desk and plugged it into the large monitor. Immediately her heartbeat slowed.

She'd seen the TV ads for a new online bingo site at the

weekend and she knew what that meant – special promotions. She'd already exhausted all the offers open to new players on every other site – and there were dozens of them. Sure enough, this site was offering a twenty-five-pound bonus to new players. The only problem was, you had to deposit ten pounds to qualify for it – and part of her current financial plan involved restricting herself to five pounds a day: thirty-five pounds a week. She frowned, but her hesitation was momentary – after tonight's humiliation, she deserved a treat.

When the money was gone, Lucy sat staring at the debit card lying on the table. If she deposited another ten pounds she would earn a fifty per cent bonus. She liked that word 'deposit'. It sounded safe, reassuring – and it reminded her that this was an investment in her future. She picked up the card and keyed in the number . . .

Later still, she sat on her bed, the music now thumping so loudly, she felt the vibration through the soles of her feet. The money was all gone and she'd won nothing. She tried not to feel disheartened. It was only a temporary setback. She looked at her watch. The girls would not leave the house until ten o'clock, maybe later, and they would not come home until the early hours. She could not bear it a minute longer. She grabbed her purse and keys and ran out of the room.

'I didn't think this would be your scene,' said Amy, handing Lucy a glass of orange juice. There was wine – an unopened bottle of red and another of white on the sideboard – but no one seemed to be touching it so Lucy didn't either.

She took a sip of the lukewarm drink and tried to ignore the wet jeans sticking to her thighs – she'd had to walk all the way over here in the rain to gatecrash this party. The party, if you could call it that, was in the lounge of a student house on Stranmillis Gardens, much the same as the house Lucy shared. Except this one was clean and it didn't smell of chip fat and stale cigarette smoke. And this shindig was nothing like the parties the girls at Wellington Park Avenue threw. For a start, no one was smoking, shouting, vomiting or snogging someone they hardly knew on the sofa.

People stood around in small groups talking quietly and laughing, some kind of acoustic guitar music playing softly in the background. A smiling girl came round carrying a tray of cocktail sausages. Lucy took one and nibbled it thoughtfully. There was something else that marked these people out from her housemates, apart from their wholesome appearance – they were friendly. Yet Lucy felt as alien here at she did at Wellington Park Avenue.

'You know what the girls in the house are like, Amy. They were getting stuck into vodka and cranberry juice,' she offered to explain her presence. 'The music was so loud I couldn't stand it. I had to get out.'

Amy raised her right eyebrow, the same colour as her flaming red hair. With her sharp features, small pale eyes behind wire-framed glasses and translucent skin so white it almost glowed, Amy was not beautiful. But she had an inner goodness that drew people to her and she was a kind and loyal friend. She read Pure Mathematics and they'd known each other since the start of first year. And while Lucy had known from the outset that Amy was a committed Christian, she had only ever tried to force her beliefs on Lucy in the gentlest of manners, occasionally inviting her along to special events run by the Christian Union.

'I don't know why you share with them, Lucy,' she said at last, shaking her head ruefully. 'They're not like you.'

Who is? thought Lucy. She wished for a moment that she had faith like Amy, so that she might feel connected to the people in this room. She wanted to belong – to feel *part* of something. But, while she believed in God, she could honestly say that she had never felt personally touched by His spirit. The compulsory religious studies she'd done in school had always felt like an interesting, but academic, exercise.

'Well, I don't have much choice. I'm tied in by the lease agreement until the end of the academic year,' said Lucy. Even if she extricated herself from the house, where would she go? Amy couldn't help – she lived with her parents in East Belfast. She could live at home she supposed, but her parents would want to know what was wrong. They claimed university was as much about 'the student experience' as it was about academic achievement. They had no idea what it meant in reality for Lucy.

'Well, I'm really sorry to hear that,' said Amy, looking into her drink. 'I know how much you hate it there.'

A loud ripple of laughter broke out on the other side of the room, giving Lucy the opportunity to look away, effectively bringing the depressing conversation to an end.

A small group of girls near the door to the kitchen were clustered around a very tall, well-built man, maybe six foot four, with a straight choppy fringe of light brown hair and a broad, clean-shaven face. His big hand encircled a pint glass of coke and he was casually dressed in distressed jeans and a faded rugby shirt with the collar turned up around his thick neck. He looked older than the rest of the group and the way he held himself – straight-backed and square-shouldered – combined with his imposing physique gave him an air of authority. His reserved, lopsided smile suggested that he was the source of the sudden mirth.

The laughter died away and the tall man glanced up, his eyebrows knitted together in an amused expression. His blue-eyed gaze, as bright and piercing as a spear, met Lucy's and she felt a strange, unfamiliar sensation in her stomach.

Her heartbeat fluttered momentarily, then stabilised again. Startled, she put a hand to her chest as if holding it there might steady her heartbeat.

'I can't stay long tonight,' said Amy, glancing at her watch, and Lucy looked over her shoulder to see who the man was staring at. But there was no one there. When she turned round again, he was standing right in front of her. She let out a little silent gasp and, shyly, looked up at his face.

'Hi, I'm Oren Wilson,' he said, the smile replaced with a searching, curious look as if he was trying to remember if he'd met her before. To Amy he said, without looking, 'How's it going, Amy?'

'Good. This is Lucy Irwin, Oren,' said Amy absentmind-edly, and she waved at someone on the other side of the room. 'Did you win today?'

'Fifteen-three,' he said and, taking in Lucy's blank face he added, 'Rugby. We were playing against Malone.'

'Oren's captain of the first eleven,' interjected Amy.

Lucy, impressed, said, 'Oh.'

'Yep, a couple of my team-mates are over there.' Oren pointed at two ruddy-faced, muscled blokes amongst the group he'd been talking to. 'They're sound lads. The rest of them are out getting smashed somewhere.' He rolled his eyes and his smile, when he shook his head, conveyed a kind of benign disapproval.

'Look, would you two excuse me a moment?' said Amy. 'I have to speak to Carolyn about Talkshop on Thursday night. We're nearly out of coffee and biscuits.'

Amy disappeared and Oren, who had not taken his eyes off Lucy, said, 'So, are you a first year?'

'N . . . No,' said Lucy and she tried to smile but her heart was inexplicably full of a feeling akin to, but not quite the same as, dread. 'I'm second year, like Amy. I'm doing Applied Mathematics and Physics.'

'You must be very clever,' he said, his tone one of mild amusement rather than conviction. Was he making fun of her?

'Are you?' she squeaked.

He laughed easily at this. 'With humility comes wisdom. In that sense, I hope I have insight.'

She blushed, tongue-tied by confusion and said at last, 'I . . . I meant are you a first year?' And then she blushed again at the stupidity of her question while Oren looked on, his thin closed lips almost smiling. He was too old to be a first year; he must be a mature student, or a lecturer even. 'So, what are you doing? I mean studying? If you're a student, that is . . .' Her voice trailed away and she looked at the floor, wishing it would open up and swallow her whole. Not only was she stupid, she could hardly string a coherent sentence together.

He nodded thoughtfully and said quietly, 'I have a degree in Law. But I'm still a student.' At this she lifted her face, and he smiled down on her. 'I'm in my first year of a degree in Theology at The Irish Baptist College.' In response to her blank face, he added, 'The college in Moira is a constituent part of Queen's.'

'I see,' she said and, unable to think of anything more to say, she downed the rest of the orange juice. Law and Theology! He was far too clever to be interested in someone like her.

'Lucy,' he said and paused. He stared at her for what seemed like a long time, and though it was uncomfortable, it was mesmerising too – she was unable to turn away. She stared into his eyes, as blue and all-encompassing as the sky on a cloudless day, and time ground slowly to a halt. She was aware only of the sound of her breathing and the pulse throbbing in her clenched jaw.

And then, slowly and deliberately, he extended his right

hand, big as a plate, and placed it on her shoulder as though bestowing something on her. His fingers, pressing lightly into the taut muscle between her shoulder and her neck, induced an exquisite tender pain. She blinked and, at last, he said, 'It's okay.'

The weight of his hand and the simple words of reassurance – which seemed to convey a much deeper message than mere acknowledgement of her nervousness – flooded her veins like the vodka she'd once drunk to try to escape her life. She felt the muscles in her neck and shoulders relax.

'You're amongst friends here. You don't need to be afraid.'

She blinked, stunned by this uncomplicated truth. She *was* afraid. Fear defined her. She was afraid of rejection, afraid of failure, afraid to be herself.

But how could Oren see this? He didn't know her. How could he see what no one else seemed to, even her own family? Even Matt. If he could see what she was really like inside, why was he still standing there talking to her?

She glanced nervously into the bottom of her empty glass, her hand shaking. Was this what people meant when they talked about making a connection with someone? An awful feeling of terror and joy all muddled up so that she didn't know what to say or think. It was as if her heart had suddenly been laid bare. She swallowed and tried to summon the courage not to turn tail and run.

'It's okay,' he whispered again and his hand slipped from her shoulder.

Her legs suddenly felt too weak and she stumbled to the nearest sofa where she sat down, oblivious now to everyone in the room but Oren. Her heartbeat pounded in her ears blocking out the sounds around her. Was it possible that the impossible had happened? Had she finally found someone who understood her? To her amazement, he came and sat on the edge of the sofa beside her, sitting slightly forward and at an angle, his long muscular legs buckled awkwardly like a grasshopper's.

He looked directly into her face. 'Are you okay?' she lip-read rather than heard.

She thought about this for some moments as the rushing sound faded away and at last, calmer now, she nodded and smiled for the first time. Realising he was waiting for her to speak, she said, 'Yes, I'm fine, thank you.' She paused and added, looking at the dark, damp patches on her jeans, 'I'm sorry. I don't do small-talk. At least not very well.'

He roared with laughter at this, throwing his head back so that his Adam's apple protruded like a fleshy rock. When the laughter had subsided he said, 'That's hardly a fault, Lucy. I wish there were more people like you in the world.'

She brightened and lifted her head. He was smiling at her, his eyes crinkled up at the corners. No one had ever said anything like that to her before. Her reserved, awkward nature, which she had always seen as a failing, suddenly felt like an asset.

'Tell me about yourself, Lucy. Where do you live?'

Breathlessly, as though she couldn't get the words out fast enough, she told him about the girls she shared with and how she didn't fit in. He shook his head sadly and fixed her with a pained look that marred his fine, open countenance. 'They don't sound like the sort of people you should be consorting with, Lucy.'

'You're so right, Oren! They're not,' she cried and shook her head vigorously, wondering that she had ever desired their haughty friendship.

He rubbed his chin thoughtfully. 'Is that why you're here tonight? To get away from them?'

She nodded. 'I knew they wouldn't go out to Kremlin until late and I couldn't stand it a minute longer.'

'Kremlin?' he said, and tucked his chin against his chest,

the way Dad did when he had a bout of indigestion. Talking as if he'd swallowed something unpleasant, he said, 'Did you say Kremlin?'

'Yes,' she said and smiled. 'Have you really never heard of it?'

He looked into his glass of coke and said, 'Oh, I've heard of it all right. Belfast's first nightclub for gays.'

She shrugged. 'Well, yes. But lots of straight people go there too. I've been.'

'Well, you shouldn't,' he said, sharply, setting the coke on the coffee table.

'Why ever not?'

'Because homosexuality is a sin. Simple as that,' he said sadly, clapping his hands together with enough force to make a loud sound.

'Oh,' said Lucy who knew no gay people personally, but held fairly tolerant views on the subject – or thought she did. 'But that sounds so . . . so judgemental.'

'Don't get me wrong, Lucy,' he said, his eyes burning with passion, 'I'm not a homophobe. I don't hate them, not like some awful bigots calling themselves Christian. I don't hate anyone or anything, only sin itself. God loves everyone and I pray that all sinners might find redemption through Jesus Christ Our Lord.' He paused and added, his voice breaking, 'You must understand that the reason I care so much is that I know that if they don't repent they'll go to Hell.' He formed his right hand into a tight fist.

Lucy, both moved and alarmed by the strength of his feeling, touched him on the back of his strong forearm. 'But don't you think that nowadays, we should be more tolerant of people who are . . . different? Isn't that one of the things that defines a civilised society?'

'Oh, Lucy,' he said, sounding so disappointed it pained her. 'Don't you know your Bible?'

She shook her head wordlessly, feeling for the first time ever as if she ought to, if only to make him happy.

'It's written clear as day in Leviticus, chapter eighteen, verse twenty-two. *Thou shalt not lie with mankind as with womankind. It is abomination.*'

If this was what the Bible said, then fair enough. But she wasn't sure she agreed with it, even though she admired Oren for his convictions. She wished she had some of her own.

'You do read the Bible, don't you?'

'I don't even own one,' she said and heard his sharp intake of breath. Then hot, damp palms closed over her right hand like it was something precious and the troubled look was replaced with a confident smile. 'Promise me you'll not go to Kremlin again, Lucy,' he said and closed his eyes momentarily. When he opened them again, the smile was gone and he was staring at her as if he never wanted to look on another living creature all his life.

'Please,' he said and her heartbeat quickened. The idea that what she did actually mattered to him, thrilled her to the core.

'Okay. I never liked it that much anyway.'

He grinned, patted the back of her hand and placed it gently on her knee. 'Thank you,' he said as if she'd just relieved him of a great burden. And even though he did not smile, he said, 'You've no idea how happy it makes me to hear you say that.'

She basked in the steady, blue-eyed gaze of his approval, her heart brimming over with a joy she had not felt since before her parents separated. Oren cared for her, he accepted her just the way she was, and that was more than any man had ever done before – with the exception of Matt. She realised then that she would do everything within her power to make Oren look upon her always the way he was looking

96

at her now – as if she were something to be cherished.

'I see goodness in you, Lucy Irwin,' he said, and her stomach made a sudden, nauseating flip. She wasn't good. She harboured a horrible, shameful habit that had led her to lie to her parents. She wrapped her arms around herself, suddenly cold. 'Oh, Oren, you don't know me. You don't know me at all. I . . . I'm not good. I . . . I . . .'

'We're all sinners.' He patted her lightly on the knee. 'There's no shame in admitting it. Trust in the Lord, Lucy.' He removed his hand and lowered his voice to a whisper. '*For the truth shall set you free.*'

A long, anguished pause followed, during which she pressed her hands between her knees to stop them shaking. Oren averted his gaze and stared at the worn carpet with a benign, encouraging smile on his lips. She wanted to be honest with Oren. If the Lord could forgive her, then he would too. She was certain of it. And yet she had not told anyone, not a soul, about her secret, private life. Finding the right words was difficult. At last she glanced around, checked no one was close enough to hear, and breathed quietly, 'I . . . I gamble.'

He nodded, still staring at the carpet. His hands, clasped together loosely, tightened just a fraction. She blushed with shame and closed her eyes, knowing that if she continued to look at him, she would not be able to carry on. And yet she wanted him to know the truth. If he could forgive her, she could forgive herself.

'On bingo websites,' she said, pressing her knees into the backs of her hands until it hurt. But she determined to go on. To break this curse once and for all. 'And I lied to my parents to get them to give me money that I then gambled.'

'Hmm,' he said thoughtfully and was quiet for some time. 'The love of money is the root of all evil, Lucy.'

She frowned. 'I . . . I don't do it for money. Not really.'

'What then?'

She thought hard for a few moments, fighting back tears. 'Escapism. I want to escape from my life, from being Lucy Irwin.'

'Oh, Lucy,' he said and leaned over and took her hand once more. 'You might hate yourself but God loves you. And He is ready to forgive you. You do know that, don't you?'

She nodded and sniffed as silent tears crept down her cheeks. 'Do you think less of me now that you know?'

He shook his head and said delightedly, 'Let the Lord Jesus Christ into your life, and believe me, it will get a whole lot better. There's hope for you yet, Lucy Irwin,' he beamed and she returned his smile with a hesitant one of her own. She believed him. *He* was her hope and her salvation.

He stared at her for some moments as if making his mind up about something. 'I think you and I are going to be seeing a lot more of each other.'

She bit her bottom lip. It was almost too good to be true. And yet she believed every single word that came out of this good, kind man's mouth. Her reply, slipping out easily, was the absolute truth. 'There's nothing I want more.'

Chapter 8

Jennifer worked alone in the functional workroom at the back of the small property she rented on Pound Street. It wasn't so much a shop as an office, the place where she kept her sample books and portfolio to show prospective clients. She sat at the old but reliable Brother sewing machine, guiding burgundy fabric into the relentless path of the surgically sharp needle that rose and fell like a piston. Through the skylight, the October sky was grey and lifeless and she wore a thick woollen cardigan to ward off the chill.

So happily absorbed was she in her task, that she never heard Ben come in.

'So this is where it all happens,' said his Belfast voice behind her, slightly teasing, and Jennifer froze momentarily, horrified to be discovered by him, doing this.

She swore silently and expertly released the pressure on the foot pedal so that the fierce needle ground almost immediately to a halt, coming to rest inserted in the fabric. She gathered up the bundle of fabric on her knee, dumped it on the table, and stood up as she turned. She found Ben, in jeans, red t-shirt and a casual canvas jacket, standing in the doorway that led through to the front of the premises. His hands were in the front pockets of his jeans and he was grinning at her, dimples, like scars, in both cheeks.

Suddenly she realised why – she was still wearing her reading glasses. Foolishly, she'd forgotten to slip them off at the sound of his voice. They were stylish, rectangular ones with funky green metallic frames, but she hated them. They were a constant, painful reminder to Jennifer that her youth had quietly, and unnoticed, slipped away.

Quickly, she whipped the glasses off and held them behind her back between both hands and smiled self-consciously.

'I didn't know you made the curtains yourself,' he observed, looking past her, and she felt her face redden.

She tried to position herself in front of the sewing machine, Alan Crawford's horrible put-down about her being a 'one-woman band' ringing in her ears. This was not the professional image she wanted to convey to any client, least of all Ben. 'Uhh, I don't normally,' she said, inching backwards and managing to deposit the glasses on the workbench. 'It's just that one of my sewers, Janice, has let me down. It's not her fault. Her husband's ill.'

He nodded approvingly and grinned. 'Good to know you're so versatile.'

'Well, needs must,' she said snippily, like a pair of scissors closing, not sure if he was laughing at her. 'Anyway,' she said, brushing past him and leading the way back into the cosy office, where she shut the frosted door into the work-room very firmly behind them both and shed the frumpy cardigan. 'What can I do for you, Ben?'

He followed her over to the small, glass-topped table squeezed into the corner of the room, the old varnished wooden floorboards creaking under his rubber-soled shoes. Deep shelves containing her unwieldy collection of sample

100

books, all shapes and sizes, lined the wall facing the window. In front of a small glass coffee table sat two velvet wing-backed chairs she'd upholstered herself in a berry and green check from Designers Guild. The walls were painted in Farrow and Ball's Saxon Green and hung with a selection of stylish architectural prints in black frames.

He looked around. 'This place has a nice feel to it.'

'Thanks.' Jennifer clasped her hands behind her back, remembering the last time he'd held her hand. Had she imagined the chemistry between them?

She was attracted to Ben, but a relationship with him was, well, it was inconceivable. If he really had flirted with her before, it was just a harmless bit of fun. And there was nothing wrong with that. So long as she didn't read too much into it. Because the idea that he might be seriously interested in her seemed, frankly, a bit ridiculous.

'Ahem,' he said, clearing his throat and flicking absent-mindedly through the thick, vibrant pages of a Roma wallpaper book that lay open on the desk. 'I was just passing and thought I'd drop by and see how things were going.'

'Good. It's all going to plan,' she said, which wasn't exactly true. She was having difficulty sourcing just the right trimmings for the window blinds and, though she'd been promised a delivery of upholstery fabric today, it hadn't yet turned up. 'The plumbing work's almost done. The new fittings went in today. We can get started on the actual decorating soon.'

'Yeah, I saw the bathrooms today. Very Philippe Starck,' he said, as if he didn't much care. She cocked her head to one side, a bit perplexed by his attitude to the restaurant, which seemed to blow hot one minute and cold the next. She found that she was slightly annoyed by his flippancy. He'd no idea the trouble she'd had getting the Duravit fittings at such short notice – or persuading Danny, the best plumber in Ballyfergus, to fit the job into his busy schedule. That had cost her a bottle of Black Bush whiskey.

'I was also wondering if you'd like a lift to the meeting tonight?' he said, closing the sample book with a flick of his long fingers, and Jennifer's breathing quickened. Last time they'd spoken on the phone, she'd invited him along to tonight's meeting of the Ballyfergus Small Business Association, of which she was a member, as a way of helping him get to know the local community. She was perfectly capable of driving herself there and she knew how it would look if she arrived with him. The members of the Association were the biggest bunch of gossips in town.

'I don't much fancy going on my own,' he went on. 'It'd be nice to arrive with a friendly face.' He looked at her imploringly and Jennifer felt like a fool for reading too much into the invitation. He wasn't trying to chat her up – he was simply looking for a companion to accompany him to the meeting.

'Well, why don't you pick me up at seven? The meeting starts at a quarter past and we always meet at The Marine Hotel.'

He smiled secretly at this and she said, 'What?'

'Oh, nothing. It's just that it's one of our hotels. It's part of the Crawford Group.'

She nodded, wondering what it must be like to be part of a famous business family.

'The members of the Small Business Association won't mind me just turning up?'

Jennifer grinned, thinking about how they struggled for members and people willing to take on committee posts. 'Of course not! With the way businesses are closing these days, we need all the new blood we can get. I promise you, Ben, you'll be very welcome.'

Later, as she was putting the finishing touches to her make-up in the bathroom mirror, Jennifer examined her smile critically and decided it was time to whiten her teeth again. This involved three weeks of wearing a gum-shield in bed every night with peroxide gel on it, causing painfully sensitive, but fabulously white, teeth. Which, as every Hollywood movie star knew, knocked several years off. She frowned at the way the flesh under her eyebrows was starting to sag like her mother's – and the only solution for that was surgery . . .

She'd never thought of herself as vain but the truth was, she'd always taken her youth and relative good looks for granted. When she'd been younger, she could pass a mirror several times day without so much as glancing at her reflection. But, now that her looks were starting to fade, she scrutinised her face ceaselessly, paid attention to ads for anti-ageing cream on TV and drank water like a fish to keep her skin hydrated.

Her thoughts were interrupted by the sound of the doorbell. She ran barefoot onto the landing and hollered down the stairs, 'Can you get that, Matt? It'll be Ben.'

Normally she wouldn't have bothered changing but she couldn't very well appear in the same clothes Ben had seen her in earlier. She pulled on opaque black tights, a knitted grey dress, black boots and a necklace – and could not resist one last peek in the mirror. The woman that looked back was smart and stylish and, if her bloom was starting to fade, Jennifer reminded herself that there were a lot more important things in life. It was just a pity that, for women anyway, it counted for so much . . .

Ben, chatting in the hall with Matt, looked up and smiled when Jennifer appeared self-consciously at the top of the stairs, a green patent bag thrown over her right shoulder. She noticed that he too had changed – into smart, black

103

trousers and an open-necked pale blue shirt under a plain black pea-coat. Her stomach flipped at the sight of him and she pressed her nails into the palms of her hands, reminding herself that this was not a date.

'Me and the lads can show you round,' said Matt, capturing Ben's attention once more. Jennifer descended the stairs and stood looking up at the two men, the earthy smell of Ben's aftershave filling her nostrils. She said breezily, 'Sorry to keep you waiting. What're you two talking about?'

'I was just saying that Ben should come out for a few beers sometime with the lads.'

Jennifer tried to keep the smile on her face, hoping that her stunned expression didn't betray the stupid, irrational jealousy that took her by surprise. It was a nice gesture on Matt's part, and she ought to be pleased that he liked Ben well enough to ask him along on a night out. But where did that leave her and her friendship with Ben? If he was young enough to go out with Matt and his pals, did that mean he was too young to be her friend too?

Matt folded his arms comfortably across his broad chest and winked at Ben. 'If you're going to be living down this way, you need to start checking out the local talent.'

Jennifer pretended to look in her bag for something and Ben laughed. 'I'd love to, though I know from experience that I'll be living like a monk for the first few months.'

'Come out for a few beers anyway. You can stay the night here if you like, can't he, Mum?'

Jennifer, too embarrassed to speak, nodded. She wasn't sure which she objected to more – Matt calling her 'Mum' in front of Ben, which made her feel so *old*, or Matt treating Ben like one of his pals who he had invited to sleep over when she, well, she saw him in a different light altogether.

'I'd like that,' said Ben with a cautious glance at Jennifer. 'But let's wait till I move into my flat.'

'When'll that be?' said Matt.

'I get the keys at the end of November. Which reminds me,' he added thoughtfully, looking at Jennifer, 'I need to get some furniture sorted.'

'You'll get everything you need at Hilary's on Bank Road,' she offered. 'They're a family firm that's been in business for over thirty years. Ian Hilary's going to be there tonight. He'll see you right.'

'Thanks,' he said. 'But I don't even know where Bank Road is. Maybe you could show me.'

'Yeah, sure.'

'And help me pick some furniture.'

'Sure, I'd love to,' said Jennifer casually, while the blood pounded in her ears. Like tonight's offer of a lift, she didn't know how to interpret this invitation.

Ben looked at her from beneath lowered eyebrows. 'It's been a long time since I bought a double bed. We'll have to test it out.'

Jennifer was too embarrassed to speak. Matt frowned and glanced sharply at Ben and then at Jennifer. He said, looking at his nails and sounding ever so slightly put out, 'Need a woman's touch then, does it, this flat?'

'Something like that,' replied Ben, without taking his eyes off Jennifer who could not get out the door fast enough. Pulling the latch closed behind them, she wished he wouldn't flirt with her, especially in front of Matt.

Ben's car, parked across the end of her drive, provided a welcome distraction from these thoughts. It was a two-tone cream and moss green saloon car from the fifties that wouldn't have looked out of place on *Heartbeat*. 'This is your car?'

'Yeah,' he said chirpily, pulling keys from his pocket. 'She's a 1955 Rover 90.'

'It's not what I expected,' she said over her shoulder as she led the way down the drive.

'What did you expect?'

'Well, to be honest,' she said, coming to a halt in front of the passenger door, 'I imagined you in a modern sports car. Something flashy. Expensive maybe.'

He walked round to the driver's side of the car and, pausing to look at her over the car roof, said, 'Then you don't know me.' And how she wished she did.

Eight members of the Ballyfergus Small Business Association, plus Ben, met in a room at the front of The Marine Hotel, a handsome Victorian building which had been completely refurbished a few years ago. When everyone was seated around the circular table and had a drink in front of them, the bald-headed chairman, Ed O'Donaghue, called the meeting to order and introduced Ben, who received a subdued round of applause. His face coloured a little in embarrassment – unlike his father, he clearly did not relish being the centre of attention.

The content of the meeting was the usual humdrum stuff; a loyalty competition to encourage people to shop locally; new safety legislation that jeopardised the Christmas lights; and a lengthy, heated debate about all-day parking on the high street by some shop owners – to the detriment of shoppers.

At long last, Ed O'Donaghue closed the meeting. Jennifer's stomach growled: she'd not eaten since lunchtime.

Everyone stood up to go and Ed came over and shook Ben firmly by the hand. 'We're very excited about the new restaurant, Ben. The town could do with a bit of a culinary boost.' With an eye on the backs of the people leaving the room, he lowered his voice so only Ben and Jennifer could hear, and said, conspiratorially, 'Since The Highways closed last year there's nowhere decent to eat. No offence meant to other eateries in the town, but unless you want Indian or Chinese or chips with everything, there's not much choice.'

Ben laughed good-humouredly. 'Well, I hope we can put that situation right. Why don't you come to the opening night in December? I'll make sure you get an invitation.'

'That's very kind of you. Now, I hear that you've done a lot to raise funds for the Sick Kids' Hospital in Belfast.'

Ben pulled his jacket off the back of the chair and slipped it on. 'I've done a bit.'

'Ah, now, you've done more than that. I heard you're personally responsible for raising over two hundred thousand in the last two years.'

Jennifer, stuffing a folder into her bag, gasped and glanced up at a red-faced Ben. This news suggested caring and maturity beyond his years – and put her charitable and volunteering efforts on behalf of local good causes rather in the shade.

'That,' said Ben with a quick, uncomfortable glance at Jennifer, 'was a joint effort. My mother was involved. She knows lots of influential people with deep pockets.'

'But you were the driving force behind the fundraising, weren't you?' persisted Ed.

Ben pulled at his bottom lip and frowned, neither admitting nor denying the claim. 'Why do you ask?'

'Well, you see, I'm on the board of Glenvale, the special school here in Ballyfergus, and we're trying to raise money for a hydrotherapy pool. At the minute we can't get funding for it – cutbacks, you know. The kids come from all over East Antrim. Some of them have severe learning difficulties.

I was wondering if I could pick your brains about the best way to go about raising funds.'

Ben's face suddenly broke into a smile. 'You can do more than pick my brains. I'd be delighted to get involved, especially as it's for kids. Tell you what. I was planning on donating all the proceeds from our opening night to a local charity. Why don't we kick-start the fundraising effort by making it Glenvale?'

Ed beamed and the two of them walked out together, heads bent in conversation, while Jennifer followed behind. In the car park, Ed said goodnight and got into his car, leaving Jennifer and Ben standing alone.

'Well, that was quite an initiation into the business world of Ballyfergus,' he said with a wry expression, car keys dangling from his hand. 'I thought that argument over car parking was going to end in fisticuffs.'

Jennifer giggled and Ben said, 'Look, I haven't had anything to eat yet.'

'Neither have I,' said Jennifer, a little too eagerly.

'Why don't we talk over dinner, then?' he said tossing the keys in the air as if he'd just won something.

'Chinese or Indian?' said Jennifer.

'Or chips with everything?' said Ben and they both burst out laughing again.

When they'd finished eating curry and rice, downed half a bottle of Pinot Grigio and exhausted the subjects of Carnegie's and the Ballyfergus Small Business Association, there was a pause. Jennifer, who'd been holding her curiosity in check since they'd left The Marine Hotel, asked, 'What's it like being part of Ulster's high society?'

He ran a hand through his thick wavy hair and shrugged. 'I don't know.'

She said, 'But you are, aren't you? I bet you went to private school.'

'Campbell College,' he conceded, and though his cheeks coloured a little, he smiled.

'And played *rugger*,' she said, putting special, posh emphasis on 'rugger'.

'Rugby,' he corrected.

'And went to university.'

'Of course. Queen's.'

'What'd you study?'

'English Lit.'

'Mmm,' she said, 'interesting.' It made sense in terms of him as a person. He was thoughtful, a little introspective perhaps, and perceptive. 'Who's your favourite author then?'

'Martin Amis.'

'Oh, too clever for me,' she grimaced. 'I like something more accessible. Like Colm Toibin, Margaret Atwood, Joseph O'Connor, Barbara Kingsolver.'

'I like all them too,' he said earnestly. 'I read everyone and everything. But you did ask me who my favourite was.'

'True. Ever try Umberto Eco?'

'Oh, yes.'

He was an intellectual then, for try as she might, the books were unintelligible to her.

'But I didn't succeed.' His bracken-coloured eyes twinkled mischievously.

She giggled. 'I'm so relieved you said that! I'm glad it's not just me.'

When their laughter had died down she said, thinking of Alan Crawford and Carnegie's, 'Seriously though, what's someone with a degree in English Literature doing in the hospitality business?'

He shook his head but this time there was no smile on his face. He swilled the wine around in his glass, then took a long gulp as if fortifying himself for something. At last he said, 'That's a very good question, Jennifer.'

She waited. He turned the glass slowly, staring at the pale yellow liquid like it might hold the answer to the question. 'I started working for my father six and a half years ago, just after I graduated from Queen's.'

Jennifer blinked, while her brain processed a swift mental calculation. English Literature was a three-year degree course – he would've started at eighteen, graduated at twenty-one. He must be twenty-eight now. She felt a horrible sinking feeling in her tummy, like hurtling downhill on a roller coaster. She'd known he was a lot younger than her, obviously, and she'd originally estimated that he was in his late twenties. But over the past few weeks she'd found herself recalibrating this estimate, speculating that he could be in his early thirties, not only because he seemed mature but also because she wanted it to be so.

Now she had to face the fact that not only were there sixteen years between them, the yawning gap straddled three decades.

'What about you?' he said, interrupting her thoughts. The waiter arrived with two cups of coffee and set them carefully on the white damask tablecloth. He smiled his thanks and added, 'Did you go to uni?'

She poured milk in the coffee and told him all about her degree course in Design and Textiles at the University of Ulster and her first job designing products for Ulster Weavers, a family-owned home textiles company based in Holywood, County Down. 'I loved my job but it only lasted a few years. I gave up work when I had Lucy.'

He frowned. 'So, you must've been quite young when you had her.'

She smiled at this and said, 'I was twenty-four when I had Lucy, twenty-six when I had Matt.'

He looked away and blinked. She wondered if he was doing maths, as she had done only a few moments ago.

110

'That's quite young,' he said, and he paused to take a swig of coffee. 'I mean most of my friends aren't even married, never mind having children.'

There was a pause and Jennifer said, scratching the table-cloth with her nail, 'It was too young. I feel as if I didn't have time to live before the kids came along. And once you have kids, well, life is never the same again.' She cleared her throat and brightened, not wanting to dwell on past mistakes. 'Anyway, enough about me. Can I ask you something?'

'Go ahead,' he said, without looking up.

She placed her coffee cup carefully on the saucer. 'Who's Ricky?'

He looked so startled when she said this – almost knocking over the glass of wine and grabbing it just in time to prevent a spillage – that she blushed, ashamed of her eavesdropping.

Hurriedly, she provided an explanation. 'I'm sorry, I didn't mean to alarm you. It's just that I overheard your Dad call you Ricky. That day in the restaurant when I came to look round. I just wondered if it was an affectionate nickname, perhaps?' she added feebly, watching the colour leach from his cheeks.

He swallowed and looked at the back of his hands laid flat on the table. 'Ricky was my elder brother.'

'Oh,' she said and put a hand to her mouth. It wasn't so much the use of the past tense, as the toneless sound of his voice that filled her with dread of what he would say next.

'He died in a car crash.' He smiled grimly and nodded several times, as if these brutal words required a gesture of confirmation to reinforce their truth.

A waiter carrying a sizzling metal platter at shoulder level walked past, the hot, smoky spices catching in her throat. She

111

should not have pried. The back of her tongue swelled up and she said thickly, 'I'm so sorry, Ben.' She had a sudden urge to embrace him, to place her lips on his and kiss away the pain so clearly etched in the grim set of his face. 'I had no idea.'

'Of course you didn't,' he said evenly, sliding his hands off the table onto his lap. 'But I'd rather not talk about Ricky tonight. I . . . would you mind if I told you another time?' He raised his eyebrows like a question mark and he seemed, in spite of the pained expression on his face, much more in control of his emotions than her.

She coughed. 'You don't have to tell me at all. I'm so sorry. I didn't mean to cause you any distress.' She put the corner of the napkin to her mouth and took a sip of water.

'It's okay,' he said. But she knew, from the way his jaw muscle flexed and the corner of his left eye twitched, that it wasn't. Desperately, she clambered for safer ground.

'Well, to go back to our earlier discussion,' she said, trying to inject some light-heartedness back into the conversation while her heart pounded against her ribcage, 'the life of a champagne-swilling Ulster socialite sounds like a glamorous one to me. All those balls and parties and black-tie dinners. I could get used to that.'

'You'd be surprised,' he said drily, peeling the gold foil off the small square of plain chocolate that had come with the coffee. 'The novelty soon wears off. Though not for my father, apparently. He does a lot of socialising, well, networking really. He never stops. Not for one minute. I don't know where he gets the energy.' He shook his head and popped the chocolate in his mouth.

'And you?' she asked, more comfortable now that they'd dropped the topic of Ricky.

'It's not really my scene,' he said out of the side of his mouth. He finished the chocolate and then stared hard at her. 'I'll be honest with you, Jennifer,' he went on, making her feel like he was confiding specially in her. 'I can't bear the falseness of it all, pretending to be friends with people you don't even like. It's all very . . . superficial and competitive. And for all my father's wheeling and dealing it's never brought him much happiness. My parents divorced when I was twelve and my father's remarried twice. Mum's had plenty of admirers but I don't think she'll ever marry again. She says once was enough and I kind of understand where she's coming from, having been married to my Dad for fifteen years.' He gave a hollow laugh. 'Truth is, we stopped being a family a long time ago.'

Listening to this observation Jennifer's heart contracted in empathy. She thought guiltily of Lucy. Was this how she'd felt when she and David divorced? For while Matt had coped, Lucy had taken it very badly, reverting to tantrums and other behaviours more befitting a toddler.

'And being rich isn't all it's cracked up to be,' he went on, looking at her with a direct, searching gaze. 'It is a blessing, but it's a curse too.'

'What do you mean?' said Jennifer doubtfully. As far as money was concerned, too little had always been far more problematic than too much.

'Well, sometimes you wonder if people only like you just because of who you are. Like Rebecca.'

At the mention of his girlfriend, the muscles in Jennifer's back tensed. He rolled the foil into a hard little ball and threw it into the empty wine glass with a ping, while she arranged an indifferent expression on her face. 'Your girlfriend?' she managed to get out, and she held her breath.

'She's not my girlfriend any more.' He looked straight at her and Jennifer felt the tension across her shoulders evaporate, the good news momentarily overshadowing her misgivings and allowing her hopes to rise.

'What happened?' she said eagerly, pushing the coffee cup away.

He shrugged his shoulders. 'She was a . . . she was immature.' He thought for a moment and then added, diplomatically, 'No, I take that back. It's not fair. We simply weren't suited, that's all. It just took me a while to realise it.'

The waiter came with the bill, folded in half on a small round metal plate, and Jennifer rummaged around in her purse for some cash. She admired his self-restraint in refusing to be drawn on Rebecca – a lesser man might've indulged in a character assassination.

By the time she'd found her purse, Ben had already paid the bill.

'I'd like to pay for mine,' she said, a little indignantly.

He stood up, the faint smell of aftershave wafting across the table, and slipped his wallet into his back pocket, the front buttons of his shirt straining against his well-defined chest. She couldn't take her eyes off this or his slim, black-trousered hips. 'Tell you what. Why don't you pay next time?'

'Next time? Oh, I'd love to do this again,' she blurted out, a little too eagerly and bit her lip. Embarrassed by a sudden wave of desire that made her face burn, she dropped the purse into her bag and suppressed a secret smile, rejoicing in the fact that there would be a next time. She liked so much about him already – the thoughtful, honest way he answered a question; his quiet humour; his modesty; the fact that, like her, he loved books. And his transparency was a startling, welcome, surprise.

But these attributes were not what stirred the yearning in her and made the skin on the back of her neck prickle with electricity. When he stared at her so intensely with his melted-chocolate brown eyes, and gave her one of his shy,

114

half-cocked smiles, the right corner of his deep red mouth turned up like a question mark, her body ached for his touch. She took a deep breath, stood up and met his smile with a confident one of her own, while she tried very hard not to visualise what lay beneath the blue shirt and the black trousers.

Chapter 9

Lucy sat at the kitchen table happily slathering soft garlic and lemon butter into diagonal slits in a French baguette. Outside the wind howled round the corners of the house like a banshee – October, which had come in like a lamb, was going out like a lion.

Watching her, Jennifer smiled. It was nice being indoors, in the warm and cosy kitchen, on this wretched night. It was heart-warming to see Lucy relaxed and happy – and to have harmony in the house once more. Over the last few weeks there had been a marked improvement in Lucy's mood. Calmness had replaced her habitual anxiety – she'd stopped biting her nails and, though she spent as much time alone in her room as before, she seemed altogether more contented with the world and with herself. And she no longer asked for money. What could be responsible for this transformation? Was it, thought Jennifer guiltily, simply because the weight of financial worry had been lifted from her shoulders? Perhaps her father had been right, after all, to bail her out.

Jennifer tipped some salt into the pot of bolognese sauce. She turned the flame down to a simmer and set about clearing up. They worked companionably in silence for a while and then Jennifer, keen to make the most of Lucy's good mood, spied the book on the table. Though it looked relatively new, it was traditionally bound with a leather-look burgundy cover.

'What're you reading? Tolstoy?'

Lucy looked up and followed her mother's gaze. She smiled, more to herself than her mother, for when she lifted her eyes to glance briefly, almost condescendingly, at Jennifer, the smile was replaced by a secretive smirk. 'No. It's the Bible.'

'Oh,' said Jennifer and she went over and picked up the book. 'That's an . . . unusual choice,' she said, examining the King James Bible. She could see now that, though not old, it was a well-worn second-hand copy.

It did not come from any bookshelf in her house and, weighing the tome in her hand, it occurred to her that that was a failing. She herself did not possess a deep personal faith – at least not one strong enough to make her seek out the written word of God on a regular basis – and David had taken the family Bible with him when he'd left.

Lucy unrolled a large sheet of metal foil, and ripped it rather savagely against the serrated edge of the box. 'What's unusual about it?'

Her defensive tone warned Jennifer to tread warily. 'Only that you've never shown any interest before?'

'That's because I didn't understand what I was missing.' Lucy wrapped the foil tightly around the bread like a swaddling blanket and set the ceramic bowl, knife and board noisily in the sink. 'Better late than never though.'

'Mmm,' said Jennifer thoughtfully, flicking through the pages and coming to a halt at the bookmark, with the Lord's Prayer inscribed on it, lodged in Corinthians. 'Maybe you're right, Lucy. It is one of the most influential books ever written, there's no doubt about that.'

'That's not why it's important,' said Lucy, and she held out her hand and looked at the book. Jennifer gave it to her and Lucy pressed it against her chest, her hands splayed across the cover like a mother nursing a precious baby's head. 'The Bible is important because it's the word of God.' She fixed her mother with a steady, sure gaze as surprising to Jennifer as her daughter's self-assured words. Lucy had always been lacking in confidence and uncertain in her convictions. It was good to see her standing up for something she believed in, but odd too as they rarely, if ever, talked about spiritual matters.

She smiled and, seeking clarification, said, 'Well, yes, of course. But not *literally*. It's the word of God as laid down by scribes over the centuries. An interpretation, if you like, of God's spiritual teachings by man. And as such, it's open to different interpretations too. Look how many versions of the Bible there are.'

Lucy shook her head sadly. 'Jesus and the Apostles took the Old Testament literally. What makes you think you're above them?'

Jennifer opened her mouth but nothing came out, so dumbfounded was she by Lucy's response. It was clear that Lucy had been studying hard over the past weeks, but not maths. Jennifer had been prepared for a lot of things as a parent – drugs, alcohol, depression, promiscuity, self-harm even – but not a religious conversion, not the adoption of beliefs alien to her own.

She and David had raised Matt and Lucy within a set of morals largely based on Christianity. They'd always agreed that the children should be free to choose their own religious path in life. And now that moment was, apparently, here she was not ready for it. If this new-found faith was responsible for Lucy's recent happiness, then it was a good thing, wasn't it? She should support Lucy's choice, even if she could not embrace her beliefs.

'The Bible isn't an allegorical story, Mum,' said Lucy with fire in her eyes and passion in her voice. She held the Bible up in her right hand and stared at it, her eyes shining. 'It's the actual word of God, clear as the living day. It's a blueprint for how to live our lives today in His image.'

Jennifer swallowed as she watched the space between herself and her daughter widen, pushed apart like continents on the earth's crust by the rising mantle of Lucy's budding faith. She'd thought over the last weeks that she and Lucy were moving towards the intimate mother-daughter bond she had always craved. But she saw now that the shift she'd perceived had been all to do with a change in Lucy's character, and nothing at all to do with a change in their relationship. Lucy had been pleasant and co-operative because she had much more important matters on her mind, that was all. Aiming to calibrate just how big the disparity was between them on this subject, Jennifer ventured, 'But what about all the inconsistencies in the Bible?'

'There aren't any.'

Jennifer blinked and pressed on, even though she feared the answer. 'Are you saying that you believe everything in the Bible actually happened? That God, for example, created the universe in seven days?'

'Absolutely. It's in Exodus. Twenty eleven,' she said, holding out the Bible in one hand and laying the other atop, like a divine sandwich made from human hands instead of bread. '*For in six days the Lord made heaven and earth, the sea, and all that in them is.*'

'But what about science? What about evolution?'

'There's as much scientific evidence to support the Bible as there is to dispute it.'

'That's simply not true, Lucy,' said Jennifer in astonishment, unable to let this pass unremarked.

Lucy smiled warmly. 'How can you challenge something

you've barely read since childhood, Mum? It's only when you come to really know the Bible that you understand.'

Ignoring this, Jennifer, driven to pursue this field of questioning by morbid curiosity asked, 'Let me ask you something.'

'Okay.'

'So what about the age of the earth? How old is it?'

'Oh, that's easy,' said Lucy flippantly, though Jennifer in her despair could not even raise a smile. 'According to biblical chronology, the universe and the earth was created about six thousand years ago.'

Jennifer put her hands, hot and sweaty, to her suddenly chilled cheeks. How could Lucy possibly think this? She was a scientist, studying Mathematics, a subject of logic and reasoning. It had been proven beyond a doubt that the earth was more than four billion years old. 'Are you telling me that you're a Young Earth Creationist?'

'Oh, labels don't interest me, Mum,' said Lucy airily. 'I'm only interested in the truth. And everything I need to know is in here.' She held the Bible in both hands across her chest and sighed. 'You should read it. I think you would be amazed, if you just got over your prejudice.'

Prejudice! Jennifer's eyes opened wide in disbelief at what she was hearing. As far as Jennifer was concerned, choosing to adopt a literal interpretation of the Bible meant closing your mind to every reasoned argument and scientific advancement of the last century.

The doorbell went and Lucy said brightly, 'I'll get it. That'll be Grandpa.' And she skipped lightly out of the room with the book still clasped in her hands as if she hadn't a care in the world.

They had dinner in the kitchen, the windows steamed up from the cooking and the room filled with the smell of garlic and dog. Jennifer's father, Brian, chatted to Matt about his new job. Lucy served herself salad and dressing out of a bottle while Jennifer brooded silently, trying to come to terms with the monumental discovery about her daughter. She passed Matt the parmesan and glanced at Lucy who returned her look with a steady, unnerving one of her own. Jennifer pushed the corners of her mouth into a smile.

'You'll need to get that hair cut,' chuckled Brian who, at seventy-six, had a deep and gravelly voice honed by a forty-a-day Benson and Hedges habit. Though long retired, he still had a thick head of grey hair, a matching close-trimmed beard and the wiry, lean build of a man who'd laboured all his working life. He'd been a bricklayer (until his knees gave out at the age of sixty-four), liked a pint and had outlived his clean-living wife by four years. He adored Lucy and Matt, his only two grandchildren.

'No,' said Matt, shaking the curls that now touched his shoulders. 'Ben says I can just tie it back in a ponytail.'

'Ben this. Carnegie's that,' chimed in Lucy. 'Honestly. Matt, that's all you talk about these days.'

'Well, it's a big step for your brother, Lucy,' said Brian. 'Starting his first proper job. You'll know how it feels when it's your turn.'

Matt gave his sister a smug look, reached over and pinched a slice of cucumber off her plate. She stabbed the back of his big hand with her fork.

'Ouch, that hurt!' he cried, wincing.

'It was meant to,' she said, her nose wrinkling up in a cheeky grin. Matt, more swiftly this time, grabbed another piece of cucumber in revenge. Lucy let out a world-weary sigh but did not attempt to retaliate. Jennifer smiled warmly, the playful affection between her children filling her with pleasure.

'What's a fella like you doing with a ponytail anyway?'

said Brian, pausing with a mound of chopped-up spaghetti and sauce balanced precariously on a fork in front of his mouth. He had come late to Italian cuisine and never mastered the art of twirling spaghetti round a fork. 'Do you think you're Samson?'

'Maybe,' said Matt, his right cheek bulging with a chunk of garlic bread.

Brian chewed and swallowed. 'In that case,' he said, with a wink at Jennifer, 'where's your Delilah?'

'I'm currently between girlfriends,' said Matt, who had so many girls chasing him Jennifer could barely keep up with them all.

When the laughter had died down, Brian asked, 'And how are you getting on at university, Lucy?'

'Good,' said Lucy and, chewing, put her hand over her mouth. She swallowed, crossed her knife and fork on her plate like swords and said, looking at Jennifer, 'I might not come home next weekend.'

Jennifer took a drink of red wine and considered this news. Lucy always came home at weekends. She said there was nothing to do.

Lucy's face went red all of a sudden and Matt pointed his fork at her accusingly and cried out through a mouthful of food, 'Hey, you've got a boyfriend, haven't you?'

Jennifer put the glass down, her interest quickened. If Matt was right, this *was* news – good news. Her secret, unvoiced fear was that Lucy would never meet someone to love her.

'Well, I have met someone I like very much,' admitted Lucy, looking down at her hands, her narrow brow as smooth and white as an egg. 'And he likes me.'

Her quiet voice was so vulnerable, that Matt dropped his teasing tone immediately and said kindly, 'That's great, Lucy.'

Lucy looked directly at Matt. 'We've only been seeing

122

each other properly for a couple of weeks but we both feel we're made for each other.'

They all stared at Lucy, dumbstruck, while the gravity of this announcement sank in. Her normally pale cheeks were pink-tinged, her lips were turned up in a secretive smile and when she blinked and brought her gaze to bear on Jennifer, her eyes sparkled like sun on moving water. She had never looked as pretty, even her skin was clear and radiant, the spots that had lingered for weeks on her chin, all gone.

'Ah, that's lovely, pet,' said Brian at last and Jennifer swallowed the lump that suddenly appeared in her throat. Lucy, so desperate for approval, was in love.

'Oh, Lucy, I'm so pleased for you.'

Matt, finding his voice, asked, 'What's his name, then?'

Lucy beamed. 'Oren Wilson. He's studying for a Theology degree.'

Jennifer thought of the burgundy Bible, with its well-leafed pages, and said, quickly, 'Did Oren give you the Bible?'

'What Bible?' said Matt, looking at Brian.

Lucy nodded. 'Yes. I've been studying it. It's the most amazing thing I've ever read.'

'Are you going to become a Christian?' said Matt in his direct way.

'Yes,' said Lucy and gave him an indulgent smile, 'I most certainly am.'

Matt's eyebrows knitted together momentarily and then his face brightened again. 'Cool,' he said, with a shrug.

'So, I take it this Oren is a Christian too, if he's studying Theology,' said Brian, carefully peeling the crust off the buttered bread like orange peel.

'Yes and he's really, really clever,' effused Lucy, who had barely touched the food on her plate. 'He's already got a Law degree – he got a two one, you know. After graduating he volunteered out in Peru, helping to build a church and

123

teach the local kids, and then when he came back he worked for a law firm down in Enniskillen – that's where he's from – for a few years before deciding that it wasn't for him. He jacked it all in to study Theology. And I think that takes real guts, don't you think? To follow God's calling.'

Matt and Brian, his mouth full of bread, nodded in agreement.

She carried on a little breathlessly, 'He feels his calling might be to minister in some capacity.'

'What? Like become a minister with the dog caller an' all?' said Matt.

'Oh no, you don't have to be a pastor to minister,' she replied patiently. 'There's all sorts of ways to serve God.' She paused to deliver an aside, 'Ministry comes from the Greek word *diakoneo*, which means to serve. Every Christian should be in the ministry of helping others.'

Jennifer smiled faintly, weighed up this heavy information like the knife she held in her hot and sweaty hand. As a CV she couldn't fault it – he sounded socially responsible, kind, giving and highly motivated. But he was clearly Lucy's senior by several years. Maybe she needed someone older, and wiser, to accompany her on life's great journey.

And yet, something niggled. Jennifer swallowed a big gulp of wine and tried very hard to hone in on what, exactly, bothered her. Was it that Lucy sounded so *infatuated* with him? So love-blinded that, Jennifer suspected, had Oren any fault at all, Lucy would be utterly incapable of seeing it?

'If you've found faith, Lucy, love,' said Brian, pressing his hand over his granddaughter's.

'I have, Grandpa.'

'Then you've found true happiness.'

'As well as a man, by the sounds of it,' said Matt rather coarsely and Brian and Lucy laughed.

'You're not saying much, Mum?' said Lucy.

'I . . . ahem . . . I'm delighted that you've met someone, Lucy. Tell you what. Why don't you bring Oren down the weekend after next so we can all meet him? He's very welcome to stay over on Saturday night,' she went on. 'That's if you don't mind him bunking in with you, Matt.'

Matt, easygoing as always, shrugged. 'So long as he doesn't mind sleeping on a roll-mat. Or you can both stay over at Dad's. He's got more room.'

'Sure, whatever suits,' said Jennifer smoothly, doing her best to hide the fact that this innocent suggestion irked. She wanted her home to be the centre of her children's lives (until they moved out at least), not David's.

'That's a brilliant idea, Mum!' said Lucy, her cheeks all aglow. 'I'll text him straight away.' She pulled her mobile out of a back pocket and busied herself pressing buttons with her thumbs.

When the plates were cleared away, Matt took an ice-cream cake he'd made earlier out of the freezer. Standing up, he began to carve slices of the frozen dessert peppered with chunks of nuts, dried fruit and splinters of golden honeycomb. He handed a wedge to his grandfather and said, 'Where'd you go with Ben after the meeting last night, Mum? You didn't come in till nearly twelve.'

'We went for a meal at the Indian,' she said evenly, scraping the remains of Lucy's dinner into the bin.

'What meeting was that, love?' said Brian, as he regarded the dessert with a suspicious look over folded arms.

'It's only ice cream with bits in, Grandpa,' said Matt, passing a plate to Lucy and setting one down at Jennifer's place.

'You'll like it,' said Lucy, laying the phone on the table, her eyes fixed on it with the same rapt attention a mother affords her newborn.

'Ballyfergus Small Business Association,' said Jennifer,

busying herself with handing out dessert forks and spoons.

Brian put the loaded spoon in his mouth, pulled it out and licked it. 'Mmm . . . not bad, son.' Jennifer sat down at the table and Brian said, 'Have they sorted out what's happening with the Christmas lights yet, Jennifer?'

She opened her mouth to explain what had happened at the meeting but Lucy said, sharply, 'You don't mean Ben Crawford, Matt's new boss?'

'Uh-huh,' said Jennifer, closing her lips over a spoonful of the rapidly softening ice cream.

Lucy stared at her mother and the frown deepened. 'But why?'

Jennifer shrugged and rearranged the napkin on her knee, glad of the sickly sweet ice cream filling her mouth and giving her time to think. She swallowed and said, 'I thought it was the friendly thing to do. He's a stranger in town and I thought he might benefit from being part of the local business community.'

'So this meal out,' said Matt, with sudden, sharp interest and a hard stare. 'It was purely professional?'

Jennifer let her napkin slide to the floor and dived after it. 'Of course,' she said from under the table.

'What are you suggesting, Matt?' said Lucy, as Jennifer straightened up, her stomach twisted like a wet rope and her face hot and damp. 'That Mum has the hots for this guy?'

Brian chuckled, 'Sure the fella's only a pup, isn't he, Jennifer?'

'I don't know how old he is,' she lied, praying that everyone attributed the redness in her cheeks to her exertions under the table.

'He's twenty-eight,' said Matt flatly, scraping his plate.

Brian chuckled. 'Far too young for your mother, Lucy.'

'Oh, that's okay then,' said Lucy and she put a hand on

her breast and, looking round at the others, giggled. 'I thought for one awful minute that you were more than friends. And no disrespect, but that would be a bit gross, wouldn't it?'

Jennifer looked at her blankly, a chill creeping up her spine.

'After all,' said Lucy, tilting her head to one side and emitting a little snort of derision, 'he is young enough to be your son, Mum.'

Jennifer tried to swallow but her mouth was suddenly dry. Lucy was right. Her happiness melted away like the remaining ice cream on her plate. Realising everyone was looking at her, she waved the napkin in front of her face like a fan. 'It's awful hot in here, isn't it? What with the cooking and all. I'll open a window.'

While she fiddled with the window handle, she silently admonished herself for fantasising about Ben Crawford. She was a middle-aged mother of two grown-up children, for heaven's sake. She'd had her chance at life, at happiness. It was time for the next generation. It was time to stand aside and let her daughter take centre stage romantically, and stop chasing ludicrous fantasies of her own.

Lucy's phone bleeped and she cried out, 'Oh, that'll be Oren!'

Grateful for the distraction, Jennifer leaned against the worksurface, with her back to the opened window, the cool night air on her back.

Lucy's eyes scanned the message and she beamed. 'Yes, he says he'd love to come.'

'Great.' Jennifer's tense shoulders relaxed a little – it was a good sign that Oren was keen to meet Lucy's family. She'd be more worried if he wasn't.

'Fantastic,' said Brian, 'I look forward to meeting him, love.'

'Don't suppose he'll be up for a pint, then?' said Matt. 'What with him being Christian and all?'

Lucy gave her brother a withering look, though there was warmth in it too, and said sarcastically, 'Well, what do you think?'

'But he does like music, yeah?' said the ever-sanguine Matt.

'Of course.'

'In that case we'll get on just fine,' said Matt reassuringly and Jennifer wished that she shared his sense of optimism. As a questioning liberal, she couldn't imagine finding much in common with a teetotal, Young Earth Creationist, Christian. But maybe Lucy was right – maybe she was prejudiced after all. She ought not to judge Oren before giving him a chance. She would make him welcome in her home, and if he really was the one for Lucy, she would do everything in her power to love him.

Chapter 10

Lucy heard Oren give his testimony for the first time the following weekend in a small, half-full lecture room in the university on Saturday night. She sat in the middle of the brightly lit room, her eyes fixed on Oren, her emotions see-sawing with the inflections of his voice – quiet and reflective one minute, hot tempered and passionate the next. But it wasn't just his delivery that transfixed her and the rest of the audience. He told how he'd drunk and smoked and even dabbled in drugs. He described a life of wild parties and promiscuity, how he turned his back on his Christian upbringing and neglected his family. A life that Lucy could not reconcile with the Godly man she loved.

He lowered his voice until it was little more than a whisper. 'I hated myself, I hated my life. When I wasn't being distracted by sinning, I was fearful. And then one night, lying in my own vomit in an alleyway outside a pub,' he paused and everyone gasped, 'I asked the Lord to come into my life. And in His wisdom and His mercy, He did. I heard a voice say, "*I am the resurrection, and the life: he that believeth in me, though he were dead, yet shall he live.*"' He placed a flat palm gently on his breast. 'And I knew it was God calling to me, showing me the way.' He paused again and bowed his head. 'I was a sinner and I still am. We all are.' He raised his head and looked at the crowd and Lucy felt that he was looking only at her, straight into her unworthy heart. 'But from that moment, when I committed myself to Christ, my life was transformed. I pray, that with the grace of Jesus Christ, yours will too.'

Oren walked Lucy back to her digs, her arm linked in his. She barely noticed the smell of the musty air, the slippy mulch of leaves underfoot, or the damp chill that penetrated her bones. She tried to concentrate as he told her about his growing interest in missionary work, but all she could feel was the heat of him through her clothing and the reassuring solidity of his arm.

'I was so proud of you tonight,' she said, sneaking a glance at his profile as they walked.

'I'm not proud of myself,' he said sharply. 'And you shouldn't be either, Lucy.'

'Oh,' she said, a little taken aback.

'The Lord hates pride.'

'I only meant I admire you for what you did tonight, standing up in front of all those people and sharing your testimony. It took a lot of guts.'

'Well,' he said, sounding mollified. 'If my witness brings someone to God, then praise the Lord. But I don't do it to attract praise to myself. *Everyone that is proud in heart is an abomination to the Lord.*' There was a pause and he added, 'Book?'

Lucy, desperate to please, bit her lip and tried to recall but could not.

'Proverbs. Chapter sixteen, verse five,' he supplied blithely.

'I don't think I've read that yet,' said Lucy despondently. The Bible, she had discovered, was over one thousand five hundred pages long, difficult to read and even harder to

130

understand. She was following a Bible study programme recommended by Oren which, confusingly, involved reading a number of chapters every day from different parts of the Bible rather than reading it from start to finish like a traditional book. 'In fact, to be honest, I'm finding it hard. All those thees and thous. Wouldn't it be easier to use a modern translation? And parts of it, like Job for instance, well, there's whole chapters that are just questions. And there's no answers.'

Oren stopped dead in his tracks and turned to face her, taking both her hands in his. He looked at her levelly and said, 'God has the answers, Lucy. You have to open your heart to Him so that He can reveal them to you. The King James Bible is from the preserved Hebrew and Greek texts. It is the best and most accurate translation. Pray for guidance, Lucy, and remember that nothing really worth doing is ever easy.'

She nodded glumly, not having a clue what he was talking about, but unwilling to reveal her ignorance.

'You're not thinking of giving up, are you?'

'Oh, no,' said Lucy, eagerly. 'Of course not.'

'Good. Because the Lord would be so disappointed if you did. And so would I.'

Oren let go of her hands and they fell into walking side by side as before. 'But how do you know so much?' she said. 'I mean you can quote from the Bible on every subject, just like that, without a moment's hesitation.'

He laughed. 'I've been studying it a lot longer than you.'

'Most of your life,' she observed. 'You know I get quite cross when I think about my childhood and the fact that my parents didn't take me to church.'

As he quite often did, Oren answered this observation with a quotation. '*Provoke not your children . . . but bring them up in the nurture and admonition of the Lord,*' which

Lucy took to mean that her parents had, as she suspected, failed her. Then he brightened and added, 'But isn't it fantastic that you've come to the Lord now?' He patted her arm with his free hand and added, making her glow with happiness, 'And you're making real progress with your scripture reading.'

Back at the empty house Lucy made instant coffee and they took refuge in her room. She sat primly on the old office chair she'd nabbed from Dad's surgery, nursing a mug. Oren sat opposite her on the bed, using the wall as a backrest. The bed sagged in the middle with the weight of him, his long, well-built legs stretched out across the grubby pink carpet.

'There's something I want to ask you, Lucy.'

'Go on,' she smiled.

'Have you ever had a boyfriend before?'

She shook her head and blushed, embarrassed to admit to it. 'No.'

He set the mug down carefully on the carpet, got off the bed and knelt down in front of her, all this accomplished in one smooth movement, so small was the room. He put a hand on each arm of the chair, and stared at her very long and hard while her heart pounded against her chest and she struggled to hold the coffee cup steady in her hands.

'You have a good heart, Lucy. And one day, you're going to make some lucky guy very happy.' Her heart soared and she held her breath, her entire body tensed nervously, ready for the kiss she had been anticipating these last few weeks. She tilted her chin up slightly and momentarily closed her eyes but, when she opened them again, Oren was on his feet, peering over her shoulder at the books on the desk behind her. 'Now show me these passages you're having trouble with and I'll see if I can help.'

She swivelled round, praying that he hadn't noticed her

foolishness, picked up the Bible and handed it to him. 'There's plenty to choose from,' she said drily, looking at the many coloured Post-it notes peeking out from every section of the book. Each one marked an unintelligible passage.

He opened the Bible at one of the pages. 'Ah, Hebrews. That's a tough one.'

Lucy watched his brow pucker in concentration as he read, his lips moving but no sound coming out. They'd held hands and Oren had even hugged her on several occasions but that was as far as physical intimacy between them went. Lucy had seen enough soaps on TV to realise this was unusual – and she yearned for more. 'Oren,' she said and paused.

'What?' he said distractedly, not looking up.

She swallowed, summoning up the courage to speak. 'Don't you want to kiss me?'

He looked up abruptly, let out a sigh and knelt down on the floor again, the Bible clutched in one hand. He smiled at her indulgently. 'Of course I *want* to, Lucy.'

'Then why don't you? I want you to.'

He grinned and let his head fall like a puppet then raised his gaze to her once more. 'Woman,' he said teasing her, 'are you trying to lead me into sin?'

She pressed her hands between her knees. 'No, but I don't see what the harm is in a kiss.'

'A kiss is one thing but it leads to others. Believe me. Look, I know this is going to sound ridiculously old-fashioned but one of the things I like about you most is your purity, Lucy. I've a great deal of respect for you and I don't want you to do anything that you – or I – might later regret. Does that sound crazy?'

It didn't sound crazy to Lucy at all. It sounded rather romantic.

He found one of her hands and pressed his big, hot palm to hers, their fingers interlacing like a puzzle fitting together. 'What we have is special, Lucy, and I don't want to spoil that or rush things. Sex outside marriage is a sin. I feel it's best if we avoid temptation. Okay?'

Lucy, blushing, nodded. She had never felt so cherished, so loved, in her life. Her heart swelled with joy. She had interpreted Oren's apparent aversion to intimacy as a sign that he wasn't interested in her. But the complete opposite was true. It was *because* he cared for her that he wanted to take things slowly. He'd even mentioned *marriage* for heaven's sake!

'Come and sit beside me,' commanded Oren, patting the space beside him on the duvet where he'd sat down again. 'And we'll go through this passage a verse at a time.' Lucy willingly obeyed and, as she sat with her shoulder brushing his rock-hard bicep and the clean soapy smell of him filling the room, she could not believe how her life was transformed. Only a few weeks before she had despaired of a normal life, of love, of marriage. And now she had Oren, good and gorgeous and dependable.

The skies were heavy with black clouds and a bitter November chill was in the air when Lucy and Oren pulled up outside the red-brick house in Oakwood Grove. Most of the leaves had fallen from the oak trees that surrounded the house and they lay in banks against the walls and fences like mottled brown snow.

Mum opened the door to them with a big, wide smile before Lucy had even rung the bell.

Guided by his faith, Oren was conservative in most things, and Lucy was therefore relieved to see that her mother had dressed soberly for the occasion, in a patterned skirt, low-heeled boots and a modest green crew-necked knit. Not

134

mumsy exactly, but not as trendy as the jeans and white shirt combo she usually favoured – which Lucy secretly thought had the whiff of mutton dressed as lamb about it.

In the past Lucy had often wished that she had the confidence to dress as fashionably as her mother but, since meeting Oren and coming to know God, that longing had dissipated. She had no desire to compete with her mother in the looks department – she had come to realise that inner beauty was far more valuable than outer appearance. She liked the fact that Oren didn't approve of women wearing make-up or revealing clothes because it took away all the pressure to conform to society's ideal of female attractiveness. But although Oren liked her as God had made her, without artifice or adornment, this knowledge did little to boost her fragile ego. For, while Lucy no longer fretted about her outer appearance, she now worried about her inner goodness. She feared that, in spite of prayer and application to her Bible studies, she would fall short of Oren's exacting spiritual standards. And, when it came to God, Oren had no time for slackers.

'You must be Oren,' said Mum, not waiting to be introduced. 'It's lovely to meet you. Lucy's told us so much about you.' She reached out her hand eagerly. Oren took it and said, politely, 'Pleased to meet you too, Mrs Irwin.'

'It's Ms. Murray, actually. But there's no need for formality. Call me Jennifer, please.' She stepped aside, opened the door fully and waved them both inside. 'Come in, both of you.'

In the cramped hall they took off their coats and the three of them stood awkwardly, Oren looking around him, and Mum said, 'Lunch is ready. Why don't we eat?'

In the kitchen, which smelt strongly of wet dog, Muffin lifted his head when they came in but didn't get out of his basket. Lucy went straight over, knelt down by his bed and stroked his damp fur. She looked up at Oren and said, 'This is Muffin.'

'Yep?' he said, examining the collection of photos, post-cards, and other detritus pinned to the notice-board by the door.

Turning her attention back to the dog she tickled him under the chin and said quietly, 'Hey there, boy.' Then, addressing her mother, 'Is he okay? He didn't get up when I came in. That's not like him.' She noticed, but didn't add, that he smelt a bit more whiffy than usual.

'He got a bladder infection,' said Mum and Lucy gasped and pressed her lips to Muffin's bony head. 'But don't worry,' she added, hastily. 'Your Dad gave him tablets and he should be better soon. He says it's very common in dogs his age.'

'Oh, that's good,' said Lucy, relief flooding through her. She tickled Muffin in his favourite spot behind the left ear.

'Does he stay in here when you're eating?' said Oren.

'Where else would he go?' Mum eyed him suspiciously. 'Don't you have dogs on the farm, Oren?'

'Of course,' he said, 'but they're working dogs. They live outdoors.'

Lucy laughed. 'Well Muffin's a pet, aren't you, boy?' She cooed soothingly into the ear on his good side, which Dad said still had some hearing left, and then added, 'And pets get treated differently. More like one of the family.'

'That's exactly what he is,' said Mum firmly while Oren squeezed himself into the chair in front of the kitchen door. Lucy went over to the sink and washed her hands, while Mum banged about with bowls and a soup ladle. 'It's not much I'm afraid. Only soup and sandwiches. I got some nice cheese though and that chocolate cake you love from the bakery, Lucy. Maggie'll give you a proper meal later – you'll enjoy that.'

She took a bottle of sparkling mineral water out of the

fridge and placed it by a basket of bread. Then she surveyed the table and dusted her hands together. 'Right, I think that's everything. Oh, there you are, Matt. Just in time.'

Matt stood in the doorway in a grey t-shirt and sweat-pants which looked like he'd slept in them. His hair stood up on end and he clearly hadn't shaved. 'Hi Lucy,' he said, coming over and giving her a peck. He smelt of sweat and last night's stale booze.

Lucy made introductions and Matt said, 'You'll have to excuse me,' with a downward glance and an unrepentant grin. 'Bit of a heavy night last night.' He yawned and stretched his arms over his head, revealing dark patches of sweat on the armpits of his t-shirt, and Lucy was suddenly embarrassed by her brother. Why hadn't he made more of an effort? She didn't need to look at Oren, well turned out in smart trousers and a clean shirt with his hair carefully combed, to know what he was thinking.

Oren took the lead by saying a short nicely phrased grace and then, over lunch, he told Matt and Mum all about his Theology course. Afterwards, they had coffee in the lounge. Mum opened a box of Lir truffles and handed them round. Lucy took one, bit it in half, and then wished she hadn't. For when it came to Oren, sitting across the room on one of the big armchairs, he held up the flat of his hand like a shield and said with a pleasant smile, 'Not for me, thanks. I don't take alcohol.'

Lucy swallowed the chocolate with difficulty and quietly set the remaining half on her saucer. Oren assured her that God disapproved of alcohol in all forms but she'd momen-tarily forgotten. Temptation was everywhere. Thank God she had Oren to keep her on the right side of it.

'What? Not even a tiny bit?' said Matt, examining the truffle he held between his fingers, turning it this way and that as if looking for some flaw.

'Alcohol, in any form, is a transgression of God's law.'

Matt raised his eyebrows, shrugged and popped the truffle in his mouth. Mum, sitting on the edge of her seat, made a funny noise and cleared her throat. 'More coffee, anyone?'

They all shook their heads and Oren leaned back in the chair, stretched out his legs and crossed them at the ankle. 'Lucy tells me you're an interior designer, Jennifer.'

Oren had the knack of making people feel at ease and Mum was no exception. She chatted happily about her work for a good ten minutes, apparently oblivious to the fact that Oren was just being polite in asking. Lucy could tell he was bored because his gaze was drawn to a coy female nude, sketched in charcoal, that had hung to the right of the fireplace for years.

'And you decorated this room yourself?' he said, inadvertently cutting across Mum, who was still babbling on.

'Why, yes,' said Mum with a little frown, following his gaze. 'Ah, yes, an artist friend from my uni days drew that for me. Isn't it well done?'

'Well, I am surprised. I hardly think it appropriate to display the naked female form in a family drawing room. Do you?'

Lucy, startled, looked at the picture in a new light. The seated model had her back partially turned to the viewer, but her drooping left breast and her full, rounded buttocks were on display. She blushed. Oren was right. It oughtn't to be hanging there. It oughtn't to be on display at all. There was a long uncomfortable pause, during which Mum glared at Oren and he stared evenly back at her. Thankfully, Matt chipped in and told Oren all about his new job. At the mention of Ben Crawford's name, Oren's interest quickened.

'I went to school with Ben Crawford at Campbell College. We were in the same year, but our paths didn't cross that much. We had different . . . interests.'

'Norn Irn is a small place,' said Matt, using the vernacular pronunciation of Northern Ireland, in which four syllables were compressed into just two, and everyone laughed.

'It's true though, isn't it?' said Mum with a strained smile. 'No matter where you go in the province, or who you meet, you always find someone in common.' Matt left the room to take a call on his mobile and Mum, clearing her throat, went on, 'And what about your parents, Oren? Are they both well?'

Oren told her that his father and mother still worked the family farm, aided by his elder, unmarried brother, who would, one day, take over the place. The way he played it down was typical of his modest character. From what he'd told Lucy, the family holding was extensive, much of it leased out to tenant farmers.

'It's nice that they're still together. So many people get divorced these days,' observed Lucy, unable to resist making a dig at her mother. When her parents had first separated they'd told her and Matt that it was no one's fault. But this wasn't true. She'd subsequently learned from her father that he'd never wanted the divorce.

'My parents are still together because they believe in the sanctity of marriage,' said Oren firmly.

Mum stiffened. 'Well, I think we all do, don't we? In principle anyway.'

'Some more than others,' said Oren wisely and he leaned forward and added gently, in that lovely caring way of his, 'Lucy tells me you got divorced twelve years ago. I'm sorry for you. I take it you tried for a reconciliation with your husband?'

Lucy held her breath and waited to hear her mother's response. Dad had offered to go for marriage counselling but Mum, apparently, wouldn't have any of it.

Mum's face went the colour of the pink flowers on her

139

skirt. She looked at Lucy, then Oren, with an expression of astonishment on her face. 'With the greatest respect,' she said, sounding more than a bit peeved, 'I really don't think that's any of your business.'

'It affected Lucy a great deal,' went on Oren, and Lucy blushed. How had he divined this? His insight was incredible. She had only mentioned the divorce in passing, even though it had been the defining moment of her life. 'Children,' he went on, 'are always the ones to suffer in these sad situations. That's one of the reasons why the Bible prohibits divorce.'

'I'm sorry, Oren, but I find this conversation intrusive,' said Mum snippily, tugging at the hem of her skirt. 'These are private matters concerning Lucy and her family, not outsiders.'

Oren's face clouded and Lucy was furious. Oren was only trying to help. Why was she so reluctant to talk about the divorce? Was it because she was ashamed? Lucy got up and went and sat on the arm of Oren's chair. 'As far as I'm concerned, my family matters *are* Oren's business.' Oren squeezed her hand.

'Well,' said Mum, sounding flustered. 'Yours might be, but mine aren't.'

A long awkward silence followed which Oren eventually broke by letting go of Lucy's hand and standing up. He hitched his trousers up by the waistband. 'I'll just use the bathroom if you don't mind.'

Mum pointed the way. 'First on your left.'

As soon as he'd left the room Lucy hissed, 'Why did you over-react like that? You know, Oren's got a real talent for pastoral care. Most people find him really easy to relate to. If you just –'

'I don't need him ministering to me,' said Mum, with a scowl. 'And if I did find myself in need of spiritual guidance, he certainly wouldn't be my first port of call.'

Lucy narrowed her eyes. 'I know what you're trying to do. You're trying to find fault with Oren just so that you can ruin my relationship with him. Well, it won't work. Me and Oren are like this.' She held up her right hand, her index and middle fingers entwined.

Jennifer's shoulders sagged. 'Don't be ridiculous, Lucy. I'm not trying to ruin anything.' She pressed the heel of her hand on her forehead momentarily and let out a dramatic sigh. 'I just don't want you to make a mistake. I can see you're very . . . fond of Oren.' She paused then, as if reluctant to spit out what she was really thinking.

'But?' demanded Lucy. There was always a 'but' with Mum.

Mum glanced at the empty doorway. Lucy heard the sound of a toilet being flushed. 'Well, all right then,' said Mum, 'I'm just not sure he's right for you.'

Lucy snorted. 'In what way?'

'You don't seem to be yourself in his company. You hardly said a word over lunch.'

Lucy folded her arms, resentment bubbling up. 'Well, that's rich coming from you, isn't it?' she said bitterly. 'Given your track record, you're hardly qualified to dish out relationship advice.'

'Oh, for heaven's sake,' said Mum, striking the seat of the sofa with a dull thud. 'Will you stop banging on about something that happened to me and your father twelve years ago?'

'Well, that's where you're wrong, you see,' said Lucy flatly. 'The divorce didn't just happen to you and Dad. It happened to me and Matt too.'

Mum flashed dark brown eyes at Lucy and sealed her lips in a thin, tight line. Lucy heard the toilet door opening and, seconds later, Oren came back into the room.

'I think it's time we headed over to Dad's,' said Lucy.

'What about your bags?' said Mum, getting to her feet. 'Do you want to bring them in now – or later?'

'I think,' said Lucy with a meaningful look at Oren, 'that we'll be staying at Dad's.' He raised his right eyebrow a fraction but said nothing. And to save him any further embarrassment, she added, 'He's got loads more room.'

Mum cleared her throat and forced a hollow laugh. 'Yes, it'll be better than sharing a room with Matt, that's for sure. I can't vouch for what you'd find on the floor in there.'

'Hey, what are you trying to say?' interjected Matt, lounging in the doorway with his right shoulder propped against the door jamb. He pulled a hurt-looking face and everyone laughed, breaking the tension.

Mum gave him an indulgent smile and delivered what could only be described as an understatement for Matt's room. 'Well, let's just say that you and the cleaning caddy aren't best acquainted.'

In the car on the way across town, Lucy said, 'I'm sorry she was rude to you back there, Oren.'

He paused before speaking, a habit that infused everything he said with gravitas and made Lucy hang on every word. 'You have to make allowances for the fact that she's been on her own for the last twelve years. And that's a hard road for a single woman to walk, with no man at her side helping and guiding her. And she's not a Christian. Well, you and I both know that without Him we have no strength.' He paused again and glanced over at Lucy. 'She's a troubled woman, but you can help her, Lucy.'

'I can?' said Lucy in surprise. The notion that her mother might need her help had never crossed her mind. It had always been the other way round.

'You can pray for her.'

'Oh, yes, of course.' In her dim-witted slowness she had not thought of the obvious.

They drove the rest of the way in silence and, thankfully, things looked up when they got to Dad's.

'What a lovely house,' said Oren, as the car crunched up the gravel drive and came to rest in front of the Edwardian façade of Dad and Maggie's red-brick home. The mansion had once belonged to a prosperous sea captain and had fine views, facing east, over the Irish Sea. And when he smiled at Lucy she breathed easy again, knowing that the incident at her mother's had been forgotten.

Dad took to Oren straight away, perhaps because of the similarities between them. Both had played rugby at university and Dad was no stranger to the scriptures. While Lucy helped Maggie in the kitchen, and the girls ran about excitedly, Oren and Dad sat together in the high-ceilinged lounge discussing the dangers inherent in modern biblical translations.

Later, while Oren stood chatting to Maggie in the kitchen as she loaded the dishwasher, Dad took Lucy to one side in the handsome dining room and held both her hands in his.

'He's a great fella, Lucy,' he said with a happy, satisfied air, staring straight at her. 'Intelligent. Well read. I can't believe . . . well, let's just say I'm delighted that you've found each other,' he went on and the hairs on the back of Lucy's neck stood up in exhilaration. And when he added, with a twinkle in his eye, 'I like him very much. Very much indeed,' she realised this was the seal of approval she had waited for all her life.

Chapter 11

'Where shall we start?' asked Jennifer, as she stood with Ben close beside her, just inside the door of Hilary's vast furniture store. She tried to keep her mind on the task in hand but it was difficult. Ben's arm brushed the sleeve of her wool coat and the smell of his pine-scented aftershave filled the air. Just being in his presence sent her heart racing and she could not look him in the eye, for fear of betraying her feelings. She took a deep breath and looked around.

Before them stretched a sea of sofas, dozens of dining table sets and rows of bookcases, cupboards, sideboards and desks. And in the far corner, the finishing touches that make a house a home – curtains, rugs, lamps and cushions. People flocked here from all over East Antrim and yet, on this dull November morning, the place was almost deserted. The only other customers were a white-haired elderly couple who sat on matching sofas facing each other, as if by their fireside at home, having a good chat.

Ben, in a navy reefer jacket, turned to face her and gave her one of his devastating, dimpled smiles. His presence overpowered her like a drug, distorting the world around her, making her feel like she was in a dream. 'I haven't a clue,' he laughed. 'That's why I asked you along. Tell you what, why don't you pick things out for me and I'll tell you whether I like them or not?'

She swallowed and smiled. 'And you trust me to do that?' she said, in a voice that implied, teasingly, that he might regret it.

'That, and more,' he said enigmatically and, though she blushed, she boldly held his gaze. 'I feel as if I really know you, Jennifer,' he said, touching his heart with the tips of his fingers.

Jennifer's stomach flipped. 'I know what you mean, Ben. I feel as if I've known you all my life.' Suddenly shy, she broke eye contact, afraid she had revealed too much of her feelings for him. Feelings that she feared would not be reciprocated. What if he only wanted to be friends? 'Well, let's get to work, shall we?' she said briskly.

He was an easy customer to please and fifty minutes later, they'd chosen all the living room furniture, curtains and accessories plus a blind and bar stools for the kitchen. Ben threw himself onto an L-shaped grey sofa, his lanky legs stretched out before him, and said, 'Enough! I can't take any more.'

Jennifer giggled. Choosing furniture with David, who had rarely let her have her way in anything, had never been this much fun. Ben, in contrast, seemed more than happy to let her choose everything.

Ben rolled his eyes. 'How do you do this, day in and day out?'

'It's fun! That's why. Come on, lazybones.' She grinned, picked up a nearby brochure and whacked him on the leg but he did not move. He only smiled, rested his head on the back of the sofa and closed his eyes.

She watched his eyes flicker under pale blue, thin eyelids, and his chest rise and fall gently beneath the thick coat. She longed to lean over and kiss him, to touch the hard line of his jaw and the dark stubble that already, so early in the morning, shadowed his cheeks. She wondered what his mouth would taste like.

He yawned, his eyes still closed.

'Busy weekend?' she said.

'Work. Not much else. You?'

Jennifer recalled the events of Saturday and sighed. 'Lucy and her new boyfriend were supposed to come for the weekend and stay over, but in the end they only came for lunch.' She paused, the disappointment catching her by surprise, and ran a hand through her hair. 'His name's Oren Wilson. He says you two went to school together.'

Ben sat up, opened his eyes and his face clouded. 'Oren Wilson from Enniskillen? Farmer's son?'

'That's the one,' said Jennifer, leaning forward, keen to hear Ben's opinion of the man.

'His family own half of County Fermanagh.'

'I was wondering how he could afford to fund a second degree,' mused Jennifer. 'So, were you friends at school?'

Ben shook his head and was quiet for a few moments, staring off into the distance, his hands clasped loosely between his legs. When he spoke he was uncharacteristically stony-faced, though no less handsome. 'Oren Wilson was a troublemaker at school and a bully. I didn't have much to do with him. He wasn't well liked.'

'Oh,' said Jennifer faintly. This was not what she had hoped to hear.

'But,' he added, hastily, seeing the dismay on Jennifer's face, 'maybe he's changed.'

'I didn't like him,' said Jennifer sadly, 'though I really wanted to, for Lucy's sake.' She paused, looked into Ben's eyes, and knew that what she said next would go no further. 'I thought he was arrogant and over-confident. And I felt

146

uncomfortable with his evangelicalism. It seems to me that he's determined not only to save Lucy, not that she's putting up any resistance, but the rest of the world as well. That sounds awful, doesn't it?' She put her face in her hands momentarily, then looked up again. 'I'm not against Christianity – I just don't like it being rammed down my throat along with a hefty dose of self-satisfied morality by someone like Oren Wilson.' She let out a sigh, glad to have gotten that off her chest.

Ben frowned. 'Oren Wilson wasn't a Christian when I knew him. In fact, quite the opposite. He got expelled for smuggling vodka into school in fifth year, mixing it with blackcurrant cordial and forcing a first year to drink it. The wee fella had to be taken to hospital with alcohol poisoning. It damn near killed him. Oren thought it was funny.'

'What an awful thing to do,' said Jennifer, appalled.

'Yeah, well,' said Ben looking at his hands. 'Oren never forgave me for that.'

'For what?'

'I called the ambulance when I found the wee lad lying in the toilets and reported Oren to the housemaster. He was expelled and went back to Enniskillen to do his A-levels. I brushed shoulders with him once or twice at Queen's when he was doing Law. I haven't seen him since we graduated.'

'Well, he's studying for a Theology degree now. He must've had a religious conversion.'

Ben gave his head a little twist to the left and said sceptically, 'He must be a changed man indeed.'

'I hope so,' said Jennifer, and she bit her bottom lip. 'Oh, Ben, I'm really worried for Lucy. She's completely besotted with him.' She looked away and struggled for a few moments, torn between loyalty to her daughter and the truth. In the end she settled for the latter and, addressing the toe of her boot, said, 'I don't know how to put this without sounding like a heartless mother but Lucy's never had a boyfriend before. I think she's just grateful to Oren for paying her attention. And I can see what attracts him – Lucy's vulnerable and open to influence. Just the sort of girl who'll put him on a pedestal. She'd do anything for him.'

Ben looked at his hands, and sounding more hopeful than convinced, said, 'Well, it's over ten years since I had anything to do with him and he might well have changed. Who knows? Maybe he does genuinely care for Lucy, Jennifer. We might both be completely wrong about him.'

'I hope so,' said Jennifer, without much assurance. Her gut instinct had served her well over the years. And just as she got bad vibes from Oren, she got very good ones from Ben. But it wasn't fair to burden him with her family worries. 'I'm sorry. I don't know why I'm telling you all this, especially here. But it's good to talk to you about it. The only other person I feel I can talk to is Donna. We're going away for a weekend together soon. I'll see what she makes of it all.' She glanced around the empty space, stood up and added brightly, 'We're not going to get your flat furnished sitting around chatting, are we? Come on, what's next?'

'The bedroom.' He gave her a sultry glance, his dark eyebrows rising infinitesimally. Jennifer blushed like a school-girl.

'Ahem . . . that'll be upstairs then,' she mumbled, and at a brisk pace, led the way up a set of industrial metal stairs in the corner of the building, wishing that she could retain a bit of composure in his presence.

At the top of the stairs, the first thing she came to was the bed department. Jennifer tested the springs of a nearby double divan bed with the palm of her hand and said, 'You'll need a bed of course.'

'We have to test it properly,' grinned Ben.

Jennifer looked at the bed, then back at Ben, imagining what it would feel like lying on the clear plastic dust cover beside him.

'Come on,' he cried out, and suddenly grabbed her hand and pulled her down onto the bed with him. They landed on the soft mattress in a tangle, Jennifer's heart pounding, her jean-clad leg wrapped around his. His legs were strong and hard against her soft flesh; her arm, trapped between their chests, pressed against warm, firm muscle. Quickly, she extricated herself and rolled, laughing, onto her back. They lay side by side staring at the ceiling, a tangle of dusty pipes and exposed silvery air ducts. She blinked and giggled nervously.

Ben rolled onto his side, rested his head on his elbow and looked down at her. 'What do you think?'

'It's a bit soft,' she said, hoping that her foundation, slapped on in a hurry that morning, was living up to its promise of 'ageless perfection'. She hoped too that the harsh showroom lighting didn't show up the lines around her eyes and the deep rift between her brows.

'Oh, no it's not,' he said suggestively and, as soon as she clocked his double meaning, she blushed furiously.

Ben, grinning playfully, rocked his body so that she inched closer to him, and she laughed as much out of nerves as at the sensation. And then she found herself right up against him, his face hovering inches above her own. He smelt of oranges and fresh laundry and, underneath those wholesome smells, she detected the faint tantalising whiff of musky male pheromones. She breathed in and held her breath. She watched his black pupils dilate; his breathing became shallow. She could see the intent in his eyes and smell the want on his hot, sweet breath. She realised that he was going to kiss her and her body arched involuntarily in response. She closed her eyes.

And then, suddenly, she came to her senses. She opened her eyes and let out a little gasp. Wriggling out from underneath Ben, she sat upright on the edge of the bed with her back to him. What was she doing?

This moment was what she'd dreamed of. And now that it was here she realised that it was all wrong.

He came and sat beside her on the edge of the mattress. 'Jennifer, look at me.'

She obeyed, sheepishly, and he took both her hands gently in his. He stared deep into her eyes and her heart pounded like a drum. 'Can you tell me what's going on, please? Because I got the very distinct impression that you liked me. I wasn't imagining it, was I?'

'No,' she squeaked.

'So why are you now giving me the cold shoulder?'

She shrugged helplessly and looked away. 'I'm sorry. You don't deserve to be mucked around like this. I do like you, Ben. I like you very much. It's just that . . .' Her voice trailed off and she pulled her hands away.

He folded his arms. 'What?'

She took a big gulp of air and blurted out, 'Well, there's an awfully big age gap between us. Do you realise that I'm forty-four?'

He shrugged. 'I'd worked it out.'

'And I've two grown-up children, one of whom is only eight years younger than you.'

Another shrug. 'So?'

'And I . . .' She glanced around the sea of beds, searching for inspiration. A brochure lay on a nearby bedside table. On the front a middle-aged woman sat reading in bed, glasses perched on the end of her nose. 'I wear glasses because of age-related deterioration in my eyes.'

'I think you look very attractive in glasses,' he smiled. 'Miss Moneypenny meets school secretary.'

150

'You're not taking me seriously,' she said as his eyes wandered down her legs.

He lowered his voice and met her gaze again. 'I am. I'm taking you very seriously.'

'So, let me get this straight. You're telling me that my age doesn't put you off?' she said incredulously.

He shook his head. 'Nope.'

'Well, it puts me off,' she said. 'I don't want people to think I'm your mother.'

'Oh, don't be ridiculous, Jennifer,' he said sharply and there was a flash of anger in his eyes. 'Lots of men date older women. And what does age matter anyway, if two people like each other? What does it matter what other people think?' He paused, his Adam's apple moving up and down and his voice was low and husky. 'I've never met anyone like you, Jennifer. I've never wanted anyone as much as I want you.' He placed a hand on her thigh and gave it a hard squeeze, sending a wave of desire up her leg. 'You are absolutely gorgeous.'

Jennifer blinked, her head reeling with disbelief and delight. Momentarily stunned by this declaration, she struggled to keep a hold on reality. She must make Ben understand why a relationship between them would not work, even though she desired it with all her heart.

'My kids won't approve, Ben. Nor my father. You happened to crop up in conversation and they were only too happy to tell me how disgusting the idea was of me dating a younger man.'

'They've no right to tell you what to do, Jennifer,' he said crossly. 'And truthfully, is it any of their business? You're a free woman, you can do what you please.'

'Why does it not feel like it then?' she said sadly.

'Because you're used to pleasing other people all the time. That's what mothers do, isn't it? But your kids are adults now. It's time for them to get on with their lives and you to get on with yours. Are you going to let them dictate who you go out with and who you don't?'

She shook her head. Put like that, it did sound a bit pathetic.

'And isn't Matt moving into his own flat soon?'

'So he says.' Jennifer had surprised herself with her calm acceptance of this news, delivered only the other night by Matt. She contented herself with the knowledge that he was very lucky to have found a good job locally – and his new home was only down the road. It was time to let go of the apron strings – for his sake, and for hers.

'Well, there you go. Lucy's making her own way in life too by the sounds of it and I bet your father would come round to the idea eventually.'

'But your family won't approve either,' she said, recalling Alan's frosty reception.

'Hang them all!' he cried. 'You've not presented one valid reason why we shouldn't go out, fall in love and get married even, if that's what we both want.' He grabbed her hands again and squeezed them and staring into her eyes with a sort of tender fury, he said, 'Answer me one thing and one thing only.'

'Okay,' she said solemnly, her eyes locked with his.

'Do you think that you could love me?'

'I'm certain of it,' she said without hesitation, without blinking, happiness folding round her heart like a soft blanket, muffling the objections clamouring for attention in her brain.

'I'm certain too, my darling,' he said.

The corners of her mouth turned up in a delighted smile. No one had ever called her 'my darling'. It sounded so tender, and romantic, to her ears.

He leaned towards her and their lips met in a sensuous

152

kiss. And something in Jennifer stirred, a part of her that David had never touched – nor the men that had followed him. And she wondered at her stupidity in very nearly letting him slip through her fingers.

Chapter 12

Donna, at the wheel of her luxurious Saab, turned the Madeleine Peyroux CD down and the heating up. Outside, dusk was falling and the wipers glided soundlessly across the windscreen, erasing the fine, cold rain that had fallen all day. 'I started my Christmas shopping this morning,' she said cheerfully, and went on to list what she had bought and for whom.

Jennifer, in the passenger seat, surrounded by the smell of new plastic and leather soft as a baby's bottom, felt a fleeting sense of panic. Christmas was only weeks away and she'd done nothing. But she thought, relaxing again, she had much more important things on her mind than Christmas shopping. She closed her eyes. The heat in the car, and the swish-swish sound of the wipers made her drowsy. She found it hard to concentrate on what Donna was saying – her mind drifted.

'Are you listening to a word I'm saying?' demanded Donna, and only then did Jennifer notice that they were already heading south on the A8 towards Belfast. They were on their way to the upmarket Ballykillen cookery school, in the grounds of a castle on the shores of Loch Erne in

Fermanagh, a county famous for its beautiful lakes. The trip was Donna's birthday present to her.

'Sorry. I was thinking about the restaurant,' she said, a half-truth. Because while one part of her brain *was* thinking about the logistics of the Carnegie project, the other was full of Ben Crawford and her heart-to-heart with him in Hilary's. She would forever think of that prefab warehouse as the most romantic place on earth.

'Now,' chided Donna, 'the whole point of a weekend away is to forget about work.'

'I'll try.' Jennifer smiled secretly to herself, knowing that she would not succeed. Work, for the time being anyway, was intrinsically linked to Ben Crawford and she couldn't but think about *him* every minute of the day.

Donna, misunderstanding the cause of Jennifer's preoccupation, let out a resigned sigh and said, 'Well, go on. You might as well tell me how the job's going.'

Jennifer filled her in on the Carnegie project and voiced a reservation. 'I've introduced a few jazzy elements just to bring it into the twenty-first century – cowhide rugs, some funky chandeliers and lampstands, quirky prints. I know it sounds odd, mixing traditional and modern, but I really think it'll work. I just hope Ben – and his Dad – like it.'

'Course they will,' said Donna confidently.

'I hope so,' said Jennifer and, steering the conversation away from Ben, added, 'Did I tell you Matt's got a room in a house lined up? He moves in next week.'

Donna glanced over in astonishment. 'You're taking that news remarkably calmly. I thought you were dreading it.'

'I was,' responded Jennifer, thoughtfully. 'I guess I've had time to get used to the idea.'

Donna chewed her bottom lip thoughtfully for a few

seconds and then said, 'Well, it'll do him good to fend for himself.'

'Yeah, it will.' Jennifer coloured and looked out the window, though it was now pitch black outside and there was nothing to see. It was time for changes in her life too.

'So, tell me about Lucy's new man,' said Donna, overtaking a van. 'You said on the phone the other night that the visit hadn't gone well.'

'Hmm,' said Jennifer thoughtfully, running over the events of that wretched weekend in her mind. She pulled the neck of her coat tight, suddenly chilled by the memory. 'It was a disaster. And now Lucy's saying she doesn't want to come home for the Christmas holidays.'

'Really?'

'She's talking about spending Christmas with Oren's family where we're headed right now. They have a farm somewhere down Fermanagh way.'

Donna's head snapped round. 'That's not at all like Lucy. What's got into her?'

Jennifer sighed. 'We had words.'

'You and Lucy?'

'And Oren.'

Donna let out air noisily through her mouth 'Okay, tell me all about it.'

Jennifer told Donna everything that had transpired. 'He took the hump when I told him that my private life was none of his business and they left shortly after that. There's a sort of conceited arrogance about him that I can't stand. He comes off with biblical quotes in the middle of a perfectly normal conversation and assumes everyone else thinks the Bible is the ultimate authority he clearly thinks it is. You should see Lucy. She thinks the sun shines out of his arse.'

Donna tittered and the Saab swerved a little towards the

ditch. Quickly, she regained control of the car. 'Oh, Jennifer, you are awful!' She wiped a tear from the corner of her left eye and said, 'He's an evangelical, that's all.'

'He's a Bible thumper.'

'It's his mission in life to spread the word of God and save souls. It doesn't make him a bad person.'

'And there's something else,' said Jennifer, and she paused, unable to articulate her feeling of uneasiness about Oren.

'What?' said Donna.

'Oh, nothing,' said Jennifer, rubbing her calf. 'I was just going to be horrible about Oren again. But I think I've said enough already.'

'Well, all I can say is that lots of people I know would be over the moon if their daughter brought home a guy like Oren.'

'They're welcome to him,' said Jennifer with a dark glance at Donna who suppressed a smile. In no mood to see the funny side, Jennifer added sharply, 'You haven't met him. Look, I know he sounds like a dream come true. But I'm concerned about Lucy. He seems to . . . to overshadow her. She's subdued in his company, sort of subservient. He's so zealous, I wonder if he's more interested in saving her than – well, you know what.'

'He sounds entirely honourable,' said Donna but, when her mischievous grin failed to rouse a response from Jennifer, she added more soberly, 'Well you and I both know that when you're in love with someone, you're blind to their faults.'

'That's what Ben said,' said Jennifer, thinking fleetingly of her ill-fated marriage. She'd certainly gone into that with blinkers on.

'Ben Crawford?' said Donna in surprise. 'You discussed Lucy with Ben?'

'Turns out Oren and Ben went to school together,' said

Jennifer, dodging the question and taking a sudden interest in a hangnail. 'I was keen to hear what Ben thought of him.'

'And?'

Jennifer related all that Ben had told her and Donna's eyebrows furrowed. 'That's quite damning. Do you trust Ben?'

'I'd believe him before Oren any day,' said Jennifer at which Donna raised her eyebrows. 'But when I tried to raise my concerns with Lucy she accused me of trying to break her and Oren up.'

'Well, she will take any criticism of him badly, Jennifer. It's only natural. Tell me, how'd he get on with David and Maggie?'

'I don't know what Maggie thought, but David came on the phone waxing lyrical about him. Thought he was God's gift. Intelligent, talented, Godly.' Jennifer snorted, and shook her head. 'Apparently they all went to church together on Sunday morning.' She picked at a loose thread on her coat sleeve and added, unable to stop herself coming across like a petulant teenager, 'And they stayed over at David's when they were supposed to be staying at mine.'

'Ah.' Donna paused. 'I see.'

Jennifer looked over at Donna and let out a long sigh. She wound the strap of her handbag, lying in her lap, round her fingers. 'You know things between me and Lucy have never been great.'

Donna nodded in acknowledgment and waited for her to go on.

'Well, I'm worried that this Oren is going to drive a wedge between us.'

'He can only do that if you let him.'

Jennifer considered this for a moment and then said, sullenly, 'I'm not sure how I can stop him.'

158

'First of all you need to face the facts.' Donna tapped the middle of the steering wheel with an index finger. 'Fact one: the more you go against this chap, the more she'll cling to him.' She moved on to the middle finger of her left hand. 'Fact two: she's chosen him and if you want to continue being part of her life, you're going to have to find a way to get on with Oren, no matter what you think of him.' She paused. 'You also have to assume the worst. She could marry him. Have his kids.'

'Heaven forbid,' said Jennifer, raising her eyes to heaven. She sat for a few moments, grim-faced, staring at Donna's profile. 'I don't know how to build bridges with him. I dislike him so much.'

'Well, a good start would be to avoid discussions about religion altogether.'

'Easier said than done with Oren. I'm not sure he has any other topic of conversation,' said Jennifer drily.

'And stop listening to hearsay,' said Donna, referring to Ben's story. 'Innocent until proven guilty. Right?'

'Yes, you're right,' said Jennifer with a sigh, letting the strap go and running a hand through her hair.

Just then the mobile phone inside her handbag vibrated and she pulled it out, thinking it'd be a text from Matt. But it was from Ben. 'Come to mine on Monday night for supper?' it said. Jennifer's heartbeat quickened. This was it. Their first proper date. Or was it? She recalled his hand on her thigh, the pressure of his lips against hers. Did he want a relationship – or did he just want sex? Perhaps the kiss, which had meant so much to her, was just meaningless flirting to him. She frowned – and shoved the phone back in her bag.

'Who was that?' said Donna, flicking on the indicator.

'Oh, it was nothing,' said Jennifer dismissively, as the car slowed and turned right into a leafy drive. She craned her neck to peer into the canopy of dripping leaves ahead. 'Are we here already?'

They retrieved the keys from reception at the castle and found the rented cottage where they were staying, a conversion in an old stone courtyard. Inside, the accommodation was compact and cosy – two comfortable sofas framed an open fire in the lounge and, upstairs, there was a small, but perfectly adequate twin bedroom, and a bathroom.

In the pale wood kitchen, Jennifer rustled up a simple meal of pasta and salad while Donna found logs and kindling and got the fire going. After they'd eaten, Jennifer curled up on one sofa, and Donna sat on the other, two glasses of white wine between them on the coffee table, the fire roaring in the grate. Jennifer realised she needed this break more than she thought she would.

Donna picked up the glass of wine and took a drink. 'So, are you going to tell me what's going on between you and Ben Crawford?'

Jennifer looked up and gave Donna a weak smile. 'What?' she said quietly, embarrassed by her fledgling relationship with Ben. She ought to be proud of him; she ought to be telling the world about him. But she couldn't, not when she felt the world would laugh right in her face.

Donna set down her glass and said matter-of-factly, 'Every time his name's mentioned you go all gooey-eyed. And your face goes bright red. It's a dead giveaway.' She frowned and considered Jennifer for some moments. 'Are you seeing him?'

Jennifer blushed. 'Well, I . . . eh, I think so. He just texted to ask me to supper at his place on Monday night.'

Donna clapped her hands together with such a loud, unexpected noise it made Jennifer jump. 'You crafty cow!' she chuckled. 'You've been dating Ben Crawford, the hottest thing on two legs in Ballyfergus, and you never told me?'

'It only just started,' said Jennifer apologetically. 'And I was going to tell you. Honest.'

Donna shook her head in disbelief and added, in mock seriousness, 'I guess that means you won't be signing up with an online dating agency, then?'

Jennifer grinned, grateful that her friend had reacted so well, both to the news and to the fact that she had not been entirely straight with her. Donna picked up her glass, settled into her seat and said, 'Well, you'd better tell me all about it. Right from the start. And don't miss out a single thing.'

'Okay,' said Jennifer, a little shyly, holding a cushion across her stomach. She recounted everything that had transpired between her and Ben, culminating in the kiss on the bed in Hilary's.

'Oh my God,' said Donna, clutching at her chest with one hand. 'That's so romantic. Tell you what, girl, he must be really keen on you.'

'What makes you say that?'

'You practically told him to get lost, didn't you?' She thought for a moment and added, 'Either that or he likes a challenge. He could be one of these guys that likes to bed cougars. Move over Demi Moore and Madonna!'

Jennifer picked up the cushion and threw it at Donna. It hit the edge of the sofa before landing on the floor. 'I'm not a cougar. And he hasn't bedded me,' she said, suppressing a smile born of relief. Donna hadn't condemned her and Ben. Underneath that teasing was approbation.

'Yet,' said Donna and Jennifer threw another, equally poorly-aimed cushion across the room. 'What do Matt and Lucy think of you dating Ben?'

'I haven't told them,' said Jennifer, staring into the fire, conscious that her cheeks were colouring yet again. 'And I don't want to until, well, until I've a clearer idea of

161

where this is going. It might peter out after a few dates. And with Ben being Matt's employer and all, it's a bit awkward.' She looked at Donna and wrinkled up her nose to indicate the delicacy involved. Donna nodded and Jennifer asked, 'Seriously, though, you don't think he's too young for me?'

Donna shrugged her big shoulders and opened her eyes wide. 'Absolutely not. And don't you listen to anyone who says he is.' She sighed contentedly as if she was the one with the new boyfriend and not Jennifer.

'So you think he's hot, then?' ventured Jennifer, angling for some more affirmation.

Donna set her glass down. 'Hot? He's the best looking guy in Ballyfergus, my Ken excepted of course. But looks don't matter, really, do they? What matters is that you've met someone you like and he likes you. I'm so pleased for you, Jennifer.' She paused and when she spoke again there were tears in her eyes. 'You deserve happiness, pet. And I truly hope you find it with Ben.'

When Ben opened the door to Jennifer she was stunning in a festive red skirt, black ribbed polo and high-heeled black boots. She presented a bottle of white wine along with a nervous smile and he was overcome with a desire to hold her. Wordlessly, he took the bottle out of her hand and put his hand on her hip. She seemed uncertain what to do, hesitating there in the doorway, the chilled-out sound of soulful Jack Johnson playing in the background.

'Jennifer,' he said and gently he slipped his arm around her little waist and pulled her to him. Her back arched, she raised her face to him and their lips met in a melting kiss. When they finally parted, she smiled up at him through half-closed eyelids and said, touching her lips with exploratory fingers, 'Well, that was quite a welcome. You know, I

162

wasn't sure, after the last time, if –' She broke off and her cheeks coloured.

'What?'

'If you were serious about what you said about me. About us.'

He laughed and kissed her on the forehead – and pushed the memory of what his father had said about Jennifer being too old for him out of his mind. 'Never more serious in all my life.' And she laughed too, and a beautiful smile lit up her face. Then, the tension between them broken, he took her by the hand and led her indoors. He gave her a tour of the one-bedroomed flat, which took all of five minutes, and she presented him with a housewarming gift – a set of brown leather coasters.

'The place looks good,' she said, when they were back in the lounge. 'Everything works really well together. It'll look even cosier when you put up Christmas decorations.'

'I don't usually bother.'

'Well, you should! I'm going to put mine up next week.' She went over to the bookcase and ran her hand along the creased spines of the books. 'A Suitable Boy,' she said, reading the title of a thick, white doorstop of a paperback. 'Have you read it?'

'Not yet. I'm saving that one for a long holiday. You?'

She shook her head, 'I've never gotten round to it. But I intend to. Did you read The White Tiger?'

It was his turn to shake his head. 'Aravind Adiga, isn't it?' he said, offering up the name of the author like the answer to a quiz.

'That's right,' she grinned delightedly. 'Oh, you must. I learnt so much about Indian culture, especially the class system. I'll lend you a copy if you like.'

'I'd like that.' He held up the bottle of wine. 'Red okay?'

'Mmm.'

He pulled the cork out of the bottle. 'Thanks for helping me with the furniture. If you hadn't been with me I don't know what I would've ended up buying.'

She gave an embarrassed little smile. He said, 'No really, you've a great eye.'

'I hope you think the same once you've seen the finished Carnegie's,' she said, walking behind the sofa and stroking the burgundy chenille throw that lay across its back. He handed her a glass of red. 'Thanks,' she said, took a sip, and he watched her slowly circle the room, picking things up and putting them down. 'Well, I like everything you've done so far at Carnegie's,' he said. 'The curtains are fabulous. And I love those quirky mirrors. I never would've thought of that.'

'Creates the illusion of more space without losing the feeling of intimacy. I'll bring over the rest of the lamps and ornaments this week.'

'What's the latest on the tables and chairs?'

She sat down on the sofa. 'The suppliers are promising to deliver them on time.'

'Let's hope they don't let us down.'

'They'd better not,' she said, a steely undertone to her voice that he'd not heard before. She was soft and maternal in some ways and yet she was tough – she had, after all, embarked on a risky start-up business while raising two kids alone.

'I admire you, you know. For setting up your own business and making a success of it. You're living your dream, aren't you?'

'I guess I am,' she smiled and then added thoughtfully, 'It wasn't always easy, though, especially when the kids were young, trying to juggle everything. But it's a lot easier now I've only myself to think of.' She paused. 'And you? Are you living your dream?'

He gave her a grim smile and said, 'Let's just say that I never planned to go into the family business,' and then, changing the subject, 'I made us a bit of supper. Nothing fancy, just ham and cheese. Shall we sit in the kitchen?'

They went through and Jennifer climbed onto a stool at the breakfast bar as he laid out the little feast. 'Eat, you must be hungry.' He pointed to a semi-soft cheese with a pinky rind. 'That's Gubbeen from County Cork and that one's Burren Gold.'

'And that's Blue Rathgore,' she chimed in, indicating the blue-veined goat's cheese. 'You've been shopping locally, I see,' she said. Blue Rathgore was made in County Antrim.

He grinned. 'I'm going to serve it in the restaurant. As well as Ballybrie, Ballyoak and Cooneen from Fivemiletown Creamery in County Tyrone. I went down to sample the cheeses last week with Jason. Absolutely fantastic. But we've only the two artisan cheesemakers in Northern Ireland. I'd like to see more.'

Jennifer sipped her wine and said thoughtfully, 'For a man who never planned to go into the restaurant trade, you sound pretty enthusiastic.'

'I'm enthusiastic about food. But I'm enthusiastic about lots of things, like books and running. Doesn't mean I want to make a career out of them. And the family business isn't really about restaurants anyway. It's mainly about property and hotels and I have no interest in that whatsoever. We only have the two restaurants and, in terms of the bottom line, they contribute peanuts.'

Jennifer buttered a slice of baguette with precision. 'So why bother with them?'

He sighed. 'My Dad encouraged me because he thought it might interest me. I wasn't doing so well in the traditional business. My father's a clever man. Every time he senses I'm losing interest he gives me a new challenge. And, on the whole, it's worked. It's just that, no matter how enthusiastically I throw myself into a new job, I never feel completely fulfilled. And that's because my heart's elsewhere.'

'So,' she said carefully, 'if you never wanted to go into the family business, what did you want to do?'

'I wanted to be a teacher,' he said, loading some Gubbeen onto a cracker. 'An English teacher. I still do.'

She looked confused. 'So go and do a teacher training course.'

He sighed, looked at her for a few long moments and said, 'It's complicated, Jennifer.'

'How so?'

He ran his hand through his hair, his elbow resting on the table and said, 'It's all to do with Ricky.'

Jennifer put down her knife and the bread and was still. 'Your brother?'

He swallowed and his heart pounded against the wall of his chest. He never talked about Ricky. Not to anyone except his mother and father. And even with them, he found it so hard. And yet there was something about Jennifer that made him *want* to tell her. He stared into her big brown eyes, so open and honest, and he knew he could trust her with his darkest secrets.

'I don't often talk about this,' he said and put a closed fist to his mouth, looking round the still unfamiliar room. Every year, as the anniversary of Ricky's death approached, it was the same. His mother went off to the Caribbean and his father buried himself in work. And Ben sank into a period of iron-clad grief.

'The beginning's as good a place to start as any,' she said softly.

He could not keep from her the most significant thing that had ever happened to him, an event that had changed

166

the trajectory of his life. He nodded and took a deep breath, feeling now that he not only wanted to tell her about Ricky, but that he must.

'Ricky was older than me by three years. For as long as I can remember, probably even before I was born, he was destined to follow in our father's footsteps. He adored Dad in a way I never did and he was really interested in the business. They used to sit for hours and talk about overheads and room occupancy rates and all the rest of it. I never envied Ricky that intimacy with Dad. I was grateful for it. With Ricky carrying on the family tradition, I was free to do whatever I wanted. So, I went to uni and planned to do a teaching qualification after that.'

'So what happened?'

'Ricky died.'

Jennifer nodded and bit her bottom lip. 'I'm sorry.' She paused. 'What was he like?'

'What was he like?' repeated Ben. He looked at the ceiling and fought back the tears. 'He was brilliant, funny, loyal. Everybody wanted to be his friend. He had this magnetic charm that attracted people, men and women. Girls loved him.' He smiled and shook his head, remembering the time Ricky had three girlfriends on the go at once – and the mayhem that ensued when they found out about each other.

'But?' said Jennifer.

'There was this other side to him . . . how can I describe it?' He thought of the time a twelve-year-old Ricky started a fire in a pile of dry leaves that destroyed a wood shed, and then pleaded innocence; a slightly older Ricky flashing at the horrified Bosnian maid who'd handed in her notice shortly thereafter; and older still, Ricky stealing drink from the drinks cabinet and topping the bottles up with water. 'He didn't know how to moderate his behaviour and he'd no sense of responsibility. He wouldn't listen to my parents when they tried to get him to stay on and do A-levels. He didn't see the point, not if he was going into the family business. So he left school at sixteen with just five O-levels. He was stubborn, hot tempered and wild. There was nothing he liked more than a party. And Dad didn't help. He spoiled him. Ricky got everything he wanted without earning it and he took it all for granted. As soon as he passed his driving test, Dad gave him a brand-new BMW and he had a penthouse apartment overlooking the Lagan by the time he was twenty.'

Jennifer gasped and said, 'And what about you? What were you doing when all this was going on?'

He shook his head. 'That flashy lifestyle didn't appeal to me. Dad paid for me to go through uni and bought a flat near the university which I lived in until I moved here. That was all I wanted.'

'So what about Ricky?'

'By the time he was twenty-four, he was driving that damned Ferrari.'

'And is that the car he . . . he crashed?'

'It was the car he died in, yes,' said Ben and curled his fist into a tight ball. 'Seven years ago this month. Dad never should've given it to him. These sports cars are difficult to handle even for an experienced driver.'

'I'm sorry,' said Jennifer in that soft voice of hers. 'I can see how much it pains you to talk about this and I appreciate you telling me.' She waited a few moments and added, 'But what does Ricky's death have to do with where you are today?'

'You met my father, Jennifer, you know what he's like.' Her cheeks coloured and she lowered her eyes, her lids a pale shimmering shade of coffee. He took this to mean she had not liked him. It came as no surprise; not many people did.

'My father's a tough man, physically robust. He never had a day's sickness in his life. And he's mentally strong too. In all my years growing up, I never saw him display a shred of self-doubt. As a little child I thought he was invincible.' He paused, and hesitated, the memory of the time following Ricky's death painful to recount.

'You don't have to tell me any more,' said Jennifer and she placed a hand on his forearm.

He stared deep into her calm, chocolate brown eyes, searching there for the peace he could not find in his own heart. 'No, I want to. I want you to . . . to understand, Jennifer. After Ricky died, my father fell to pieces. He stopped going to work. He wouldn't even get out of bed. It was just awful. We were all so worried. His wife Cassie couldn't do anything with him and even my mother came round to try and talk him into coming out of the bedroom. The doctor put him on anti-depressants, but it made no difference.'

'So what happened?'

'It was the end of January and I was sitting on the bed one day talking to him. He'd given up talking himself by this stage and he had a beard – he wouldn't let anyone shave him, let alone do it himself. And he'd lost so much weight. It was as much as Cassie could do to persuade him to shower. And then he came out with it, just like that. He asked me if I would join him in the business. It was the most animated I'd seen him in weeks. There was such wild hope in his eyes. What could I say? I said yes. And he was back to work within a week, completely restored.'

Jennifer bit her lip and looked very solemn.

'I felt that I didn't have a choice,' he said, gently releasing her hand. 'We agreed that I'd finish my degree – I was in my final year – and then go into the business. But I wasn't any good at it. I'm still not.'

'I'm sure that's not true,' she said loyally, withdrawing her hand onto her lap.

'I was weak, wasn't I? I should've stood up to my father.'

She looked surprised. 'Quite the contrary. You put your father before yourself. If you hadn't agreed, what would've happened to him?'

'I honestly don't know.' If he had saved his father, as Jennifer implied, he'd sold his soul in the process.

She played with a ring on the middle finger of her left hand. 'But I also think your father manipulated you.'

He looked away, unable to confess all of it, unable to explain why he felt so beholden to his father. Why the debt could never be repaid, no matter what he did.

'Ricky died almost seven years ago, Ben,' she went on quietly. 'You've done your bit. But isn't it time you moved on? Did what you wanted to do?'

'But you don't understand, Jennifer. I'm Alan's only heir. And he's obsessed with handing on the business to his descendants. That ambition is the driving force behind everything he does, every decision he makes.'

'Ah,' she said, exhaling softly, as understanding took hold. Her pupils contracted and the smile faded slowly from her pretty face. 'That's why he doesn't like me. He thinks I'm too old for you, doesn't he? He knows I could never give you children.'

He grasped her hand and squeezed it, desperate to see her smile restored. 'How can he dislike you when he doesn't even know you?' he said flippantly, avoiding answering her question. He could not bear to see her hurt. But she was right. His father had made his feelings about her very clear – and left Ben doubting his own judgement. Should he be more concerned about the age gap between them? Given that she had a grown-up family, Jennifer would probably not want more children – even if she could have them. But he didn't want them either. He wanted only her.

She turned her face away from him. He touched her chin with the curve of his finger. 'Look at me,' he said and when she raised her eyes to his they were full of tears. 'Oh, darling, why are you crying?'

'I'm so sorry about Ricky,' she said, brushing away tears. 'And about you.'

Wordlessly, he went and stood by her then, still perched on the bar stool. He enveloped her in his arms and she wrapped hers around him and clung to him so tight it hurt. He pressed his lips to the crown of her head, his nostrils filled with the heady, feminine scent of perfume and shampoo. He felt desire rise in his groin, but his feelings for her were more than just lust. He wanted to hold her in his arms every day, to protect her, to know she was his. He was, he realised, starting to fall in love with her.

And yet, though he felt such a strong connection with Jennifer, deeper than any he'd known before, and he wanted to tell her everything, he could not. Something held him back. He could not explain his part in Ricky's death. The words simply would not come. He knew that had he made different choices that night, things would've turned out very differently. Ricky would still be alive.

He wanted to explain this to Jennifer but fear held him back. Fear that she would judge him as harshly as he judged himself. And he could not bear to lose her good opinion. He was trapped, like a car caught the wrong way in a traffic jam, between duty and guilt, unable to turn, unable to

171

escape. Sandwiched between these disempowering emotions, slowly inching forwards along a tedious road he had never wanted to travel.

He clung on to Jennifer all the tighter, and tears pricked his eyes. If only she would love him, he felt certain that he could find the courage to break free of his father and change his life.

Chapter 13

Jennifer stood with a glass of champagne in her hand, smiling inanely as people trooped into Carnegie's from the bitterly cold December night. She'd dressed smartly in a uniform of sorts – a knee-length, long-sleeved black dress from Phase Eight, a wide leather belt, high-heeled patent boots. She'd piled on the make-up and jewellery and all in all she felt well, and appropriately, dressed for a winter restaurant opening. But her appearance wasn't responsible for her nervousness.

Nor was it fear that people might not like the interior design. Ben had loved it and she thought it one of her most successful commissions. It was breathtaking, there was no doubt about it. Sparkling chandeliers cast a flattering glow on the scene below – windows layered in gorgeous fabric, rich berry-coloured candles burning in each window recess; deep carpet the colour of crushed blueberries; chairs upholstered in richly textured, zany fabric and leather; the finest crisp, white Irish linen; and tasteful prints adorning the walls. The room was classic and timeless without being old-fashioned.

No, Jennifer's anxiety stemmed entirely from Ben's

presence in the room and the fear that they might somehow, inadvertently, betray the fact that they were seeing each other. Their heart-to-heart in Ben's flat a fortnight ago had confirmed all her doubts about the long-term sustainability of a relationship between them. One day soon Ben would want children and she could not give him that. Not because she was barren – plenty of women popped babies out in their forties – but because that chapter of her life, as a mother, was over. Initially she'd been upset, but she was trying to be more sanguine about it. Marriage might not be on the cards but, as Donna said, 'Stop agonising over it, Jennifer and just have fun!' But she couldn't help wondering if, given her relationship with Ben was ultimately doomed, she should finish it. She searched for Ben's mop of wavy hair amongst the crowd, but he was nowhere to be seen.

'Hi, Mum,' said Matt's voice and Jennifer turned to find him standing beside her, dressed in immaculate chef's whites with a black chef's cap on his head. He gave her a peck on the cheek and shifted his weight nervously from one foot to the other.

'Don't worry, sweetheart,' she whispered, leaning in to adjust his skewed and spotless black-and-white checked neckerchief. He was so preoccupied he didn't even seem to notice her doing it. 'It's going to be fabulous.'

'It'd better be. Jason had me in here at six o'clock this morning prepping.' He filled his cheeks with air and blew it out, rubbing his hands together.

'I'm proud of you, son,' she said and he beamed.

'Thanks, Mum. Look, I'd better get back to the kitchen. Just wanted to say hello. Oh, and by the way, this doesn't look too bad,' he said with a wink, holding out his hands to indicate the surroundings. 'You did a really good job,' he added and disappeared back to the kitchen.

She grinned, just as pleased with his approval as she had

174

been with Ben's. Matt had moved out the week before and the house was weirdly quiet. She missed him terribly. Lucy hadn't been home since Oren's visit, but she and Jennifer were back on speaking terms. Lucy was spending next week with Oren's folks down in Enniskillen and then coming home for the rest of the holidays. With Donna's words of advice to make a friend of Oren ringing in her ears, Jennifer took a drink of champagne. Easier said than done. But still she must try. She worried how Lucy would react to the news that she was dating Ben Crawford. Fearful, not just of Lucy's reaction but that of her father and Matt, she'd asked Ben to keep their budding relationship a secret for now.

The room began to fill up with well-dressed men and glamorous women Jennifer didn't know – but who clearly knew each other. The air was filled with high-pitched shrieks of recognition between women who acted as if they'd just discovered each other on a desert island. In order to fit in as many people as possible for the opening, Ben had opted for a hot buffet and some tables had been cleared to make standing room for guests. At last she recognised a face amongst the crowd – Ed O'Donaghue, chairman of the Ballyfergus Small Business Association. She was so relieved to see a friendly face that she kissed him on the cheek, only to discover his face unpleasantly filmed with sweat.

'I don't mind telling you that I'm a bit nervous, Jennifer,' he said, getting out a cotton handkerchief and dabbing his round face, while she discreetly did the same to her lips with a hankie. 'Ben's asked me to say a few words about Glenvale, you see. He's going to put a collection box out for the course of the evening.'

'You'll be just fine, Ed.'

She glanced around appraisingly and compared herself to the well-heeled guests, feeling suddenly drab in her all-black outfit. Most of the women wore bright dresses, either

175

floor length or very short indeed, and there were lots of fake-tanned, bare shoulders on display. 'I expect people here will contribute quite a bit,' went on Ed, clearly excited. 'It could boost our coffers substantially.'

Jennifer caught a glimpse of Ben and her stomach flipped. He was moving easily through the crowd, in a smartly cut black suit and an open-necked white shirt, with a ready smile and a few words of conversation for everyone, grand or humble. She watched the curve of his high, faintly coloured, cheekbones when he smiled and the way his long, black lashes brushed his cheek. How could she have contemplated finishing with him only a few moments earlier? No matter that her heart might be broken later, she would trade the future sorrow for a few, snatched weeks of happiness now.

When he moved towards her, she glanced up with a carefully prepared look of polite neutrality on her face.

'Jennifer, I'd like you to meet my mother, Diane,' said Ben, guiding a very tall, tanned redhead by the elbow. It was hard to believe she was Ben's mother. Her face was flawless and her rich red hair fell about her face in youthful, flattering waves. Jennifer sucked in her stomach.

Diane, dressed in a diaphanous halterneck gown in shades of green – shamrock, pine, viridian and emerald – held the bottom of the champagne flute in both hands like a chalice. 'Ben tells me that you're responsible for the interior design.'

'That's right.' Jennifer summoned a smile, utterly intimidated by this beautiful creature. The nails on her long elegant fingers were painted with iridescent green varnish, like the plumage on a mallard's head. She held her long neck erect like a swan and looked down curiously at Jennifer, a professional, practised smile on her face.

'She did a fabulous job, don't you think?' Ben beamed

and placed a hand on Jennifer's shoulder. The familiar gesture which, under other circumstances might have produced a thrill in Jennifer, made her recoil in self-consciousness.

'Superb,' said Diane, the smile fixed like glued dentures. Ben said, looking towards the door, 'If you'll excuse me, I have to go and speak to someone.'

He walked off and Jennifer tried very hard not to be intimidated. Finding her voice at last she said, 'Ben tells me you run a model agency. That sounds interesting.'

'It has its moments.' Diane twirled her long hand in the air like a dancer – everything about her was elongated – and said, conspiratorially, 'Though some of the girls can be a real pain sometimes. They expect it all to happen without hard work on their part. I used to regularly put in twelve, thirteen-hour days when I was modelling.' She ran an appraising eye down Jennifer.

'Still it has its compensations,' she went on, touching the folds of her dress with long, bony fingers. Jennifer noticed the crêpy skin on the back of her hands and the prominent veins on her sandalled feet, both of which betrayed her years. 'I do like the fashion side of it.'

'I read something quite interesting in the paper the other day about women in the fashion industry increasingly forgoing make-up,' said Jennifer, keen to get Diane talking so she could learn a bit more about Ben's mother.

Diane laughed. 'Yes, it started in New York with the Make-up Free Mondays.'

'Well, it's all very well if you're a natural beauty with flawless skin,' scoffed Jennifer, unclenching her stomach muscles a little. They were starting to hurt. 'But how many ordinary women fall into that category?'

'Not many I should think. And, once we're over forty,' said Diane, continuing with her conspiratorial tone, 'we need all the help we can get, don't we?' And she finished off with a friendly wink, her eyelid slicked with eyeshadow the same colour as her nails.

Jennifer smiled thinly. Throughout this conversation, not a single line had appeared on Diane's forehead, leading Jennifer to the conclusion that her handsome looks might well have been assisted by surgical means, and she felt uncomfortable with Diane's 'we're-in-the-same-camp' tone.

As if Diane could read her mind she said, 'I do wish Ben would hurry up and marry, though.' There was a pregnant pause. Jennifer blinked under Diane's close scrutiny – and prayed that the heavy layer of foundation she'd applied earlier was enough to hide her red face.

'I want to be the mother-of-the-bride before my face and figure go,' went on Diane, flicking a lock of flame-coloured hair off her face. 'And I certainly want to be a grandmother before I'm too old to be considered glamorous! You'll understand that sentiment, I'm sure.'

Jennifer tried to laugh but, when she opened her mouth, nothing came out. Her tongue was thick and the roof of her mouth dry. Did Diane know – or suspect – that something was going on between her and Ben? Was this her way of warning Jennifer off? She took a sip of the champagne, licked her lips and fanned her face with her hand. 'Goodness, it's hot in here.'

'Is it? I don't feel it,' said Diane with a dismissive shrug of her insubstantial shoulders. She frowned disapprovingly at Jennifer's dress and said, 'Mind you, you are a bit over-dressed in those long sleeves.' Without drawing breath, she went on, spearing Jennifer with that intense, unsettling gaze of hers, 'Do you have any children?'

'Two. I have a son and a daughter,' said Jennifer, falling on the change of subject with relief, in spite of Diane's catty remark about her attire. She remembered that Diane had lost a child and compassion softened her anger.

'Was the young chef I saw you talking to earlier your son?'

Jennifer nodded and Diane added swiftly, with a laugh like broken glass, 'I almost mistook him for Ben. They're so alike, don't you think?' She scanned the crowd, her eyes settling at last on her son, who was talking to a gorgeous looking young woman, with a skirt practically up to her knicker-line. Diane spied them, smiled on one side of her face and said, 'There can't be much between Ben and Matt age wise.' She paused, pursed her lips, and slowly brought her gaze back to Jennifer. 'Can there?' she added pointedly.

'I . . . eh . . .' mumbled Jennifer, who preferred not to see the resemblance and felt slightly nauseous. There was a point to this conversation and Jennifer did not like it one little bit.

Diane craned her neck to look over the crowd – she must've been over six foot in heels – and her face burst into a radiant smile. She nodded and, having caught the attention of whoever it was she wanted, she said idly, all chummy again, 'I'm starving. I can't wait to sample the food. Jason's a remarkable chef.'

Jennifer nodded dumbly, believing the first part of this statement anyway. Diane looked as if she could do with a good, square meal inside her.

To her surprise, Alan Crawford appeared at his ex-wife's side. 'Ah, there you are, Alan,' she said, draping her arm over his shoulder like a shawl. They must've made an odd married couple, for Diane towered over her ex by several inches. 'This is Jenny . . . sorry I didn't catch your surname?'

'We've met,' said Alan without warmth, his gaze some-where else, though he did take her hand limply and kiss her perfunctorily on the cheek. His mobile features twitched, and he said, 'Well, I suppose I've got to hand it to you, Jennifer. You did a first-class job on the place. Top-notch, and better than that Calico woman.'

Though grudgingly bestowed, Jennifer lapped up the compliment and, putting her business hat on, she said bravely, 'I hope you'll think of me for future commissions then.'

There was a pause. Diane pressed her bony fingers into Alan's shoulder hard enough to make him visibly wince. 'Most of what Crawford Holdings does is on a . . . a commercial scale, Jennifer,' she said. Alan looked at her sharply.

'Alan?' said Jennifer, her voice unintentionally, pathetically pleading. She had hoped that this would lead to more jobs like it and, God knows, she could do with the business.

'Diane's right,' he said brusquely, shaking his head. 'We don't usually do one-offs like this.'

Diane narrowed her eyes like a cat. 'Didn't Ben tell you? I'm a major shareholder in Crawford Holdings. And I have a seat on the board. So I do actually know quite a lot about the business.'

Jennifer stretched her lips into an approximation of a smile, feeling like her face was about to crack. 'Of course. I see.'

'But I'll certainly recommend you to my friends,' said Diane lightly. 'My girlfriends are always refurbishing. Fashions change so quickly, don't they? Apparently black sanitary ware is going to be the next big thing.' And she wrinkled her nose like Samantha out of *Bewitched*. 'Do you have some business cards I could hand out?'

Jennifer had no desire to procure business from Diane's friends, not if they were anything like her. But she wasn't good at thinking on her feet. Instead of pretending that she'd forgotten them, she heard herself saying, 'Of course. Thank you.'

She'd just pulled a handful of cards out of her bag when Danny, the tweed-suited photographer and sometime journalist from *The Ballyfergus Times*, interrupted with, 'Do you mind if I take your photograph, Jennifer? The three of you, if you don't mind?'

They huddled up together, all smiles, as if they were the best of buddies. Danny took the shot, scribbled their names into a notebook, thanked them profusely and moved on to the next group.

'Well, it was lovely to meet you, Jennifer,' said Diane, as soon as Danny was gone. She acknowledged Alan with an abrupt nod, turned her back on them both and walked off.

'Got to catch up with some people over there,' said Alan and he too disappeared, leaving Jennifer standing alone, clutching a bunch of damp business cards in her sweaty palm. The party should have been a celebration, but it had turned instead into a painful lesson in humiliation. She looked around desperately for Ben but he was engaged in animated conversation with two men about his own age. The confidence had been knocked out of her, like the stuffing of Lucy's first teddy bear, that now lay limp and bald in a box in the attic.

Though she tried very hard to fight against them, tears pricked the back of her eyes. She could not, would not cry in public. Pasting a stupid, false smile on her face she made her way to the ladies' toilets with walls finished in pink plaster, the floor tiled in pink-veined marble and hand beaten brass sinks from India. She locked herself in a cubicle, sat down on the closed toilet lid and let the tears flow.

Diane and Alan had both known about her and Ben, that much was obvious, and clearly, one of their objectives in coming here tonight was to deliver their unequivocal message – you are not welcome in this family.

But how had they found out? She stopped crying, dabbed her eyes with toilet paper and thought hard. She could think of only one explanation. Ben must have told them. She shook her head in disbelief. Maybe she'd misjudged him. Maybe he was more like his parents than she'd thought, or wanted to believe. Her heart hardened. If he could break such a simple promise, then how could he be trusted? Jennifer pulled herself together, collected her coat and left the party without, it seemed, anyone even noticing.

It was very late when the doorbell rang. Jennifer turned over in bed, pulled the duvet over her head and tried to ignore it.

But it kept on ringing. Two doors down the German Shepherd began to howl and Jennifer threw back the covers. 'Oh for God's sake,' she muttered irritably. 'You're going to wake all the neighbours.' She went over to the window, pulled back the curtain and looked down onto the street. Ben's car was parked haphazardly outside her house, the front wheel up on the kerb. She marched downstairs, not caring that her face was bare of make-up and she looked an absolute fright.

She flung open the door. Ben was standing there looking distraught and a little dishevelled, the collar of his suit jacket turned up.

'What do you want?' she said crossly. 'Do you realise what time it is?' she demanded, though she'd no idea herself. The street was deserted and every house in the cul-de-sac bar the Richmonds' directly opposite was shrouded in darkness, cars nestling neatly in well-kept driveways, side by side.

'You left without saying goodbye.' His speech was slurred. 'I'd no idea where you were. I spent ages looking for you.'

'You're drunk.'

He shrugged his shoulders.

'I had a headache. I had to come home.'

'But you're all right now, darling?'

'Yes,' she said tersely and folding her arms, realised that she was wearing an unflattering pair of pink and grey leopard print flannel pyjamas that were too big for her. She'd bought them for Lucy last Christmas but she'd hated them. And, Jennifer's mantra being waste not, want not, they'd ended up in her wardrobe.

'You told your parents about us, didn't you?'

He looked at her in astonishment. 'I did not.'

'Hmm,' said Jennifer, this rebuttal somewhat taking the wind out of her sails. She folded her arms and scowled, not knowing what to say next.

'Can I come in?'

She paused and scowled again and the dog started to bark once more. 'Oh, all right then.'

Inside, she sat on the bottom of the stairs, dimly lit by the light from the landing above. She rested her elbows on her knees, while the rage quietly ebbed away like the receding tide to be replaced with a wretched sadness.

'What's wrong with you?' he said, neutrally, standing over her with his hands in his trouser pockets, swaying slightly.

She squinted up at him. 'How come they know about you and me?'

'They don't. How could they?'

'Well, someone told them. Diane went to great lengths to let me know how much she was looking forward to you marrying and providing her with grandchildren. And she was at pains to point out how close in age you and Matt are. She made me feel like some sort of . . . of paedophile,' she blurted out and rubbed her brow with a closed fist.

He burst out laughing and shook his head. When his mirth had died down he wiped a tear from the corner of his eyes and said, 'Oh, Jennifer. Don't be ridiculous.'

'I'm not being ridiculous. And it's not the least bit funny,' she said crossly, nervously picking little pills of grey wool off her bedsocks.

'You're reading too much into it.' He sighed heavily and she glanced up at him. He ran a hand through his hair – a dark, unruly curl flopped down in front of his left eye, and her stomach lurched. 'I'm sure her comments weren't directed at you.'

'They were. Believe me,' she said flatly. What she did not tell him was how deeply Diane's words, aimed with all the precision of a sniper, had wounded her. And Alan's too.

'Well, if she did appear to know about us,' he conceded, 'she's only guessing. Or maybe someone saw us together in the Chinese last week. My parents know people everywhere.'

Both scenarios were entirely possible, she thought, grudgingly. Alternatively, Diane might well have been acting on pure instinct and conjecture, as might Alan. Ben held her gaze unflinchingly. Her stomach flipped, the hurt transformed suddenly into desire.

'You mean they have spies everywhere? Like MI5?' she smiled.

'Something like that. Budge up.' He sat down heavily beside her on the stair, their arms pressed together in the confined space. She rested her head on his shoulder, put a hand on his thigh and he sighed contentedly.

'You shouldn't have driven over here.' She lifted her head and looked up into his face. His breath smelt of alcohol and the illicit, tantalising aroma of cigarette smoke rose from his jacket, a smell she'd always thought manly. 'You've been smoking too.'

He did not answer but stared instead at the top of her head as if fascinated by it. And then, gently cupping the back of her head in one of his hands he brought his lips down onto hers. The kiss was long and hard, and when he

184

finally released her from it, Jennifer's head was spinning and her entire body tingled with want.

'You'd better stay the night,' she said hoarsely, the heat of his thigh searing her hand through the fine wool fabric of his trousers.

He said not a word but his lips travelled across her cheekbone and found their way to her left ear. She squirmed with pleasure. His breath was damp and he whispered her name feverishly, his voice creaking with longing.

She removed her hand from his thigh and pressed her palm against his toned chest, feeling the fast thud of his heart against his ribcage. His lips inched down her neck, sending a delicious tingling sensation shooting down her left side.

'I want you more than I've ever wanted any woman, Jennifer Murray,' he whispered hungrily.

She closed her eyes. Her heart moved in her chest like a trapped bird; blood rushed to her groin. The entire world contracted into the tiny space on the stairs that held them both. There was only the here and the now; his fingers pressing into her skull; the heat and the smell of him; the swooning dizziness in her head.

And then, abruptly, he pulled away, leaving her panting, aching for his touch. He stared at her, his eyes as dark and wide as the night, the smell and touch and taste of him filling up all her senses. And he said, deadly serious, 'This isn't just a fling for me, Jennifer. You do know that, don't you?'

She nodded dumbly.

'You understand that I love you?'

'I love you too,' she said, as a pulse of desire threatened to overwhelm her, the yearning so strong and unfamiliar that it frightened her. She had never craved a man's body the way she needed Ben's. And she could not resist the

185

impulse to satisfy that craving, even if she had wanted to.

Jennifer had no idea how much time had passed but, when she heard the insistent knocking on the bedroom door, she sat up and looked at the clock. It was two forty-five and Ben, naked in the bed beside her, did not stir.

'Mum,' said Matt's voice from outside the door and she bit her lip.

'Shit.' Instinctively she pulled the covers over her bare breast and looked at Ben again. He was lying on his stomach, in a deep, drink-induced slumber. He would not wake. The room smelt of sex and she wrestled with the feeling that he ought not to be here, that she should be ashamed. Her heart fluttered uncertainly in her chest and there was another tap, sharper now, on the door. Yellow light seeped under the door like luminescent fog.

'Mum, are you all right?' came Matt's voice again and this time there was a note of concern in it.

She had nothing to be ashamed of, she told herself firmly, yet still, it would not do for Matt to find them like this. Noiselessly, she got out of bed, pulled on a dressing gown and padded out onto the landing. She closed the door silently behind her, pausing momentarily to lay her right palm against the woody grain of the door. She smiled involuntarily, the tenderness in her sated body an exquisite reminder of their energetic love-making. Arranging a blank expression on her face, she turned and whispered to Matt, 'What are you doing here?'

'I got locked out. Harry's gone to Dublin on a stag weekend and I waited for ages for Andy to come home but he didn't turn up. If the damned flat wasn't on the second floor, I'd have broken one of the windows.'

Jennifer rubbed her right eye with one hand, keeping a

tight hold on the collar of the dressing gown with the other. 'Jesus, Matt. It's nearly three a.m.'

'Sorry, Mum.'

'What'd you wake me for?'

'I dunno really. It's just, well, I thought I'd better check you were okay. You see, Ben Crawford's car's been abandoned outside our house. Really weird.' He walked over to the small window on the landing, looked down onto the street and frowned. 'Looks like he was drunk when he parked it.'

Jennifer pulled the dressing gown even tighter round her neck and glanced at the bedroom door, wishing that Matt would hurry up and cotton on before she was forced to spell it out in black and white. 'So?' she said and held his gaze.

He looked from her face to the bedroom door, then back again. She raised her eyebrows and tried to smile, as a hot flush of embarrassment crept up her neck. At last, slow understanding, agonising to watch, spread across his handsome features, blanching them white.

'Don't tell me,' he said and paused.

She wished the ground would open up and swallow her whole. This was certainly not the way she'd have chosen to tell her son about a new lover.

'Mum,' he said at last, the disappointment in his voice more hurtful than the disbelief. 'You have got to be kidding.'

Downstairs in the kitchen, Jennifer stirred sugar into a mug of hot cocoa and pressed it into Matt's hands. 'Here, drink this.'

Muffin, annoyed at the rude interruption to his beauty sleep, sat up and gave up a doleful, wolf-like howl. 'Shush,' snapped Jennifer crossly and he lay down in his basket again, closed his eyes and let out a long, heartfelt sigh. Matt sprawled on a kitchen chair, and Jennifer, plucking fretfully at her bottom lip, tried to put herself in his shoes.

187

How would she have felt if she'd come home to find her forty-four-year-old mother in bed with her boss, a man young enough to be her son, and only eight years older than herself? She frowned. It wasn't an attractive image. But she wasn't her mother and times were different. She reminded herself firmly that she had, actually, done nothing wrong; no one had been hurt, taken advantage of or misused. Not without consent anyway.

He set the mug down on the table, pulled his checkered neckerchief off – the black cap was gone – and shook his head as if still not willing, or able, to assimilate the truth. 'What were you thinking, Mum?'

It was a good question. She hadn't been thinking at all. It hadn't occurred to her that the neighbours would see Ben's distinctive car in the morning. Or that there was no chance of Ben sneaking out of the house unnoticed. She'd been driven entirely by a primeval need for sex. And, oh, what sex! She had never really enjoyed sex with David, or any other man for that matter, apart from the actual brief moment of orgasm. Ben's sensual love-making, stemming from a desire to please her first rather than himself, was something completely different.

'What are you smiling at?' he demanded.

She wiped the smile off her face and pulled out a chair. She sat down, clasped her hands together on the top of the table, and said, 'I know this has come as a bit of a shock.'

'You can say that again.'

'And, I don't mean to sound harsh, but it really isn't your business.'

He looked at her sharply.

'Any more than it would be my business to cross-examine you about who you sleep with,' she went on.

He scowled at her from under dark eyebrows, the hot cocoa untouched on the table. Bolstered by Ben's declaration of love still ricocheting around inside her head, she continued. 'Think about it, Matt. I'm a single woman. And you and Lucy are adults now. I never brought men home when you were young. But, now that you're both grown, I don't think it's unreasonable for me to have a life of my own.'

'I'm not saying it is. It's just . . . well, for one thing he's my boss.'

'Yes,' she said, looking at the red nail polish she'd put on specially for the opening night. A night that had see-sawed between misery and rapture. 'That does make things a bit complicated.'

Matt scratched his head and let out a loud sigh, his anger deflating. 'I guess it's going to take some getting used to. It never occurred to me to see you two as a . . . a couple. But, hey, I like Ben, I really do, and if he makes you happy, then that's all right with me, I guess.'

Touched by this answer, and the fact that he had clearly struggled to reach this accommodation, she got up, and went and stood behind him. She put her arms around his shoulders and kissed the top of his head. His hair smelt of kitchen grease. 'It makes me so happy to hear you say that, son. You've no idea.'

Matt yawned. 'Come on, Mum. It's late. We should both get to bed.' He stood up.

'Matt, will you do something for me?' she said, looking up at him.

'Sure.'

'Don't tell Lucy or your Dad about Ben just yet. Or anyone else.' He opened his mouth to protest but she silenced him with, 'Just for the time being. I'll tell them all before Christmas, I promise, but it has to be the right time.'

Matt considered this for a moment. 'Okay. But don't leave it too long, eh, Mum? You know I'm rubbish with secrets.'

189

'I won't. I promise.' She placed a hand on his cheek. 'I was proud of you tonight, son, you do know that, don't you?'

He grinned and said, 'Yeah, Jason said I did really well.'

'That's fantastic, Matt. Congratulations.'

And she gave him a big hug, hoping with all her heart that Lucy, when she found out about Ben, reacted just as positively as her kind, big-hearted brother had done.

The weak winter sun shining through the wide crack in the curtains woke Jennifer the next morning. Ben was already awake, lying quietly on his side staring at her, his chin dark with stubble and sticky hair matted to his head. She hoped she hadn't been snoring and she wished she'd woken up first. She would've snuck into the bathroom and put on a bit of discreet make-up.

'Morning, my darling.'

Her heart soared at the simple words of endearment. 'Morning,' she smiled dreamily.

'Any regrets?'

'Nope. What about you?' She lowered her eyes to his chest, thick with dark hairs, and blushed at the recollection of her forwardness when she'd suggested he stay the night.

'Last night was the best thing that's ever happened to me. And I don't just mean the sex.'

She blushed more deeply, and her gaze drifted to the top of a well-toned bicep, just peeking out under the duvet. 'You were drunk. I think I might have taken advantage of you.'

'You did,' he agreed and she glanced up at his face, stricken with mortification. But he was smiling widely, the corners of his eyes all crinkled up like he was squinting into the sun. He leaned up on one elbow and she rolled onto her back, letting the covers fall away from her breast.

'You're a brazen hussy,' he said and slipped a hand under

190

the duvet, found the side of her hip and gave her a playful slap.

'But you like brazen hussies, right?' said Jennifer hoarsely.

In reply, he pulled the duvet over their heads, plunging them into darkness.

Later, while they were still in bed, and rain battered the window, she told him about Matt's nocturnal visit to her room and Ben said, 'I'm glad he knows.'

'But it could make things a bit awkward between you two.'

'No, it'll be fine,' said Ben. 'There'd be something wrong if he wasn't a bit protective of you. But he'll be cool once he knows that I'm not going to muck you about. Now, come over here and give me a cuddle.'

He rolled her gently onto her side and lay down behind her, moulding his body to the shape of hers, so that they lay together like spoons in a drawer. He ran a hand lightly down the curve of her hip and said, 'God, I love your body.'

She laughed, bunching the pillow under her head. He nibbled the back of her neck and said, absentmindedly, 'What're you doing on the twenty-ninth of December?'

'I don't know. Nothing much I imagine.' She usually filled the dead time between Christmas and New Year by dutifully traipsing round relatives. But Christmas, she suddenly realised, would be different this year. She pictured them having long lazy lie-ins, curling up in front of the fire drinking mulled wine in the warm glow of Christmas tree lights, and taking brisk walks in the bracing sea air.

He trailed his fingers along the curve of her shoulder, sending shivers shooting down her arm.

'Well, how would you like to come with me to my cousin's wedding? It's at Galgorm.'

'A winter wedding,' she said, the invitation taking her by surprise. Galgorm, opened a few years ago, was one of the province's finest hotels. She'd heard fabulous reports about it, but she'd never been. She sat up in bed and pulled the duvet over her breasts. 'To the evening reception?'

He rolled onto his back. 'No, the whole day.'

Jennifer, suddenly facing the prospect of being propelled from obscurity into the limelight of the Crawford clan, was terrified. Everyone would be curious about her, judging her suitability as partner to Ulster's most eligible bachelor. Ben's parents would no doubt be there and would not be well pleased to see her on the arm of their only son. 'It's still early days for us, Ben. I'm not sure it'd be right for me to be there.'

He too sat up then, the duvet falling away to reveal a muscled chest thick with wiry black hair. 'I want you to be there. I want to show you off to everyone. To the entire world! Please say you'll come,' he pleaded and, when she hesitated, he grabbed her hand and pressed it to his red lips. The black stubble that shadowed his face was rough against her skin and he stared up at her with immense brown eyes. 'Look, if we're going to be a proper couple, then you have to come. I want you to be there at my side.'

She smiled and all her objections melted away in the hazy warmth of his love. How could she say no to him? Why should she let his parents stop her going? He loved her and that was all that mattered. With him at her side, she could face anyone.

'Okay,' she heard herself say, 'I'd love to.'

Chapter 14

Oren seemed unusually preoccupied as they drove the eleven miles, along winding country roads walled with high hawthorn hedges, from the isolated farmhouse he called home into Enniskillen. Bereft of their lush green summer leaves, only a handful of red haw berries clung stubbornly to the orange-brown skeletons in the vicious westerly wind.

'Where are we going?' said Lucy, watching the dark belly of a cloud sag ominously over the mud-blotted landscape like the seat of an old chair. In the distance, the hills were curtained with rain pressing in from the Atlantic and, in a nearby marshy field, tufts of reeds sprouted from the wet grass and sodden sheep sheltered from the wind in the lee of the hedge.

'I thought I'd show you Enniskillen,' he said. 'The walk along the river by the castle is spectacular.'

'You want to go for a walk in this weather?' she said incredulously and his smile slipped momentarily to be replaced with a look of mild irritation that Lucy had come to expect when she displeased him in some way.

Oren's patient smile returned and he said, confidently, as a spat of rain plopped on the windscreen, 'It's only a shower. And we can always take shelter in the castle.'

'Yes. And it's nice to get out of the house for a bit, isn't it. Just the two of us,' said Lucy who'd quickly discovered that the best way to restore harmony between them was to agree with Oren.

'You do like my family, but,' he said, slipping into the Ulster dialect his parents spoke.

'Of course. They're lovely and they couldn't have made me feel more welcome.'

His mother, in a sober knee-length dress with greying hair scraped into a tight bun, had welcomed her with tea and a mound of home baking that would've fed the entire population of Oakwood Grove. His father was a quiet, serious man with work-roughened hands and a face scoured red by a life outdoors. He was tall like Oren and shared the same thick neck and big hands. After tea on the first night, he'd offered her his favourite seat by the peat-blackened fireplace – a great honour, Oren had later confided. The large farmhouse was homely inside despite its austere grey-harled exterior and black slate roof. It had been in the family for four generations and was crammed full of ancient dark wood furniture, crazed pottery and worn patterned carpets. The farm itself was immaculate, the vast barn outside filled with shiny brand-new machines, the only evidence that this modest family were one of the wealthiest in the county. Lucy was getting used to grace before every meal, the animal smell of the farmyard and a very different daily rhythm to the one she was used to. Life on the farm started early, long before dawn, and the house was closed up for the night at ten every evening.

They'd spent the last few days visiting Oren's relatives scattered across the county. Together, they'd explored the grounds of Florence Court, the historic home of the Earls of Enniskillen with its breathtaking views over Benaughlin and the Cuilcagh Mountains. One of Oren's uncles had taken them out in his boat on a chilly sightseeing trip on Lough Erne and they'd all attended church together on Sunday where the congregation greeted her like some long-lost member of their flock.

'And you don't miss TV?'

'Not at all,' she said truthfully. There was a television in the drawing room but it was very rarely switched on – the family got their news and weather from the sun-yellowed white plastic radio that sat on the kitchen windowsill along-side the eggs Mrs Wilson collected from the henhouse every morning. At night, while Oren and Lucy played board games on the coffee table, Mrs Wilson did cross-stitch and Mr Wilson read the Bible. 'There's something nice about the serenity of your parents' house. It's very peaceful.'

'Yes, the outside world is very much kept outside,' he said. 'The way it should be.'

'The only thing I find a little odd is the lack of books in the house.' There were no bookcases and the only books she could find, apart from cookery books in the kitchen, were on a shelf in the drawing room. There were gardening books, an atlas, books on birds and DIY, dog-eared copies of farming magazines, several copies of the Bible and religious tracts, but no novels at all. 'And they don't buy a Sunday newspaper either.'

The car came to an undulating, straight stretch of road. Oren thrust the car into fifth gear, and accelerated so fast Lucy felt a nauseous tug in her stomach. 'That's because the Bible is the only book you need, Lucy. The original blueprint for this short life on earth.'

She turned her face to the window and stared out at a muddy field, thinking guiltily of the Tess Gerritsen thriller she'd brought with her and which had remained in her attic room, a secret bedtime treat.

'Oh, look, there's a fairy tree,' she said, pointing at a

195

gnarled and ancient hawthorn tree in the middle of the field. It was boxed in by a new fence of raw wood, erected to protect the tree from grazing animals. 'Apparently some of them are four hundred years old. I wonder how old that one is.'

'You don't believe in fairy trees, do you?' he said, sounding horrified. 'All that nonsense about fairies bringing you bad luck if you cut down the tree.'

Lucy, who wasn't sure whether she believed in fairies or not, said dreamily, 'But I think it's a sweet tradition, the idea that fairies live in the tree. And it's harmless, isn't it?'

'Superstitious folklore,' he tutted and glanced grudgingly at her. 'That's McQuillan's land. Silly old papist fool. I daresay when the old man dies, his son'll have more sense and cut the thing down.'

Oren's mood improved as they neared Enniskillen on the western approach road dominated by views of the imposing castle. Once they'd parked and got out of the car, he seemed positively and uncharacteristically buoyant, hurrying Lucy along by the elbow.

'Enniskillen,' he said, gripping her tightly by the arm and propelling her along the grey gravel path beneath the dark grey walls of the castle, 'is the only island town in Ireland. And this castle was once the medieval home of the Gaelic Maguire clan.' They paused for a moment to look up at the perfectly preserved castle walls, and he let go of her arm. He was wearing a black hiking jacket but no gloves or scarf. He seemed impervious to the cold. 'This bit,' he said, pointing at a distinctive twin-turreted section, 'is the Watergate and it was built by William Cole in the seventeenth century. The family moved to Florence Court in the eighteenth century after which it became a military barracks.'

'It's a handsome building,' said Lucy, pushing her gloved hands deeper into her pockets and wishing she'd worn a hat. A hank of her hair whipped up by the wind blowing across the River Erne slapped across her face. She tucked it behind her ear, only for another length to break free.

'I love it here,' he said.

'I'd like it too if it was a bit warmer. I imagine it's lovely in the summer,' said Lucy, wondering how soon she could suggest retiring to a tea-room without incurring Oren's wrath.

Oren turned his gaze from the castle wall to the inhospitable-looking river. Lucy huddled against him, doing her best to shelter from the wind.

'I used to love coming here as a boy,' he went on, obviously lost in memories, for he had completely ignored her when she'd spoken. 'I imagined I was a soldier fighting for King and Country.' He glanced nervously over his shoulder at the path they'd just travelled, then peered ahead in the direction they were going. They were completely alone. 'And I still like coming here to think and talk to Him upstairs. You'd think I'd be able to do that best in a church.' He favoured her with a whimsical thin-lipped smile, the right corner of his mouth turned up. 'But no, for me, it's here.'

Lucy examined him closely, registering his flushed pink cheeks and his eyes glinting like wet flint in the cold wind. He was looking at her but yet he seemed to be looking through her. Alarmed by his apparent agitation, she said, touching him lightly on the arm, 'Are you all right, Oren?'

He started a little and his eyes came into focus. He smiled. 'I guess I always liked the idea of serving, except now I know my role in life is not to serve an authority here on earth, but in heaven.' He paused, raised his eyes momentarily to the steel-grey clouds skittering across the sky, then focused on her once more. 'Things are suddenly clear to me, Lucy. I've prayed long and hard for God's guidance and He's answered my prayers. Now I know where my duty

197

lies. But it's a path I don't think I can walk alone. I need a partner to do it with me. Someone who loves Jesus as much as I do.'

'What path is –' she began but suddenly, with a scuffle of gravel underfoot, Oren dropped to the ground. Lucy, thinking he must've somehow slipped and lost his footing, held out both hands to assist him to his feet. 'Oren, are you okay?' she tittered, torn between genuine concern and amusement.

And then, noticing the annoyed solemnity of his expression, her laughter died away. He made no attempt to struggle to his feet, but remained where he was with his right knee digging into the sharp, glittering gravel. It could only mean one thing. Her heart battered the inside of her chest and she took a small step backwards, overwhelmed by the idea that he might be about to propose. She had not expected this.

She was not worthy of Oren. She fell so far short of his goodness every day. It seemed inconceivable that he should choose her. But yet, she still believed in fairytales. And deep in her heart, somewhere way beyond consciousness, she had allowed the hope to blossom that one day he might look on her and see a woman good and holy enough to be his wife.

And yet, now that moment appeared to be upon her, she looked around wildly, torn between the inexplicable impulse to run and the urge to stand her ground. For wasn't this the dream that had sustained her through long nights of Bible study, when she'd racked her brain to decipher the meaning of incomprehensible passages that seemed so crystal clear and unambiguous to Oren? He held out his hand and gestured her towards him. She took a deep breath and stepped forward.

His eyes gleamed with the hard intensity he usually

reserved for talking about God and, when he grasped her hand, his grip was tight and his hand was shaking. 'Lucy. Will you marry me?'

'Marry you?' She worshipped the ground he walked on, but she had never allowed herself to believe he felt the same about her. 'You love me?' she said, her heart pounding now to a mad, chaotic rhythm.

He glanced momentarily to the left and said, 'I wouldn't be asking you to marry me if I didn't love you, now would I?' Then he smiled, a disarming, nervous smile and he said, 'You'd better hurry up and give me an answer, or I'm going to end up with a punctured kneecap!'

'Yes! Oh, yes, I'll marry you!' she cried and the next thing she knew she was in his arms, sobbing with joy – and relief. The lonely future she had so often steeled herself to accept was not to be her destiny after all. Instead, she would have love and companionship and a family – all the things she had thought would never be hers.

'Why are you crying, Lucy?' he said, smoothing the hair back from her forehead and planting a chaste kiss on her brow. 'I thought you would be happy.'

'I am happy. I'm sorry,' she said, sniffing back tears. 'I'm just being foolish. I'm happier than I've ever been in my entire life.'

'Good, because so am I,' he said and he held her tight against his body, as hard and solid as a tree.

'Oh, the ring,' he said suddenly, releasing her. He fumbled in his pocket for a few moments and pulled out a small, battered burgundy velvet box. He opened it and there, nestling inside on a tiny bed of rumpled silk, lay a port wine coloured garnet ring, encircled by a wreath of small, dull diamonds.

'Oh, it's very . . . unusual,' said Lucy. In style it was very like her grandmother's emerald engagement ring which now lay, unworn, in her mother's jewel box at home.

'It was my grandmother's. Here, try it on.' He plucked the ring from the box and slipped the glove off her left hand.

'It won't fit,' she said, slightly embarrassed, clutching both fleecy gloves in her right hand. Why did everything about her have to be big and ungainly? 'I have thick fingers.'

'Nonsense.' He tried to wrestle the ring onto her ring finger but it would not fit. He settled on the little one instead. 'No matter,' he said brightly. 'We can have it re-sized.'

She stared at the ring and tried to suppress her ungrateful disappointment. It was too small and delicately wrought for her large hand, and she would never have chosen such an old-fashioned stone, or setting. The garnet stared at her lifeless and glassy like a fish eye and she could see now that the dirty diamonds clustered around the garnet were only diamond chips.

'My grandmother would've loved you, Lucy. She was level-headed like you. I think you'd have gotten on well.'

Lucy swallowed her dismay and blushed with shame. Clearly, Oren believed that bestowing this hideous ring on her was a great honour. She ought to be thankful.

He grinned at her then and said, 'Oh, you and I are going to do wonderful things together, Lucy.' He tucked her arm under his and went on, leading her along the path once more, 'And with you at my side to support me, I feel ready to take on God's next challenge and change the course of my life.'

'What challenge?' said Lucy, as a drop of cold rain splattered on the crown of her head. Another one followed almost immediately, this time on her cheekbone. It trailed down her face like a cold tear.

Oren looked at the sky and said, 'We should be making tracks. Let's find a coffee shop, shall we?'

200

'You are going to be a minister, aren't you?' said Lucy.

'Not necessarily,' said Oren, patting her on the arm.

Lucy pulled her arm from his grasp and standing still, forced him to do the same. 'I thought that's what you wanted?'

'It was what I wanted,' he said, turning to her with a small, secretive smile, 'but it turns out it wasn't what God wanted.'

'I don't understand,' she said stubbornly, ignoring the rain that was falling heavily now, gusting on the bitter wind.

'I don't either. But God works in mysterious ways. And it turns out that He has a different plan in mind for us. Oh, don't look so worried, Lucy,' he said, and he threw back his head and laughed. 'When you're engaged in the Lord's work, you have nothing to fear.'

'What work, Oren? What are you talking about?'

He swept his arm in a wide arc across the vista of castle and river. '*Go ye into all the world, and preach the gospel to every creature.*'

She stared at him dumbly, not understanding, as a trickle of cold water worked its way down the collar of her thick winter coat. 'But you're already an evangelist,' she said.

'I'm not even that, Lucy. I'm a revivalist, speaking to people who've already heard the Word of God.' He shook his head sadly in disbelief and then brightened. 'But I want to spread the Word in the true biblical sense amongst peoples who have never heard it. Can you imagine how that would feel, Lucy? To bring the good news to people for the very first time? Just like Jesus.'

He clasped her hand to his breast. 'You and I, Lucy Irwin, are going to be missionaries in Peru.'

Jennifer picked up *The Ballyfergus Times* for the umpteenth time and scowled at the grainy photograph of her

201

sandwiched, like a dwarf, between Diane Crawford and Ben's father. She was smiling too hard in the photo so that her eyes all but disappeared and the black dress, which she'd thought so flattering, made her look pale and fat. Or perhaps it wasn't the dress, perhaps it was standing beside Diane Crawford that was the problem. Diane sported a flirty, knowing smile and inclined her right bronzed shoulder slightly towards the camera, making her look even slimmer. Alan looked like any other bald-headed man of advancing years.

Jennifer threw the paper down on the workbench, refusing to let the unflattering picture put a dampener on her good mood. With a bit of luck, she told herself, no one would notice the photo hidden away on page twenty-three, except perhaps Ben who would surely look for it. She touched the smooth wooden surface of the bench and smiled. Five days had passed since the first wonderful romantic night they'd spent together and, even with Matt's rude interruption, it was the happiest day of her life. The speed with which she'd fallen in love unnerved her slightly. There was still so much she didn't know about Ben. But they had the rest of their lives to find all that out. They'd met twice since Carnegie's opening night. On Sunday they'd gone for a sedate drive and lunch and yesterday he'd called in at the shop.

She blushed as she recalled their tryst in this very room where he'd bent her over the workbench amidst a pile of feather cushion pads and made hard, passionate love to her while she bit down on her hand, moaning in ecstasy. And later, he'd sat her on his lap and held her tight and told her she was the most beautiful woman in the world. She shuddered, weak-kneed at the memory, and walked out of the room.

Across the street, in the steamy window of the internet

202

café opposite, brightly coloured Christmas lights pulsed as if to the beat of music around the shiny plastic head of a jolly Santa Claus. Jennifer smiled at the display although her homage to the festive season was much more subdued. A string of blue-white LED fairy lights with white feathers attached round every bulb were artfully draped in the window.

The phone rang abruptly, startling her. She took a deep breath, went into work mode and picked it up.

'Saw you in the paper,' said David's gleeful voice and Jennifer cringed. So much for her hope of the photo passing undetected. 'I see you're brushing shoulders with the great and the good.'

'What can I do for you, David?'

'Can you come over to ours on Sunday for lunch? Lucy's bringing Oren down and she wants us all to be there. I asked her why and she went all mysterious on me and said I'd have to wait to find out.'

'How odd,' remarked Jennifer, bothered by the short notice as much as the fact that Lucy hadn't asked her to stage this event. Of course, where a big party was involved, it made a lot more sense for Maggie and David to host, not only because they had more room, but because it would be a lot more relaxed for everyone if the girls were in their own environment.

'She wants your father there too,' said David, cutting across her thoughts. 'I've already texted Matt.' Odder still. Was Lucy trying to create the illusion of one big happy family? Family get-togethers at Maggie and David's weren't unprecedented, but they were unusual. The last time they'd all been together was for Matt's eighteenth and the time before that was Lucy's. Maggie and David were always generous hosts but, in spite of everyone's best efforts, these occasions were, naturally, a bit awkward.

'You'll come then? Maggie'll lay on the food. You just have to turn up.'

'Of course I'll come, David, but I'll bring a couple of dishes. It's not fair to expect Maggie to do it all. Tell her I'll give her a ring later and we can talk about it.'

'Okay. Look, I have to go. My next patient's just come in. And he's not very happy by the sound of it.' Jennifer could hear the scraping of claws on the smooth hard floor of the veterinary practice.

As soon as she came off the phone, Jennifer tried calling Lucy but there was no reply. She texted her asking for a chat but got a cheery message back almost straight away saying that she was very busy but she was looking forward to catching up at the weekend. How could she be busy? She'd finished university and was staying down at Enniskillen on a farm in the middle of nowhere by all accounts. She'd never been too busy to phone her own mother before, thought Jennifer. She frowned. Whatever Lucy was up to she would have to wait until the weekend to find out.

Meantime, she had a more pressing problem on her hands. She dialled Donna at work and, when she answered said, 'Can you talk?'

'I've got a few minutes before my next meeting.'

'I know it's short notice, Donna, but can you come late night shopping with me on Thursday night?'

'Wardrobe crisis?'

'You could say that. Ben's asked me to his cousin's wedding at Galgorm on the twenty-ninth of December.'

Donna sucked in air through her teeth and said, 'Oh, that'll be quite a do. A society wedding. You'll definitely need a hat. Luckily, I'm free on Thursday. I can meet you in the city centre straight after work. Let's hit Victoria Square.'

'Thanks Donna. You're an absolute life saver.'

'Does this mean that you and Ben have gone public?'

'Not yet,' said Jennifer. 'Matt knows but he's sworn to secrecy. I've still to tell everyone else and, in the interests of ongoing diplomatic relations, I'd like them to hear it first from me. I just have to pick the right time.'

Chapter 15

At Maggie's, Jennifer arranged her colourful contributions
of orange and fennel salad, stuffed red peppers and a side
of smoked salmon amidst platters of ham, chicken, beef and
cocktail sausages. As well as this, the dining table groaned
with all manner of salads – warm potato, coleslaw, tomato,
rice and couscous, spinach with toasted pine nuts and crumbled white cheese. Maggie, generous to a fault, always went
overboard with catering, and even now she was hovering
in the doorway in a Chanel-style navy jacket and matching
knee-length skirt, fretting. Jennifer too had made the effort
in a royal blue military-style belted dress and black heels.
Maggie had always been a slightly anxious person but these
days she seemed positively neurotic, an impression reinforced
by her whippet-thin figure and the way she stood wringing
her hands as if she were at a wake.

'Do you think there's enough food, Jennifer?' she said,
coming over to the table and fiddling with an already perfect
arrangement of holly-covered napkins fanned out like cards
on a dealer's table.

Jennifer, peeling the cling film off the salmon, glanced
sharply at Maggie. Her shoulder-length brown hair was both

voluminous and smooth and her make-up, especially around her pale grey eyes, was magazine perfect.

'It's just that David likes things to be perfect.'

Jennifer scrunched the thin plastic into a tight pale green ball remembering how she used to run herself ragged trying to live up to David's high standards and expectations. He hated to see the children in anything other than pristine clothes, liked the house to be immaculate and expected her to look groomed and tidy all the time. When they'd divorced, the relief of no longer having to live by these strictures had been indescribable. 'I don't think you've anything to be worried about,' said Jennifer kindly, feeling sorry for Maggie. 'You've enough here to feed an army!'

Maggie's facial muscles relaxed for the first time since greeting Jennifer at the door. 'Thanks. I really appreciate you helping out with the food, Jennifer.'

'I can't expect you to cater for everyone, it wouldn't be fair, especially with Matt's appetite. He'll eat you out of house and home if you don't watch him!' laughed Jennifer, trying not to let the fact that the party was here and not at her home, annoy her.

'I just want Oren to feel welcome.'

Jennifer surveyed the laden table, then shot Maggie a wry smile. 'I just hope he's hungry.'

Maggie giggled and some of the tension went out of her. Then a series of high-pitched shrieks coming from the adjoining room drew both women towards the door. Matt, in casual jeans and a hoodie, was chasing the children round the room. He lunged at Rachel across the back of the gold sofa with a roar that made Jennifer jump. Rachel shrieked, slipped his grasp and ran over to join Imogen, who was hiding behind the wing-backed chair in front of the crackling log fire. Both girls wore old-fashioned velvet party dresses in navy with broad pale blue sashes at the waist and white tights, and their long straight hair was tied up with ribbon. Where on earth Maggie got the outfits, Jennifer had no idea. She thought people had stopped dressing girls like dolls way back in the eighties. It occurred to her that the Christmas gifts she'd bought the girls – modern leggings and tunic-style tops in bright colours – might not be welcomed.

'Get him to stop, Auntie Jennifer!' implored Rachel, breathlessly, but she had her eye on Matt and a mischievous grin on her freckled face. 'Follow me,' she commanded her little sister and both girls crawled across the floor – completely oblivious to their white tights and Maggie's remonstrations – to take refuge behind the enormous, lavishly decorated Christmas tree, while Matt carried out a thorough search of the area near the fire.

The sight of Matt playing with his step-sisters delighted Jennifer. Maggie and David's beautiful daughters were the one good thing to have come out of the divorce, a sort of compensation to Matt and Lucy for the trauma of their parents' separation.

She glanced around the room, which, like the rest of the house, was stunning, and Jennifer couldn't help but feel a pang of jealousy at David and Maggie's good fortune. But, though she'd given up this lifestyle along with her wedding band, she would not make the trade back again.

David and Brian were chatting companionably by the tall bay window and Jennifer acknowledged with a little pride that everyone made a good job of papering over the cracks in this family. And much of the credit for that went to Maggie. Not many women would tolerate so graciously the presence of their husband's ex-wife and ex-father-in-law, nor be as kind and loving to step-children as Maggie had been over the years. Moved by this realisation, Jennifer turned to her former friend and smiled warmly. 'This is really nice.

Thank you for hosting.' Maggie beamed with pleasure.

The doorbell went, David and Brian looked up and the girls made a beeline for the door. Moments later, amidst much giggling, Oren was dragged into the room by the two girls with Lucy following behind, looking severe in a long-sleeved dark green dress that Jennifer had not seen before and flat shoes. Oren, very respectable in a grey suit and tie, laughed good-humouredly. 'Hey steady on, Rachel, you'll pull the arm off that sleeve if you're not careful!'

'Have you brought us any sweets like the last time, Oren?' said Imogen. 'Please say you have!'

'Don't be so forward, girls,' cried a horrified Maggie, advancing and brushing her daughters off Oren with brisk efficiency, as if they were naughty puppies. She gave him a peck on both cheeks, and said, 'I'm afraid they're a bit over-excited what with Christmas just round the corner. Every day Rachel marks off the number of sleeps on her calendar.'

'That's quite all right,' said Oren genially.

While David and Brian descended on Oren, Lucy produced two colourful tubes of Smarties from her handbag and gave them to the girls which sent them tail-spinning around the room in paroxysms of delight. Everyone laughed, Maggie called out, 'Save them for after lunch now!' and the girls ran off. It took a good ten minutes for everyone to say hello and, to Jennifer's relief, there was no trace of any animosity from either Oren or Lucy. Perhaps they too had wiped the slate clean and were ready to start afresh.

Maggie shepherded everyone over to the three sofas arranged around the fire in a horseshoe shape, a massive upholstered footstool serving as a coffee table in the middle. Once Maggie had handed out glasses of soft drinks and non-alcoholic mulled punch (in deference, Jennifer presumed, to Oren, for David and Maggie liked a drink as much as the next person) David stood by the fire, raised his glass and said, 'Let's have a toast. To family.'

Everyone mumbled a response, took a sip of their drinks and David sat down. Oren looked at Lucy sitting beside him, nodded and patted her hand. Only then did Jennifer notice the dull, old-fashioned ring on Lucy's finger and the rather dazed, slightly apprehensive look on her face. Her heart began to race.

'Ahem,' said Oren, clearing his throat and commanding silence. Everyone, even the girls nursing their glasses of flat lemonade, quietened. They all stared at him and waited and Jennifer felt certain that she knew what was coming next.

'Lucy and I have something to tell you,' said Oren. 'We're engaged to be married.'

Jennifer put a hand over her mouth to stop herself crying out. This couldn't be happening. But the ring was already on Lucy's finger and Oren was holding her hand like he owned her.

She wasn't the only one stunned by this news. The silence lasted a few long moments. And then David, consummate as always, was on his feet with a warm handshake for Oren, a kiss for Lucy and a ready smile to hide his surprise. Jennifer, reeling from shock, tried to take it in.

Her precious daughter was to marry this man? The toddler who used to come into her bed for a cuddle when she'd had bad dreams, the little girl who used to kiss her on the lips and tell her she was the best Mummy in the world? It couldn't be. He would never be right for her.

But marriage was a contract between two people. What right did she have to pass judgement or criticise? She knew she ought to accept Lucy's choice and give the couple her full support. That's what Donna would advise, she was sure of it. But she couldn't. A lump formed in her throat and tears filled her eyes. She simply couldn't.

'Well, that is a surprise,' said David, nodding at the surrounding company, while Jennifer's mouth went dry and she fought back the tears. Clearly, he had not been expecting this announcement either for his smile did not quite travel all the way to his eyes. David would've expected to be asked for Lucy's hand before any engagement took place – and evidently that had not happened.

'We're delighted for you both, even though it is a bit unexpected, aren't we, Maggie?' he went on. Maggie beamed her approval and Jennifer, staring at Lucy's shining face, decided that she must dissuade her daughter from marrying this man. But now was not the time, nor the place. Her best chance of success would be to speak to Lucy alone. Meantime she would have to keep her reservations to herself. She set down the glass of sickly-sweet punch, got unsteadily to her feet and went over to Oren and Lucy, who were now both standing up.

Mustering as much enthusiasm as she could, and a smile that made her face ache, she said, 'Well, congratulations to you both,' and hugged them.

'What do you think of the ring?' said Lucy, holding out a trembling hand. 'It belonged to Oren's grandmother.'

'Oh, is that a garnet?' said Jennifer, unable to say anything positive about the ugly, dated ring.

'Uh-huh,' said Lucy, and Maggie, examining the brown-red stone, said with her usual diplomacy, 'It's an unusual colour, isn't it?'

'Oh, they come in all colours, apparently,' said Lucy.

Feeling like a fraud, Jennifer averted her eyes while Maggie, unable to find anything complimentary to say about the horrible garnet, enthused instead about the setting of tiny diamond chips.

Brian pumped Oren's hand. 'Congratulations, son,' he said.

Matt gave his big sister a fierce hug, then held her at arms' length. 'That's just great news, so it is, Lucy. I can't quite believe it though. You getting married?'

Lucy laughed and Matt gave Oren a bear hug, while Brian and Maggie stood watching with beaming smiles. Even David seemed to have recovered from the slight of not being asked for his daughter's hand, and chatted happily to Lucy whilst holding both her hands. And the girls were positively ecstatic, arguing already over whether Lucy should have a train and wear a veil.

'Can I be a bridesmaid?' said Rachel. 'I want to wear pink.'

'Me too!' exclaimed Imogen, bouncing up and down on the carpet like a wound-up toy.

Lucy laughed and looked at Oren. 'They can be bridesmaids too, can't they?' she said, a pleading note in her voice. 'As well as your niece? That wouldn't be too ostentatious, would it?'

Oren sucked air in through his teeth and shook his head doubtfully.

Warning bells rang inside Jennifer's head. 'Surely the decision over bridesmaids belongs with the bride and her family?' she heard herself say, the words bursting out of their own volition. 'After all,' said Jennifer, directing her comments entirely at Oren, 'when Lucy gets married, her father will be paying for the wedding.'

Oren didn't even look at Jennifer. He flashed Lucy the briefest of frowns, his lips pressed together like he was holding something back. 'Of course, Lucy. Whatever you want.'

Matt said, with a twinkle in his eye, 'Well, you're a brave man, Oren, taking *her* on.' Oren put his arm round Lucy's waist and Lucy gave Matt a playful, but painful-looking, whack on the arm.

Maggie then clapped her hands softly and her thin voice rose, only just, above the din of everybody competing with each other. 'Food's ready. Let's eat, everyone, before it's spoilt.'

Once everyone had helped themselves to the buffet, they sat on the sofas in the drawing room once more, balancing the plates on their knees. Immense responsibility weighed down on Jennifer. From everyone else's reaction to Oren, it looked as though she was the only one who objected to him. So, it would fall to her, and her alone, to try and dissuade Lucy from this union. She pushed food around her plate and listened, with increasing despair, to the conversation.

'So Matt, how're you getting on at Carnegie's?' said David. 'You know I've booked it for our staff night out?'

'Yeah, Ben told me,' said Matt, shovelling food enthusiastically into his mouth.

'Ben?'

Matt chewed and swallowed. 'Crawford. He runs the place. Owns it too. Isn't that right, Mum?'

Nervously, Jennifer speared a cherry tomato with her fork; an ill-advised move that sent juice squirting over her dress. She dabbed it with the napkin.

'How would your mother know that?' said David.

'Because she did the interior design, Dad,' said Lucy.

'Yes,' said Matt, waving his fork in the air like an old-fashioned cigarette holder. 'But they're seeing each other as well, aren't they?' he went on, as if this was common knowledge and they were all dunces for not knowing it.

All eyes turned to Jennifer. She felt a creeping heat start below her collarbone and work its way up her neck. She closed her eyes briefly, feeling faint, then opened them again. Suddenly there wasn't enough air in the room and her face was aflame with embarrassment.

Matt, realising what he'd done, clapped his hand over his mouth, fork still held between forefinger and thumb. 'Oh, Mum. I'm sorry. It just slipped out.'

She shook her head and attempted to smile. She was annoyed with Matt but the slip had been unintentional. And if she'd not prevaricated about telling everyone, he never would have been placed in the unfair position of having to keep her secret. 'It's okay, Matt. I would've told everyone eventually anyway.' She set her plate on the big footstool, folded her napkin and dropped it on top of the remains of her meal. She adjusted the skirt of her dress, then waited.

'But your mother can't be going out with Ben Crawford,' said Oren. 'He's far too young for her, isn't he?'

Jennifer lifted her head and, in spite of her flaming cheeks, said, with as much poise and disdain as she could manage, 'I am in the room, Oren. And I think you'll find that if you direct your questions to me, I'm perfectly capable of answering them myself.'

In response, he glared at her with unblinking gimlet blue eyes, a look of distaste on his face.

'Well, are you going out with him?' said Lucy, her face a picture of incredulity.

Jennifer took a deep breath. 'Yes, I am as a matter of fact,' she said smoothing down her skirt with the flat of her hand. 'We've been seeing each other for a few weeks.'

'But . . . but . . .' stumbled Oren, for the first time stuck for words. 'That's just plain wrong.'

'How dare you,' said Jennifer, her calm, measured reply concealing the rage beneath.

'Girls, why don't you come and eat at the kitchen table?' squeaked Maggie, standing up and addressing her daughters as if someone had just said something indecent. 'You're getting food on the front of your frock, Rachel.'

214

Rachel looked down at the pristine dress. 'No, I'm not, Mummy.'

'You will, if you're not careful.' Maggie glared at her daughter and David said, 'Do as you're told. Go with your mother.' Immediately, the two girls scampered out of the room, followed by Maggie. When she reached the door she paused to glance back at Jennifer and gave her a small, encouraging smile. Then she was gone, leaving Jennifer feeling like she was in a lion pit.

'Seems to me that Jennifer can go out with whoever she likes, Oren. She's a free woman,' said Brian, throwing her a lifeline. Jennifer shot him a grateful look.

'But Mum,' said Lucy. She hugged the tops of her arms and said in an uncertain horrified whisper, 'He's young enough to be your son.'

'What age is this man?' demanded David.

'Twenty-eight,' said Oren, at the same time as Jennifer said, 'It's none of your business.' Oren and Jennifer locked eyes and glared at each other.

'Oh my goodness, you are cradle snatching, Jennifer!' said David and he slapped his thigh and laughed uproariously for a long time while Jennifer fumed and glared at him.

Eventually Matt said, 'Look Dad, I don't see what the problem is. Older men go out with younger women all the time, so why not the other way round? And I've a lot of time for Ben Crawford.'

'Thank you, Matt,' said Jennifer while David wiped tears of mirth from his eyes.

'The problem is, Matt,' said Oren evenly, in a patronising tone, 'that this relationship is an abomination in the eyes of Our Lord. It's demeaning to your mother, it's inappropriate and she should end it immediately.'

'Don't you tell my Mum what to do!' cried Matt.

'Now steady on,' said Brian.

'And where exactly does it say that in the Bible, Oren?' demanded Jennifer.

In response, he simply shook his head sadly and smirked.

'And that aside,' she went on, 'my private life is none of your damn business.'

'Yes, it is,' said Lucy, blinking back tears and holding tightly on to Oren's arm. 'Oren's part of the family now.'

'Not yet, he isn't,' snapped Jennifer.

'Hey, let's just calm things down a bit, shall we?' said David. Oren leaned back, threw an arm over the back of the sofa, and looked out the window with a scowl.

'Jennifer,' said David, his voice gentle and full of measured reason, 'I know we're divorced, but I do still care about you, you know. And I don't want to see you making a fool of yourself. I mean it's embarrassing, isn't it?' He paused to glance around, looking for support, and gave a little laugh. 'You going out with a man so much younger than yourself. I mean, how on earth can you have anything in common?'

Jennifer inhaled deeply and counted to five. 'I've more in common with him than I ever had with you. And I bitterly resent your attempt at interference in my life, David. You have no right, none whatsoever.'

'She's right, David,' said Brian's quiet but firm voice. 'You've no more right to poke your nose into Jennifer's business, than she has to poke her nose in yours.'

'Time for coffee!' said Maggie's tinny, sing-song voice from the doorway, bringing a welcome shift in the dynamic of the room. She shuffled across the old varnished floor-boards with a big silver tray in her arms.

'Here, let me help you with that,' said Matt, and he got up and relieved Maggie of the heavy tray. Jennifer, with hands shaking uncontrollably, collected the plates and cutlery. A little later, she stood in the kitchen stacking dirty dishes in the dishwasher, while she composed herself. The girls were nowhere to be seen. The faint sound of a blaring TV came from some distant corner of the house, while unintelligible whispers and mumblings drifted in from the drawing room. They would all be talking about her in her absence of course; Matt and Brian defending her, Maggie saying nothing and the rest criticising.

It was utterly humiliating that an independent woman of her age should be subjected to such insults, especially from Oren who was nothing to her and, if she could have her way, never would be. But, though her heart pulsed with anger, it was also full of self-doubt and her face still burned with shame. Was she making a fool of herself in dating Ben? Did people snigger behind her back when they were out together? She feared that their relationship was ultimately doomed. Would he still love her, think her beautiful, when she was sixty-four and he only forty-eight? She stood by the window and put her hand on her belly, as a desperate sadness enveloped her, and her stomach twisted with worry. When she came back into the room, Maggie pressed a cup of coffee into her hand and she took her place on the sofa again, avoiding eye contact with everyone.

'I do so love a wedding,' said Maggie cheerfully, perching on the sofa opposite. Jennifer gave her a grateful smile for the change of subject, even if it was, to her anyway, a painful one. 'So, Oren and Lucy, when's the big day?'

'We were thinking of a Spring wedding,' said Lucy.

'Plenty of time to plan then,' said Maggie, brightly.

'She didn't mean next year,' said Oren flatly.

'What? This Spring?' said Jennifer incredulously, spilling a little coffee into her saucer.

'Yes. We thought May,' said Oren.

'But Lucy has exams in May,' said Jennifer.

'After Lucy's finished her exams, then,' said Oren coldly.

Jennifer looked sharply at Lucy taking in her pale complexion, her nervousness, her lack of eye contact. Good God, was she pregnant? She stared at Lucy's flat belly and felt as if she might throw up. 'But why the rush to get married?' she blurted out. She feared Lucy would live to regret marriage at such a young age – just as she had done.

'There's no rush,' said Oren evenly, fixing her with a steely gaze and, finding Lucy's hand, intertwining his fingers with hers. 'But when two people are as certain as we are,' he said, pausing to smile at Lucy, 'what's the point in waiting?'

'Oh, that's so romantic,' said Maggie dreamily.

'But,' said Jennifer, reddening, 'the timing of the wedding aside, Lucy has another year of uni to complete and you've no means of support. You're a student too, Oren.'

'Your mother does have a point, Lucy,' said David, his common sense kicking in at last. 'It might be wise to wait until you both graduate.'

Oren leaned in towards Lucy and squeezed her hand so tight her knuckles went white. 'We're not going to be students for much longer, are we, Lucy?' She shook her head obediently.

'What?' said David sharply.

Oren eyeballed David and said, 'Lucy and I have been called to join a mission in Peru, David. We'll be working amongst the natives, spreading the Word in places where the Lord's light hasn't shone before.'

'Oh my God,' said Jennifer under her breath. So Lucy wasn't pregnant. The pressure to marry so quickly was coming from Oren – so that he could fulfil some Godly evangelical fantasy.

'Huh? Called by who?' said Matt, who up until now had been sitting quietly, looking bored.

'By the big man, of course,' said Oren cheerfully, 'Him upstairs! We leave at the end of June.'

'What, like, on holiday?' said Matt.

'No. We've signed up for a year. We'll be following the voice of the Holy Spirit into one of Peru's remotest locations. We'll be based out of Nauta and spending a large part of our time travelling up the Amazon to spread the Word.'

'Sounds awesome,' said Matt. 'Can I come visit?'

Jennifer was momentarily speechless. Places like Peru were rife with malaria, yellow fever, typhoid, tuberculosis, cholera, rabies – and God knows what else. And hadn't she heard a brief report on the radio only the other day about ongoing civil unrest in Peru between cocoa farmers and the police? Lucy had never been to a third world country – she had no idea what she was letting herself in for.

'I don't think this is wise,' said David, 'Lucy can't just walk away from her degree course like that.'

Jennifer closed her eyes and said a prayer in thanks. David would put a stop to this nonsense.

'Yes, she can,' said Oren quickly, and Jennifer opened her eyes. 'She can take a year out and pick up where she left off. People do it all the time.'

'But what about you, Oren? You're in the middle of a degree too,' Jennifer pointed out.

'Oh, the college understand the position. In fact, they've been very supportive. They understand that God moves in mysterious ways. There'll be a place for me when we come back.'

'But why not just wait, Oren?' argued David reasonably. 'It's only another year and a half until you both finish university. Wait till Lucy finishes her degree and you finish yours, get married and if you still want to, go to Peru then.'

Oren laughed derisively. 'You make it sound as if this is something about which we have a choice, David.'

'You have to understand that God's called us now, Dad.

219

Together,' said Lucy, gripping Oren's hand. 'And it'd be wrong of us to go against His plan.'

'What if I promised you that Lucy will finish her degree when she comes back, David?' said Oren. 'Would that make you more comfortable?'

'I . . . well . . . I suppose so,' said David, his resolve weakening as Jennifer became increasingly incensed. Why did Oren insist on addressing David alone? Was her opinion, as Lucy's mother, of no account whatsoever?

'But what if something went wrong?' cried Jennifer, appealing to David, Maggie and Brian. 'What if Lucy gets sick? Healthcare in these places is rudimentary at best, and possibly unavailable in the place they're planning to go to. And what if they get caught up in civil unrest? The police and legal systems in these countries are riddled with corruption.'

The colour drained from Lucy's face and Oren actually laughed. 'I think you're being a bit melodramatic, Jennifer. We're going out to an established mission that I've visited before. We'll be there under the auspices of the BMS.'

'The what?' said Matt.

'It used to be called the Baptist Missionary Society but nowadays it goes by the name of BMS World Mission.'

'Well, that's a comfort,' said David. 'It's clear you've given this a great deal of thought.'

Jennifer placed a hand on her heart and found it hard to get the words out, so constricted was her throat in anger. 'You cannot be giving this your sanction, David,' she said, her voice barely above a whisper.

'I know you're worried about Lucy,' said Brian gently. 'We all worry for her. It's only natural.' He beamed at his granddaughter. 'But she's an adult, and if this is what she's set her heart on, well, then you mustn't stand in her way.'

Jennifer glared at her father, angered by his lack of

support, and appealed directly to Lucy. 'You can't be serious about this, Lucy. You told me you never wanted to leave Ballyfergus, let alone Northern Ireland. And now you've suddenly decided to head off to a place you've never been on the other side of the world, where you've no connections, no contacts, no protection.'

'I'll have Oren – and the protection of Our Lord Jesus Christ. That's all I need.'

'Oh, for God's sake,' said Jennifer rolling her eyes. 'Will you please stop talking like some kind of religious fanatic?'

Oren, looking furious, opened his mouth to speak, but David cut across him. 'I know you've never been a religious woman, Jennifer, but the rest of us in this room are.' He looked at Maggie and gave her a grim smile. 'And not only do I believe in what these two young people want to do, I'm proud of them. So, Oren and Lucy,' he said, having finished admonishing Jennifer, 'as far as I'm concerned, you have my blessing.'

Chapter 16

The day before Christmas Eve found Jennifer fidgeting nervously in the kitchen over a lunch of hot smoked salmon and roasted veg. Ben was coming for lunch to meet Dad and Lucy for the first time and Matt would be there too. Jennifer thought Ben and her father would get on just fine. But Lucy was another matter.

Oren had gone down to Enniskillen the day after the engagement announcement, but, over a week later, Jennifer still hadn't plucked up the courage, nor found quite the right moment, to raise the subject of the engagement with Lucy. She spent so much of her time either on the phone to Oren, or locked away in her room, reading scripture. She was almost a stranger to her.

'Mmm, something smells nice,' said Lucy, coming into the kitchen and lifting the lid on a small saucepan of dill sauce.

'Oh there you are. Did you have a lie-in?'

'Nope. I was up early. Reading in my room.'

By now Jennifer knew not to ask 'What?' as, invariably, Lucy's reading material was the Bible itself or some other religious tract. She'd also become very selective in her choice of TV viewing. Soaps, for example, which Lucy had lately judged as too morally lax, were out.

'You will make an effort with Ben, won't you?' said Jennifer, adjusting the thin red belt around the waist of her smart black dress, and regarding Lucy thoughtfully. In old jeans, a shapeless cardigan and worn slippers, she'd made no effort whatsoever with her appearance. 'I think you'd like him, if you gave him a chance.'

Lucy shrugged. 'Of course I'll be civil to him.'

'I want you to be more than civil. I want you to be nice to him.'

Lucy sighed loudly. 'I'll be nice.' She paused and added with a deep frown, 'You're sleeping with him, aren't you?'

Jennifer slipped oven gloves over her hands, and busied herself with trays in the oven so that Lucy could not see her blushes. Matt must've told her, then, about the night he came home and found Ben in her bed. She'd been careful since. Ben hadn't stayed the night again. They had sex only at his place and she always came home to sleep in her own bed.

'You're not denying it then,' persisted Lucy.

Jennifer straightened up, placed her gloved hands on her hips and gave Lucy a steady stare. 'I don't have to explain myself to you or anyone else.'

When Jennifer opened the door to Ben, dressed in jeans and a round-necked navy sweater over a checked shirt, her heart flipped. He grinned cheekily, pressed a bottle of wine into her hands, and kissed her full on the lips. She backed away and ushered him in with a furtive, 'The neighbours'll see you.' He laughed, while the knot in Jennifer's stomach tightened.

In the lounge a fire crackled merrily in the grate and a Christmas tree sparkled in the corner of the room. Brian and Matt greeted Ben warmly but, when he offered his hand to Lucy, she shook it limply and mumbled something unintelligible. She did not offer him her cheek for a kiss, nor did she look him in the eye. Anger jostled with disappointment in Jennifer's belly.

When they were all seated round the kitchen table eating, Ben addressed Lucy directly. 'So, how's your course going? Your Mum tells me you're studying Applied Mathematics and Physics.'

Lucy pushed a piece of salmon round her plate and said, truculently, 'Fine.'

'Not for long though,' remarked Matt, who'd already cleared his plate and was helping himself to seconds. 'Once her and Oren get hitched, they're going out to Peru.' He paused to laugh and shake his head in disbelief. 'Of all places.'

'So I hear,' said Ben quietly with a concerned look at Lucy. 'Are you sure that you'll be safe? I read recently that areas where cocoa is cultivated are particularly dangerous.'

Lucy looked Ben directly in the eye for the first time. 'I know what I'm doing. And with respect, Ben, I really don't think that it's any of your business.'

Ben glanced around uncomfortably and despair filled Jennifer's heart. For the first time in her life Jennifer was ashamed of her daughter.

'No . . . I . . . eh,' stumbled Ben.

'So how are you spending Christmas Day, Ben?' said Brian pleasantly, saving the day.

Ben smiled in relief and went on to explain how he would be having Christmas lunch at Alan and Cassie's. His mother wasn't due back from Barbados until Boxing Day. The conversation revolved round Christmases past and present and, as soon as the meal was cleared away, Jennifer suggested coffee in the lounge. Lucy stood up. 'I'll skip the coffee if you don't mind. I've got a . . . a headache coming on. I'm going to lie down.' And without another word, she left the room.

The next day, Jennifer and Lucy walked Muffin in the crisp and frosty Town Park. Jennifer, whose anger with Lucy had mellowed to a sort of quiet despair, decided she could put off the subject of Oren no longer.

Lucy had stopped walking and turned around to wait for Muffin who was trailing behind them. On the swings in the nearby play-park children squealed, and Jennifer remembered with a pang reading Clement C Moore's 'The Night before Christmas' to the children one particular Christmas Eve. Matt, a fair-haired baby with big brown eyes, had sat on her lap while Lucy, her sandy-coloured hair in a braid down her back like a spine, had knelt on the floor in a pink flannel nightgown, craning to see the illustrations in the book. She remembered how she had paused in her reading, her voice catching in her throat, to give thanks to God for that perfect moment – and for her precious children. And even though she was all grown, there was still something of the innocent about Lucy. That was why Jennifer simply couldn't stand by and watch her ruin her life.

'Come on, boy. Come.' Lucy slapped her thighs to attract Muffin's attention but he continued to sniff at a bush hoary with frost.

Eventually the dog padded up to them, panting, white drool dripping from his mouth, and sat down heavily on the path.

'I thought the walk might be too much for him,' said Jennifer thoughtfully. 'He's really not capable of much more than a stroll over to your Grandpa's.'

They both stood and regarded Muffin thoughtfully. 'Let

him rest for a bit and then we'll walk back to the car,' said Lucy.

Feeling her chance slipping away, Jennifer said, 'Lucy, I've been thinking.' Immediately the air between them crackled with tension.

'What?' said Lucy, bending down to stroke Muffin's long sleek head.

'What do you think of Ben?' said Jennifer, side-stepping the subject of Oren yet again.

'You know what I think of you and Ben,' said Lucy straightening up, but refusing to make eye contact.

'I know what Oren thinks,' said Jennifer.

Lucy sighed. 'I'm quite certain your relationship with him goes against the teachings in the Bible, Mum.'

Jennifer took a deep breath and allowed this ludicrous statement to pass unremarked. If they argued now, they would not get round to the subject of Oren and the preposterous engagement.

Lucy went on, 'Ben seems like an okay guy, but the fact that you and him are dating . . .' She paused to shiver and finally looked Jennifer in the eye. 'Well, I just think it's creepy that you're dating a man the same age as Oren. It makes you look kind of . . . well, predatory.'

'Is it inconceivable to you that Ben and I might actually love each other? And that age is completely irrelevant?' said Jennifer sharply, knowing of course this wasn't true.

'Look, I really don't want to talk about it any more, Mum. Nothing you say is going to make me change my mind. I'd just rather not be around you two when you're together, that's all.'

'Well, that's your prerogative.' Inside the pockets of her padded down coat, Jennifer clenched her fists and the effort to retain her composure made her right eye twitch uncontrollably. Lucy's callous comments hurt her deeply, but reacting now would be counter-productive. At least she was opening up about how she felt. This may be the best opportunity she would get all holiday to talk to her at a meaningful level.

When she could trust herself to speak with equanimity, Jennifer steered the conversation in the direction of her goal. 'So how do Oren's family feel about the engagement?'

'They're delighted, naturally.'

'I see.' A pause. 'And you love Oren?'

Lucy glanced at Jennifer and laughed out of the side of her mouth. 'Of course.' She unclipped a worn brown leather dog lead from around her neck, found the D-ring on Muffin's collar and attached it. 'You don't like him, do you?' she said quietly, ruffling the thick fur on Muffin's neck. 'I can tell.'

Jennifer started. For a few seconds she considered denying it, but then decided to simply avoid answering altogether. 'I don't think he's right for you, Lucy, that's all. I think you behave differently when he's around. You're cowed and subservient. And I hate the way you deferred to him over the issue of bridesmaids.'

'I call it being humble,' said Lucy, glancing at Jennifer with a pitying look. 'Accommodating. And there's nothing wrong with a woman deferring to her man.'

'Yes there is!' cried Jennifer, unable to hide her dismay. 'If your opinion doesn't carry the same value as his, how can it be an equal partnership?'

Lucy laughed and began to walk slowly along the path, Muffin hobbling along behind at a stately pace.

'Of course, a husband and wife are of equal worth before God,' said Lucy, as Jennifer fell in beside her. 'But husbands and wives have different functions. It's the man's God-given responsibility to provide for, protect and lead his family. And it's a wife's responsibility to respect and submit to her husband's authority.'

Jennifer's heart sank. Did Lucy really believe in this out-dated view of marriage? 'Is that what Oren told you?'

'It's in the scriptures, Mum. I don't need Oren to tell me that.'

'What scriptures exactly, Lucy? Because there are many ways to interpret them.'

'Oh, I can't think right now,' said Lucy with a wave of her hand. 'Oren's your man if you want someone to quote chapter and verse.'

'But that's not how marriage should be. A woman shouldn't be submissive to her husband.'

Lucy came to a dead halt, turned to face Jennifer and said nastily, 'What, like your marriage? Look, don't take this the wrong way, but your formula for marital bliss could hardly be described as a success, Mum, could it?'

Muffin sat down on the path between the two women and, detecting the tense atmosphere, flattened his ears against his head.

Jennifer said crossly, 'I married your father too young, Lucy.' She paused and took a deep breath, preparing to reveal details about her marriage that she had only ever admitted to herself. 'If I'm honest with myself, I don't think I loved your Dad. And I don't think he truly loved me. I think he married me out of a sense of duty.'

The words hung between them for a few moments like her steamy breath.

'But it was you that wanted the divorce!'

'That's true. Your Dad was prepared to stick it out for the sake of appearances – and for you and Matt. But he's much happier with Maggie than he ever was with me.'

'But that's not what you told us,' cried Lucy. 'You said that you and Dad fell out of love. You said it happens sometimes.'

Jennifer looked at the ground, unable to meet her daughter's eye.

'Why did you lie?' demanded Lucy.

'How could we tell you the truth when we couldn't own it to ourselves? We both tried so hard to make it work.'

'If you hadn't been pregnant with me you never would've married Dad, would you?'

'Probably not,' said Jennifer, raising her head and looking directly into Lucy's furious face. 'Look,' she said with a heavy sigh, her breath puffing out like smoke. 'The reason I'm telling you this now, Lucy, is that I think you're in danger of making the same mistake. I think you and Oren are in danger of marrying for the wrong reasons.'

Lucy pursed her lips and blinked. 'You don't know anything about us. And we both know that biblical principles are the soundest basis for marriage.'

Muffin whined and Jennifer said sadly, 'Principles don't hold a marriage together when there's no love present.' When Lucy made no response Jennifer went on, tentatively, 'Are you certain Oren loves you, Lucy?'

'Of course he does,' said Lucy irritably. She gave Muffin's lead a little tug and he got to his feet. She headed off in the direction of the car, parked on the Old Glenarm Road.

'For the right reasons?' called Jennifer after her.

Lucy twirled around, and waited for Jennifer to catch up. 'What's that supposed to mean?'

'Does he love you because he thinks you'll make him a good and dutiful Christian wife?'

Lucy nodded, walking slowly again. 'Yes, of course.'

'Or because he worships the ground you walk on? Can he live without you? Does he think you're the most beautiful creature he's ever set eyes on?'

Lucy kicked at a frosted stone on the path with the toe

of her boot and said crossly, 'No one's ever thought that of me. Even in the most favourable light, I could never be called a beauty, now could I?'

A cold chill ran down Jennifer's spine and she stopped walking. She touched Lucy on the arm, bringing the girl to a halt too, and said gently, 'That's simply not true, Lucy. You are striking. Hasn't Oren told you that?'

Lucy blushed and squinted into the distance, as if searching for something on the horizon, her wind-scorched, rose pink cheeks in stark contrast to her pale skin. 'Oren thinks,' she said thoughtfully, continuing to gaze at the view, 'that it's much more important that two people are compatible in their beliefs, values and morals. That's the sound basis for a happy marriage. Not romantic love.'

'Well, yes, they are good principles on which to build a marriage,' said Jennifer, looking up into Lucy's face, which had become resolute once more. 'But every marriage runs into difficulties at some point, and without passion at the outset, without undying love to glue it together, principles on their own aren't enough.'

'You're wrong. A Christian marriage, grounded in faith and a shared love of God, is the perfect breeding ground for compatibility.' Lucy turned her gaze on Jennifer and stared at her for a long time, her eyes filming with tears, and then she seemed to decide something. She cleared her throat. 'Before I met Oren, I hated myself.'

'Oh, Lucy,' said Jennifer, the words of self-loathing ripping her apart. 'Please don't say that.'

'It's true. I was living a lie,' said Lucy, lifting her chin.

'What do you mean?'

'Trying to be something I wasn't. I hate my course and I can barely manage to keep up. I only went to university to please you and Dad. I have no friends there, apart from Amy. I'm only finishing this year to please you and Dad and because Oren seems to think it a good idea. Personally, I couldn't care less if I never go back.' She paused to allow a shell-shocked Jennifer to take this all in. 'Before I met Oren I sat in my room alone every night. I was addicted to online gambling.'

'What?' said Jennifer, reeling from this litany of heart-wrenching revelations. How could she not have noticed that her daughter was so isolated – and so unhappy?

'Yes, that's why I was always short of money.'

'But why didn't you tell me?' said Jennifer, hurt by Lucy's failure to confide and stunned by the guilty realisation that she had failed her. Lucy hadn't felt able to confide in her – or David.

'I knew you wouldn't listen. I did try to tell you that I didn't want to go to university but you and Dad didn't want to know.'

It was true. Lucy had not been keen, but she and David had put that down to nerves. They'd both thought that Lucy, shy and introverted, would benefit from the university environment.

'I'm sorry, Lucy. I'd no idea about any of this,' said Jennifer humbly, leading the way past the old bandstand, bright blue paint peeling from the railings. 'Have you told your Dad?'

Lucy shook her head. 'No. Matt neither. But it doesn't matter now. It's all in the past. I met Oren and my life changed. I let the Lord Jesus Christ into my life and I'll be forever grateful to Oren for that. I owe him so much.'

'And that's why you're going to follow him to Peru? Because you feel you owe him?' said Jennifer carefully, taking a sideways sneak at Lucy. She looked so serious, her brow creased up in a frown like a rumpled sheet.

'No, I'm going because I love him. And because I want to serve God.'

They came out of the park, and turned right up Old Glenarm Road. The car was only fifty yards away. Jennifer took a deep breath. 'Well, maybe taking a year out to do something completely different isn't a bad idea, Lucy. It'll give you a chance to work out what you want to do with your life once you've finished your degree.'

Lucy blinked. 'But I already know what I want to do with the rest of my life,' she said stubbornly. 'I want to spend it with Oren in the service of the Lord.'

'Maybe you could look at something a little less adventurous than Peru,' Jennifer pressed on, determined to make her point, to make Lucy listen. 'I'm sure there are plenty of inner city missions crying out for help in this country.'

'But I don't want to work in an inner city mission!'

Jennifer stepped into the gutter to let an elderly woman trailing a shopping bag on wheels pass. 'And there really isn't any need for the two of you to marry straight away,' she said, mounting the kerb again. 'Not in this day and age. I'd be perfectly happy if you lived together for a bit, you know,' she said reasonably.

Lucy stared at her in astonishment. 'Oren and I would never live in sin.'

They reached the car. 'Please, Lucy,' said Jennifer, slipping the glove off her hand and groping for the car key in her pocket. 'Will you just give what I'm saying some consideration?'

Lucy said coldly, 'Can you open the car please, Mum? Muffin's getting cold.'

Jennifer found the key fob and pressed a button, unlocking the car. 'All I'm saying, Lucy, is finish your degree and if Oren wants to go to Peru, let him. If he loves you, he'll wait for you.'

Lucy opened the back door of the car and Muffin,

exhausted by the walk, hauled himself into the car and curled up immediately in the foot well of the passenger seat. 'I'm going to marry Oren Wilson,' said Lucy, 'whether you like it or not, and I'm going to Peru. And nothing you say or do will stop me.'

Chapter 17

Jennifer sat stiffly at the large round table in the Great Hall at Galgorm House on an ivory damask covered chair. A plum-coloured sash was tied around the back of it like a massive cummerbund and matching ribbon adorned the little nets of silvered sugared almonds that decorated each place setting. A four-foot candelabra, sprouting five ivory candles amid a nest of winter berries and foliage, sat in the middle of the table, partially obscuring her view of the top table where the best man was currently delivering his speech. Ben, gorgeous in a dark navy suit, sky blue shirt and striped tie sat beside her, his left arm thrown casually over the back of her chair and a happy smile on his face.

No detail had been overlooked. Everything about the venue was stunning: the vista of lawn studded with trees, rather like an upmarket golf course; the string quartet that had greeted them on arrival; the beautiful table set in fine linen and silverware. And the five-course meal of salmon, soup, Irish lamb, cheese and pudding had been divine. But Jennifer had struggled to enjoy it.

For one thing, the wedding was not the huge event she'd anticipated – at which she'd imagined she could blend in with the crowd – but a much more intimate affair. She couldn't help but feel that everyone was staring at her and Ben. Diane and Alan were seated at separate tables, yet, in spite of the relatively small size of the party, neither had yet exchanged a word with her. Every time she glanced in the direction of either of them – outside the church; in the reception area where they'd had tea and munched on shortbread while the bridal party had their photographs taken; as they took their seats in the Great Hall – they were engaged in lively conversation with people she didn't know.

When the speech was over Jennifer leaned across, the front of her navy pillbox hat partially obscuring her vision, and whispered to Ben, 'I don't know anyone here apart from your parents. Are you sure Hannah doesn't mind you bringing me? I mean, this must be costing her family an arm and a leg.'

'Of course not. It's the perfect opportunity for you to meet my family. And maybe next year we can spend Christmas Day together.' He patted her reassuringly on the knee and glanced at her wrist. 'The bracelet looks great on you. I knew it would.'

He'd given her the jewellery – a Bulgari eighteen-carat white gold band, embedded with pavé diamonds – for Christmas. The bracelet made her present of copies of her favourite all-time books, tied up in a thick red ribbon, seem mean in comparison. Even though Ben had appeared thrilled, and insisted that he'd never had such a personal, thoughtful gift, she was inclined to think he was just being polite. But as Donna had pointed out, both the wedding invite and the bracelet were signs that Ben was serious about her. And that was what she wanted, wasn't it? Somewhat reassured by this thought, Jennifer smiled bravely and looked around the table. They'd been seated with an assortment of Ben's cousins and their partners and some friends of the bride. Ben knew them all well and they'd made a real effort to include her in the conversation. But Jennifer felt desperately out of place; not one of them had reached their thirtieth birthday.

The girl sitting beside her, in a flowery dress that barely covered her thighs and ballet pumps, looked like she'd just left her teens behind. The other women wore unstructured low-cut dresses with incredibly short hemlines, and plunging cleavages. Apart from her navy pillbox one, not a hat was to be seen at this table – just little feathery fascinators sprouting from the side and tops of heads like expired exotic birds. Jennifer had struggled to find an outfit amongst the sparkly, sequinned party dresses in the shops and had been forced, through lack of choice, to settle for a fitted dress with a sweetheart neckline and long sleeves. She liked the flattering ruching across the stomach area, the just-below-the-knee hemline, and the way it made her chest look bigger and more pert than it was. She wasn't so sure about the colour but Donna assured her that pillar-box red was perfect for a winter wedding. As a nod to current trends, the saleswoman in the shop had persuaded her to go for a pair of nude high heels worn with the sheerest skin-tone tights.

Jennifer looked at the bride sitting at the top table, radiant in a mass of white netting, and bit her lip. 'That could be Lucy sitting at the top table in a few months. If I can't persuade her otherwise.'

Ben's brow furrowed and he shifted uncomfortably in his seat. 'I shouldn't have told you about Oren's schooldays.'

'No,' she said hastily, 'I'm glad you did. It only confirmed what I already thought. I think Oren's latched on to Lucy because she's impressionable. Let's face it, there aren't many women who'd be prepared to chuck in university to follow their man around the world while he evangelises pagans.'

Ben's raised his eyebrows. 'You mean you wouldn't do that for me?'

Jennifer grinned, a little of the tension seeping away, and said grudgingly, 'I suppose there's a certain charisma about him.' She paused. 'Donna says I should go out of my way to befriend him so that, if Lucy marries him, I don't end up estranged from her.'

'Mmm,' said Ben. 'I can see the logic. Why don't you ask the two of them down for a few days? No Matt or Brian or any of the rest of the family. Spend some time together and try to build some bridges.'

'Yeah,' said Jennifer thoughtfully. 'That's a good idea.'

'Oh, there's Auntie Liz,' said Ben, a warm smile spread across his face.

Jennifer watched the well-built woman approach with mounting horror. She was in her late sixties and wore tan tights and sensible black court shoes with a low heel. Her black straw boater hat had a cluster of net and pearls on one side and looked very similar to the type of hat regularly sported by the Queen.

Jennifer had noticed the woman earlier, in the foyer, where everyone had peeled off their coats. She'd turned away quickly and hoped she could manage to avoid her for the rest of the day. For they were wearing exactly the same, bright red dress.

Under normal circumstances, Jennifer would've laughed about the coincidence and even approached the wearer to comment light-heartedly upon it, perhaps taking comfort in the fact that she looked somewhat better in the dress. But today it served only to highlight how big the age gap was between her and the people around the table. None of the young women here today would've chosen such a modest, fitted style. Far from being chic and classy as she'd believed, it was the sort of dress a granny would wear to hide her rounded belly, bingo arms and saggy knees.

Auntie Liz made her way round the table until she came to Ben. She clasped his head in her hands and planted a big, noisy kiss on both cheeks, Italian-style. 'How's my favourite nephew?' she said, grinning. Her face was heavily lined and the leathery skin on her neck and chest spoke of too many holidays abroad in the sun.

'I want you to meet my girlfriend, Jennifer,' said Ben and Jennifer felt herself flush with embarrassment as Auntie Liz sized her up.

'Oh, I see we're wearing the same dress, dear,' she said straight away. She leaned in and gave Jennifer a friendly squeeze on the arm, and chuckled, 'Though I have to say it looks a damn sight better on you than it does on me!'

Jennifer smiled weakly, grateful for her kindness. Aunty Liz moved away, and Ben went off to the gents, leaving her alone at the table. The people on either side of her had disappeared.

'Well, this is a surprise, Jennifer,' said a woman's voice and Jennifer turned around to find Ben's mother standing behind her holding a glass of champagne in her hand and looking utterly beautiful. She wore a long, elegant, pale blue coat dress, the sleeves encrusted with embroidery and baby blue, pearlised beads. On her head she sported an enormous ivory wide-brimmed hat. Of course, she had the looks and the height to carry off such a stunning piece of headgear.

She slipped into the seat just vacated by Ben and crossed her long, slim legs. 'Well, we were all dying to find out the secret of Ben's mystery guest.' She turned her cold, green-eyed gaze on Jennifer, as clear and unblinking as a cat. 'And imagine our surprise when it turned out to be you.' She smiled and then said abruptly, 'How's business these days?'

'Excuse me?'

'Oh, it's just that I was thinking interior design must be a bit like the restaurant trade. A mad rush in the run-up to the festive season and then dead. Nobody wants to spend money come January.' Diane clinked the rim of her champagne glass with the hardened tips of perfectly French-manicured nails.

'Well, not really,' said Jennifer, with an awful sinking feeling in her stomach. 'I get Christmas and the New Year off.' Why was Diane asking her about business? Why weren't they admiring the bride's elegant ivory gown? Or passing judgement perhaps on the guests' outfits?

'Of course,' said Diane, as if she hadn't heard Jennifer. 'In Ben's case, what he earns is more or less irrelevant.' She paused to smile and wave at the father of the groom, in tails, on the other side of the room. As soon as he broke eye contact, the smile fell from her face. 'It's what he's set to inherit that will make him a rich man.'

Jennifer stared at Diane in astonishment, the penny finally dropping. Diane thought she was after Ben's money! She hadn't come to talk out of friendship, or even politeness, after all. She'd come to deliver a message. The muscles in Jennifer's left jaw twitched and she pressed her teeth together until they hurt, the hot, hard lump in her throat making it impossible for her to speak.

Diane blinked, then opened her eyes wide in a startled expression. 'Oh,' she said dramatically, a flattened hand hovering over her heart, being careful not to actually touch the dress lest she mark it. 'Of course, I didn't mean to suggest that *you* were after the Crawford fortune,' she said earnestly. 'Like me, you're used to being independent and supporting yourself. But doing it for yourself can be a lonely existence. I've got to hand it to you, Jennifer,' she said, her voice full of anything but admiration. 'What better way to dispel the loneliness than a short-term fling with a younger man? And why not? I might even try it myself.' She laughed out loud at this notion.

Jennifer looked desperately around the rapidly emptying room as everyone made their way slowly to the bar or up to their rooms to rest before the evening entertainment. She squirmed in her seat, damp sweat forming under her arms, anxious to escape Diane and her offensive insinuations. Where the hell was Ben?

'Isn't this a lovely venue?' said Diane, suddenly changing direction like a speedboat, leaving Jennifer confused and disorientated in her wake. 'Though, of course, when Ben gets married he'll have a much bigger wedding. Alan will insist on it. After all he is our only son. Oh, I do hope he meets the right girl soon.'

'Oh, hello darling,' cried Diane in an affected voice and Jennifer looked up to find Alan standing there. He gave her a curt nod and Diane stood up. 'I know Alan's dying to talk to you, Jennifer,' she said, placing a hand like a restraint on Jennifer's shoulder. 'Why don't you two sit down and have a little chat?' Diane removed her hand and Jennifer looked quickly from left to right, trying to conjure up a means of escape. She opened her mouth to excuse herself to go to the ladies', but Diane said, 'I'll go powder my nose,' and Jennifer's escape route was blocked.

Very deliberately Alan pulled Ben's chair around and sat down, so that they weren't sitting beside each other but facing in opposite directions, like a lovers' seat. Bracing herself, Jennifer sat back in her chair and took a deep breath, the smell of expensive aftershave filling her nostrils.

They were both stubbornly silent for a few moments. Eventually, Jennifer peeked at Alan and was astonished to see a single tear fall freely down the man's ruddy cheek. Making no effort to brush it away, he stared straight ahead. He looked as she had never imagined Alan

240

Crawford could: vulnerable, weak, broken. And her heart went out to him.

'Everyone expected Ricky to take over the business one day,' he said, still staring straight ahead, as if talking to thin air. 'I was training him for it. He was hungry for success.' His face lit up with a brief, radiant moment of happiness, then it was gone, like an extinguished candle.

Jennifer looked away, unable to bear the man's grief. 'I'm sure you can imagine what it's like to lose a child.'

'I think so,' she said softly, full of pity for the man, but wondering why on earth he was sharing this highly personal information with her?

Alan sighed, took a white hankie out of his pocket, patted his cheek and put the hankie away. At the entrance to the function room, Jennifer saw Diane accost Ben, who was coming back into the room. She whispered something in his ear, took him by the arm, and dragged him away. Jennifer's heart sank.

'Ben is all I have left,' went on Alan, the softness in his voice slowly giving way to something a little more steely. 'Everything I have will be his one day and then his son's and then his son's after that.' He paused, giving plenty of time for the implications of this statement to sink in. Jennifer's breathing grew shallow and she suddenly felt sick and light-headed.

'So you see, Jennifer,' he said and she knew that he was looking at her, but she could not meet his eye. 'I've nothing against you personally, dear, but you are forty-four years old. You are never going to provide Ben with a son, are you?'

Jennifer shook her head. That part of her life was over. She could not do it again, not even for Ben, who fund-raised endlessly for children and never missed an opportunity to spoil Jason's little daughter. She'd found out through Matt

241

that Ben had bought the child a massive rocking horse for Christmas.

'You seem to have some sort of hold over him.'

Finding reserves of strength she did not know she had, Jennifer looked him squarely in the eye. Ignoring the storm raging in her stomach, she said evenly, 'I think they call it love, Alan.'

He looked away and sniffed dismissively. 'In my experience, romantic love is highly overrated.' He shifted in his seat, leaned forward and cradled his hands in one another. 'Ben thinks he's in love and you're having a good time together and, hey, there's nothing wrong with that.' Alan raised his palms in the air to demonstrate his open-minded acceptance of the affair, diamonds winking on the cuffs of his shirt. Jennifer's face burned as he ploughed on, clasping his hands together tightly. 'But you must see that it would be morally wrong to deny a young man like Ben the chance of having a family of his own. Of experiencing the joy of fatherhood. And as for Diane and I, well, he's our only hope of ever having grandchildren, Jennifer. Without an heir, all my life's work will have been for nothing. And Ricky's death will have been in vain.'

Jennifer could not speak. He was wrong on so many levels. He was wrong to load all his expectations onto Ben's shoulders; to hijack his life like that. He was wrong to interfere in her relationship with Ben. And Diane was completely wrong about the money.

And yet he had a point. She'd had her crack at family life, at raising kids. Motherhood had brought her the greatest joy she'd ever known, an enduring satisfaction and happiness that did indeed transcend romantic love. If Ben chose her, he would never experience the joy of holding a child of his own in his arms for the very first time – the moment when you were changed forever. Could she deny him this utter sense of fulfilment, of completion? And if she did, the time might come when he would resent her for it.

'The longer your relationship with Ben goes on, the harder it'll be to end. It doesn't have a future, Jennifer.'

'If it's not going to last, then you have nothing to worry about, Alan, do you?' she said icily, rising at last to her feet, the spell of pity finally broken. Alan's eyes narrowed, and he opened his mouth to speak. But it was Ben's voice that arrested them both.

'Sorry, I got held up, Jennifer,' he said, coming up to the table briskly. 'So many people to talk to – and all wanting to know who you were! I must introduce you.'

Jennifer smiled weakly, emotionally drained by the awful truth of what Alan had said. Ben paused, his hands frozen in mid-rub and looked from Jennifer to Alan. 'What have you two been talking about?'

'Just chatting.' Alan leapt to his feet. 'Now, I must go and find Cassie. You two have a good time.' He placed a hand on Ben's shoulder momentarily – proprietorially, Jennifer thought – then walked off.

Jennifer looked up at Ben's open, honest face and smiled wearily. Ben loved her, of that she was certain, but had he given their future together any serious consideration? The menopause was already knocking on her door – her periods were becoming increasingly erratic in frequency. In a few years' time, her looks would go and she would, eventually, lose the battle with her midriff. When that time came, when she was old and completely barren, would he still love her? No matter how much she loved Ben, Jennifer couldn't see a future for them. She could not give him what he so richly deserved. She ought to let him go.

'What're you thinking, my darling?' he said.

'I was just thinking that you're so very different from

243

both your parents,' said Jennifer, wondering how on earth two devious, manipulative individuals like Alan and Diane had managed to create someone so thoroughly decent.

'Look, I'm really sorry to have to do this, Ben, but I have the most awful headache. I'm afraid I'm going to have to ask you to take me home.'

Chapter 18

'What the hell did you say to her?' demanded Ben, as soon as his father walked into the enormous drawing room of his rural home in Dundonald, on the south-eastern fringes of Belfast city. He'd built the modern mansion for himself and Cassie when they'd married four years ago. Ben thought the house, with its glass walls and minimalistic décor in neutral tones (without a single splash of colour to relieve the monotony) was cold and unwelcoming. A bit like Cassie.

'I don't know what you're talking about.' Alan, who'd just come in and was still wearing his outdoor wool coat over a suit, had kicked off his shoes at the door. He shrugged off the wet coat, raindrops glistening on the shoulders like jewels, and threw it carelessly over a black leather sofa with chrome legs.

Cassie, with hair like Dolly Parton and a chest to match, teetered in after him (she always wore heels), draped in a floor-length black jersey dress and a flowing grey cashmere cardigan. Ben acknowledged her presence with a nod. Ever since Alan's sixtieth two years ago, when Cassie had thrown a huge surprise birthday party to which she'd invited half of Northern Ireland, but not Ben, they'd both dropped the pretence of being friends.

'I'll have a large one,' said Alan gruffly, falling heavily onto the sofa, his pot belly straining against the buttons of his shirt. Wearily, he lifted his feet onto the glass coffee table and placed his hands, palms down, on the cool leather. Cassie went over to the curved glass and chrome bar, lifted the lid on the beaten metal ice bucket and stood with tongs poised like a dagger over the ice. 'Can I get you a drink, Ben?'

'No thanks.' Ben sat down on the matching sofa placed at a right angle to the one Alan occupied, and tried to calm himself by staring at the view beyond the floor-to-ceiling triple-glazed window. The sodden green pastureland of County Down rolled away from the house like waves and sheep dotted the smudged landscape like daubs of white paint in the distance.

Something had happened between Alan and Jennifer at the wedding. He was sure of it. In the car on the drive back to Ballyfergus Jennifer had been withdrawn and reticent and, two days later, he'd only just managed to persuade her to see him. He was planning to go over to her house, tonight, on New Year's Eve, after he'd finished at the restaurant. He'd wanted to spend the whole evening with her – they'd been invited to a party at Donna's house – but of course he had to work. He hated the intrusion Carnegie's made into his private life. He couldn't even spend New Year's Eve proper with the woman he loved. But he planned to make it up to her. Nestled deep in the pocket of his navy corduroy jacket was a Bulgari ring he'd just picked up from the premier jewellers, Lunn's, in Belfast. The ring matched the bracelet he'd given her for Christmas and, on Valentine's Day, he planned to complete the set with the matching necklace.

He'd given girlfriends expensive things before – he had little need of money himself and it gave him great pleasure to spend on other people. But never before had a woman

246

been so surprised, so wowed by a gift as Jennifer had been with the bracelet. He couldn't wait to see her face when she saw the ring, because never before had he wanted to please a woman so much. But first, he had to deal with his father. He would not permit him to upset his beloved Jennifer.

Cassie clip-clopped her way across the specially imported maple wood floor, and handed Alan a crystal tumbler of straight whiskey. Then she scooped up Alan's coat and retreated from the room.

'When I left the table at the reception,' said Ben evenly, 'Jennifer was perfectly happy. When I came back fifteen minutes later she was suddenly unwell and wanted to go home. I can't help but think that your conversation might have had something to do with that.' He gave his father a hard stare and folded his arms across his chest. 'Why do you not like her?'

'I don't dislike Jennifer,' said Alan, his gaze sliding off to the left. 'Quite the contrary. She's a very pleasant, attractive lady.' He brought his gaze back to Ben and smiled. 'I wouldn't say no to a roll in the hay with her myself.'

Ben stiffened and Alan said, quickly, 'Relax, I'm only teasing.' The smirk fell from his face, and he stared into his drink for a few moments, then turned his grey eyes, as hard and cold as his surroundings, on Ben. 'Tell me, is she just a passing fancy, Ben? Or something more serious?'

'I love her,' Ben said easily.

'That's what I feared,' said Alan with a grave expression, swirling the amber-coloured whiskey round in the glass. 'Let me ask you something. Who's going to take over the business, Ben, if you don't produce an heir?'

'Are you trying to tell me who I can and cannot date on the basis of fertility?' said Ben incredulously.

'You can date whoever you like, Ben. Just don't marry a woman too old to give you a family.'

'I'll marry who I damn well like,' said Ben, standing up and walking over to the window. Cold spits of rain splattered the glass. His heart was pumping fast now, like this morning when he'd upped his pace on the run out to Ballygally and back along the coast road. Alan had told him what to do all his life. But this was one step too far. He shoved his shaking hands deep into his pockets and tried to retain his composure.

'I didn't realise that I wanted children either, Ben,' said Alan, his voice softening. 'But when Ricky came along, and later you, I was glad. Children . . .' said Alan, stumbling a little over the sentiment, 'Well, they complete you. That's the only way I can think of to describe it.' He laughed lightly. 'You're the man of words, not me.'

Ben turned around. There was no smile on Alan's face and a deep frown creased his brow as he dug deep for words. 'You and Ricky gave my life a meaning it didn't have before. And I've never loved anyone before, or since, as much as I loved you two.'

A lump formed in Ben's throat. He swallowed and looked at the floor, both moved and embarrassed by his father's extraordinary confession. Though he had never doubted his father's love, he could count on the fingers of one hand, the number of times he'd expressed it openly.

Alan's expression hardened. 'If you continue with this relationship, if you marry her, Ben, I'll have to reconsider my position.'

Ben looked up sharply. The old Alan was back – heartless, cold, mercenary. A man not used to being thwarted.

'I'll write you out of the will, Ben.'

Ben laughed, hating his father with the same force that he loved him. 'When you say things like that, Dad, it just reinforces how different we are. How little you understand me.'

'I mean it,' said Alan, grimly.

Ben laughed again. 'I know you do. That's what's so sad about it.' He paused and held his father's unflinching gaze, glad that he was standing and Alan sitting. It made his father seem less threatening. 'Do you actually think a threat like that will stop me seeing Jennifer?'

'It'll make you think twice about it,' said Alan confidently.

Ben shook his head. 'You just don't see, do you? I don't care about the money, I don't give a damn about Crawford Holdings. It can be broken up. Sold. And I don't care if I never see a penny of it.'

Alan's face paled. 'You don't mean that.'

'Yes I do,' said Ben, unable to prevent his voice rising, glad to see that he had, at last, unsettled his father. He had never stood up to him like this before. He had never had the strength. Alan rose to his feet. 'If he was still alive, your brother would've been glad to be in your shoes. You're selfish and ungrateful!'

'Me?' said Ben and he stabbed his chest with his index finger, choking over the words, his throat constricted with emotion. 'I'm selfish? I sacrificed my future – my dream of becoming a teacher – to please you. Every day I drag myself to a job I hate, trying to fill Ricky's shoes. Trying to be the son you want me to be. And not the one I am.'

Alan shook his head, his face puce with rage. He marched over to Ben and stood in front of him looking up, a solid, squat ball of fury. 'It's taken me my entire life to build the business up from nothing,' he spat into Ben's face. 'I won't stand for strangers taking it over. I won't let you break it up.'

'Then find someone else to leave it to, Dad,' said Ben quietly. 'I don't want any part of it. And I won't let you use it to blackmail me either.'

Alan stood there in his socks, his hands clenched tightly

by his sides, like a furious soldier under parade ground inspection. And Ben, his own anger spent, felt suddenly sorry for him. His voice softened. 'The things I want in life don't cost money. And your money comes with too many strings attached.'

Alan blinked and his bottom lip quivered slightly. 'You don't know what you're talking about, son. You've never known hunger.' He pressed a clenched fist to his stomach. 'You don't know what it feels like, gnawing at your insides like a rat. You've never walked five miles along snowy country lanes to school carrying your shoes so as not to wear them out, or had to hide when the rent man came calling.'

'I know. And I'm grateful for the life you've given me,' said Ben humbly. 'But I'm not Ricky, Dad,' he said quietly. 'And I'm sorry, but I never will be.'

When Ben finally pulled up at Jennifer's house one and a half hours into the crisp, freezing cold New Year, he breathed a sigh of relief. Jennifer's car was in the drive and the light in the lounge was still on. He hoped Lucy wasn't there. The girl was hard going, bordering on the downright rude. So unlike her brother Matt whom he'd left behind at Carnegie's celebrating the New Year with his work colleagues and the half-dozen bottles of Moët et Chandon champagne Ben had given the staff. There would be a few sore heads in the morning.

The encounter with his father had left him emotionally drained. He wanted nothing more than to hold Jennifer in his arms; to feel her, taste her, to know that she loved him. She gave his life a purpose that it had not had before.

The door was unlocked and he slipped in quietly, clutching a chilled bottle of Bollinger by the neck. The ring he planned to give Jennifer burned a hole in his pocket. He couldn't wait to see her face when he gave it to her. Inside, she was waiting for him in the lounge, still in a sparkly party dress and heels, sitting cross-legged and cross-armed on the sofa. The lights were burning a little too brightly and he was disappointed to see that there was no fire in the grate and no candles lit as he'd imagined. But no matter, it was late. She stood up and he went over and set the champagne on the coffee table. Then he gathered her to him, pressing her against his body, loving the way she felt small and vulnerable in his arms. He kissed the top of her head – her hair smelt faintly of coconut and fruit – and tipped her chin up with his index finger.

'Happy New Year,' he smiled.

'Happy New Year,' she said, and he kissed her on the mouth – but there was something a little perfunctory about the way she returned his kiss. Gently she pulled away.

She stifled a yawn and said, 'I'm tired. You must be exhausted, working so late.'

But he didn't feel it. He felt as if he could stay awake all night just looking at her, drinking her in, marvelling at the fact that she was with him. 'Shall we just go to bed, then? We can have a mother of a lie-in in the morning and have the champagne tomorrow night.'

She hesitated and looked at the ceiling. 'I'm not sure you should stay the night,' she said, and he imagined Lucy in the room above them, curled up in bed with her disapproval and old-time morals.

'We shouldn't have to sneak around Lucy, acting as if we're doing something wrong,' he said, unable to stop himself.

'Lucy's not here,' she said flatly, going over to the sofa and sitting down. He stood stupidly for a few moments. 'So,' he said at last, sounding thick and slow, 'you don't want me to spend the night?'

251

She looked him straight in the face then, her miserable expression sending deep waves of fear through him. Immediately he went over and sat down beside her. 'What's wrong? Have I done something to upset you?' He racked his brain but he couldn't think what.

'No, it's not that,' she said with a heavy sigh and looked away once more, sliding her cool, dry hands gently out of his grasp and laying them on her lap. 'I've been thinking of something your father said to me at the wedding.'

'I knew it! I knew he was trying to poison your mind against us.'

Jennifer looked at him sadly. 'But your father's right, Ben. The business is your birthright. You can't turn your back on it because of me. You can't let your family down like that.'

'I'm not turning my back on anyone! He's the one forcing me to make a choice.' He paused and glared angrily at Jennifer, annoyed with both of them – Alan for injecting poison into his relationship with her, Jennifer for apparently allowing him to succeed. 'I thought you'd be pleased,' he said, hating the sullen, resentful way he sounded. 'I thought you'd be proud that I put you first, above fortune and family.'

She gave him a small, sad smile. 'I'm not sure you truly realise what choosing me means. It would mean sacrificing more than money, Ben. And you should never underestimate the importance of family. Sometimes, family is all you have.'

'Jennifer,' said Ben, becoming a little exasperated, 'what on earth are you talking about?'

'You love kids, Ben. Look at the amount you raised for the children's hospital.'

'That's because of Emily.'

'And Glenvale. And I've seen you with Emily, that day Jason's wife brought her into the restaurant and I happened to be there.'

'So?'

'You'd make a great father, Ben.' A pause. She lowered her head. 'And I can't make you into one.'

Ben snorted. 'He's really got to you, hasn't he?'

Jennifer lifted her chin and sniffed. 'It's only natural to expect grandchildren one day. Everyone does . . .' She blinked at him, her eyes full of tears. 'I can't be responsible for you doing something I think you will one day come to regret. And I can't watch you become estranged from your parents because of me. They've lost one son already.'

'But that's my decision to make, Jennifer, not yours,' he said, his voice hoarse with the awful realisation that he was losing her.

His words seemed to fall on deaf ears for she simply shook her head. 'You're wrong about your father, Ben,' she said softly. 'We did talk about these things at the wedding reception, yes, but that wasn't the first time they'd crossed my mind. I've had . . . doubts, and though I love you, Ben, with all my heart . . . I can't honestly see a long-term future for us. I'd –'

'Don't say it!' He raised a hand in the air as if he might parry her words with it like a tennis racquet.

But she pressed on regardless, relentless, as if she'd had this speech rehearsed all along. 'I'd rather end it now before we get any more involved.'

His hand dropped to his side, brushing the bulge in his pocket where the Bulgari ring lay, a reproach to his folly, his belief that love could, and would, conquer all. 'You don't love me?'

'Of course I love you, Ben,' she said, the tears spilling over at last and running down her cheeks. 'But I'm ending it, Ben. It's over,' she said, with cold finality.

'No, you can't do this to us,' he said, as a terrible weight pressed down on his chest, making it hard to breathe, hard to think clearly. It was impossible. It was wrong. He came and knelt in front of her on the floor, and put a hand on her shoulder. 'You can't let him win, Jennifer. This is exactly what he wants to happen.'

But she turned her head away and lifted her shoulder, shrugging his hand off as if she couldn't bear his touch. 'It's not just your father, Ben. It's everyone. Everywhere I go I feel as if we're out of place. Like at the wedding. The people around the table were your peers, Ben, but most of them were half my age.'

'You're exaggerating.'

'I felt conspicuous and uncomfortable. I felt as if everybody was talking about us.'

'So you're letting what other people think break us up.'

'No,' she said, and she turned her red-rimmed eyes on him. 'Not what other people think.' She paused, gulped back tears and dropped her gaze. And when she spoke again her words were barely audible. 'It's what I think. I don't want you to look back one day and regret not having family. Or look at me one day and wonder how on earth you ended up with an old woman on your arm.'

He stood up then and stared down at the top of her head while she sniffed quietly into a tissue she'd conjured from somewhere. And his compassion turned to bitter disappointment.

'When I first met you, I thought you were like no woman I'd ever known. Independent, self-possessed, self-sufficient. I loved the way you weren't at all impressed by money or status. You accepted me for who I am and I loved you for that.'

She looked up at him with dark eyes like bottomless pools of grief, but her wretched gaze, even though it tore at his heart, did not soften his anger. 'But you're not what I thought you were, Jennifer. You're weak.'

She flinched as if he'd struck her.

'I'd have given up everything for you, Jennifer, and I still would. If only you had believed in us enough.'

'Oh Ben, it's not like that.'

But he would not listen to her excuses. 'You talk to me like I'm a fool who doesn't know his own mind, second guessing what I *might* one day want, or regret.' He moved away and stood with his back to her, trembling with sorrow and rage. 'Has it occurred to you that I have thought long and hard about us? That I actually might not want children of my own and that I thought like that long before I met you?'

There was silence broken only by the sound of his blood pounding in his ears.

'I've spent the last seven years trying to please my father. A difficult enough task.'

He paused again to allow a wave of grief to wash over him, so strong he could not speak for some moments. 'But pleasing you has proved absolutely impossible.'

Chapter 19

Upstairs, Jennifer flicked open a fitted white sheet and stretched it over the single mattress in Matt's old room. When she was done making the bed, she sat down on it and stared out the window at the washed-out blue February sky. It was the colour of the pastel blue shirt Ben had worn the night they'd gone for an Indian after the Ballyfergus Small Business Association meeting. An evening she now thought of as their first date. How long ago was that? Only a matter of months, yet it felt like a lifetime. So much had happened – and so much had gone wrong.

She smoothed the surface of the red and white striped duvet, exhausted by the exertion of preparing the room, now spick and span, for Oren's stay. Not that the task was especially onerous but, since New Year's Eve a month ago, a sense of hopelessness had settled on her shoulders like the weight of the world. Her life, rattling around this empty house alone, terrified her. A life of unremitting loneliness, work and duty, punctuated with fleeting interludes of companionship in the form of family and friends – and her beloved Muffin. There was no soulmate, no one to share the little highs and lows that defined a life, no one to wake up with in the morning or drift off to sleep with at night. She would not look for that again because no man would ever be able to live up to Ben. Her quest for love was over.

Sadness consumed her like a fever, leaving her dried up, parched. She was barely able to get out of bed in the morning. The simplest of tasks, like cooking a meal or making a cup of tea, required such focus and concentration they left her exhausted. She'd spent the last two days in her pyjamas with a constant headache that pressed against the back of her eyes like her brain was suddenly too big for her head.

She ran her hand through sticky, unwashed hair and thought of what Ben had said on New Year's Eve. He'd been angry but he was wrong. She wasn't weak. Giving him up was the greatest sacrifice of her life, requiring every ounce of strength she had within her. She'd tried to do the right thing by him and by his family, though Ben did not see it that way. Not now. But he would one day – and he would be grateful.

So even though it didn't feel like it, she told herself she'd done the right thing. And not just by Ben, but by herself too. Try as she might, she just couldn't picture a long-term future for them. Like Alan said, one day he'd leave her. And she couldn't bear to live with that threat hanging over her.

She looked at her watch and sighed. Oren and Lucy would be here in a few hours and she had so much to do. Wearily, she rose from the bed and went and stood under a hot shower. When it came to selecting an outfit, she reached automatically for her favourite jeans then remembered Oren's views on such constrictive clothing, so settled for a sombre, grey wool dress instead. And she just remembered to don the necklace Lucy and Oren had bought her for Christmas. She liked the stylish wood and bead necklace well enough but hadn't quite got used to the idea of exchanging gifts with Oren. She'd bought him a pair of socks, terribly unimaginative, but what did you buy a man whose only hobby appeared to be God?

Downstairs, she set the fire for later, and in the kitchen, put a ready-made chicken pie in the oven under the watchful eye of Muffin who, picking up on her mood, lay in his basket with his ears flattened against his head, and his chin on his paws.

Setting the table for lunch, she paused, clutching a sheaf of cutlery in her hand, and practised a welcoming smile that felt like a mask. Suddenly the phone rang, making her jump.

'How are you, pet?' Donna's voice was so full of concern that Jennifer's eyes welled up with tears. She blinked them back.

'I'm okay. Oren and Lucy should be here in about an hour.'

'Are you sure you don't want me to come over for moral support? I can be there in five minutes.'

Donna's kindness made Jennifer feel weepy again but she fought back the tears. 'No, it's okay. This is something I have to do by myself.'

'Good luck, pet. Ring me later,' said Donna and she hung up.

Jennifer stood with the phone pressed against her chest. Her heart felt like it had been spliced in two, but she would talk and act the way she always did, even though she felt scraped out inside, like the pumpkins Matt and Lucy used to hollow out with spoons at Halloween.

'Did you make this?' said Lucy, poking at the pastry on the pie suspiciously with her fork. 'It tastes different.'

Jennifer smiled weakly, worn out with the effort of keeping up appearances; of looking interested while Lucy chattered on about the details of the wedding; and trying so hard to like Lucy's big, brooding fiancé. 'It's from the supermarket. I didn't have time to cook.'

'That's not like you,' said Lucy with a frown.

Jennifer shrugged, the heat in the kitchen making her dozy. Her eyes were gritty with tiredness – she'd slept badly this last month and was constantly exhausted. 'Nothing tastes as good as homemade,' said Oren with authority, his elbows on the table and his shirt sleeves rolled up like he was about to go milk a cow. 'My mother always says shop-bought pastry tastes like cardboard.'

Jennifer smiled thinly. 'What an interesting observation.'

'Dad's booked The Marine for the reception,' blurted out Lucy with a furtive glance at Jennifer, while Oren speared a baby potato with his fork.

'Great,' said Jennifer, trying to inject some enthusiasm into her voice.

'And I was thinking that I might pick up a dress in the sales.'

'Make sure you get something suitable now,' warned Oren and Jennifer paired her cutlery noisily on the plate, her appetite vanished.

'Oh, don't worry,' said Lucy, patting the back of his big hairy hand, 'I'll get something white and traditional. Would you help me choose, Mum?'

'The dress. Why yes, of course,' said Jennifer colouring, realising that she, as the bride's mother, ought to have proposed this idea. 'We'll make a day of it,' she said, deciding to step up to the plate no matter what her reservations about this union. 'And have lunch out somewhere nice in Belfast. In fact, why don't we make a weekend of it and go to Dublin? Maybe Amy would like to come too?'

Lucy grinned excitedly and Oren said, 'Is such extravagance necessary?'

The smile fell from Lucy's face and she bowed her head.

'I'm buying the dress,' said Jennifer flatly, throwing the snap decision down on the table like a gauntlet.

Oren shrugged and Lucy glanced anxiously from her mother to Oren, reminding Jennifer of her earlier resolve to try and build bridges. She blinked and took a deep breath. 'Is there anything in particular you fancy doing while you're in Ballyfergus, Oren?' she said pleasantly. 'I thought you would like to meet some of Lucy's relatives. Maybe we could take a run over to Ballymena to meet my brother and his wife.'

'Sure,' said Oren wolfing down a big forkful of pie like he hadn't seen food in days. So much for his aversion to shop-bought food. He sniffed and rubbed his nose and Jennifer looked away, repulsed by his crude manners.

'Maybe I'll walk Muffin over to Grandpa's this afternoon,' said Lucy and Muffin, asleep in his basket, stirred at the sound of his name.

'He'd like that. He hasn't been out today.' She glanced out the window at the grey snow clouds gathering, boiling up on the horizon. 'Wrap up warm. Snow's forecasted for later.'

'I'll come with you,' said Oren, filling Jennifer with relief. Maybe Brian would offer them tea and they'd stay most of the evening.

'We'd better go soon then,' said Lucy. 'It gets dark so early.'

'I'll stay here if you don't mind. I've fallen behind with . . . er . . . my paperwork,' said Jennifer, as Lucy stood up. 'I could do with a couple of hours to catch up.'

Oren pushed his scraped-clean plate into the middle of the table. 'That was delicious.'

'Even if it was shop-bought?' she smiled, offering the joke as an olive branch.

He grinned and looked almost handsome. 'Yes. Even if it was shop-bought.'

They all laughed and harmony was once more restored.

Oren was hard work, there was no doubt about it, but this little exchange heartened Jennifer. It proved that she and Oren could find common ground, a way to get along. They may have little in the way of shared values but they could share humour at least.

Lucy stood up and went and got Muffin's worn lead from the brass hook by the back door. 'Come on, Muffin. Let's take you for a walk.'

Oren pushed back his chair with a screech and stood up, filling the room with his big frame. 'On second thoughts,' he said with a hand on his stomach, 'I might give the walk a miss.'

'What's wrong, sweetheart?' said Lucy, going over to him and putting both arms round his waist. 'Are you feeling unwell?'

He moved his hand from his stomach to his head. 'Just a bit tired, that's all.' He yawned and stretched both arms over his head, touching the ceiling with his fingertips. 'Do you mind if I give the walk a miss? I might have a nap.' His arms fell to his sides and he rolled his shoulders as if he'd been sitting too long at a computer screen. 'Tell your Grandpa I'll pop in and see him before we go.'

'Okay,' said Lucy, shrugging on her coat. 'I'll not be long.' She gave Oren a kiss on the cheek and led Muffin out the back door into the bitterly cold afternoon.

As soon as she'd gone, Oren said brightly, 'I'll get the bags out of the car then, shall I?'

'Sure,' said Jennifer. She dried her hands on a towel and watched him walk up the hall with a spring in his step. He went out and the front door banged behind him.

Moments later he was back, standing at the bottom of the stairs with a grip bag held lightly in each hand. 'Where shall I put them?'

Jennifer walked up the hall, rubbing hand cream into the

dry, cracked skin between her fingers. She would have to start wearing the Marigolds that lay unused in the cupboard under the sink. 'Just leave them at the bottom of the stairs for now. We can take them up later.'

'Why don't I just take them now? Save doing it later, eh?' he smiled. He put his right foot on the bottom stair and she noticed he'd taken off his brogues in preparation for ascending the staircase. The toe of the pale beige sock on his right foot was almost worn through and his discarded shoes were lying by the front door. It was good that he felt relaxed enough in her home to kick off his shoes – wasn't it?

She looked up the stairs, the landing at the top shrouded in darkness, and said slowly, 'Well, okay, if you insist.'

'Mmm, what's that lovely smell?' He leaned over, too close, and Jennifer backed away.

'Just hand cream. Gardenia,' she said briskly, avoiding eye contact. 'Now, you're in Matt's old room,' she said pointing upstairs. 'Top of the stairs, first on your left. Lucy's room is the second door on the right, past the bathroom.'

He looked up the stairs and frowned, then shook his head. 'Sorry. I didn't catch that. Why don't you show me?'

'First on your left. Second on your right,' said Jennifer, wondering why he was playing silly games. There were only three bedrooms upstairs; he'd hardly get lost.

'Please?' he said and stared at her without blinking.

She did not want to go up the stairs with him. She had nothing concrete on which to base this vague reluctance, only a gnawing unease in the pit of her stomach that she put down to the fact that she did not like him. But how could she refuse to show him to his room? She took a deep breath and smiled brightly. 'Of course.'

'You go first,' he said and, again, how could she refuse? So she climbed the stairs, feeling his eyes on her behind all the way up, glad that she'd had the foresight to wear a modest, loose fitting dress. She made a mental note never to allow such an uncomfortable situation to arise again. She ought to have gone out with Lucy, rather than stay in the house with Oren alone. In fact, as soon as she was done here, she'd follow Lucy over to Dad's house and they could walk back together. Oren could stay here and do what he liked.

On the landing she flung open one door, fumbled for the light switch and said, 'This is Lucy's room.'

Oren cast a cursory glance around the room, then dropped one of the bags just inside the door. Jennifer opened the door of Matt's old room, flicked on the light and stood to one side, not looking at Oren. 'And you're in here.'

But he didn't walk into the room straight away. 'And the bathroom?'

'Oh, yes of course,' she said, going over to the bathroom door, pushing it open and pulling the light cord. She was rather proud of the sleek bathroom which she'd done up only last year, replacing the tired pale pink suite with a modern white one. The walls and floor were finished in slate grey tiles and the chunky chrome fittings gleamed in the bright overhead light.

'You just need to watch the shower curtain. Make sure it's inside the bath or you'll flood the place,' said Jennifer, stepping into the room and tugging at the shower curtain to illustrate her point. And then suddenly the door clicked shut behind her – and she froze.

She turned around in time to see Oren flick the lock on the door. 'What are you doing? Open that door at once,' she said, her calm, commanding voice at odds with the terror she felt inside. She was trapped. There was no way out except through that door – and between her and it stood the huge figure of Oren. He stared at her with his head cocked slightly to one side, regarding her with a mixture of curiosity and lust.

'Come here,' he said huskily and she inched backwards until she could go no further, the rim of the sink pressing into her buttocks.

He dropped the bag on the floor and advanced on her, the pupils of his pale blue eyes huge and black. 'Gone all shy on me, have you?' he leered and he snatched at her arm making her lunge backwards, hitting the small of her back painfully on the rim of the sink. He made another lunge for her and suddenly he had her in an iron embrace, the hardness of him pressing into her belly, his hot, panting breath moist in her ear. She wriggled to free herself but it was useless. He was too strong.

'Oh, stop acting as if you don't want this,' he hissed, holding her still with one arm as easily as she might restrain a newborn puppy, while he lifted her chin with his free hand. 'You're hot for me, aren't you? Look at you, all made up like a painted doll with that red lipstick. Who's that for then, if not me?' He wiped his thumb, the skin as rough as sandpaper, across her lips. Then he pressed his forehead to hers and said, 'You get off on younger men, don't you?' His damp breath was foul and cold sweat beaded his brow. 'That's why you finished with Ben Crawford, isn't it? So you could be with me. I wonder how he'll feel when he finds out I've had you too.'

'Get off me, you creep!' she shrieked and from somewhere she found the strength to break free of his grip. They separated and stood, panting, glaring at each other, her heart pounding against her ribs. 'I don't know where your delusion's come from, Oren,' she said, averting her eyes from the bulge in his trousers that made her want to throw up. 'You disgust me. You're absolutely . . . repulsive. And you're stupid too. What on earth makes you think I would welcome advances from you? I've done nothing to encourage you.'

He flinched slightly, as if wounded by her words, and then his gaze hardened. 'So I'm not good enough for you, eh?' he demanded, his lip curling up in hot anger, and she was suddenly acutely aware of his superior strength. She hadn't broken free – he'd let her go. 'You'd shag Ben Crawford but not me.'

Her only hope was to talk her way out of this room. Instinctively, she realised that she must not, under any circumstances, show that she feared him. She lifted her chin and, in spite of the dread in her heart, said boldly, 'You're not half the man he is.'

'Ben Crawford is a sneaking, lying little snitch!' he exploded. 'He doesn't know the meaning of loyalty or trust.'

Jennifer almost choked, fear giving way momentarily to astonishment. 'You talk of trust,' she said, putting a hand to her neck, where the skin burned hot under her palm. 'You're engaged to my daughter.' She let out a sob then, unable to retain her composure any longer. 'How could you touch me? How could you? How could you do this to Lucy?'

He smiled then, crookedly, and she thought that he must be mad. She looked past him at the locked door. The window was behind her but it was tiny. She'd never manage to squeeze through it. 'This has nothing to do with Lucy. She's not a tart like you.'

She ignored this. Told herself that what he thought of her was of no consequence. All that mattered now was saving her daughter from this maniac. 'It's over, Oren. Your cover's blown. The marriage can't possibly go ahead after this.'

He shrugged his shoulders and put his hands in his trouser pockets. 'I don't see why not.' He was relaxed now, the feverish passion replaced with a cool, calculating expression.

'When she finds out what you've done, it'll be over. You and Lucy are finished. And thank God for it.'

Her intuition had been right all along. If only she'd had the courage to stick to it before. She should never have invited him into her home.

'And what makes you think,' he said very slowly, running his eyes up her body from feet to head, the lust replaced with revulsion, 'that Lucy's going to believe you?'

'Of course she'll believe me,' said Jennifer, pulling herself up to her full height.

He gave a hollow laugh, turned and unlocked the door. He was leaving! She breathed out and her knees suddenly gave way. She sank down onto the edge of the bath and held on to the rim of the sink with both hands.

He stepped onto the landing, and turned round to gaze at her once more. Her stomach muscles tightened in a spasm. She held her back straight and her head erect, and tried to look strong and defiant while her insides dissolved to jelly.

'Lucy loves me. And when it comes to choosing who to believe, trust me, she'll choose me.'

He disappeared and a few moments later she heard the front door slam shut. She closed her eyes and sobbed, 'Thank God!' And then her bones seemed to turn to rubber and her muscles to elastic, unable to support her any longer. She slid onto the floor and lay on the bath mat, her breath coming in short gasps. Tears spilled out the corners of her eyes and she sobbed. She'd thought he was going to rape her. The room felt cold and she started to shake and suddenly nausea overcame her. She managed to crawl to the toilet where she threw up in the bowl. Then she sat on the floor and leant against the side of the bath, her back moist with cold sweat, and the acrid taste of vomit in her mouth. She told herself she'd had a lucky escape. She'd endured an unwanted advance, an unwelcome touch and horrible, suggestive comments. But that was all. Nothing she couldn't overcome, nothing she couldn't deal with. Except this clammy fear that gripped her still.

But what about Lucy? She glanced in the direction of the door. Was she in danger? Had he gone to find her? And do what? She must find Lucy, make sure she was all right. She struggled to her feet and looked at her face in the mirror above the sink. Red lipstick was smeared across her chin like blood seeping from an open wound. She ripped loo paper off the roll and rubbed her lips and chin until every trace of lipstick was gone and her skin was red. Then she dabbed the tears from her eyes and tried to think clearly.

Oren would not hurt Lucy, not until she was his wife anyway, of that she was certain. And he wouldn't tell her what had happened either. She would have to break the awful news to Lucy that the man she loved was a sexual predator, a morally corrupt creep. Oren would deny it, of course, but Lucy would see through him just as Jennifer had done.

In the kitchen she'd just pulled on her coat with the intention of going out, when the door burst open. Lucy, giggling, stepped in out of the cold followed by a flurry of snow, Muffin and, bringing up the rear, Oren. The door closed behind the three of them and Jennifer stood with her hand on the collar of her coat, her mouth hanging open. Oren refused to look at her and her initial fear at the sight of him turned to cold anger. How dare he cross the threshold of her house after what he had done?

'Grandpa wasn't in,' said Lucy, pulling off her hat and chucking it on the table. It skidded to the opposite edge leaving a slick of water on the surface. 'Can't imagine he's gone for a walk, though. Not in that weather. It's just started to snow. Never mind. We'll maybe catch up with him tomorrow.' She undid Muffin's lead, then looked at Jennifer. 'Are you all right, Mum? You look a little peaky.'

'Get out of my house, Oren.' Muffin crept into his basket and looked up with big, doleful eyes understanding perfectly the tone, if not the meaning, of Jennifer's words.

'What?' said Lucy and she turned and looked at Oren who instantly adopted a bewildered, hurt-looking expression.

'Get out of my house,' she repeated through gritted teeth.

'Mum! What is wrong with you?' Lucy went and stood beside Oren and hooked her arm in his. He stared straight ahead, his brow furrowed as if he were terribly confused, his pupils tiny black dots of lucid understanding.

'Oren's not going anywhere,' said Lucy. 'Now, can you tell us what on earth this is about? Why are you demanding that Oren leave?'

Jennifer looked into Lucy's face, flushed with loyal indignation, and her heart sank. This terrible news would surely break her heart. Why couldn't she have given her heart to someone worthy of her love? How could she not see Oren for what he was? She did not want to deliver this devastating news – but she must.

'Well?' demanded Lucy and she waited while Oren stood dumbly at her side.

Jennifer took a deep breath, held on to the back of a chair, and closed her eyes. 'After you left the house, Oren made a pass at me.'

There, she had said it. She opened her eyes. Lucy's head was cocked to one side and she had a blank, puzzled look on her face, as if Jennifer had just uttered something in a foreign, unintelligible tongue.

'Upstairs, in the bathroom,' went on Jennifer, for it was clear her words had not penetrated Lucy's consciousness. 'Oren asked me to show him to your rooms and then he got me into the bathroom and locked the door. And he tried to . . . to . . . force himself on me. He said that he knew I

268

wanted him.' She shook her head, unable to go on. 'It was grotesque. Awful.'

Lucy's face, pale to begin with, drained of all colour. She turned slowly to Oren and looked up into his face. 'Oren?' she whispered.

He looked into Lucy's eyes and tightened his grip on her hand. 'As God is my witness,' he said, without so much as a flicker of an eyelid, 'that is not what happened.'

'You liar,' shouted Jennifer and Oren smiled placidly. 'How can you stand there and tell barefaced lies like that? You know what I'm saying is the truth.' He wasn't just a creep overtaken by hot emotion, he was a calculating, practised liar. What else had he lied about?

Oren considered her calmly for some moments and then he turned his attention back to Lucy, who stood with her mouth slightly ajar staring at them both. 'Lucy,' he said and she looked up at him and blinked, as a tear slid out the corner of her eye and down her cheek. 'I didn't want to have to tell you this.'

Jennifer's anger subsided to be replaced with an awful apprehension. He was going to own up after all. He must realise he had no choice. But poor Lucy. It would break her heart. Tears welled up in Jennifer's eyes.

'I didn't want to hurt you, but your mother,' he said, glancing meanly at Jennifer, 'has given me no choice.'

'Oh no,' whispered Lucy. 'Tell me it's not true, Oren.'

Jennifer swallowed the lump in her throat. She hated him for what he was about to confess more than what he'd done in the bathroom upstairs. She could bear the indignation. But she could not bear to see her daughter's heart broken.

'We were in the bathroom together. You mother was going on about the shower curtain and telling me to make sure I didn't flood the floor when I had a shower. She called me over to have a look and when I got close, well . . .'

Jennifer frowned. She hadn't called him over to look at the curtain. And he'd left out the bit about shutting the bathroom door and locking it.

'. . . that's when it happened.' He put his hands over his face and sobbed. 'Oh, Lucy, I'm so sorry.'

Lucy slipped her hand from his arm and stared aghast at him while Jennifer tried to hide her satisfaction. Oren removed his hands from his face, revealing red eyes and tear-stained cheeks. He looked so contrite, Jennifer couldn't help but feel moved herself. Was this how he hoped to win Lucy round – with a show of repentance? But Lucy would see through it.

'I've always felt a little bit uncomfortable around your mother, Lucy. I didn't want to say anything before. But she's obviously got a thing for younger guys. I mean, look at Ben Crawford.'

What the hell was he talking about? What had Ben got to do with his behaviour?

'So when she put her arms around my neck and started coming on to me, I can't say I was altogether surprised.'

Lucy gasped, slapped a hand over her mouth and looked at Jennifer, her eyes wide with horror. Jennifer uttered a startled, muted cry. 'No,' she whispered.

Oren gave Jennifer a sly little glance, licked his lips and went on. 'I wasn't going to say anything. I was prepared to overlook it, pretend it hadn't happened, for your sake, Lucy.' He turned his cruel gaze on Jennifer. 'And then your mother makes up this ludicrous accusation. I can only assume she made it up out of revenge. Hell hath no fury like a woman scorned.'

'Lucy,' said Jennifer, so shocked by what she'd just heard that she found it hard to get the words out. 'He's lying. You must believe me.'

Oren bent his head down so his lips were close to Lucy's ear. 'I've never lied to you, my darling. Not ever.'

'And neither have I!' cried Jennifer, her voice rising to a high-pitched shriek. He was cleverer than she'd thought. And so believable, with that steady blue gaze of his and his oaths and quotations. Lucy stared at her strangely and said, 'You're jealous of me, aren't you? You never expected big, gangly Lucy to find a man, let alone one as handsome and good as Oren, did you?'

'Lucy, stop –'

'You've been against our engagement from the start. You tried to talk me out of marrying Oren and when that didn't work, you resort to these despicable tactics.'

'No, Lucy, that's not true. Everything Oren's told you is a lie.'

Lucy regarded her coldly. 'Can't you bear to see me happy?'

'Lucy,' said Oren sharply and then he softened his tone. 'Don't be too hard on her. I think your mother needs our help more than she needs condemnation.'

'Oh, Oren,' said Lucy and she put her hand out and touched his jaw. 'I wish I could be more like you.'

'He's lying,' shouted Jennifer, tugging now at the sleeve of Lucy's coat. 'I swear. He made a pass at me and now he's trying to cover it up by making out I was the one that acted inappropriately.'

'Ahem,' said Oren, pulling out a chair, and glancing meaningfully at Lucy, 'Jennifer, why don't you sit down and Lucy'll make us all a nice cup of tea?'

Lucy moved towards the kettle and Jennifer screamed, 'I don't want a bloody cup of tea!' She let go of Lucy's sleeve and balled her fists by her sides in impotent anger. 'I want you and your Goddamned lies out of my house now. And I never want you here again.'

'Okay,' said Oren slowly, with a fearful glance at Lucy. He put his hands up in surrender and backed away as if she was a wild and dangerous animal. And through her tears, Jennifer could see he'd won. He succeeded in portraying her as an irrational, hysterical woman – and himself as the sane and injured party. She had played right into his hands.

'Oren,' said Lucy, suddenly taking charge of the situation. 'Can you go and get our bags and meet me at the car please?'

Jennifer recoiled as he brushed past her. She listened to his heavy tread on the stairs, then said calmly, all life drained out of her, 'It's my word against his, isn't it?'

'I guess so,' said Lucy, her face a porcelain mask.

'And you believe him?'

A little frown creased Lucy's brow like wind on the surface of Ballyfergus Lough and her reply when it came was not at all what Jennifer expected. 'Don't you see? I have to.'

Chapter 20

Leaning heavily on one knee, Donna put a match to the scrunched-up paper in the fireplace in Jennifer's lounge and immediately it burst into flames, igniting the kindling sticks she'd arranged round the paper in the shape of a tepee. 'There, that's better.'

Outside, the burnt caramel February sun was disappearing rapidly below the hazy horizon. The snow was gone and delicate snowdrops pushed their way determinedly through the moist earth, but Jennifer took no delight in this harbinger of spring. Her daughter was lost to her – perhaps forever. A sob caught in her throat but she fought it back. She had cried all night and now she must think clearly, she must find a way out of this mess – and get her daughter back. Breathing audibly, Donna took her place on the sofa opposite Jennifer, folded her arms and said, 'I still think you should report Oren to the police.'

'And what would they do?' sighed Jennifer, nursing a glass of vintage port left over from Christmas. In the fireplace, the kindling sticks crackled into flame. 'Apart from throwing a few choice insults my way, he didn't actually harm me.'

'He intimidated you in your own home. Held you against your will, if only for a few minutes.'

Muffin ambled into the room and flopped down with a sigh in front of the fire. Jennifer sighed again. 'There's nothing I'd like more than to see him punished. But there's no evidence. No witnesses. Didn't Ken say as much?'

'I guess you're right,' said Donna resignedly, but she added, 'Doesn't mean a crime hasn't been committed, though.'

They sat in silence pondering this until Donna said, shaking her head, 'Tell you what though, I can't believe Lucy believed him.'

Jennifer sniffed. 'You haven't met Oren. He's very plausible.' She paused and added, 'You know, I get the feeling from something Lucy said yesterday that she feels as if she's thrown her lot in with Oren and now she has to stand by him.'

'What do you mean?'

'Well, I get the feeling that she thinks if Oren doesn't marry her, no one will. It's as if she can't walk away, even if she wanted to.'

Donna nodded thoughtfully and they were both silent for some time. Then Donna said, 'I've been thinking. Don't you think that you and Ben should have a proper talk?'

Jennifer gulped down some port and shook her head. 'Not after what he said about me. He said I wasn't the woman he thought I was.' She paused. 'It's over, Donna. I did the right thing. It would never have worked out. Even you know that.'

'No, I don't know that. Your relationship had as much chance of succeeding, or failing, as everyone else's.' Donna's face clouded a little. 'Don't you know that love conquers all?'

'Well, not in this case,' said Jennifer, drily. In this case there were just too many problems to overcome, too much doubt and too much fear. Her eyes filled up with tears. 'I just wish things had been different. That I'd fallen in love with someone more . . . more suitable. But I didn't and I can't change that. It just wasn't meant to be. And now I've lost Lucy too.'

'Oh, Jennifer,' said Donna and she brushed the corner of her eye with her fingertip.

'I really don't think I can talk about it any more,' said Jennifer. She hiccuped and added, 'It just makes me too sad.'

Donna eyed her appraisingly. 'When did you last eat?'

'Dunno. Breakfast? But I'm not hungry.' After recent events, her appetite had entirely disappeared.

Donna heaved herself out of the sofa once more and headed for the door, the sleeves of her acid lime batwing sweater flapping like wings. She moved gracefully, like a heavy-laden, majestic ship. 'I brought a few things over with me. You can nibble on whatever takes your fancy.'

The doorbell went. Donna stopped in her tracks and the women tensed and looked at each other.

'That'll be Dad,' said Jennifer and they both relaxed a little.

'I'll get it,' said Donna.

'If it's anyone else, tell them I'm not in.'

Donna went out of the room and Jennifer held her breath, relaxing only when she heard the reassuring sound of her father's voice. He came straight into the lounge followed by Donna, dumped a plastic supermarket bag on the floor and came over and kissed Jennifer on the head. The act of simple affection brought a lump to her throat.

'How are you today?' he said, shrugging off his coat and tossing it over a chair in the corner of the room. His face was the same grey colour as his hair and Jennifer worried

275

that this family dispute was putting too much of a strain on him.

'I'm fine.'

Sounding like she was in charge of a war council, Donna asked, 'What's the latest, Brian?'

'Lucy and Oren stayed the weekend at David's. I went over to David's yesterday but I couldn't get to speak to Lucy alone. Oren wouldn't leave the room even though I made it perfectly clear that I wanted nothing to do with him. They left for uni this morning and I went to see David and Maggie.'

'And?' said Jennifer.

Brian looked at the floor. 'I've tried to talk sense to him, Jennifer. But Oren's sticking to his story and David believes him.'

'So that's the family split in two, more or less,' said Jennifer dully. 'You and Matt on my side, Lucy and David on Oren's.'

'That pretty much sums it up, yes.'

'And the wedding's going ahead?'

Brian looked at Donna and bit his lip. 'Looks like it.'

'I'd better get you a drink, Brian,' said Donna with a glum expression.

'No need. I brought my own,' said Brian, glancing over his shoulder at the plastic bag.

'Food then,' said Donna and she marched purposefully out of the room.

'She's a gem, that Donna,' observed Brian, helping himself to a can of lager. He detached the ringpull with a loud pop, sat down in the winged armchair and took a sip. Jennifer, who'd normally give off to him for drinking straight out of the can, couldn't summon up the energy to object. 'And in a situation like this, you need all the friends you can get.'

Jennifer set her glass down on the coffee table and put

her head in her hands. 'Oh, this is absolutely awful, Dad. How can she go ahead and marry him? How can David let her? Can't he see Oren for what he is?'

'He had me fooled too, Jennifer. I thought he was a genuinely good guy.'

She looked up at him. 'She's going to ruin her life.'

Brain went over and put a hand on her shoulder. 'There, there, pet. It's going to be okay,' he said, without much conviction. 'Things will turn out all right, you'll see.'

'Will they?' said Jennifer. 'He'll cheat on her, Dad. I know it. They're only just engaged and he's making passes at me, for crying out loud! She's convinced that he loves her, and maybe he does in his own twisted way, but that doesn't mean he'll be loyal and true.'

Brian sighed heavily. 'Lucy's an adult, Jennifer, and free to make her own decisions – and mistakes. I know you want the best for her, we all do, but your job as a mother is more or less done. If she's determined to marry Oren, there's nothing you, or I, can do to stop her.'

Jennifer opened her mouth to speak but Brian went on, stroking the arm of the chair thoughtfully with his thumb. 'She's quite stubborn when she puts her mind to it. A bit like you.' He took a drink of beer.

'What do you mean?' she said, surprised. She'd always thought of herself as accommodating, readily altering her plans to please others or keep the peace. Hadn't she proven that over the years with David and Maggie?

He smacked his lips. 'Do you remember how your mother and I tried to talk you out of marrying David?'

Jennifer nodded, remembering her fear at the prospect of single motherhood, of coping alone. She'd chosen the safety net of marriage and respectability, only for the net to turn into a cage. Like Lucy, she'd been young and foolish, too headstrong to listen to those around her.

277

'But what's going to happen, Dad? Lucy won't speak to me. I tried phoning her.'

'If she marries him, we'll all have to bear it.'

Jennifer shook her head. How had this disaster befallen her family? How had Lucy got involved with someone as malicious and manipulative and downright scary as Oren Wilson? Jennifer thought back to the things Lucy had told her about the gambling and her miserable life at uni. It was hard to acknowledge, but she and David had failed in their parenting of Lucy. Her low self-confidence and lack of self-worth had made her easy prey for Oren.

'All you can do is bide your time, Jennifer,' said Brian, wiping his upper lip with the back of his hand, 'and be there for her when things between her and Oren go horribly wrong.'

When the phone rang the next morning, Jennifer sat up in bed and immediately regretted it. Her head was pounding with a hangover the like of which she had not experienced since Donna's hen night a few years ago. What the hell had she been drinking? Ah, yes, vintage port. That was why she'd slept like the dead last night, her slumber deep and dreamless for the first time in a week.

Tring, tring, tring went the phone downstairs in the hall, sending a sharp pain shooting through her skull. She staggered out of bed and fumbled on top of the chest of drawers for the handset. She found the base unit but there was nothing in it. She must've left it downstairs. Damn.

She sat down on the edge of the bed and waited. After six rings the phone tripped to the answer machine. Falling wearily back into bed, she pulled the covers over her head and thought miserably of Ben. Where was he? Her eyes stung with bitter tears and she blinked them away, determined not to slide into self-pity.

She poked her head out of the covers and peered at the clock. Nine-thirty! She was supposed to be working today – her first day back after the holidays – and poor Muffin was still locked inside downstairs. His bladder control wasn't what it used to be – he'd just recovered from yet another bladder infection. If she didn't let him outside now, she'd have a nasty mess to clean up.

With a groan she stumbled downstairs. Muffin was lying in his basket asleep and there was no sign of an accident, thank God. She opened the cupboard, found the yellow box of Anadin Extra and tossed two tablets down her throat. Outside, the sky was grey and heavy and the snow had started to melt, exposing dirty-looking patches of dark green, flattened grass. The dishes from last night had been washed and left to dry in the draining rack. Donna must've stayed and cleaned up, bless her.

The phone rang again, startling her and sending another pain shooting through the left side of her skull. She pressed the heel of her hand against her head, picked up the phone and croaked, 'Yeah?'

'Jennifer, is that you?' said David's voice.

Jennifer cleared her throat. 'Who'd you expect? The Pope?' she said facetiously. She could not forgive David the fact that he had chosen to side with an almost-stranger against her. After all the years of marriage, and the years since, she thought David knew her better. This single act of betrayal revealed more about his true character than anything that had gone before.

'I think we need to talk,' he said. 'I haven't got long. I'm at work.'

'Well talk, then. I'm listening.'

'I think it would be a good idea if we all got together and cleared up this, er, misunderstanding.'

'What do you mean, "misunderstanding"?' she said,

defensively, a little wrong-footed by his unexpected, conciliatory tone.

Muffin got out of his basket and padded over to the back door. He circled once, twice, then scratched at the floor, sure signs that he needed to relieve himself.

'Hang on a minute,' said Jennifer, distractedly, 'I just need to . . .' She walked over, turned the key in the lock and let Muffin into the back garden.

'Are you still there?' said David.

'Yes, I'm here.' She stood on the doorstep with the phone pressed to her ear, the bitter wind cutting through her pyjamas, the cold nipping her bare toes. Muffin disappeared round the corner of the house and the cold drove her back inside. Muffin wouldn't stay out long; he'd let her know with a bark and a scratch at the door when he wanted back in.

'I think,' went on David, 'that a simple apology from you would suffice. And then we can all forget it happened and say no more about it.'

Jennifer sank down on a chair and held the phone to her ear with both hands. 'You're asking me to apologise to Oren Wilson?'

'Well, yes,' said David, sounding slightly baffled. 'Oren's prepared to overlook what happened. And after the accusations that you made against him, I think he's being very gracious about it.'

Jennifer paused before speaking, disbelief and indignation competing with the pounding in her head. 'Why have you chosen to believe Oren's story over mine?'

David hesitated. 'Because he swore on the Bible that it was true.'

'And that makes me a liar?'

There was an awkward pause. 'Oren's a devout Christian, Jennifer. He wouldn't lie under divine witness.'

'And I would?'

There was another long pause. 'Look,' said David, 'I know you've been having a tough time of it lately. Brian told us how upset you were that things didn't work out between you and Ben. And I know you're missing Matt. Perhaps it's all just been too much of a strain. And Oren's such a likeable, caring guy, I can . . . well . . . I can see how you might seek comfort there.'

Jennifer was entranced, and rendered speechless, by this far-fetched analysis.

'Lucy believes him too,' went on David, rousing Jennifer from her stupor.

'Lucy's blinded by love, David,' she snapped. 'What's your excuse?'

'Jennifer,' said David, inhaling deeply, and she could imagine him standing in the surgery in the clogs and green coat he wore for consultations, pushing out his chest. 'I think this nonsense has gone far enough. I know you don't like the guy but you can't make outrageous assertions like that. We have Lucy's future to think about.'

'And you would see her married to a man who made unwanted sexual advances to her mother? What kind of a father would stand by and let that happen?' The doorbell went and she ignored it. She hadn't finished with David and she wasn't going to answer the door in her pyjamas to anyone. 'I believe he's capable of anything. He'll cheat on her at the first opportunity and,' she said, shivering at the memory of his fierce, brutal embrace, 'he's got violent tendencies.'

'I think Lucy's right about you,' said David.

'What?'

The doorbell went again, except this time whoever was ringing the bell pressed it again and again, each time holding the buzzer down for several seconds at a time. The noise jagged through her brain like a chainsaw.

'I do believe you might be jealous of her,' said David. 'Could you not bear to see her happy when your relationship's gone down the pan?'

'What absolute nonsense, David,' she said angrily. Fists banging on the front door finally got her attention proper and filled her with dread. She walked towards the front door and put her hand on the snib, no longer caring that she was dressed in nightwear.

'Or is it because you dislike Oren so much?' sneered David as she turned the lock. 'Did you think this alleged attack would break them up?'

'For the last time, David. I didn't make the attack up,' she retorted, grinding her teeth. 'And frankly, I'm disappointed in you. We've known each other for over twenty years. When did I ever lie to you? You've known Oren all of two minutes and you think the sun shines out of his proverbial.

'Look, I'm going to have to answer the door,' she said and opened the door wide. Isabel Duncan from next door stood on the doorstep in a knee-length wool coat, tan tights and sensible black snow boots. Her grey hair was hidden under a furry hat.

'Oh, Jennifer, thank God you're in,' she gasped, her dove grey, age-faded eyes full of tears. 'Come quickly! It's Muffin.'

'What's that about Muffin?' said David's muffled voice, as she let the phone slide from her ear. Muffin was in the garden where she'd left him, wasn't he?

'I was coming back from getting the paper. I was on the main road,' said Isabel, the words tumbling out, one on top of the other. 'And you know the way there's that blind corner as you turn into the estate?'

Jennifer nodded blankly and looked towards the end of the street. But there was nothing to see, the bend in the street where it joined the main road hidden from view by the house on the corner.

282

'Well, I came round the corner,' went on Isabel, 'and there he was. Just standing in the middle of the road. As soon as I saw him I hit the brakes as hard as I could but it was no good. I had new tyres put on the car before Christmas so it wasn't my fault. It was the ice, you see. I've phoned the council three times this winter about gritting our street, but they say it's not a priority because it's only a cul-de-sac. Anyway, the car just kept on going, sliding across the ice, and it . . . it hit him.'

She paused to catch her breath. Wordlessly, Jennifer put a hand to her mouth.

'I heard this awful thud. And now he's lying up there on the road in front of my car.'

'Dead?'

'No, no I don't think so. I think he's still alive but he's hurt, my dear.'

Jennifer put the phone to her ear. David was still talking, saying something about keeping a client waiting and how he'd give her time to think things over. 'David,' she said, interrupting him. 'Can you come over here right now? Muffin's been hit by a car.'

Chapter 21

Lucy came out of the first lecture of the day hugging a blue A4 folder to her chest with her name and 'Fluid Mechanics and Electromagnetism' written in her neat handwriting on the front. First day back and her head was swimming with Non-Newtonian fluids, the continuum hypothesis and Navier-Stokes equations. Her understanding of mathematical concepts was tenuous at best. Just when she thought she was on the brink of comprehending a concept, like Bernoulli's principle, the subject of today's lecture, it would slip from her grasp like sand through fingers.

How on earth was she going to pass the exams at the end of the year? She would have to start studying hard if she was to stand any chance. But her heart wasn't in it. Now that she had Oren, she didn't care about uni any more. Her future was hitched to his like a cart to a horse: she was only soldiering on because Oren had promised her father she'd finish second year.

And then they would be off to Peru, which Oren said would be the greatest adventure of her life.

She'd nodded in agreement, but of course the greatest adventure would be marrying him; becoming Mrs Oren

Wilson. She couldn't wait to leave university, and the bitchy girls at the house, behind and surrender herself to his protection and care. She didn't particularly want to go to Peru, but Oren's heart was set on it and she knew that if she didn't go, she would lose him. She was tired of battling alone through life, trying to fit in, pretending she was something she wasn't.

And her happiness would've been complete had it not been for the awful, deplorable thing her mother had done. Throwing herself at Oren had been bad enough but then to falsely accuse him of the very thing she'd done herself, well, that really was unforgivable. And it had spectacularly backfired.

Through it all Oren had acted with restrained dignity. After rebuffing Jennifer's advances, he'd protected her from wider censure by keeping quiet about it. He'd only owned the truth when Mum tried to turn the tables on him. He'd borne her hideous accusations stoically, displaying his true Christian nature, and exposed her mother for the liar she was. And she'd never realised that her mother, who claimed to love her, could hurt her so.

To her astonishment, Oren had offered Jennifer his ready forgiveness, an act that proved he not only loved the word of God, he lived it too. She only wished that she too could find it in her heart to forgive her mother.

'Hey, you,' said Amy, striding purposefully down the corridor. 'Let's see the ring then!'

Lucy peeled herself off the wall and tossed her hair back. The ring on her finger made her feel special, wanted, superior. Even the girls she shared a house with had stared at it in awe, their hard, mean faces glazing over in jealousy. She held out her left hand and said proudly, 'It was Oren's grandmother's. I'm sorry, I meant to call you but things were a bit manic over the holidays.'

'Oh, that's all right.' Amy took her hand and examined the ring. 'That is gorgeous,' she said. 'I'm so happy for you both.'

'Thanks. You will come to the wedding, won't you, Amy? It's the last Saturday in May.'

'Wouldn't miss it for the world,' she beamed happily.

'And will you help me choose a dress?'

Amy frowned. 'Won't your Mum want to do that with you?'

'No,' said Lucy firmly, 'I'd like you to.'

'Oh, okay. Sure.' Lucy blinked and looked away and Amy, always quick to smooth over awkward moments, added brightly, 'Now what's this rumour going round that you and Oren are joining the mission out in Peru? Is it true?'

Lucy blushed, thrilled by the novelty of being the subject of gossip for the first time in her life. 'Yes,' she said confidently, 'they've accepted our application. We're going out as soon as the exams are finished. The plan is to go for a year and then come back and finish our degrees.'

'Oh my word, that is just amazing! I'm not sure I could be that brave. From what I hear it's pretty basic out there you know,' she said with a worried look. 'You'll need all your jabs before you go and you'll have to take malaria tablets.'

'Well, yes,' said Lucy, realising that she had not given the practicalities of the trip much consideration. All Oren talked about was the God's work they would be undertaking – he wasn't a details man.

Her mobile rang. 'That'll be Oren,' she said with a secretive smile and pulled out the phone. But it wasn't Oren's mobile number displayed on the screen. 'No, it's Dad,' she stage-whispered to Amy who nodded, gave her a little wave goodbye and disappeared.

Lucy put the phone to her ear, wondering briefly why her father was calling her at this time in the morning. Shouldn't he be at work?

'Hi Dad,' said Lucy, turning to face the wall as if this might provide some privacy. 'Is everything all right?'

'No, darling, it's not,' he said in the same voice he'd used to tell her that he and Mum were getting divorced. Her heart stilled. 'It's Muffin,' he went on. 'He's been hit by a car up at your Mum's.'

'Oh, Dad,' said Lucy, dry-eyed, blinking.

'He's alive, Lucy. But only just. And I'm afraid it's not good, pet. His right hip's broken and he has internal injuries. I'm going to have to put him down.'

'Oh no, Dad, please don't,' she cried breaking down and sobbing into the phone. 'He's my best friend.' She closed her eyes and saw him as a puppy, a fluffy ball of two-toned mischief and mayhem who went on to chew all the chair legs in the house. She smiled, remembering holding him for the first time in her arms, feeling the slight weight of him, so skinny under all that fur, and the nipping bite of his sharp little teeth.

Dad cleared his throat and said a little shakily, 'I have to, darling. It's not fair to let him suffer. Even if he was a younger dog, stronger, fitter, he couldn't survive these injuries. His time has come and we all have to be brave.'

Lucy wiped the tears from her face. Students emerging from a nearby lecture room streamed along the corridor, filling it with noise. 'I don't want him to die like this, Dad, without me. I thought that when the time came, I would be there.'

There was a long pause on the other end of the line and some muffled conversation she couldn't quite make out. 'Okay. You still can. He's heavily sedated at the moment and I can keep him that way for a few more hours so that

287

he's not in any pain. How quickly can you get home? I don't want to leave Muffin in case his condition worsens.'

'No, you must stay with him.' She looked up the corridor hoping to see Amy, to call her back, but she was long gone.

'Maggie's got to pick the girls up shortly for lunch, and I'm afraid your mother's in no fit state to –'

'It's okay,' interrupted Lucy, 'I'll get Oren to drive me. It'll be much quicker than someone coming for me.' No way would she get in the car with her mother, even in this emergency.

As soon as she'd hung up she rang Oren. Thankfully he answered straight away. He was somewhere quite noisy – there was lots of laughter in the background and a female voice hissed 'Shush.' She ran a hand through her hair and got straight to the point, telling him about what had happened to Muffin.

'I'm so sorry to hear that,' he said, moving away from the noise.

His compassion brought on more tears. How she wished she was in his arms right now, with his big hands on her back and her face buried in his neck. She wasn't sure she was brave enough to do this without him. 'Oren, I have to get home as fast as possible. I don't want him to suffer unnecessarily.'

'Of course you don't. You know, it might be best just to tell David to go ahead and euthanise him straight away. It might be the kindest thing to do.'

'Oh,' said Lucy, a little taken aback. Didn't Oren know how much she loved Muffin? Even though he might be unconscious, she could not let him die without her at his side, where she had been all his life. 'But I have to get back, Oren. I can't let him die alone.'

'He won't be alone. Didn't you say your parents were with him?'

'Yes, but he's my dog, Oren,' she said, whining disappointment creeping into her voice. 'He needs me.'

'Okay,' he said wearily, 'if you say so.'

'We'll need to leave straight away. Can you please meet me at my flat? I think we should take an overnight bag and stay at Dad's. I could tell he was really upset on the phone, even though he tried to hide it. Where are you now?'

'Er . . . in the college café at Moira, just getting a coffee. I'm about to go into a seminar.'

'You can be at my flat in twenty minutes then,' said Lucy pushing up the sleeve of her jacket and looking at her watch. 'And then we can swing by yours and pick up your overnight stuff.'

There was a short silence. She thought she heard a faint sigh and Oren said, 'I can't give you a lift, Lucy, and I can't stay in Ballyfergus tonight.'

Lucy, shocked, put a hand on the back of her neck. 'But, but I need you.'

'I'm sorry. I can't afford to miss this seminar and I've got an essay that I have to hand in tomorrow. I'll be burning the midnight oil to get it done in time. I've already asked for an extension. I can't ask for another one.'

'You shouldn't leave things so late, Oren. You should be better organised,' she snapped and then felt awful. 'I'm sorry. That was uncalled for.'

'Yes, it was,' he said and paused to let this rebuke sink in. 'Anyway, I don't think it would be wise for me to be there, not with your mother around.'

Lucy frowned. 'It would be awkward, I suppose, but can't you put your feelings aside for Muffin's sake? He's the priority.'

'I'm sorry, Lucy,' he said firmly. 'I can't do it.'

'But,' she said, a feeling of helplessness overcoming her. 'how will I get home?'

'Get the train,' he said in a voice that suggested this was blatantly obvious.

'Yes, yes, I suppose I could. I have a timetable somewhere.' She set her bag on the floor, crouched down and started rummaging in it with one hand, the other still holding the phone to her ear. 'I can't find it!' she cried.

'Calm down. Do you not think you're over-reacting a bit, Lucy? He is only a dog, after all.'

A cold chill ran down her spine and she stood up, abandoning bag and folder. 'But don't you understand? He's always been there for me. I used to tell him things I never told another living soul. Until you came into my life.'

Oren made a noise like he was sucking air in through his teeth. 'He hasn't got a soul, Lucy. He's a dumb animal.'

Lucy's face burned and she wanted to tell him to shut up.

'And it sounds to me like you love that animal more than you love God.'

Was this true? She certainly loved Muffin as much as God, as much as Oren. Was that a sin? 'What's wrong with loving something God created?'

'The problem with sin, Lucy, is that it manifests itself in so many different ways. That's why we have to be vigilant all the time,' he said, jumping on the opportunity to deliver a mini-sermon, rather than answering her question. 'Nowhere in the Bible does it say that animals have souls. If they did they'd be our equals and they're not. They're there to serve mankind. If you were familiar with Genesis, you'd know that. *Be fruitful, and multiply, and replenish the earth, and subdue it: and have dominion over the fish of the sea, and over the fowl of the air, and over every living thing that moveth upon the earth.*'

'But . . . if Muffin doesn't have a soul then he won't go to heaven.'

290

'Of course he won't go to heaven,' chuckled Oren. 'Honestly Lucy, you crack me up sometimes.' And when she didn't say anything, he added, mockingly, 'You didn't seriously think he would, did you?'

'I don't have time for this, Oren,' she said quickly. 'I have a train to catch. I'll be back tomorrow.'

'Ring me,' he said. 'Ring me and let me know how it goes, will you?'

She hung up and scowled at the phone, finding fault with Oren for the very first time. How could he be so cold and unfeeling? He was wrong about Muffin. Muffin did have a soul and an understanding beyond human comprehension. Even when her parents never noticed, Muffin knew when she'd been teased at school, when she was sad and lonely. All his life he had given patient love, enduring friendship and he had asked nothing in return. She would not let him down now. Being there at the end, as he breathed his final breath, was the very last thing she would do for him. She picked up her bag and folder, and started to run.

Lucy knelt on the floor of the surgery recovery room with Muffin's head on her lap. The room was warm and smelt of disinfectant and animals. Lucy looked up at her father, her face encrusted with dried tears, her eyes swollen and sore. She'd kept the promise she'd made to herself on the train from Belfast – she had not wept nor sobbed nor clung hysterically to Muffin. She'd cradled him in her arms and whispered to him softly while he took his last breath and stilled. Dignity in death was her last, loving gift to him.

'He's gone,' said Dad simply and Lucy nodded and looked down at Muffin again. His mouth was slightly open revealing yellowed teeth and creamy drool dripped onto the thigh of her jeans. He looked peaceful, as if he was asleep. She stroked the top of his head, feeling the bone underneath the thin layer of skin and fur, noticing how grey he'd become behind the ears. Then, very gently, she eased his head off her lap and onto the blanket. Matt stood with his head bent, one hand in his trouser pocket, the other around Jennifer's shoulder. She pressed a scrunched-up handkerchief to her mouth and she looked awful – she'd no make-up on and her hair looked like it needed a good wash.

Lucy got to her feet and the four of them stood silently for a few moments staring down at Muffin's body. And Lucy was filled with a wave of panic. Muffin was the last link with her childhood, the last connection to the only time when she had been truly happy. He'd been there for her through her parents' divorce – and the subsequent horrible teenage years. She felt suddenly, desperately alone.

Dad, who had been so brave up until this moment, let out a stifled sob. Lucy took his hand and he smiled thinly. 'Why don't the three of you go next door to the waiting room?' he said, professional once more. 'Mary'll get you a cup of tea while I get Muffin ready.'

'What's going to happen to him?' asked Lucy.

'We'll have him cremated.'

The three of them shuffled out to the waiting room and sat on green plastic chairs in the corner furthest from the door, nursing cups of tea provided by David's assistant Mary.

'I really ought to get back to work,' said Matt, taking a sip of tea and looking at his mobile phone.

'Don't go just yet,' said Lucy putting a hand on his knee. She did not want to be alone with her mother. She was only here in the same room as her because of Muffin.

They sat in silence for some long minutes and then Lucy, unable to keep the image of Muffin's horribly misshapen rear end out of her mind, asked, 'Do you think he suffered an awful lot?'

'His injuries were severe,' said Jennifer, plucking at the sodden hankie she clutched in her hand. 'But he wouldn't have suffered. Your Dad was there in a matter of minutes. He was wonderful. He injected him right there and then, on the road at the entrance to Oakwood Grove.'

Lucy winced – Muffin always cried like a baby when he had his annual booster injections – and Jennifer went on, 'Morphine, I think, for the pain and then later, something to knock him out. After that, he wouldn't have felt a thing.'

'But what was he doing in the middle of the road? Who was with him?' said Lucy. Was she imagining things or did Jennifer smell of stale drink? She looked at her face closely. There were faint black smudges under her eyes, the kind the girls in her shared house sometimes sported in the morning, when they'd gone to bed the night before without taking their mascara off properly. But Mum was always so fussy about her cleansing and toning routine – it was a standing joke between Jennifer and Lucy, who had no need of cleansers because she never wore make-up in the first place. Jennifer shook her head and rested her chin against her chest. 'No one.'

'No one! Why was he off the lead?' persisted Lucy. 'He's never off the lead near roads.' It was a rule Dad had laid down when Muffin was a young and lively puppy and one that the family had never wavered from.

Jennifer said nothing for some long moments and then, finally, raised her head and stared straight at the posters on the wall ahead. 'He escaped from the garden. I let him out to go to the toilet. The side gate had been left open from the night before.'

'You left the side gate open?' accused Lucy. 'And then you let him into the garden?'

'It was an accident,' said Matt quietly, who up until now had been largely silent, caught up in his own thoughts.

'You were drunk last night, Mum. I can smell it on your breath and see it in your eyes.'

Jennifer looked away. 'It could've happened to anyone,' she said, not answering the charge.

'If you hadn't been drinking you would've shut the gate last night. And if you hadn't have had a hangover this morning you would've checked it when you put Muffin outside.'

'Don't give Mum a hard time, Lucy. Anyone can make a mistake,' said Matt, setting his mug on the floor as a look of utter misery came over Jennifer's face. 'Muffin's escaped before and he never got knocked down by a car, Lucy. You remember the time we found him at the old quarry, nearly half a mile away?'

It was a place she and Muffin used to escape to. The summer they moved into Oakwood, they'd spent many long hours lying in the long grass together around the rim of the quarry. She'd lain with her head on Muffin's panting chest, and squinted up at the blue sky, listening to crickets and the hum of bumblebees – and the fast, steady beat of Muffin's heart. She swallowed. 'So?'

'He was old. He'd lost most of his hearing and his eyesight was bad. He might not even have known he was on the road.'

Lucy blinked and said incredulously, 'What are you saying? It was Muffin's fault he got knocked down because he was old?'

Jennifer interrupted with, 'No, of course not. He never should have been out on his own. And I'll never forgive myself for that.' Her face twisted up as if she was about to

294

burst into tears but she bit her bottom lip instead and her brows knitted together the way they did when she was concentrating very hard on something. 'But he was very near the end of his life. His arthritis was really bad this winter and he's had three bladder infections in the last four months. Life was becoming a struggle for him. He couldn't enjoy his walks the way he used to and he must've been in pain a lot of the time.'

'Are you saying that to make yourself feel better?' said Lucy.

'Lucy,' implored Matt, folding his ankles under his chair and his arms across his chest. 'I think Mum's trying to make us all feel better.'

'Well, I don't,' said Lucy, tearfully, addressing Matt. Her hands started to shake. 'Did you see the state of him? The way his legs were all bent and that awful gash on his shoulder.' She turned to Jennifer and stared straight into her eyes. 'I'll never forgive you for that. It's your fault Muffin's dead.'

Everyone fell silent. Dad came through the door at the end of the room. 'Look, why don't you all come back to the house with me for a bite of late lunch? Janice is going to reschedule my next client. I'll give Maggie a call and she'll rustle up some sandwiches or something. And while we're all together, it might be a good opportunity to . . .' he paused and glanced at Jennifer, '. . . clear the air.'

'I'll need to give Ben a ring,' said Matt, standing up and pressing buttons on his phone. 'I'm so late for work as it is.'

'Okay, son,' said David and Jennifer, who'd been sitting staring at the floor, looked up, suddenly alert. Matt went over to the window and began talking quietly into the phone, and Jennifer never took her eyes off him. She may have been the one to finish things with Ben Crawford, thought Lucy, but she was far from over him.

'Will you come, Jennifer?' said David and Jennifer dragged her eyes away from Matt.

'Oh, I don't know,' she said with a wary glance at Lucy. 'If Lucy's not prepared to believe me about what Oren did, I'm not sure there's any point.'

David scowled and Lucy said, 'So you're still flogging that old horse, Mum. Well, there's no way I'm going to sit in a room and listen to any more of your lies about Oren.'

Jennifer pressed her lips together in a thin, hard line and Lucy was filled with a sudden, desperate need to see Oren. She should not have ended the phone call on a sour note. She must get back to him, to tell him that she was sorry for her earlier truculence.

'I have to get back to Belfast,' she said abruptly. 'I need to see Oren.'

'Well, yes, of course,' said David with a slightly nervous glance at Jennifer. 'That's understandable, darling. But maybe he could come down to Ballyfergus later? You could both stay the night if you like.'

She glanced at her bag and the blue folder lying on the floor, both cast aside when she'd rushed in earlier. 'Oren can't come down tonight. I've already asked him and I left in such a rush I didn't bring any overnight things with me.'

'Won't you come for lunch at least?' said Dad, and she could tell he was getting a bit short with her. But she'd much rather incur his anger than Oren's.

'I can run you up to Belfast later if you like,' offered Jennifer and when she saw Lucy's face go red, she added, 'Seeing as your Dad has to work.'

Lucy picked up her bag and threw it over her shoulder.

'It's okay, thanks,' she mumbled, crouching down and picking up the folder. She stood up, held it against her chest and rested her chin on the edge. 'I'd really rather get the train. Can you give me a lift to the station now please, Dad?'

Chapter 22

In the train on the way to Belfast Lucy consoled herself with the thought that though it had ended horribly, Muffin had enjoyed a good, long life in a loving home and she knew that they would one day meet in heaven. She would keep this to herself, of course, for Oren clearly disapproved of such a notion.

But as far as Lucy could make out the Bible was, as with so many other subjects, rather ambiguous on the matter. In fact, there were many ways to interpret the scriptures, and wasn't the proliferation of different churches proof of that? By the time the train pulled into Belfast Central station and Lucy emerged into the cold, dry night, she was all out of tears and the sharp pain of loss had eased to a dull ache. The earlier rush of adrenaline that had propelled her along the streets of the city that morning had left her exhausted. She boarded the bus back to her digs and climbed the stairs inside the house wearily, ignoring the shrieks of laughter and loud music coming from the lounge.

In her room she rested on the bed and a sudden thought struck her. Unless Mum was prepared to drop the ludicrous allegations against Oren, they might never be reconciled. A lump of anxiety formed in her stomach. She didn't want to be estranged from her mother. She loved her, yet she hated her for what she'd done in forcing Lucy to choose between her and Oren. And she hated her even more for clinging stubbornly to her story when everyone was prepared to forgive and forget the hysterical imaginings of a lonely, middle-aged woman.

She must look to Oren now, for her future lay with him. She imagined him, toiling over his essay with the end of a pen in his mouth and the perplexed expression on his face that she loved so much. She smiled, and decided there and then to pay him a surprise visit. She would take one of those Chinese or Indian meals from the supermarket over to his flat – there was never anything half decent to eat in his house. She would tell him about Muffin and ask forgiveness for her earlier rudeness. And, after she'd prepared the meal and they'd eaten, she'd join him at the dining table and study quietly alongside him, the way she imagined they would sit together in the evenings when they were married and study passages from the Bible.

Enthused by this idea, she jumped up and changed into a pale green jumper that Amy had once admired. She checked her reflection in the mirror with one quick glance, pausing only to register the redness of her eyes. She never lingered long on her face these days for she understood that true beauty came from within, from the goodness in one's heart.

An hour later, Lucy stood in front of a detached Victorian building that had been converted into three flats way back in the seventies. The walk had taken longer than she'd expected, and the handles of the supermarket bags she carried in both hands cut painfully into her palms, shutting off the blood supply to her fingers even though she wore thick woollen gloves.

It had started to rain a fine mist, the cold damp air cutting

299

through her wool coat like a knife. And though her head was protected by a woollen beanie her cheeks stung with the cold. She was looking forward to the warmth of Oren's flat and his embrace.

She was relieved to see the lights on in Oren's ground-floor flat and his car parked outside. She couldn't wait one minute longer to see him. She imagined his surprise, and the big warm smile that would spread across his face when he saw her. She took the few short steps to Oren's front door and rang the doorbell. No answer. She pressed the bell again, a little longer, a little harder, and waited, staring at the elaborate Victorian tiled floor. Still no answer. Oren might be annoyed with her for coming over, but she had come all this way and was starving; she'd not had anything to eat since breakfast. She would just give it one more try. Putting a gloved index finger on the bell she gave it one long, last buzz.

A long time passed and she was just about to abandon her visit, when she heard whispered voices from inside. Then the sound of the lock being scraped back. 'I've told you before, Phil. If you forget your key one more time . . .'

When he saw her the words died on his lips. He was barefoot with a towel wrapped around his waist. His smooth well-defined chest looked a little red and damp and his hair was tousled, as if he'd just stepped out of a shower. Lucy, imagining herself naked, her small breasts pressing against his taut, bare flesh, blushed. She yearned for the day when they would be man and wife and he would take her, possess her in the deepest, most meaningful act between two people. Since the engagement, intimacy between them had progressed to the odd chaste kiss. But, if Oren hadn't been so principled, she would've given herself to him long ago.

'Surprise!' she said, suppressing these lustful thoughts.

'Lucy,' he said under his breath, staring at her as if she were an alien just landed on his doorstep.

'Yes, it's me!' She laughed, took a step forwards and pecked him on the cheek, but he was so shocked by her appearance he did not return the kiss. 'I thought I'd surprise you,' she said, to fill the silence as Oren continued to stare, dumbfounded.

'But . . . but I thought you were staying in Ballyfergus tonight?' he said, taking a step forward and pulling the door partially closed behind him.

'I changed my mind.' She sighed. 'After Dad put Muffin to sleep, I just wanted to get back to Belfast. You should've seen Muffin. He was in a bad way, Oren.' She sniffed and tears seeped out of her eyes, already so sore with crying. She brushed the tears away with a gloved hand and went on, 'I stroked his head and talked to him until he passed away. I'm so glad I was there.'

'That's . . . er . . . good. And it's better that he's out of his misery.'

She smiled bravely, to show that she did not love Muffin more than God or Oren, and waited for him to invite her in.

'Lucy,' he said and paused, contorting his mouth into all sorts of odd shapes before finally spitting out, 'why are you here?'

'Oh,' said Lucy. Wasn't it obvious? She was upset by Muffin's death. And they were engaged to be married. Did she have to have a reason? 'I . . . er . . . I wanted to see you and to apologise for giving you a hard time about not giving me a lift up to Ballyfergus. I brought us an Indian meal,' she said, looking down at the bags at her feet, the contents spilling out onto the floor.

'But I have to work.'

'I know,' she smiled. It wasn't like Oren to get all wound

up about coursework. He could clearly do with some moral support. 'I won't disturb you, I promise. I'll get the meal ready while you work and afterwards, I'll just sit with you and study.'

He glanced furtively over his shoulder and it occurred to Lucy that early evening was an odd time to be taking a shower unless he'd been playing rugby. But he hadn't said anything about training, or a match, earlier. 'Are you going to keep me standing here all night?' she said, peering past him into the hall and noticing then that, though his hair was dishevelled, it was not wet.

'You can't come in,' he blurted out.

'What?'

'I need the flat to myself. I need complete peace and quiet. You should have called.'

Lucy's face flushed with embarrassment and the cruel pain of rejection, compounded by her raw grief, made her bottom lip quiver. She had overstepped the mark in coming here. She should have called. But he was supposed to love her. How could he leave her standing here like this? It had taken her forty-five minutes to walk all the way here from her house.

'But what about all this food?' she said pathetically while inside the flat someone flushed a toilet.

Oren tensed, the muscle on his jaw tightening, and Lucy said, 'Who's that?'

'Phil.'

'But,' she said slowly, 'you thought I was Phil.'

He looked at her curiously, a deep frown between his eyebrows.

'At the door. Just a second ago,' she said.

'Simon,' he said, understanding her meaning at last, 'I mean Simon.'

'You said you needed complete peace and quiet. If Simon's home, what difference does it make if I'm here too?'

Oren did not answer. His face was rigid and he would not look at her – his eyes flickered right, then left. Something was not right. He was hiding something, someone, from her. She looked at his naked torso, now rough with goose-bumps. Was that sweat and not water on his chest? Her stomach flipped and her throat went dry and she managed to blurt out, 'What's going on, Oren?'

But he did not need to answer, for a female voice from somewhere inside the flat called out, 'Who is it?' and Lucy froze, while everything fell into place. The girlish laughter she'd heard on the phone that morning; Oren's refusal to drive her to Ballyfergus; the essay that had to be finished. Had he been to Moira at all? Did the essay exist?

'Oh, Oren,' she whispered, as her heart turned to lead and all her dreams to dust.

'It's not what you think,' said Oren hastily and she shook her head.

'Don't,' she managed to squeeze out of lungs that did not want to work properly. 'Don't make it any worse than it already is.'

And he had the grace, that at least, to hang his head. 'I'm sorry,' was all he said and Lucy turned and fled.

'I brought you some beef casserole,' said Maggie with a big smile, standing on Jennifer's doorstep with a red coat on, black leather gloves, and high-heeled shoes she wore because she had a complex about being so much shorter than David. 'I didn't think you'd feel like cooking after yesterday. I know how much you loved Muffin.'

Jennifer, who had spent most of the previous night sobbing into a cushion, blinked, so pleasantly surprised by this spontaneous act of kindness that she almost forgot her manners. 'I . . . er . . . why, Maggie,' she bumbled. 'That is so very nice of you. Please, won't you come in?'

303

Once inside Maggie placed the still-warm dish in Jennifer's hands.

'Thank you,' said Jennifer, while Maggie looked about, in the manner of a roosting bird intending to settle for a while. Jennifer didn't want to be rude but she wished Maggie would leave. She was wrung out emotionally, too tired and depressed by Muffin's death and everything else in her life that had gone spectacularly wrong to make small-talk.

'I see you've redecorated the hall,' commented Maggie. 'It looks nice. What's that lovely colour on the walls?'

'Elephant's Breath,' said Jennifer, trying and failing to remember the last time Maggie had been in her house. She was a little ashamed that it had been so long. 'It's a Farrow and Ball paint,' said Jennifer, forcing a smile. 'They go in for weird names. How do you fancy Dead Salmon or Cat's Paw?'

Maggie laughed and there was a pregnant pause. Because it would've been unforgivably rude not to, Jennifer asked, 'Would you like to have a drink with me, Maggie? If you have time.'

'Do you know what? I'd love one. A nice cup of tea, if it's not too much bother. I so rarely get one made for me. Which probably sounds like an odd thing to say.'

'Not at all,' reassured Jennifer, as she led the way into the kitchen and put the kettle on. 'I'd love a cuppa too. If it's any comfort I felt the same when my kids were young. But the good news is that you can look forward to them making you cups of tea when they're older. Before they fly the nest, that is.'

With Muffin gone, she really was all alone. She hardly saw Matt these days and it looked like her relationship with Lucy was all but over. Swallowing hard, she set the mugs down and got out a packet of chocolate digestives.

'I'm sorry about Muffin.' Maggie was staring at Muffin's

304

empty basket and beside it, his food and water bowls. Her eyes filled with tears and Jennifer gulped.

'Thank you,' she said, her heart heavy with sorrow and guilt. 'You know, I'll never forgive myself, Maggie.'

'It was an accident, Jennifer.'

Jennifer, pouring boiling water into the teapot, was grateful for Maggie's compassion. But it didn't alleviate her grief. 'You know Lucy blames me. She was so angry.'

Maggie, her face unreadable, did not answer.

Jennifer set a plate of biscuits on the table and poured two mugs of tea. 'Does David know you're here?'

Maggie screwed up her nose. Jennifer sat down and pushed one of the mugs across the table. 'Thanks,' said Maggie, cradling it with both hands. 'And in answer to your question, no, not exactly.' Then she looked Jennifer in the eye, her own the colour of brushed steel. 'I told him I was taking the meal round to a widow from the church who's not been well. She's got senile dementia so if David ever mentions it, I can always claim she's forgotten.'

Jennifer opened her mouth in astonishment. She didn't need to ask why Maggie had used subterfuge to cover her tracks; that was obvious. Ever since the Oren incident things between Jennifer and David had been tense, yesterday's armistice aside, and no doubt Maggie didn't want to be caught up in the middle. Maggie poured milk into her tea and Jennifer asked slowly, 'So why are you here?'

Maggie slid a biscuit off the plate. 'I wanted to talk to you about Oren.'

'Oh, that again,' said Jennifer defensively, pouring milk in her mug. Had she come of her own volition – or had David sent her?

'David, well, he can be difficult to live with at times,' said Maggie with a resigned sort of smile and Jennifer's mouth hung open in surprise. This was the first time she'd

305

heard Maggie admit that all might not be well between her and David.

'You know that better than anyone,' went on Maggie. 'And we have a very . . . how shall I put it . . . traditional marriage. When I took my vows I promised to love, honour and obey.' She looked at Jennifer's blank face and added, 'What I'm trying to say is that David wouldn't take too kindly to me being here.'

'Why's that?' said Jennifer.

'Because I don't agree with him. I don't believe Oren's story. I believe you. And I just wanted you to know that. I've tried to persuade David that Oren's lying but he doesn't want to hear it.'

Maggie paused to bite a chunk off the biscuit and Jennifer put a closed fist to her mouth, tears springing to her eyes. 'You don't know how much it means to hear you say that.'

Maggie swallowed a sip of tea and said simply, 'I think I do.' And then she went on, as if delighted, at last, to air her opinion. 'David says he senses the hand of God on Oren,' she said with a scoff, 'if you can believe that. He's terribly impressed by Oren's ability to quote chapter and verse from the Bible on any subject.'

'And you're not?'

Maggie shrugged. 'The more I get to know him, the less I like him. He seems to have an inflated sense of his own worth.'

Jennifer nodded in agreement, delighted to hear that she was not the only one who saw through Oren's façade and knew him for what he truly was – a liar and a cheat. 'I think I'm going to lose her, Maggie. She won't talk to me. I even tried going to her digs in Belfast but she wouldn't see me.' She paused and added hoarsely, 'If she marries Oren Wilson, I might never see her again.'

306

Maggie nodded gravely. 'Well, let's just hope and pray that some miracle occurs to prevent it.'

'You know I gave Ben up because of Lucy and Oren,' blurted out Jennifer. 'Well, partly anyway.'

'Because they objected to the relationship?' said Maggie, a crumb falling out of the corner of her mouth onto the table.

Jennifer nodded. 'It wasn't just that, of course. I worried what would happen to us in the future. I overheard someone at a party on New Year's Eve call me a cougar. I was so embarrassed I left the party early. I couldn't bear to be a figure of fun, with people laughing at me, at us, behind our backs.'

'I'm sure they weren't.' Maggie stared thoughtfully into her tea. 'But I know exactly what you mean about caring too much what other people think. You know I turned David down three times before I finally agreed to have dinner with him?'

Jennifer shook her head. She knew nothing about how David and Maggie got together, though of course David had known Maggie as Jennifer's friend for years.

Maggie looked up at Jennifer. 'It wasn't that I didn't want to.'

'So what held you back?'

'I felt that I was stealing your husband, taking advantage of your misfortune. That it was somehow distasteful, back-stabbing. And that people would judge me for it.'

'But that's nonsense,' cried Jennifer. 'We were divorced.'

'I know. But still, it didn't feel quite the done thing. It was David who persuaded me in the end.'

'Well, I'm glad he did,' said Jennifer firmly. 'I would've hated to see you miss out on happiness because of a misplaced sense of loyalty to me. Or because of gossip-mongers.'

307

'It's good of you to say that, Jennifer. Not many women would.' Maggie paused and smiled gently. And then she leaned forward and laid a hand on the table. 'But don't you see that you've done just that with Ben, Jennifer? You've let your own self-doubt and what other people think destroy your happiness.'

Jennifer leaned back in her chair and sat in stunned, quiet silence. And then she said, 'I . . . I think you're right, Maggie. I have, haven't I? And it's brought me no closer to Lucy. Ben didn't want to end it, you know. He begged me to stay with him.'

'Is it too late to start over?'

'I . . . I don't know,' said Jennifer, as panic took hold. She rested her elbows on the table and put her head in her hands. 'Oh, Maggie, what have I done? I've been so stupid and shallow. Ben must hate me.'

'I doubt that very much,' said Maggie placidly.

'Oh, I don't know what to do!' she cried and she pushed back her chair. But before she could rise from the table, the back door burst open with a blast of freezing air, and Matt walked in still wearing his chef's whites.

'Hi Maggie. Hi Mum,' he said, throwing his cap petulantly on the table.

Jennifer stood up, her hand on the back of the chair. 'What's wrong? Why aren't you at work?'

Matt snorted and shook his head. 'Because Ben Crawford's just gone and cancelled all the bookings and closed Carnegie's, hasn't he?'

'What?'

'And we're all out of a job. For the time being anyway.'

'But he can't do that, surely?' said Maggie with an alarmed look at Jennifer.

'He can and he has. He says he doesn't know when Carnegie's will reopen. Jason says not to worry. He says

308

Alan Crawford will get a new manager in, but I don't know,' he added with a shake of his head and a quiver of his bottom lip. 'It was all going so well.'

'But why?' said Maggie. 'The restaurant's been a roaring success. Why on earth would he close it?'

Matt shook his head in exasperation and put his hands on his hips. 'Maggie, all I can tell you is that he has and he's down there now, on his own, drinking.' He looked at Jennifer, then looked away.

'Tell me,' she said, as the blood drained from her face.

Matt folded his arms and stared directly at her. 'Some people are saying it's due to personal problems. Since you and him finished, Mum, he's been like a bear with a sore head. And I don't know if this has anything to do with it, but he came in today with a shiner. His right eye was almost swollen shut.'

'Ben's injured?' She went over to the door and grabbed the first coat that came to hand – an old jacket she used for walking Muffin – and the car keys, lying on the counter.

'Mum, where are you going?'

She paused with her hand on the doorknob. 'I have to go to Ben. He needs me.' Then she opened the back door and walked out into the night.

Chapter 23

Ben sat at the back of the restaurant with a bottle of Jack Daniel's and a glass on the table in front of him. The temple above his right eye throbbed and the vision out of the narrow, swollen slit was slightly blurry. But he didn't mind the black eye. It was a reminder that, for once in his life, he had done the right thing. Something he could even be proud of.

The roller blind on the door was pulled down and most of the lights were off so that, from the outside, the place looked empty. One or two customers whom he'd failed to contact by phone earlier had come knocking on the door, eventually turned away by the sign he'd scrawled in black marker, 'Restaurant closed until further notice'. He felt bad about that, but he felt even worse about the staff. He'd never felt like such a worthless shit as when he told them he was closing the restaurant – and saw the look on their faces. Especially Jason, whom Ben could not look in the eye. He couldn't make them any promises, but he knew Alan wouldn't let a little goldmine like Carnegie's go down the pan.

And then he would be free to go. To leave this wretched town where his hopes had been raised to the heavens and then dashed to the ground. He looked about the room, the gilded mirrors and shiny chandeliers that had gleamed with so much promise on opening night, now dark and dull, the way he imagined the tarnished furnishings in Miss Havisham's room in *Great Expectations*. He shook his head. Who would he share such an insight with? Who, of the people he worked with and the friends he had outside work, would identify with the reference? Jennifer would, but she had made it clear she never wanted to see him again. He took a swig of whiskey, grimacing at the taste, hoping that it would be enough to dull the pain in his heart that was so much worse than the pain in his head.

He could not face one more night of meeting and greeting with a plastic smile on his face when his heart was cracked open like a nut. He'd read so many books on the subject of love but he'd never understood, not until he'd held Jennifer in his arms and looked into her eyes. Love, he now realised, meant caring for someone more than you cared for yourself. If he was asked, even now, he would lay down his life for her.

He'd loved her enough to defy his father and his mother and would've turned his back on them both without hesitation, if that meant he could be with her. But that wasn't enough for Jennifer.

He took another swig of whiskey. Because in the end she wasn't prepared to do the same for him.

And now he wished he had not met her, for he could've gone on living in ignorance, thinking that the life he lived was as happy as any man could expect. Now he knew better.

A sharp tap on the front window drew his attention and in the gloom he saw a small figure, that of a woman he guessed, peering through the big glass pane. Her nose was pressed up against the glass, her hands cupped around her face. Why wouldn't she just go away and leave him in peace? Couldn't she read the sign?

'Hello,' shouted the woman, and his heart stood still. It was Jennifer, he was sure of it. He set the glass on the table, stood up, and the sudden movement made a pain shoot across his forehead.

Her shadowy figure moved to the door. 'Ben, please open the door. I know you're in there.'

His heart began to race like it did when he ran up the Grammar Brae, forced by the gradient to shorten his stride and open his mouth wide to gulp in air. He moved towards the door, propelled by the need to see her once more, to look upon her one last time before he left this Godforsaken place. She rattled the door handle again and, impatient, called out, 'I have to talk to you. Please let me in.'

He reached the door and turned the key in the lock. Moving slowly on account of his swollen eye, he slid the bolts top and bottom, then opened the door.

She looked up at him with a sorrowful smile, placed a hand on her heart, and said, 'Oh, thank God.' He wanted to hate her, but she looked so vulnerable, it was impossible.

'Come in,' he said and turned and walked back to the table. He so wanted to embrace her, to press his lips against her soft mouth, but she did not want him. Being here with her now, in the same room, knowing he could never have her, was intolerable.

The door clicked shut. 'It's awfully dark in here,' she said.

'Turn the lights up if you want. You know where the switches are.'

She wove her way through the tables to a panel of switches on the back wall and flicked one. Immediately all the floor and wall lights came on bathing the room, and Jennifer, in a soft yellow glow. She wore trainers and grey marl trackies under an unflattering old jacket and her face was bare of make-up. He couldn't help but notice the grey shadows under her eyes and the sallowness of her complexion.

He poured some more whiskey with shaking hands, sloshing the rust-coloured liquid over the sides of the glass and onto the pristine tablecloth.

'Can I sit?' she said sheepishly, pointing at the chair beside him.

He nodded and she sat down on the edge of the seat and looked at the table, set for six. 'Want some?' he said, gesturing at the whiskey.

She shook her head, sandwiched her hands between her knees and stared at his right eye. 'What on earth happened to your face? It looks so painful,' she said, wincing as if it were she who bore the injury and not him.

'I got into a fight with someone.'

'I wonder what the other guy looks like,' she said, her half-hearted attempt at humour falling flat like a beach party in the rain.

'You'll find out soon enough. If Oren doesn't tell you himself I'm sure Lucy will.'

'You fought with Oren?' she gasped.

'Yeah, I did.' And he had certainly come off worse. Oren was a huge man and Ben had been no match for him. He'd managed to land a few ineffectual punches before Oren had punched him full just above the right eye, rendering him unconscious.

'But . . . when?'

'This morning. I went to his flat.'

'But why?' said Jennifer. 'Why would you fight with Oren Wilson?'

He gave her a twisted smile. 'Matt told me he made a pass at you and, when you rejected him, he accused you of doing the same to him.'

'You did that for me?' Jennifer's eyes filled up with

313

tears and she reached a hand across the table. Her hand hovered uncertainly in the air, then settled on the table, palm down.

'You're still my girl,' he said, his words coming out slow and thick. 'Even if you don't want to be. That's why I'm leaving Ballyfergus. I can't stand living in the same town as you, knowing that I could bump into you any day.' He cleared his throat and spoke up. 'Jennifer,' he said, 'what do you want? Why did you come here?'

She hesitated, seemingly startled by the question, and withdrew her hand. 'I . . . I . . .' she began and stalled.

'Are you here to persuade me to re-open the business because you're worried about Matt's job?' he said a little harshly. 'I'm leaving. But I daresay Alan will keep the show on the road. Matt's a brilliant chef. He doesn't have anything to worry about.'

'No,' she cried. 'No. I'm here because I want to say that I'm sorry. I made a mistake.'

He stared at the wall, turning his head away from her so that she would not see the despair on his face. What good was an apology? What was the point of analysing what had gone wrong and why? It would not mend his broken heart, nor restore him to the man he had once been.

'I shouldn't have listened to other people,' she went on. 'Or cared what they thought. I should've had the strength and the belief in us to follow my heart. And I'm sorry that I didn't have the guts to do that.' She paused and added, her voice oscillating with emotion, 'Please Ben. Look at me.'

He turned his head then and stared into her eyes, which shone like polished mahogany. She reached out hesitantly and touched his arm lightly. 'Can you forgive me, Ben?'

He looked at her hand, startling white, like the tablecloth, against his black shirt. Was that what she came for? Absolution for her foolishness? Forgiveness for the hurt she had caused him? He swallowed. 'Of course I forgive you,' he said thickly, and he waited for her to rise, to kiss him lightly on the cheek perhaps, and leave.

But she did not move. He turned his head towards her and looked into her face. Her cheeks were red and she blinked furiously. 'Do you think . . . can we . . . will you take me back?'

He held his breath, not certain that he had heard her correctly. Wondering if, in his desperate grief, he had heard only what he wanted to.

'What did you say?' he said, his throat tightening so he barely got the words out.

'Will you give us another chance, Ben?'

He stood up abruptly and her hand fell from his arm. He walked away quickly and stood in the middle of the restaurant with his back to her, his shaking hands in his trouser pockets, the blood pounding in his head. There was nothing in the world he wanted more. But could he trust her? He turned round and looked into her unblinking eyes and found that he was angry with her. 'Don't play games with me, Jennifer.'

She stood up. 'I'm not playing games, Ben. I love you. I want us to be together.'

'We *were* together, Jennifer. You broke us up.'

She opened her mouth to speak but only a stifled sob came out. Putting a hand to her lips, she steeled herself and whispered, 'I know. And I was wrong. But I can't change the past, I can only try to make it right now.'

He shook his head and fought against the urge to sweep her up in his arms and make her his again. It would be so easy to ignore the difficult questions he knew must be answered. 'How do I know you'll not leave me again?'

315

'Because I just won't. Not ever,' she said firmly.

He looked at her pale, stricken face and said bitterly, 'What's changed, Jennifer? You're still sixteen years older than me. And my parents, and your daughter, are still just as opposed to us as ever.'

'They haven't changed. But I have,' she said, placing her hand over her heart. 'I've been such a fool.'

He looked at the ceiling and blinked back tears. 'I wish I could believe you, Jennifer. You've no idea how much you hurt me.'

'I'm so sorry, love.'

'You broke my heart.'

Suddenly, she was standing in front of him, looking up dolefully. 'And I want to mend it again. I know I can. Please don't let your anger come between us.'

'I want to believe you, Jennifer. I really do.' He shook his head as he spoke and would not look her in the eye.

'What do I have to do to make you believe me, Ben?' She took a step closer, placed the flat of her palm against his chest and he looked into her eyes, brimming with tears. 'I see now what I didn't see before. We are made for each other and a life without you is pointless and futile. I don't care what other people think any more because my love for you is more important to me than what they say. Please let me show you how much I love you.'

Shaking, he took both her hands in his and stared deep into her eyes. 'I tried to stop loving you, you know. I told myself you were too old for me, you came with too much baggage and I was a fool for giving up my inheritance. But it didn't make any difference.' He brushed the hair from her forehead and touched her cheek. 'I can't stop loving you.'

Hope flickered in Jennifer's eyes. 'Will you give me another chance?'

He nodded, his love for her far stronger than anger or fear. And when she came into his arms, and he wrapped his around her, he knew that he would never love another woman.

Later, when she'd taken the bottle of whiskey away and made him drink several cups of strong coffee, she came over to him at the table, all animated and happy, her loveliness restored. 'You're a real hero, you know,' she beamed, leaning over and very gently kissing his smashed face. 'Defending my honour like that.'

'No, I'm not.' It had all been rather pathetic actually. He'd taken a swing for Oren as soon as he opened the door of his flat. A scuffle in the hall followed, watched from the doorway by a bookish bloke in glasses, which resulted in the blow to his eye. He'd woken up, face down, on the grimy tiled floor outside Oren's front door, with Oren nowhere to be seen.

She sat down beside him, their chairs sitting at a forty-five-degree angle to each other, knees touching. 'A real knight in shining armour,' she went on dreamily as if he hadn't spoken.

He sighed happily and tried to raise both eyebrows but the right side of his face wouldn't move. 'If you say so.' He took her hand and pressed it to his lips. 'Let me ask you something. What made you come here tonight? What made you change your mind about me?'

'One of the reasons I finished with you,' she said, placing a hand on his knee and giving it a squeeze, 'was to try and please Lucy. I know. That sounds ridiculous. But I was trying to be the mother that she and Oren obviously expected me to be. But after Oren made that lunge for me, and Lucy believed him, I –'

'What?' he said sharply, cutting her off. 'Lucy believed *Oren*?'

317

'That's right.'

He shook his head in disbelief.

'Well, I realised then that she was probably lost to me. Oren's never going to tell the truth, is he? But I shouldn't have let Lucy manipulate me like that. And then Muffin died and she blamed me for his death.'

'Oh, my darling, I'm so sorry. What happened?'

She smiled sadly and told how Muffin had been hit by a car and David had to put him down. She stared sadly into the distance for a few moments, then sighed heavily and brought her gaze back to Ben. 'Anyway, I thought about what you said to me on New Year's Eve and I realised that you were right. I *was* second guessing what was right and best for you. I shouldn't have done that. I should have listened to what you wanted.

'And then out of the blue Maggie came to see me tonight. She made me see how foolish I'd been in letting you go. When Matt came in and told me that you were down here drinking, and that you'd been like a bear with a sore head since we split up, that was the clincher. I knew then that you still loved me.'

'I never stopped.'

She grinned, looked around and said brightly. 'So, now that we're back together, are you going to re-open the restaurant?'

He followed her gaze. The room, so beautifully designed by Jennifer, was the talk of Ballyfergus and beyond. And the kitchen, under Jason's expert direction, was now working like a finely tuned machine. The restaurant would be a success with or without him. If only he had the courage to walk away.

'I suppose so,' he said and she looked at him sharply.

'You don't sound very enthusiastic.'

'I'm not. I've come to realise this past month or so just how much I hate my job.'

'Well, then, you mustn't go back to it,' she said lightly, as if walking away was an option.

'It feels as if I haven't any choice.'

She watched him for a few seconds then clasped both his hands in hers. 'You said something to me a while back and it stuck. You said that what you wanted to do more than anything was to be an English teacher. Well, this is your opportunity. Go to Stranmillis and get your teaching qualification.'

'Do you think I could? Haven't I left it too late?' Becoming a teacher was a pipe dream, so far from where Ben found himself that he could not imagine ever realising it.

'No, of course not. Sure they're crying out for mature teachers. And people change careers all the time. Look at me. I only started my business twelve years ago.' She regarded him thoughtfully and then added, in that pragmatic way of hers, 'Are you going to spend the rest of your life asking "what if?" and living with regrets? Because if you are, I don't want to live with you. I want to live with a man who's fulfilled by what he does for a living, who takes pride in his work and takes pleasure from it every day.'

'That's the kind of person I want to be.'

'Well, then, do something about it!' She lowered her voice, looked deep into his eyes and said, 'I don't know what kind of hold your father has on you, Ben. I know it's not money because you don't give a fig about that. But whatever it is, believe me, you've paid your dues. He's had seven years of your life.'

'Oh, my darling,' he said, tears welling up. Jennifer was right. Seven years was too long to harbour secrets and guilt that should've been shared long ago. He brushed the side of her face with the back of his hand and said in wonder, 'What did I ever do to deserve you?'

But he never heard her reply, for the front door exploded

319

open and Alan stormed in wearing a winter overcoat, his chest pushed out like a sergeant major and a determined expression on his round face. They both stood up, with Jennifer grabbing his hand as they met Alan in the middle of the restaurant.

Ignoring Jennifer, Alan growled, 'I just got a phone call from Jason McCluskey to say that you sent the staff home and closed the restaurant. What the hell's going on?' He hesitated momentarily, 'And what the hell did you do to your face?'

'I got in a fight. It's just a black eye.' Ben took a deep breath, his heart pounding in his chest. This was his chance to break free of him, to make his own life, find his own way. He must find the courage from somewhere to stand up to him. Jennifer squeezed his hand and glancing over, she nodded her head in encouragement. He took a deep breath, stared his father directly in the eye, though his right knee was shaking uncontrollably, and said, 'I've decided to jack it in, Dad. I don't want to manage Carnegie's any more. I quit.'

Alan looked at him in bewilderment. 'But the place is a roaring success, son. We're getting a two-page spread in *Ulster Tatler* next month. And we're on course for winning a Taste of Ulster Award this year. Anyway, you can't leave me in the lurch like this. I don't have anyone to run this place.'

'I'm sorry. I should've given you more notice,' said Ben.

'Please Ben. You can't do this to me.'

Ben's resolve hardened. Alan would use any means, including emotional blackmail, to get what he wanted. Ben had fallen for this ploy in the past, but not any more. 'But I've made my mind up and that's it. Surely you can pull a manager out of one of the hotels meantime until you get someone permanent?'

'Well, yes, I suppose so,' said Alan, grudgingly, 'but that's not the point. You've only been here two minutes and you're fed up already. Can't you stick at anything?'

'I've been fed up for a long time, Dad,' said Ben darkly. 'I think you know that.'

Alan sighed and the anger went out of him. 'Okay, what job do you want to try now? How about a spell in Head Office?'

'I don't want any job working for Crawford Holdings.'

Alan's face drained of colour. 'Don't be a fool. You don't mean that,' he said, but his voice lacked conviction. He pulled out the nearest chair, sat down heavily and glared at Jennifer. 'I should have known she'd have something to do with this,' he said, jabbing a stubby finger at her. 'She's only after your money, you know.'

'Enough!' Ben put his arm protectively round Jennifer's shoulders. She shook with rage but, remarkably, held her tongue. 'Jennifer's here to stay, Dad. And I'll thank you to give her more respect.'

'Ben, son, what are you thinking?' said Alan, shoving cutlery aside and putting his elbow on the table. He bent his head and rubbed his brow with his hand. 'You know the future of the business rests with you. There is no one else. You can't walk away from it. You just can't.' He lifted his head and his small, grey eyes squinted at Ben as if he was looking at the sun. 'Who do you think I do it for, huh? Not for myself but for you – and the generations that'll come after you. One day the Crawford name will be famous all over Ireland and beyond.'

'It might be what you want, Dad. But it's not what I want,' said Ben quietly. He let go of Jennifer's hand, went over and put a hand on his father's shoulder. Ben wasn't sure if it was because he was standing and his father sitting, but Alan seemed diminished somehow; the crown of his head, bereft of hair, looked so vulnerable. 'I've spent the last seven years trying to fill Ricky's shoes and I can't do it any longer, Dad. I'm sorry. I've decided to become a teacher.'

Alan's head shot up. 'What would you want to do that for? Sure everybody knows there's no money in teaching.'

Ben laughed and his hand slid from Alan's shoulder. 'Well, maybe that's exactly why I want to do it, Dad.'

'I won't fund it, you know,' said Alan, his beady eyes blinking rapidly. 'I won't pay for you to go to teacher training college.' He sat back in the chair with a triumphant look on his face and folded his arms.

'You won't have to,' said Jennifer, speaking for the first time and both men snapped their heads round to look at her. She pulled herself up to her full height, lifted her chin and stared imperially at Alan, her dark eyes flashing with anger. 'Because I will.'

Ben's heart swelled at this selfless act of generosity. Jennifer's income was not great, he guessed, and yet she was prepared to support him for an entire year.

'That is so sweet of you, my darling,' said Ben, taking her hand again and giving it a tight squeeze. 'But you won't have to. I have a small trust fund from my maternal grand-mother and some savings. It'll be enough to put myself through college.'

'And then what?' said Alan. 'Do you think you'll be happy living in some hovel together on what she earns and a teacher's salary? Don't make me laugh.'

Ben and Jennifer looked at each other and did exactly that – they burst out laughing. 'Well, yes, as it happens,' said Ben. 'It won't be a palace but it won't be a hovel either. But that's okay, isn't it, my darling?'

'Yes,' said Jennifer firmly, looking up at his face and clinging on to his hand as if she would never let go. 'We'll be happy no matter where we are, so long as we have each other.'

Alan stood up. 'Then I wash my hands of you, Ben,' he said, the old steeliness back, 'and on Monday morning I'll have my solicitors write you out of my will. Maybe that'll make you see sense.'

And with that he stormed out, slamming the door behind him. Ben watched Alan disappear out of sight. He let out a loud sigh and the tension in the room immediately dissipated.

His heart was still pounding and his hand, holding Jennifer's, was damp with sweat. But he also felt an incredible elation, a lightness of heart and spirit that he had not felt since before Ricky's death.

'Well, that's the toys thrown out of the pram,' observed Jennifer and Ben laughed far more than the joke merited. Alan's red Porsche roared out of the car park, brakes screeching. 'Do you think he will write you out of his will?'

'Probably. But it'd be a relief in a way. Then I wouldn't feel the way I have done all my life – as if I owed him.' He tutted, annoyed with his clumsy attempt at articulating his feelings. 'I don't mean that I don't owe him – I do – of course I do. He's my father and he gave Ricky and me a very happy, privileged upbringing. And I love him.' He felt himself choking up.

'But he wanted to own you.'

He nodded and Jennifer put her arm around his waist and tucked her head against his shoulder. 'I'll go and see him when he's calmed down a bit,' said Ben, pensively.

'Yes, you should.'

'There are things I need to tell him,' went on Ben, talking more to himself than Jennifer. 'Things I should've told him a long time ago.'

Chapter 24

A week and a half had elapsed since the earth-shattering moment when Lucy had stood on Oren's doorstep and her world had crumbled beneath her. And now she stood on a bright and sunny Wellington Park Avenue, with a weekend bag in her hand, looking up at the window of her room, the place where she'd sat on many a winter's evening with Oren, trying to let God into her life, while Oren took occupation of her heart. She'd thought him her saviour, come to rescue her from a life of lonely despair. And he had, for a time, but it was all a mirage. Like the foolish man in Matthew, chapter seven, who built his house on sand, she'd built her hopes of happiness on a faithless hypocrite.

She turned slowly and walked to the end of the street where she stood at the bus stop. She put her hand on the outside pocket of her jacket and felt the small, square box containing her engagement ring. Her heart lurched and she felt like she might be sick. She clung to the bus stop sign, let out a single wretched sob, and the nausea passed. A woman with a baby in a blue pram walked past and looked at her strangely. Lucy turned and faced the wall, as a single glassy tear trickled down her cheek. She had loved him with all her heart and soul. But her devotion to Oren, and to God, had not been enough. Why did he want to marry her, when he could not be faithful? And why did he want her – plain, gangly, boring Lucy – when he could have any girl he wanted?

Did Oren think that because she was plain she would tolerate his behaviour? Lots of girls would, she supposed. She might even, had she believed it a one off. But she knew that it wasn't. He'd made a pass at her mother and she was ashamed that she had not believed her. She could only hope and pray that her mother would forgive her.

She thought back to all the times he'd not answered her calls or responded to texts, the times he claimed to be studying or playing rugby or preparing a speech for church – all opportunities for unfaithfulness. If she married him, is this how her life would be? Always looking over her shoulder, doubting him, never being able to trust him? Her confidence, and her love, slowly eroded by each betrayal, every time she looked away or turned the other cheek? Lucy did not yet know what God intended for her life but she was quite certain it wasn't this.

She saw Oren as soon she entered the high-ceilinged concourse of the train station, standing on the pale grey tiled floor, close to the frosted ticket barrier as if he might catch her trying to slip past him. Behind him, train times and messages flashed up in bright red on the black notice-board. He wore jeans, white trainers and a battered brown leather jacket that he loved, and he was standing perfectly still, towering above the crowd like a rock. People flowed around him like a stream and, while her heart leapt at the sight of him, tears sprung to her eyes. He cut such a fine, handsome figure with his rod-straight back and those broad shoulders, she had to fight back the tears, determined to see this through with dignity and poise. It was all she had left.

'Why didn't you answer my calls?' he cried as soon as he saw her. He touched her lightly on the elbow and guided her over to a row of perforated, moulded metal seats fixed to the floor. 'Oh, Lucy, I've been so worried.' And looking into his watery eyes, she could so easily believe him.

'I've been driven mad with worry. Amy hasn't seen you in over a week. I called at the house loads of times but they said you were out.' For that small kindness she would forever be grateful to her housemates.

When she could not answer, her reply stuck in her throat like a chicken bone, he went on, 'Why did we have to meet here? I really, really want to talk to you, Lucy. Listen, why don't we find a coffee shop or something nearby where we can talk, you know, properly?'

She did not want to sit in a coffee shop somewhere, listening to a web of smooth-tongued lies, fearful that he might entrap her once more. For though she knew he was a cheat and a liar, she still loved him. She found her voice at last and said, 'I have a train to catch in twenty minutes.' A sharp pain stabbed her heart and her legs felt as wobbly as her voice. She put a hand out and steadied herself by holding on to the back of a seat.

'At least sit down with me?'

She looked at the seat of the chair nearest to her, all shiny with use, and shook her head. Sitting with him would indicate a willingness to converse, to listen, to understand. And, after days of agony and sleepless nights, she had come here for none of those things. She looked up at his broad face, not as handsome as she'd remembered it. 'I can't see you again, Oren.'

'I know I've let you down, Lucy. I'm sorry. I've let myself down. Please forgive me.' He bowed his head the way he did in church when he prayed and she wondered if he meant for her to touch his crown, like a faith healer. Or a Catholic priest absolving him from his sins.

He looked up and stared at her with such a desolate expression on his face, she had to remind herself that he was the architect of this situation. 'I've thought of nothing else these past ten days, Oren. But I can't forgive you.'

'You can, Lucy. Please. I love you. I still want to marry you.'

'Please, don't . . .' she said, looking away, and folding her arms miserably across her chest. He still loved her. He still wanted to marry her. Her stomach tightened in a knot and his soulful eyes were trained on her like a puppy. Her heart was bruised with hurt like a fallen apple, but worse was the terrible, aching sense of disappointment. 'You're not the man I thought you were. I thought you were faithful. I thought you were *good*.'

'Oh, Lucy, I never claimed to be good,' he said holding out both hands, palms upwards. 'I always told you I was a sinner. And aren't we all? *For all have sinned and come short of the Glory of God.*'

'Don't bring God into this.' His hypocrisy in quoting the Bible at her grated, like the screech of a train somewhere in the background. 'God has nothing to do with this. Only the devil.'

'No, you're wrong, Lucy,' he said earnestly, and fleetingly she closed her eyes, bracing herself for one of his persuasive arguments. 'The devil put temptation in my way and I succumbed. But didn't God teach us how to forgive? *Be ye therefore merciful,*' he quoted, his eyes shining bright as they always did when he recited Scripture, '*as your Father is also merciful. Judge not, and ye shall not be judged: condemn not, and ye shall not be condemned: forgive, and ye shall be forgiven.*'

'I know I should forgive you, Oren. And I hope that, with God's grace, one day I can.'

His face brightened and his hands dropped to his sides. 'Don't let my sins tarnish you, Lucy.'

'What?' she said, removing her hand from the back of the seat.

'But if ye forgive not men their trespasses, neither will your Father forgive your trespasses.'

She was stunned into silence for a few moments. How had his sin suddenly jeopardised her chance of entering the Kingdom of God?

'I don't want you to incur the Lord's wrath,' he went on. 'Forgive me, Lucy, and all will be as it was. We can be happy together as man and wife.'

'Oren,' she said evenly, spite stirring in her breast. 'If I thought that what happened in your flat was a one off, then maybe I could find it in my heart to forgive you.'

'Oh, Lucy, I knew you would!' He moved towards her and she took a step back, the heel of her boot clanging on the metal bin. 'It was a moment of madness. A mistake. I promise you, it'll never happen again.'

She shook her head, watching his features closely. 'But what you did to my mother was wicked and evil. You lied and you stood by, watching, while my family nearly tore itself apart.'

He bit his lip and took another step towards her until he was standing too close, crowding her against the bin, his breath on her face. 'As God is my witness,' he said, his eyes boring into her like a drill, 'I never laid a hand on your mother.'

'Don't you dare say another word,' hissed Lucy, and she placed both palms on his chest and gave him a sudden sharp push backwards. He could have stood his ground but he didn't; he stepped backwards, giving her space to think and breathe. 'I don't believe you. And let me tell you something. I'm glad it happened. Because without that proof, I might have been tempted to give you another chance.'

His left eye twitched. 'Lucy, you've got this all wrong.'

'No, Oren, I've got it exactly right,' she said, simmering rage powering through her veins. A verse came suddenly to mind and she smiled crookedly. '*And immediately there fell from his eyes as it had been scales,*' she quoted, taking delicious pleasure in reciting it to him, mimicking one of his favourite techniques in an argument – hijacking Scripture to support his point of view. '*And he received sight forthwith.*'

'Acts, chapter nine,' he said, almost admiringly. 'I taught you well.'

'I taught myself. I see you for what you are, Oren. A hypocritical liar and a cheat.'

She put her hand in her pocket and pulled out the jewellery box, the burgundy tooled leather worn with age. 'Take it,' she said, holding it out to him. 'It's your grandmother's ring, not mine.'

Slowly he extended his hand, looking sheepish, and she pressed the box into his palm, sadness enveloping her as she let go of the symbol that had carried with it all her hopes and dreams. 'Let me just ask you one thing,' she said, watching his fingers fold over the domed lid of the little box. 'Why did you want to marry me?'

He slipped his hand, and the box, into his jacket pocket. 'Isn't it obvious? Because you're pure in body and in spirit. And humble and good.'

'Everything you want in a good Christian wife, then?'

'Everything, Lucy,' he said and smiled sadly, 'that I'm not.'

She swallowed and blinked hard several times. 'And what

about the girl in the flat? Who's she? Will you marry her instead?'

'She's nobody, Lucy.' He made a funny noise, almost like a laugh and added, 'You don't marry girls like that.'

It had been a long time since Lucy had visited her mother's shop on Pound Street. She used to go there sometimes after school when Mum had to work late and Matt was in after-school club. That was one of the things she hated most about the divorce – Mum going out to work.

Lucy hadn't wanted to go home to an empty house, even though she was old enough to fend for herself. So she'd go to the shop and curl up in a wingback chair and watch her mother work, begrudging her mother her prettiness and pondering the unfairness of her life. It had not occurred to her until the journey home on the train today, that she ought to be proud of her mother for establishing a successful business, running a home and raising kids almost singlehandedly. Looking back, she must've been exhausted. A faint flush crept over Lucy's face as she remembered some of the horrible, ungrateful things she had said.

And now she stood outside the shop, in the shadow of the old stone building, and shivered with nervousness, fearful of what might await her within. She set her bag on the ground and peered in the window, her breath steaming on the cold windowpane. And there, beyond a bright window display of daisy-print wallpaper, fuchsia pink fabric and lime green cushions, was Mum, sitting at the glass desk, wearing a white shirt and a navy cardigan with a chunky necklace of brown wooden beads around her neck. Something in Lucy's heart pinged like a broken string on a tennis racquet and she stepped away from the window quickly, fearful that her mother might have seen her.

If she ran, where would she go? Back to Belfast and that room that felt like a prison, surrounded by a world to which she did not belong? Or to Grandpa, who would sit her down and counsel her to do just what she had come here to do today. Matt lived in one room in a shared house – she could not stay with him.

Lucy took a deep breath, picked up her bag and pushed open the door of the shop.

'Lucy!' cried Jennifer. The silver Anglepoise desk lamp shone a pool of yellow light on the papers spread out in front of her.

'I thought you'd be here,' said Lucy, dropping her bag on the floor. Her mother looked at it, then back at Lucy. She set her glasses down, came round and stood in front of the desk and glanced warily at the door. 'Oren's not with you then,' she said.

Lucy shook her head and bit her lip so hard she tasted blood. She was determined not to cry, but when her mother approached and placed a hand on her arm and said, 'Lucy, what's wrong?' she could hold it in no longer. She burst into tears.

'Lucy! Whatever's the matter?' cried Jennifer and she guided Lucy over to one of the chairs where she sat down on the edge of the seat, and rubbed her back the way she used to when she was a little girl.

When the sobs had eased some, she dabbed her eyes, all sore from crying, and said, 'I'm sorry for not believing you, Mum. I know now that what you said about Oren was true and that he was lying.'

Mum let out a long sigh and placed a hand between her breasts. 'Oh, thank God.'

'I'm so sorry.'

'It's all right, sweetheart.'

Just like that she was forgiven. It felt too easy, too generous on the part of her mother, and made Lucy all the more ashamed. 'I never should've believed him over you.'

'He's a very convincing liar, Lucy. If I was you, I might have believed him too. Love really does make us blind.' She paused and her expression clouded. 'But where's Oren now? Are you . . .' She stumbled over the words, her eyes full of apprehension, 'Are you two still together?'

Lucy shook her head and looked at the floor.

'What happened?' said Mum fearfully.

'I went round to Oren's flat and found him with a girl.' Jennifer's hand stilled momentarily, then continued its circular sweep of her upper back. Lucy dabbed her nose and looked up at her mother's troubled face. 'He was having sex with her.'

Jennifer's face paled. She stopped rubbing Lucy's back and gripped her shoulder instead. 'You caught them in bed together?'

Lucy sniffed. 'Not exactly.' She looked at the floor and, even though it was difficult, she faithfully recounted everything that had happened that night.

Jennifer's hand slipped off Lucy's shoulder and when Lucy looked at her, she was staring pensively at her folded hands. It would be so easy for her to say, 'I told you so,' but she said nothing.

'You're not surprised are you?' said Lucy.

Jennifer pressed her lips together the way she did when she was trying to control her temper. She took a moment to collect her thoughts and said, simply, 'I'm sorry, Lucy. You deserve better.' And then she paused and added, fearfully, 'But what about the engagement?'

'We're finished. I gave him the ring back today.'

Jennifer put her hands to her face and cried out, 'Oh, thank God. Thank God it's over.'

'I should have listened to you when you said that he was

wrong for me,' said Lucy, staring at the scrunched-up hankie in her hand.

'Love doesn't listen to common sense.'

Lucy's eyes filled with tears and she dabbed at them furiously with the hankie. 'I did love him, Mum. I loved him with all my heart.' And she started crying all over again.

'Shush, darling,' said Jennifer, her eyes too now filled with tears, and she stroked Lucy's hair like she was a girl once more. 'I know you don't want to hear this right now. But he didn't deserve your love, Lucy. One day you'll find a man who does.' She paused and added, 'I thought I'd lost you, Lucy. I really thought I'd lost you.' Her voice broke up and Lucy realised that her mother was crying too.

When they'd both composed themselves, Jennifer asked, 'What did Oren have to say for himself?'

'He admitted he'd been with the girl but he told me it was a one off and it would never happen again. And then he swore blind that he hadn't made a pass at you. That's when I gave him the ring back.' Lucy paused and looked sheepishly at her mother. 'I can't believe he fooled me like that. How could I have been so stupid?'

'You weren't stupid, Lucy. You trusted, that's all. And you had no reason not to.'

'I suppose. But how can you forgive me, Mum, for not believing you?'

'Because you are my daughter, Lucy,' said Jennifer, with a loving smile. 'And I love you, always, and no matter what.' She brushed a stray hair off Lucy's forehead. 'Love makes us all do crazy things. I don't blame you, Lucy, for being true to him.'

Lucy blushed and rubbed her nose with her hand. 'You make me ashamed. You forgive me so easily and yet I can't find it in my heart to forgive Oren. All I feel is hate – and love – all jumbled up. And I feel terrible about that.'

Jennifer leaned forward and said earnestly, 'But you will forgive him one day, Lucy, when the hurt has faded and the pain isn't as raw. You have to come to terms with your own grief first. In time, you'll see Oren clearly for what he is and you'll find that your feelings towards him have . . . softened.'

'What do you mean?'

Jennifer gave a little shrug. 'You won't hate him any more and neither will you love him like you do now. At the moment, I hate him for what he's done to you. But I pity him too. A person like that isn't capable of finding happiness in life. No matter how much he goes about spouting verses from the Bible like a fountain.'

Lucy giggled in spite of herself and Jennifer said, seriously, 'He hasn't destroyed your faith, has he?'

Lucy paused to consider this. 'Funnily enough, all this has made my faith even stronger. Knowing God loves me has been a great comfort. I can't explain it very well, but I believe God is guiding me, and even though what's happened is painful, I believe it's for a purpose.'

'Maybe the purpose in you meeting Oren was to find God.'

'Perhaps. I have him to thank for that, if nothing else.' She sniffed. 'And I know I've had a lucky escape. Imagine if I'd only discovered all this *after* we were married.'

Jennifer shivered and rubbed her arms. 'Don't even go there,' she said and then added, 'Maybe that's why he was so keen to get you down the aisle. He was afraid that once you realised what he was really like, you'd dump him.'

'Maybe,' echoed Lucy and she rubbed her temple and yawned. She was worn out by the day's events, her heart sore and tender from the battering ram of emotions that had assailed it over the last week and a half.

334

Jennifer looked at the watch on her wrist. 'I'm almost done for today. Why don't I finish up here and give you a lift home? Assuming you want to come home, that is?'

'I'd love to,' said Lucy, thinking of her room at Oakwood Grove with fondness. Though things would be different of course – Muffin was no longer there. She looked at her mother shifting papers on the desk and blushed. She counted up the number of times Dad had had to tend to Muffin for his various ailments over the last year. Every time she'd gone home, Mum was shoving some tablet or other down his throat and it occurred to her then that perhaps Mum was right. Perhaps his death had been a blessing in a way.

'I'm sorry I blamed you for Muffin's death,' said Lucy suddenly. 'That was unfair of me.'

Jennifer stopped sifting paper and tears filled her eyes. 'Thanks for saying that, love. It means a lot.'

'It'll be strange Muffin not being there,' said Lucy.

Jennifer smiled without showing her teeth and said, 'I have to warn you.' She twirled a shiny ring Lucy had not seen before around the middle finger of her left hand and fixed Lucy with a steely stare. 'Ben Crawford's moved in.'

'Oh,' said Lucy, taken by surprise. David had sent an email telling her that Mum and Ben had got back together, but she hadn't realised things had moved this fast. 'Good,' she added and Jennifer's eyebrows rose imperceptibly. 'I . . . er . . . it's time I got to know him properly. I never really gave him a chance before.'

Jennifer grinned. 'I'm so pleased to hear you say that! And don't beat yourself up. It's all in the past now. I just know you two will get along famously.' The smile fell suddenly from her face and she said, 'You know about Ben and Oren, don't you?'

Lucy shook her head and Jennifer told her an astonishing story about how Ben had fought Oren over the allegations he'd made against her. 'Ben must love you very much to do that, Mum.'

Jennifer smiled happily and said with a confidence that Lucy one day hoped to emulate, 'He does.' She looked thoughtful for a moment, then added brightly, 'He's resigned from his job at Carnegie's, you know. His father wasn't best pleased, but he got a new manager in pretty quick and according to Matt, he's okay. Ben's going back to college in the autumn to retrain as a teacher.'

'Really?'

Jennifer smiled happily. 'Yeah, really. He's been unhappy in his work for some time.'

Lucy felt a lump in her throat and her eyes welled up with tears.

'What is it, Lucy?' said Jennifer quickly, leaning over and touching Lucy's knee.

Lucy paused and looked around the room that was as familiar to her as home. It was now or never. Was she going to go on living the life her parents wanted her to live? Or like Ben, would she follow her heart?

'What would you say if I didn't want to go back to uni?' she said, her voice full of misery more than hope. 'Not ever.'

Jennifer patted her knee, then removed her hand, and sat back in the chair. 'You can't let Oren spoil your future, Lucy. You've only four months or so of uni left this year. And if Oren goes to Peru like he's planned, you'll not see him next year anyway.'

'No,' said Lucy carefully. 'It's not because of Oren. You remember the things I said to you in the park?'

Jennifer stilled, and her face became very serious. 'How could I forget?'

336

'I meant everything I said, Mum. I hate uni. Please don't make me go back.'

Jennifer clasped her hands between her knees, stared directly at Lucy and thought for what seemed like a very long time. At last she smiled and said, 'Okay, darling, if that's what you want. But we're going to have to persuade your father first.'

Chapter 25

Ben stood with his shirt sleeves rolled up, bathed in the bright glow of the warm May sunshine, looking out of the patio doors onto his mother's garden, bursting with new growth and bright spring flowers. Four months had passed since he and Jennifer had got back together and his whole world had changed. He'd moved into Oakwood Grove; Alan had taken possession of the flat in Ballyfergus; and he was working two part-time jobs. Only now had he plucked up the courage to tell his parents what he ought to have told them a long time ago.

A young woman came out of the stables in cream riding pants carrying a brown polished leather saddle. She must've called out, for a three-year-old chestnut gelding trotted obediently over to her.

Diane, in a coral-coloured jersey dress, came and stood beside Ben and they both watched as the girl saddled up the horse.

'Do you ride him much?' said Ben.

Diane shook her head and said thoughtfully, 'Rarely. I get Julie to exercise the horses most of the time. I do ride occasionally but I find it very tiring and somehow I don't

338

seem to have the time these days. I suppose I'm not as young as I used to be.' She gave him a sad smile. 'Can't remember the last time I played tennis either. I'll maybe get the racquet out and dust it off this season. What do you think?'

'Good idea,' he smiled, noticing the way the bright sun lit up the small lines and creases on his mother's face and acknowledging to himself that she was ageing. His father was due any minute – he suddenly doubted that he should tell them at all. What was the point in reliving the worst night of their lives, tearing open the healed wounds and making them all bleed with grief once more? They'd all found a way to cope, a way to go on, and with each passing day Ricky's memory receded.

Except that he was kidding himself. Ricky was as much with them now as he had been seven years ago, not only in the photos in his mother's orangery, but in their hearts. His spirit was in the air around them, enveloping them like a mist. He haunted Ben's dreams – a red-haired boy with big green eyes and freckles across his nose, who teased Ben mercilessly because he was too scared to climb the big oak tree at the bottom of the garden. And when Ben woke from these dreams he was left with a nagging feeling that there was something left to be done. That Ricky would never be finally laid to peace until all the circumstances of his death had been laid bare.

The doorbell rang out. Diane said, 'That'll be him,' and left Ben alone in the room. He looked about, panicked. The hot sun slanted in the window, bleaching bright white squares on the floor. Overcome by the stuffy atmosphere, he went and opened the patio doors, and breathed in the fresh, warm air, the sweet scent of lilac filling his nostrils, and he was filled with calm. He said out loud, 'This is the last thing I'll ever do for you, Ricky.'

Then he went inside and stood by the fireplace, and

moments later Diane led Alan into the room. 'What's all this about, Diane?'

'I have no idea, darling,' said Diane airily, with her back to him as if she were above his questioning. She gestured at Ben with a flick of her wrist, and said superciliously, 'He won't tell me a thing.'

Alan plonked himself down on an elegant sofa, consulted his watch and said testily, 'Well, whatever this is about, Ben, you'd better make it quick. I've got to be in the city centre for five o'clock.'

'Anyone care for a whiskey?' said Diane, gesturing at the bottle of J&B, water and an ice bucket on the table.

'Can't we just get this over with?' said Alan, eyeing the drink.

'I think a drink would be a good idea,' said Ben, and gave his father a meaningful stare.

'Oh, all right then. Make it a small one, Di, will you?'

When she'd handed out the drinks in chunky crystal glasses, and she and Alan were seated on opposite ends of the same long sofa, Diane crossed her legs. 'So, Ben,' she said, looking at him across the coffee table where he sat on a matching sofa. 'What was it you wanted to talk to us about?'

'I want to talk to you about Ricky.'

Diane and Alan looked at each other and Diane said, 'What about him?'

'I want to tell you the truth about what happened the night he died.'

Alan took a big swig of whiskey, glanced quickly at Diane, who was now looking thoughtfully into her glass, and said, a little irritably, 'But we already know that, Ben. I don't know about your mother, but I'd rather not go over all that again.'

Diane shot him a stony look. 'Alan's right. It was all in your statement to the police.'

'What I told the police was only partly true.'

Alan's face went red as if he might explode while Diane's went as pale as the white marble fire surround.

'What are you saying?' Diane uncrossed her legs and leaned forward. 'You lied to the police?'

'I didn't think of it as a lie. It was more of a . . . an omission.'

She moved her head a fraction and waited.

Ben cleared his throat. 'You remember how Ricky was always getting into scrapes? Like the time he let the pet snake out of its cage and you found it in your bed, Mum?'

Alan laughed. 'I remember that one. Your mother nearly died.'

His laughter stopped abruptly and Ben said, 'Well, I used to cover for him a lot.'

'What do you mean?' said Diane.

'I used to take the flak so that he wouldn't get into trouble,' said Ben, talking to his mother. 'Like that time Scout camp was coming up and he was on his last warning and you said if he did anything, anything at all, he wouldn't get to go.'

'Yes . . .'

'Well, he put that frog in the laundry basket for Rosemarie to find. You remember, don't you?'

'But that was you!' said Diane.

Ben shook his head. 'No, it wasn't. It was Ricky. I covered for him because I knew I'd just get a warning whereas he'd get grounded. And we both got to go to Scout camp. I used to do it a lot. Sometimes Ricky asked me to and sometimes I did it because I didn't want him to get into trouble.'

'What's this got to do with the night he died, Ben?' said Diane.

'That night at the party, well, he was drinking too much,' said Ben, looking at the floor. 'And taking drugs. I know he

341

took at least one line of coke and shortly before he left he took a blue tablet. I remember it clearly. It had the impression of a four-leaved clover on it. Someone said it was ecstasy.'

Diane made a little choking sound and said quietly, 'Why didn't you tell us, Ben?'

Ben could not bring himself to look at her, so he continued staring at the carpet and said, 'Ricky was your golden boy, Mum. How could I tell you when you were suffering so much already? And what was the point? I thought it would only make things worse.'

'And you think that's why he crashed the car? Apart from driving too fast, like the police said.'

'It must've had something to do with it, Mum,' said Ben, looking at her ashen face again. 'The drugs must have impaired his judgement. But the reason I'm telling you, is that I didn't stop him. I didn't stop him taking the drugs and I didn't stop him driving home. And I could have done both. I thought about it.'

'But why didn't you?' cried Diane. 'If you'd taken the car keys off him, he couldn't have driven. And he would never have died.' She sobbed then and put a hand to her mouth.

'I tried to stop him taking the first line of coke. He told me that I wasn't his effing babysitter and to just eff off and leave him alone. And I was so angry, Ricky never knew when to stop. And when we got outside at the end of the night and I asked him for the car keys he just laughed and told me it was his car and just to get in the effing passenger seat or I was walking home.'

Diane turned to Alan who had been largely quiet throughout this entire exchange and said, 'Why aren't you saying anything?' Alan hung his head and she said, 'You knew, didn't you?'

Alan nodded and looked at his ex-wife. 'The inspector came to see me. You remember Ronnie Mair? We go way back.' Diane shook her head slowly but Alan went on regardless, with a quick, guilty glance at Ben. 'He showed me the autopsy report. They'd found traces of cocaine and ecstasy as well as speed and ketamine. It's a hallucinogen.'

So Alan had known all along. Ben had assumed the traces hadn't shown up. That someone had made a mistake somewhere. 'Oh my God,' said Diane and she put her hand to her mouth. 'Why didn't you tell me, Alan? Why didn't you show me the report?'

'I was trying to protect you, Diane.' His chin started to wobble and the muscles in his jaw twitched. 'And I didn't want Ricky's name besmirched. I didn't want his memory tarnished by drugs and for people to say that it was his own fault that he died. I asked Ronnie to suppress the report and he did.' He nodded as if to confirm to himself that he had done the right thing.

'You shouldn't have made that judgement call, Alan. I am his mother. I have the right to know the truth about how my son died.'

'I'm sorry, Diane.'

They all fell silent then, lost in their own thoughts, and Ben said, 'There's something else.'

'Oh my God,' said Diane. 'What?'

Ben swallowed and he could barely hear his own voice above the pounding of his heart. 'When the car crashed into the tree and I came to, I thought I was okay. I didn't feel the bruises or the broken rib. I remembered that there were drugs in the car. I'd seen Ricky slip a little brown paper envelope into the glove compartment. I knew the car was a write-off and the police were going to be involved. I knew I had to do something. Drink driving was one thing, but drugs . . . I knew that was serious.'

Diane gasped and Alan inched up the sofa and took her hand. She never took her eyes off Ben.

343

Tears filled his eyes, but Ben pressed on, knowing that if he didn't finish this story now he would never be able to retell it. 'His head was resting on the airbag, facing me and his eyes were closed. I reached out and I gave him a little shake. I remember the lights inside the car were still on and the headlights were shining out over the countryside and there was steam rising out the bonnet of the car.'

He paused. Both Diane and Alan were staring at him, rigid with horror. Neither spoke.

'Eventually Ricky came to and he smiled at me and his eyes were all glassy but I thought he was okay. He said something I didn't understand but I wasn't listening. But I knew the police would be along soon so I reached in under the airbag and got the envelope and I held it up and said, "I've got to get rid of this, Ricky." I opened the door and the cold air rushed in and I remember thinking that I hoped he didn't get too cold, sitting there waiting for the police to arrive. And then he reached out his left hand and clamped it on to my arm and said something again.' Ben gasped with emotion, but he forced himself to go on. 'And I said, "I'll just be a minute, Ricky. You'll be all right, mate." I didn't know that he had a metal post in his stomach. I didn't know that he was dying. I got out of the car – for some stupid reason I left the door open. And when I came back his eyes were closed and the smile had gone. He'd gone all limp and I shook him and shook him but I couldn't wake him up.'

The room was utterly silent, save for the sound of the birds in the garden. Ben closed his eyes and wished he could go back, wished he could relive those last few moments in the car park, when, if he had wrestled Ricky to his knees and got the keys off him, he would be alive today. But his judgement had been impaired by the beer he'd drunk. And he'd stood back and for once, not intervened, and thought to himself, 'Let's see how he manages without me.'

'What did you do with the drugs?' said Alan.

'Huh?' said Ben and thought for a moment. 'There was a river. You remember the crash happened just over the bridge?'

Diane and Alan both nodded.

'I could hear the river as soon as I got out of the car. I ran to the bridge and threw the contents into the water; a tablet and a tiny sachet of powder – I couldn't see them too clearly but I could feel them with my fingers. And then I ripped the envelope into tiny little pieces and threw it in too.' He paused, remembering how the little bits of paper had fluttered in the breeze like ticker-tape and then disappeared into the black swirling water below. 'I'll never forgive myself for what I did.'

'But you were only trying to protect your brother,' said Alan, displaying more understanding than Ben had expected of him. 'Keeping him out of trouble. I'd have expected no less.'

'But don't you see, Dad? I left him there to die all alone. In the freezing cold on that wretched stretch of road. I think he was asking me to stay with him. I think he knew he was dying. And I . . . I left him.'

Then Ben put his face in his hands and wept tears of relief that he had finally shared what he'd stored in his heart for seven long years. He felt Diane's weight beside him on the sofa, then her arms around his shoulder and her voice in his ear. 'But how were you to know, son? You thought you were doing the right thing. Nobody can hold what happened against you. I certainly don't. And I don't blame you either for Ricky taking the drugs – or driving. He was an adult. He was responsible for his own actions.'

Ben wiped the tears away and looked across at his father who nodded and said, 'Your mother's right. You mustn't blame yourself.'

'That's why I agreed to go into the business, Dad. I felt so guilty; I felt I had to repay you somehow. I tried to fill Ricky's shoes but I just couldn't do it.'

Alan stood up, his arms hanging woodenly by his sides, and said in a strangely detached voice, 'I'm sorry if I pressurised you into the business, Ben. I shouldn't have done that. And you have nothing to feel guilty about. You've been a good son and the best brother. If anyone's to blame for Ricky's death, it's me.'

Diane removed her arm from Ben's shoulder and they both stared up at Alan.

'I knew he was wild,' he went on. 'I even admired him for it. He reminded me so much of myself as a young man. I gave him too much money and I bought him that car and he wasn't ready for it. He couldn't handle it.' He looked at Diane then and said, 'You blamed me too.'

She turned her head to the side as if he'd slapped her across the face. 'It's true. I did. But that,' she said, bringing her gaze back to Alan, 'well, that was . . . wrong of me. Because it wasn't just the car, was it? And what good does it do to blame each other? It won't bring Ricky back.'

'You've never said a truer word,' said Alan and he looked at his watch. 'Look, I have to go now. I don't want to keep Cassie waiting.'

Ben got up and went over to his father and they shook hands. 'I hope you're happy in the life you've chosen, son.'

'You too, Dad,' said Ben softly, feeling an affection for his father that he hadn't felt in years.

Alan let go of Ben's hand and said, brightly, 'Well, I have some good news to share with you both.'

Diane, who had regained her normal composure, said, 'You've not bought another hotel, have you?'

Alan chuckled. 'Much better than that, Diane. I'm going to be a father again,' he said and he lifted his chin and stood up straight and in that instant he looked ten years younger. 'Cassie's three months pregnant.'

Ben and Diane looked at each other in astonishment and Diane said, 'Congratulations! But I thought Cassie didn't want children?'

'Oh, you know women,' said Alan. 'Always changing their minds. I promised her a holiday home in Majorca and a diamond eternity ring. I think that might have done the trick.'

'That's wonderful news, Dad,' said Ben, suppressing a smile.

'Well, mustn't keep her waiting,' said Alan, and he turned on his heel and sailed out of the room.

'What are you smiling at?' said Diane, when Alan was gone.

'You've gotta hand it to him,' said Ben, feeling a peculiar mix of awe and admiration for his father. 'He'll have his dynasty after all.' He turned to his mother and took both her hands in his, so painfully aware that she was all alone. 'I'm sorry that you'll never have grandchildren, Mum.'

'Oh, that's all right, Ben,' she said, smiling bravely, and quickly changed the subject. 'I owe Jennifer an apology, Ben. I was rather unkind to her at Hannah's wedding. I'm sorry.'

'I'm sure Jennifer will forgive you, Mum.'

'I hope so. I'll ring her.'

She linked arms with him and they walked to the door. 'Perhaps she'll give me some tips on how to bag myself a younger man. Oh, don't look at me like that,' she laughed, 'I'm only joking. Well, actually I'm not. Why not? All the men my age are a complete waste of space. You only have to look at your father.'

Ben kissed her on the cheek. 'I worry about you, Mum, being on your own.'

Diane laughed lightly, the earlier intimacy between them

gone, and said, bravely, 'Oh, don't worry about me, son. Now, I very much hope that you and Jennifer will come to my annual charity ball.'

Jennifer sat at the kitchen table, wearing a pretty cotton dress and cardigan. She fingered the necklace at her throat that Ben had given her for Valentine's Day, and smiled. She kept telling Ben that she didn't need expensive jewellery, but it was lovely all the same to receive it. And she knew that it wouldn't last. Once he was living on a teacher's salary he wouldn't be able to buy such things.

The back door opened and Lucy came in, wearing a pale blue t-shirt, jeans and trainers, her face pink from the sun. Her slim figure was more toned these days and Jennifer had persuaded her to get some highlights in her hair. But the biggest change was in her demeanour. There was only one way to put it – she absolutely glowed. 'What's that?' said Lucy, glancing at the mood board on the table.

'Oh, it's for Maggie. She asked me to help her redecorate the downstairs. I just put some ideas together for her. I'll not charge her though.'

Lucy laughed. 'Looks expensive. Dad'll not be happy at having to fork out more money, after buying me the car!' She grinned, stood by the open back door and said, impatiently, 'Come on outside, Mum. I want to show you something before everyone gets here for the barbecue.'

Jennifer followed her up the side of the house and into the sunshine. The estate car that David had bought Lucy (they'd persuaded him it was a much better investment than a wedding to Oren Wilson) was parked out front.

'Oh, Lucy, that's wonderful!' cried Jennifer, noticing immediately the sign on the side of the doors. 'Muddy Mutt Dog Walking' it said along with phone numbers and an email address.

'It's the same on the other side,' enthused Lucy, 'and look,' she said gesturing for Jennifer to follow her round the car, which they encircled like prowling wolves. 'They put paw prints all over the back and on the bonnet. Isn't it brilliant?'

Jennifer stood up on tip-toes and gave Lucy a peck on the cheek. 'It's absolutely fantastic! Wait till your Grandpa sees this!'

Lucy's phone bleeped and she pulled it out and quickly read a text. 'That's another potential customer,' she said happily, running her hand through her hair. 'At this rate I'm going to have to employ someone to help me walk the dogs!'

Ben's old Rover pulled up in front of the house and Jennifer's heart leapt. She ran over. 'How did it go with your parents?' she asked.

'We cleared the air about a few things and everything's good.' He paused and added, changing the subject, 'Cassie's going to have a baby.'

'Oh, my God. That means you'll have a wee brother or a sister.'

'Yeah, I hadn't really thought about it like that but yeah.' He grinned and two deep dimples appeared in his cheeks. 'I'll be a brother again. And Mum's very keen to talk to you. Says she owes you an apology.'

Not half, thought Jennifer, but she kept this observation to herself. 'Well, maybe we can start all over, your Mum and me.' Ben grinned with happiness.

They walked over to Lucy holding hands and Ben exclaimed, 'Hey, look at the wheels, Lucy!' She smiled shyly and they stood together, all three, and admired the car.

'I've been thinking about expanding,' said Lucy. 'You know the way I do a midweek dog walking service. Well, I've been thinking of extending that to weekends. I could

349

do a big long dog hike on a Sunday – you know, three or four hours.'

'You'll be exhausted,' cautioned Jennifer.

'No, I won't. And I'd charge well for it, twenty quid a dog. If I could take six dogs that's one hundred and twenty pounds. And even if I had to pay someone to do it for me, at say seven pounds an hour – and that's well above the minimum wage – I'd still make nearly a hundred quid. If we did that on Saturdays as well, eight times a month; that's eight hundred quid a month. Not to be sniffed at.'

'Well, it looks to me like you've found your niche, Lucy,' said Ben. 'You're talking like a real businesswoman.'

'But I've still to get the business website up and running,' she frowned, her brain so active it flitted from one subject to the other like a butterfly. It was so good to see her motivated and happy – and getting on so well with Ben.

'I might be able to help you with that,' said Ben. 'I've this friend . . .'

Just then Donna and Ken pulled up in their car followed shortly by Grandpa and Matt on foot. Everyone admired Lucy's car then squeezed into Jennifer's small back garden. Matt took charge of the barbecue while Ben did drinks and the women carried out the rest of the food.

'Do you want me to cut down these old daffodil leaves for you, love?' said Grandpa who could not bear to be still in a garden.

'Yes. If you like, Dad.'

When Jennifer finally sat down on a bench, with Brian rooting in the borders and Matt slaving over the hot barbecue, Ben said, mysteriously, 'I have a surprise for you.'

He got up without another word and disappeared around the side of the house. A few minutes later he came back with a cardboard box in his hands, and a rather concerned look on his face. 'Now, he can go back if you don't want him,' said Ben, and Jennifer's heart leapt.

Ben put the box by her feet and she heard the tell-tale scuffling sound of a new puppy. She put her hand on her heart and tears filled her eyes.

'I know we talked about getting a dog,' said Ben, unfolding the flaps. 'I just hope the timing's right. And that you like him.'

A little black face popped out of the top of the box and everybody laughed.

'What is he?' said Brian who'd stood up to observe the proceedings, a trowel in his hand.

'A black Lab,' said Ben.

'Oh, they're so good tempered,' said Donna.

'Oh, let me see you,' said Jennifer and she crouched down and lifted the little pup onto her lap. He smelt of the litter and his little pink tongue hung out one side of his mouth. His fur was as smooth as silk and his little claws dug into her flesh like needles through the thin cotton skirt. He was shaking a little, overwhelmed by the audience, and he stared at Jennifer with coal black eyes so knowing and trusting her heart melted.

'Oh, let me have him. Let me have him,' cried Lucy and she grasped the little pup and pressed him to her breast and kissed the top of his smooth black head as if he were her baby. 'Oh, he's just adorable,' she cried and she cuddled him for some minutes, then set the little pup on the ground and everyone watched as he wobbled about, like a toddler who'd just found his feet, sniffing and tugging at Ken's trouser leg.

'I wonder what we should call him?' said Lucy.

'Well, we've had a Muffin . . .' Matt's voice piped up from the corner. 'How about Doughnut?' Everyone laughed and Ben said, 'Oh, Matt, that's brilliant.'

351

As if realising that he'd just been christened, the puppy decided to mark the occasion. He squatted and a little trickle of urine ran along the join between the patio slabs, only missing Donna's smart leather bag by centimetres. Everyone roared, not least Donna, and she snatched the bag onto her lap.

'You've got a wee lethal weapon, there, Jennifer,' she teased.

Ben said, 'Are you sure you like him? I know he'll never be a replacement for Muffin. But I thought the summer was the perfect time to get him.'

'Now is the perfect time,' said Jennifer, her heart swelling with happiness. 'And he's the perfect dog.'

'I've got everything we need for him in the car,' said Ben. 'A crate, pen, puppy food. You name it, I bought it!'

'Give us the keys then and I'll get the kitchen set up for him,' said Lucy. 'He'll need a place to crash after all this excitement.'

Ben handed over the keys and big burly Ken stood up. 'I'll give you a hand, love. I'll get cramp if I sit too long.'

Lucy paused with the keys in her hand and stared at Doughnut, who was now over at the border beside Grandpa, attacking the trowel with ferocious determination. Grandpa rolled the pup on the ground and tickled his chest. 'And maybe it's time we scattered Muffin's ashes.'

'Where were you thinking of, Lucy?' said Jennifer.

'Why right here,' she said with a smile. 'At the end, this was the only place he wanted to be.'

Jennifer nodded and looked around the small, sunny garden. He had spent most of his life here in this house and garden – it was right and fitting that it be his final resting place.

Lucy and Ken disappeared and Jennifer watched the puppy hesitantly climb the steps up to the house, reminding her so much of the tentative way babies explore the world. And while the rest chatted and Matt, with a beer in one hand and a pair of tongs in the other, expertly flipped meat on the hot grill, Jennifer turned to Ben, now sitting beside her on the bench, the empty cardboard box at her feet.

She placed a hand on his knee, so bursting with joy and gratitude, that it was some moments before she could speak. 'Thank you, Ben. That little pup means more to me than the finest jewellery.'

'He's our pup, my darling,' he said interlacing his fingers with hers. 'And it's my way of saying that I'm going to be around for a long time. Forever, if you'll have me.'

She did not want to think of the future, only the here and now and this happiness that she held in her heart as fragile as an egg. 'Let's enjoy each day as it comes,' she said staring into his deep, brown eyes, mirrors to her own, while all around them everyone laughed at the puppy's antics. 'Forever is a very long time.'

Erin Kaye's thoughts on writing
Second Time Around

What inspired you to write about a cougar relationship?
The hypocrisy within society that says it's okay for a man
to date a very much younger woman, but not the other way
around. It's true that cougar relationships are more common
nowadays and less frowned on – but they've become a source
of amusement. I prefer not to use the word 'cougar' when
talking about Jennifer and Ben as it implies a predatory
relationship, whereas this love story is about the meeting of
two minds.

**Are Jennifer's fears for the future of her relationship with
Ben unfounded?**
The book ends on a slightly cautious note from Jennifer. I
think she's taking her happiness where she can find it, in
the here and now, fully aware that it may not last. But then
again, it might.

Do you think it is a child's responsibility to fulfil his/her parents' hopes and expectations?

No. We never own our children, we are only guardians for the short time they are with us. It's very hard as a parent not to harbour hopes and expectations. Loving children unconditionally and without expectation is difficult – almost impossible. And yet it's what we ought to strive for. In the story both Ben and Lucy are striving, unhappily, to be what their parents want them to be – and it backfires in both instances. The message in the book is – follow your heart. I think I learned that lesson the hard way. I had ten successful, but not fulfilled, years in banking before becoming a writer.

Who was the inspiration for Oren?

Nathan Price in *The Poisonwood Bible* by Barbara Kingsolver. I had a lot of fun with Oren and felt so sorry for poor Lucy at points in the book where she was trying to please him and kept getting it wrong! I hope Oren's fanaticism is something with which people everywhere can identify. I think it's worrying when people adhere to any creed unquestioningly. I've become increasingly alarmed by reports of the rise of Young Earth Creativism in the US.

Tell us more about Lucy?

I'm quite perturbed by the current policy of pushing more and more kids into higher education, even when they're not really suited to it. Matt's vocational career path, in contrast to Lucy's academic one, brings him happiness compared to Lucy's despair. At the end of the book we see Lucy breaking free of these bonds and following her heart, and that's how she finds true fulfilment.

Is romantic love nirvana?
It is for some people. But for others, like Ben's mother Diane, it isn't. I think Lucy's happily single at the end of the book and I don't foresee a man in her life.

Why does Lucy lack confidence?
Because her father doesn't love her unconditionally and she knows it. At the end of the book, her faith and God's love bring her contentment.

What inspired Ricky's story?
The death of a young man locally in a car crash. There was no suggestion of the involvement of drink or drugs in that case, but it got me thinking how a family would cope with such a terrible tragedy.

Do you take your inspiration then from your own life?
Yes, and things that happen to my friends and family and the gossip you hear in a small town like the one where I live. Believe me, it all happens here. You don't have to look any further. I got the idea for *Second Time Around* from a friend who was signed up with an online dating agency. She lied about her age and ended up dating much younger men! And then I began to wonder about why she wouldn't come clean about her age and realised it was because there is still a bit of a taboo about older woman/younger man couples.

Reading Group Questions

1) Do you think 'cougar' relationships are more acceptable today than they were in the past?

2) Is Jennifer over-sensitive to what other people think of her and Ben? Why is Jennifer more conscious of the age difference between her and Ben, than he is?

3) How has Ben's background shaped his character?

4) Why does Ben find it so hard to go against his parent's wishes, e.g. staying in the family business when his heart isn't in it? In what ways does Ricky's death affect each member of the Crawford family?

5) What do Ben's parents object to more – Jennifer's age or background? How does Ben find the courage to go against his parents?

6) Both Alan and Lucy, though very different characters, are both quite hard to like. Why is this?

7) What mistakes have Lucy's parents made in raising her? How have these mistakes affected her character? Why does she become addicted to online bingo?

8) What similarities are there between Lucy's father and Oren? Is this why Lucy is attracted to Oren?

9) Did you find Oren's character more laughable or sinister? Why does he have such a hold on Lucy?

10) If Lucy hadn't discovered Oren in bed with another woman, do you think she would have stayed with him?

11) Are Ben's parents wrong to place expectations on him? At the end of the book which parent do you feel more sympathy for – Alan or Diane?

12) At the end of the book we forsee a happier future for mother and daughter. Who has changed the most, Lucy or Jennifer?

13) Are Jennifer's concerns for the future of her relationship with Ben unfounded?

14) Do you think Lucy will ever find love?

It's a family affair...

ERIN KAYE · PROMISE OF HAPPINESS

Louise McNeill arrives home to the idyllic Irish town
of Ballyfergus, hoping that it will provide the sanctuary
she desperately craves. As she starts over with her
three-year-old son, Louise's heart is full of apprehension.

To make matters worse, her sister Joanne seems far from
happy as she watches Louise's little family blossom. But as Joanne
grapples with her 'perfect' marriage, is everything
as tranquil as it seems?

Meanwhile, Louise's youngest sister Sian has decided
she doesn't want children as she and fiancé Andy want
to dedicate themselves to ecological living. But is this a
mask to disguise a bigger issue? And is Andy really
on board with all of Sian's plans?

Join the McNeill family as they try to give each other
the support they all need – whether they know it or not.
Perfect for fans of **Maeve Binchy** and **Cathy Kelly**.

A V O N

£6.99
ISBN: 978-1-84756-201-2

ERIN KAYE · THE ART OF FRIENDSHIP

Fifteen years ago, chance brought them together, and friendship has bound them. Until now.

Over the years, in the small Irish town of Ballyfergus, four women have shared their triumphs and tragedy. Men have come and gone, children been born and left home. Life has taken them down paths they never expected, but through it all their relationship has endured.

But all that's about to change. This year their friendship will be tested as never before:

Widowed Kirsty falls in love with someone she shouldn't.

Patsy struggles to cope with turbulent marriage and a shocking revelation from her daughter.

Janice is forced to confront ghosts from her past.

Clare takes control of her life, only to discover that her new-found independence comes at a high price.

Can their friendship survive the strains and come through unscathed? Warm, emotive Irish storytelling, perfect for fans of Cathy Kelly and Maeve Binchy.

A V O N

£6.99
ISBN: 978-0-00-734036-1